CANADIAN MYSTERY STORIES

Edited by Alberto Manguel

TORONTO
Oxford University Press
1991

Oxford University Press, 70 Wynford Drive, Don Mills, Ontario M3C 1J9

Toronto Oxford New York
Delhi Bombay Calcutta Madras Karachi Petaling Jaya
Singapore Hong Kong Tokyo Nairobi Dar es Salaam
Cape Town Melbourne Auckland

and associated companies in
Berlin Ibadan

To Philip Berger, this inadequate expression of thanks.

Man, his essence, is but a speck.
It is that speck that Death devours.
                        —Henri Michaux

Canadian Cataloguing in Publication Data
Main entry under title:

Canadian mystery stories

ISBN 0-19-540820-9
1. Detective and mystery stories, Canadian (English).*
I. Manguel, Alberto, 1948-

PS8323.D4C36 1991   C813'.087208   C91-093228-X
PR9197.35.D48C36 1991

Selection copyright © Oxford University Press Canada 1991
Introduction and Notes copyright © Alberto Manguel 1991
OXFORD is a trademark of Oxford University Press
1 2 3 4 - 94 93 92 91
Printed in Canada by Webcom Limited

CONTENTS

INTRODUCTION

The most obvious thing about our world is that it is incomprehensible. Why the rain falls where no man is or why the gates of death are opened are questions that have remained unanswered since before the days of Job. Perhaps because of this uncertainty, throughout the ages of literature we find, scattered here and there, little pockets of perfection, seemingly impossible mysteries that, against all expectations, have marvellously logical solutions. The Arabian Nights, the Bible, the folk-tales collected by the brothers Grimm, all contain early examples of these riddles, which, pulled into shape in the mid-nineteenth century, became the genre known to us as the detective story.

It is a commonplace to say that the laws of the detective story—a.k.a. mystery, thriller, whodunnit—were established by Edgar Allan Poe (who also invented the tale of horror). Five stories written between 1840 and 1845 ('The Murders in the Rue Morgue', 'The Mystery of Marie Rogêt', 'Thou Art the Man', 'The Gold Bug', and 'The Purloined Letter') contain almost every trick later developed by the masters: the mystery set out in the first few pages, the detective whose sight and powers of deduction are keener than those of his peers, the unlikely murderer. And yet, at the time, not a soul recognized the birth of a new genre. In spite of splendid mysteries by such masters of the convoluted plot as Charles Dickens—*The Mystery of Edwin Drood* (1870), left unfinished, is the perfect puzzle because we will never know its true solution—and Wilkie Collins—*The Moonstone* (1868) was described by T.S. Eliot as 'the first, the longest and the best of modern English detective novels'[1]—the recognition had to wait until 1887. Thirty-eight years after Poe's death this immortal line first appeared in *Beeton's Christmas Annual*: 'You have been in Afghanistan, I perceive'—the first words ever spoken by Sherlock Holmes to Dr Watson. Holmes was more than the world's foremost private detective. Unlike Poe's C. Auguste Dupin, whose rational exploits lay hidden among tales of supernatural horror and could therefore be read simply as startling adventures, the characters created by Sir Arthur Conan Doyle were so blazingly unique that they demanded a new method of reading fiction. Doyle's readers were taught to expect a problem in every plot, to be wary of every detail, to suspect each and every character. He taught so well that, by the time of the last Sherlock Holmes story, in 1926, the public was ready for perfection. That same year, Agatha Christie's *The Murder of Roger Ackroyd* was published. In England, the golden era of the mystery story had begun.

In Canada, the development of the genre was slower and frankly derivative of the British model. Both in the English-speaking provinces and in Quebec there are early examples of popular fiction that can, up to a point, be classified as 'mystery stories'—even though, at the time, these texts lacked a public trained in the reading method required by the genre. Michael Richardson, in *Maddened by Mystery*,[2] proposes James De Mille's 'fine Victorian mystery' *The Cryptogram* (1871) as the first true Canadian detective story. Professor J. Hare[3] suggests, for French Canada, Georges de Boucherville's gothic tale *'La Tour de Trafalgar'* (1835) or Pamphile Le May's short story *'Sang et or'* in *Contes vrais* (1899). But they are far from the puzzling mastery of Conan Doyle's or Poe's creations.

If the place of residence or birth grants authors a literary nationality, then at least two interesting examples of British pre-golden age mystery writers are Canadian. Born in Scotland but raised in Canada, Robert Barr, headmaster of Windsor Central School in Ontario and later founder, in England, of *The Idler* magazine, showed something of the talents of both Doyle and Poe in his 1906 collection, *The Triumphs of Eugène Valmont*; one of the 'triumphs', 'The Absent-Minded Coterie', became a frequently anthologized classic. And Grant Allen, born in Kingston, Ontario, introduced a new kind of hero in his novel *An African Millionaire* (1897)—Colonel Cuthbert Clay, gentleman crook, ancestor of Maurice Leblanc's *Arsène Lupin*. Neither, however, set his stories in Canada. In fact, as Douglas Malcolm has remarked, 'Canada has always had its fair share of murder, arson, robbery, assault, fraud and assorted other crimes. We've even had the occasional case of espionage. But despite all this bona fide criminal activity, Canada until the 1970s was as empty as a Liberal gathering in Alberta when it came to crime fiction.'[4] Then, in the following years, the genre seemed to take root and flourish: the top international mystery-writing awards were given to Canadian authors such as L.R. Wright, Eric Wright, and L.A. Morse, and in the winter of 1982, under the chairmanship of Tony Aspler, the Crime Writers Association of Canada was founded, acknowledging the stupendous rise of new national genre. So numerous, in fact, are noteworthy Canadian mystery writers that I have had to make the difficult decision to leave out James Powell's memorable 'The Brim Whistle' as too lengthy for the constraints of this book.

One of the reasons for this flourishing is the consolidation of a Canadian literary landscape. For centuries, and in spite of brave romantic efforts, it had seemed as if Canada didn't possess something like the magic of London fogs, the grittiness of Los Angeles' wild side, the turbulence of New York's low life. Only when writers such as Margaret Laurence, Hugh MacLennan, Anne Hébert, Robertson Davies, Marie-Claire Blais, and Margaret Atwood had dramatized the Canadian landscape were the crime writers who followed able to take advantage of what was, by then, a place of mystery—the country of Manawaka and Deptford. But the relationship between literary and crime writers is one of mutual dependence. Russell M. Brown, in an important study of the Canadian novel,[5] remarked that writers such as Davies or Atwood use mystery plots in their fiction, and that the devices of the genre are fundamental in their work. In some cases, as in Timothy Findley's *The Telling of Lies* or Carol Shields's *Swan*, writers whose work would not normally be found on the mystery shelf of a bookstore deliberately signal the alliance by subtitling their novels 'A Mystery'. Hubert Aquin, for instance, made no bones about it: 'All novels are mysteries . . . When I open a book I cannot help searching for the cocainomaniac silhouette of the genius of Baker Street and the criminal shadow he projects even over the pale pages of fiction.'[6] *Kamouraska, Surfacing, The Manticore*, whatever else they might be, are also mystery novels, trying to solve the uncaring, cruel, violent landscape of our times.

It is not that our century is more violent, more cruel, more uncaring than any other: hell has never really been an imaginary place. But our imagination has changed. By and large, it seems to require stronger bonds to the things of this earth; it has less faith in allusion, in metaphor. Like St Thomas, our present imagination requires something to touch before it can believe. The bodies discovered by Sherlock Holmes were as dead as those stumbled upon by Howard Engel's Benny Cooperman or Eric Wright's Charlie Salter, but the former needed barely a hint of a corpse to let the reader know that a foul deed had been done. In Lawrence Gough's Vancouver-set novels there are long, loving paragraphs dwelling upon the death of this or that body. These are not gratuitous descriptions. They are necessary because the iconography of our times, with its photographic recording of brutality and evil, requires sterner stuff to lend credibility to our riddles.

Riddles are at the core of most fiction. Nothing carries a reader from page to page with more force than a question—especially a question whose answer seems unobtainable, but isn't; seems mad, but is, on close inspection, quite reasonable. Because of this, the detective story will continue, in whatever guise it may take in the future, to serve the purpose of giving us confidence in the ultimate sanity of the universe.

NOTES

[1] T.S. Eliot, quoted in J.I.M. Stewart's introduction to Wilkie Collins's *The Moonstone*, Penguin, 1966.

[2] Michael Richardson, editor, *Maddened by Mystery*, Lester and Orpen Dennys, 1982.

[3] John Hare, private correspondence with A.M.

[4] Douglas Malcolm, 'Blood on the Snow', in *Books in Canada*, June-July 1988.

[5] Russell M. Brown, 'In Search of Lost Causes: The Canadian Novelist as Mystery Writer', in *Mosaic*, Spring 1978.

[6] Hubert Aquin, in *Blackout*, quoted in Brown, op. cit.

ACKNOWLEDGEMENTS

To J.D. Singh of *Sleuth of Baker Street* and Professor John Hare for their unofficial research, to Margaret Cannon for her guidance, to Karen Mulhallen for the unforeseen editing, and to Sally Livingston for the translations. And to my editor, Richard Teleky, once again, for his confidence and patience.

GRANT ALLEN · 1848-1899

The Episode of the Mexican Seer

My name is Seymour Wilbraham Wentworth. I am brother-in-law and secretary to Sir Charles Vandrift, the South African millionaire and famous financier. Many years ago, when Charlie Vandrift was a small lawyer in Cape Town, I had the (qualified) good fortune to marry his sister. Much later, when the Vandrift estate and farm near Kimberley developed by degrees into the Cloetedorp Golcondas, Limited, my brother-in-law offered me the not unremunerative post of secretary; in which capacity I have ever since been his constant and attached companion.

He is not a man whom any common sharper can take in, is Charles Vandrift. Middle height, square build, firm mouth, keen eyes—the very picture of a sharp and successful business genius. I have only known one rogue impose upon Sir Charles, and that one rogue, as the Commissary of Police at Nice remarked, would doubtless have imposed upon a syndicate of Vidocq, Robert Houdin, and Cagliostro.

We had run across to the Riviera for a few weeks in the season. Our object being strictly rest and recreation from the arduous duties of financial combination, we did not think it necessary to take our wives out with us. Indeed, Lady Vandrift is absolutely wedded to the joys of London, and does not appreciate the rural delights of the Mediterranean littoral. But Sir Charles and I, though immersed in affairs when at home, both thoroughly enjoy the complete change from the City to the charming vegetation and pellucid air on the terrace at Monte Carlo. We *are* so fond of scenery. That delicious view over the rock of Monaco, with the Maritime Alps in the rear, and the blue sea in front, not to mention the imposing Casino in the foreground, appeals to me as one of the most beautiful prospects in all Europe. Sir Charles has a sentimental attachment for the place. He finds it restores and refreshes him, after the turmoil of London, to win a few hundred at roulette in the course of an afternoon among the palms and cactuses and pure breezes of Monte Carlo. The country, say I, for a jaded intellect! However, we never on any account actually stop in the Principality itself. Sir Charles thinks Monte Carlo is not a sound address for a financier's letters. He prefers a comfortable hotel on the Promenade des Anglais at Nice, where he recovers health and renovates his nervous system by taking daily excursions along the coast to the Casino.

This particular season we were snugly ensconced at the Hotel des Anglais. We had capital quarters on the first floor—salon, study, and bedrooms—and found on the spot a most agreeable cosmopolitan society. All Nice, just then, was ringing with talk about a curious impostor, known to his followers as the Great Mexican Seer, and supposed to be gifted with second sight, as well as with endless other supernatural powers. Now, it is a peculiarity of my able brother-in-law's that, when he meets with a quack, he burns to expose him; he is so keen a man of business himself that it gives him, so to speak, a disinterested pleasure to unmask and detect imposture in others. Many ladies at the hotel, some of whom had met and conversed with the Mexican Seer, were constantly telling us strange stories of his doings. He had disclosed to one the present whereabouts of a runaway husband; he had pointed out to another the numbers that would win at roulette next evening; he had shown a third the image on a screen of the man she had for years adored without his knowledge. Of course, Sir Charles didn't believe a word of it; but his curiosity was roused; he wished to see and judge for himself of the wonderful thought-reader.

'What would be his terms, do you think, for a private *séance?*' he asked of Madame Picardet, the lady to whom the Seer had success-fully predicted the winning numbers.

'He does not work for money,' Madame Picardet answered, 'but for the good of humanity. I'm sure he would gladly come and exhibit for nothing his miraculous faculties.'

'Nonsense!' Sir Charles answered. 'The man must live. I'd pay him five guineas, though, to see him alone. What hotel is he stopping at?'

'The Cosmopolitan, I think,' the lady answered. 'Oh no; I remember now, the Westminster.'

Sir Charles turned to me quietly. 'Look here, Seymour,' he whispered. 'Go round to this fellow's place immediately after dinner, and offer him five pounds to give a private *séance* at once in my rooms, without mentioning who I am to him; keep the name quite quiet. Bring him back with you, too, and come straight upstairs with him, so that there may be no collusion. We'll see just how much the fellow can tell us.'

I went as directed. I found the Seer a very remarkable and interesting person. He stood about Sir Charles's own height, but was slimmer and straighter, with an aquiline nose, strangely piercing eyes, very large black pupils, and a finely chiselled close-shaven face, like the bust of Antinous in our hall in Mayfair. What gave him his most characteristic touch, however, was his odd head of hair, curly and wavy like Paderewski's, standing out in a halo round his high white forehead and his delicate profile. I could see at a glance why he succeeded so well in impressing women; he had the look of a poet, a singer, a prophet.

'I have come round,' I said, 'to ask whether you will consent to give a *séance* at once in a friend's rooms; and my principal wishes me to add that he is prepared to pay five pounds as the price of the entertainment.'

Señor Antonio Herrera—that was what he called himself—bowed to me with impressive Spanish politeness. His dusky olive cheeks were wrinkled with a smile of gentle contempt as he answered gravely—

'I do not sell my gifts; I bestow them freely. If your friend—your anonymous friend—desires to behold the cosmic wonders that are wrought through my hands, I am glad to show them to him. Fortunately, as often happens when it is necessary to convince and confound a sceptic (for that your friend is a sceptic I feel instinctively), I chance to have no engagements at all this evening.' He ran his hand through his fine, long hair reflectively. 'Yes, I go,' he continued, as if addressing some unknown presence that hovered about the ceiling; 'I go; come with me!' Then he put on his broad sombrero, with its crimson ribbon, wrapped a cloak round his shoulders, lighted a cigarette, and strode forth by my side towards the Hotel des Anglais.

He talked little by the way, and that little in curt sentences. He seemed buried in deep thought; indeed, when we reached the door and I turned in, he walked a step or two farther on, as if not noticing to what place I had brought him. Then he drew himself up short, and gazed around him for a moment. 'Ha, the Anglais,' he said—and I may mention in passing that his English, in spite of a slight southern accent, was idiomatic and excellent. 'It is here, then; it is here!' He was addressing once more the unseen presence.

I smiled to think that these childish devices were intended to deceive Sir Charles Vandrift. Not quite the sort of man (as the City of London knows) to be taken in by hocus-pocus. And all this, I saw, was the cheapest and most commonplace conjuror's patter.

We went upstairs to our rooms. Charles had gathered together a few friends to watch the performance. The Seer entered, wrapt in thought. He was in evening dress, but a red sash round his waist gave a touch of picturesqueness and a dash of colour. He paused for a moment in the middle of the salon, without letting his eyes rest on anybody or anything. Then he walked straight up to Charles, and held out his dark hand.

'Good evening,' he said. 'You are the host. My soul's sight tells me so.'

'Good shot,' Sir Charles answered. 'These fellows have to be quick-witted, you know, Mrs Mackenzie, or they'd never get on at it.'

The Seer gazed about him, and smiled blankly at a person or two whose faces he seemed to recognize from a previous existence. Then Charles began to ask him a few simple questions, not about himself, but about me, just to test him. He answered most of them with surprising correctness. 'His name? His name begins with an S I think—you call him Seymour.' He paused long between each clause, as if the facts were revealed to him slowly. 'Seymour—Wilbraham— Earl of Strafford. No, not Earl of Strafford! Seymour Wilbraham Wentworth. There seems to be some connection in somebody's mind now present between Wentworth and Strafford. I am not English. I do not know what it means. But they are somehow the same name, Wentworth and Strafford.'

He gazed around, apparently for confirmation. A lady came to his rescue.

'Wentworth was the surname of the great Earl of Strafford,' she murmured gently; 'and I was wondering, as you spoke, whether Mr Wentworth might possibly be descended from him.'

'He is,' the Seer replied instantly, with a flash of those dark eyes. And I thought this curious; for though my father always maintained the reality of the relationship, there was one link wanting to complete the pedigree. He could not make sure that the Hon. Thomas Wilbraham Wentworth was the father of Jonathan Wentworth, the Bristol horsedealer, from whom we are descended.

'Where was I born?' Sir Charles interrupted, coming suddenly to his own case.

The Seer clapped his two hands to his forehead and held it between them, as if to prevent it from bursting. 'Africa,' he said slowly, as the facts narrowed down, so to speak. 'South Africa; Cape of Good Hope; Jansenville; De Witt Street. 1840.'

'By jove, he's correct,' Sir Charles muttered. 'He seems really to do it. Still, he may have found me out. He may have known where he was coming.'

'I never gave a hint,' I answered; 'till he reached the door, he didn't even know to what hotel I was piloting him.'

The Seer stroked his chin softly. His eye appeared to me to have a furtive gleam in it. 'Would you like me to tell you the number of a bank-note inclosed in an envelope?' he asked casually.

'Go out of the room,' Sir Charles said, 'while I pass it round the company.'

Señor Herrera disappeared. Sir Charles passed it round cautiously, holding it all the time in his own hand, but letting his guests see the number. Then he placed it in an envelope and gummed it down firmly.

The Seer returned. His keen eyes swept the company with a comprehensive glance. He shook his shaggy mane. Then he took the envelope in his hands and gazed at it fixedly. 'AF, 73549,' he answered, in a slow tone. 'A Bank of England note for fifty pounds—exchanged at the Casino for gold won yesterday at Monte Carlo.'

'I see how he did that,' Sir Charles said triumphantly. 'He must have changed it there himself; and then I changed it back again. In point of fact, I remember seeing a fellow with long hair loafing about. Still, it's capital conjuring.'

'He can see through matter,' one of the ladies interposed. It was Madame Picardet. 'He can see through a box.' She drew a little gold vinaigrette, such as our grandmothers used, from her dress-pocket. 'What is in this?' she inquired, holding it up to him.

Señor Herrera gazed through it. 'Three gold coins,' he replied, knitting his brows with the effort of seeing into the box: 'one, an American five dollars; one, a French ten-franc piece; one, twenty marks, German, of the old Emperor William.'

She opened the box and passed it round. Sir Charles smiled a quiet smile.

'Confederacy!' he muttered, half to himself. 'Confederacy!'

The Seer turned to him with a sullen air. 'You want a better sign?' he said, in a very impressive voice. 'A sign that will convince you! Very well: you have a letter in your left waistcoat pocket—a crumpled-up letter. Do you wish me to read it out? I will, if you desire it.'

It may seem to those who know Sir Charles incredible, but, I am bound to admit, my brother-in-law coloured. What that letter contained I cannot say; he only answered, very testily and evasively. 'No, thank you; I won't trouble you. The exhibition you have already given us of your skill in this kind more than amply suffices.' And his fingers strayed nervously to his waistcoat pocket, as if he was half afraid, even then, Señor Herrera would read it.

I fancied too, he glanced somewhat anxiously towards Madame Picardet.

The Seer bowed courteously. 'Your will, señor, is law,' he said. 'I make it a principle, though I can see through all things, invariably to respect the secrecies and sanctities. If it were not so, I might dissolve society. For which of us is it there who could bear the whole truth being told about him?' He gazed around the room. An unpleasant thrill supervened. Most of us felt this uncanny Spanish American knew really too much. And some of us were engaged in financial operations.

'For example,' the Seer continued blandly, 'I happened a few weeks ago to travel down here from Paris by train with a very intelligent man, a company promoter. He had in his bag some documents—some confidential documents': he glanced at Sir Charles. 'You know the kind of thing, my dear sir: reports from experts—from mining engineers. You may have seen some such; marked *strictly private*.'

'They form an element in high finance,' Sir Charles admitted coldly.

'Pre-cisely,' the Seer murmured, his accent for a moment less Spanish than before. 'And, as they were marked *strictly private,* I respect, of course, the seal of confidence. That's all I wish to say. I hold it a duty, being entrusted with such powers, not to use them in a manner which may annoy or incommode my fellow creatures.'

'Your feeling does you honour,' Sir Charles answered with some acerbity. Then he whispered in my ear: 'Confounded clever scoundrel, Sey; rather wish we hadn't brought him here.'

Señor Herrera seemed intuitively to divine this wish, for he interposed, in a lighter and gayer tone—

'I will now show you a different and more interesting embodiment of occult power, for which we shall need a somewhat subdued arrangement of surrounding lights. Would you mind, señor host—for I have purposely abstained from reading your name on the brain of any one present—would you mind my turning down this lamp just a little? . . . So! That will do. Now, this one; and this one. Exactly! that's right.' He poured a few grains of powder out of a packet into a saucer. 'Next, a match, if you please. Thank you!' It burnt with a strange green light. He drew from his pocket a card, and produced a little ink-bottle. 'Have you a pen?' he asked.

I instantly brought one. He handed it to Sir Charles. 'Oblige me,' he said, 'by writing your name there.' And he indicated a place in the centre of the card, which had an embossed edge, with a small middle square of a different colour.

Sir Charles has a natural disinclination to signing his name without knowing why. 'What do you want with it?' he asked. (A millionaire's signature has so many uses.)

'I want you to put the card in an envelope,' the Seer replied, 'and then to burn it. After that, I shall show you your own name written in letters of blood on my arm, in your own handwriting.'

Sir Charles took the pen. If the signature was to be burned as soon as finished, he didn't mind giving it. He wrote his name in his usual firm, clear style—the writing of a man who knows his worth and is not afraid of drawing a cheque for five thousand.

'Look at it long,' the Seer said, from the other side of the room. He had not watched him write it.

Sir Charles stared at it fixedly. The Seer was really beginning to produce an impression.

'Now, put it in that envelope,' the Seer exclaimed.

Sir Charles, like a lamb, placed it as directed.

The Seer strode forward. 'Give me the envelope,' he said. He took it in his hand, walked over towards the fireplace, and solemnly burnt it. 'See—it crumbles into ashes,' he cried. Then he came back to the middle of the room, close to the green light, rolled up his sleeve, and held his arm before Sir Charles. There, in blood-red letters, my brother-in-law read the name, 'Charles Vandrift', in his own handwriting!

'I see how that's done,' Sir Charles murmured, drawing back. 'It's a clever delusion; but still, I see through it. It's like that ghost-book. Your ink was deep green, your light was green; you made me look at it long; and then I saw the same thing written on the skin of your arm in complementary colours.'

'You think so?' the Seer replied, with a curious curl of the lip.

'I'm sure of it,' Sir Charles answered.

Quick as lightning the Seer rolled up his sleeve. 'That's your name,' he cried, in a very clear voice, 'but not your whole name. What do you say, then, to my right? Is this one also a complementary colour?'

He held his other arm out. There, in sea-green letters, I read the name, 'Charles O'Sullivan Vandrift'. It is my brother-in-law's full baptismal designation; but he has dropped the O'Sullivan for many years past, and, to say the truth, doesn't like it. He is a little bit ashamed of his mother's family.

Charles glanced at it hurriedly. 'Quite right,' he said, 'quite right!' But his voice was hollow. I could guess he didn't care to continue the *séance*. He could see through the man, of course; but it was clear the fellow knew too much about us to be entirely pleasant.

'Turn up the lights,' I said, and a servant turned them. 'Shall I say coffee and benedictine?' I whispered to Vandrift.

'By all means,' he answered. 'Anything to keep this fellow from further impertinences! And, I say, don't you think you'd better suggest at the same time that the men should smoke? Even these ladies are not above a cigarette—some of them.'

There was a sigh of relief. The lights burned brightly. The Seer for the moment retired from business, so to speak. He accepted a partaga with a very good grace, sipped his coffee in a corner, and chatted to the lady who had suggested Strafford with marked politeness. He was a polished gentleman.

Next morning, in the hall of the hotel, I saw Madame Picardet again, in a neat tailor-made travelling dress, evidently bound for the railway station.

'What, off, Madame Picardet?' I cried.

She smiled, and held out her prettily gloved hand. 'Yes, I'm off,' she answered archly. 'Florence, or Rome, or somewhere. I've drained Nice dry—like a sucked orange. Got all the fun I can out of it. Now I'm away again to gain my beloved Italy.'

But it struck me as odd that, if Italy was her game, she went by the omnibus which takes you down to the *train de luxe* for Paris. However, a man of the world accepts what a lady tells him, no matter how improbable; and I confess, for ten days or so, I thought no more about her, or the Seer either.

At the end of that time our fortnightly pass-book came in from the bank in London. It is part of my duty, as the millionaire's secretary, to make up this book once a fortnight, and to compare the cancelled cheques with Sir Charles's counterfoils. On this particular occasion I happened to observe what I can only describe as a very grave discrepancy—in fact, a discrepancy of £5,000. On the wrong side, too. Sir Charles was debited with £5,000 more than the total amount that was shown on the counterfoils.

I examined the book with care. The source of the error was obvious. It lay in a cheque to Self or Bearer, for £5,000 signed by Sir Charles, and evidently paid across the counter in London, as it bore on its face no stamp or indication of any other office.

I called in my brother-in-law from the salon to the study. 'Look here, Charles,' I said, 'there's a cheque in the book which you haven't entered.' And I handed it to him without comment, for I thought it might have been drawn to settle some little loss on the turf or at cards, or to make up some other affair he didn't desire to mention to me. These things will happen.

He looked at it and stared hard. Then he pursed up his mouth and gave a long low 'Whew!' At last he turned it over and remarked, 'I say, Sey, my boy, we've just been done jolly well brown, haven't we?'

I glanced at the cheque. 'How do you mean?' I inquired.

'Why, the Seer,' he replied, still staring at it ruefully. 'I don't mind the five thou., but to think the fellow should have gammoned the pair of us like that—ignominious, I call it!'

'How do you know it's the Seer?' I asked.

'Look at the green ink,' he answered. 'Besides, I recollect the very shape of the last flourish. I flourished a bit like that in the excitement of the moment, which I don't always do with my regular signature.'

'He's done us,' I answered, recognizing it. 'But how the dickens did he manage to transfer it to the cheque? This looks like your own handwriting, Charles, not a clever forgery.'

'It is,' he said. 'I admit it—I can't deny it. Only fancy him bamboozling me when I was most on my guard! I wasn't to be taken in by any of his silly occult tricks and catchwords; but it never occurred to me he was going to victimize me financially in this way. I expected attempts at a loan or an extortion; but to collar my signature to a blank cheque—atrocious!'

'How did he manage it?' I asked.

'I haven't the faintest conception. I only know those are the words I wrote. I could swear to them anywhere.'

'Then you can't protest the cheque?'

'Unfortunately, no; it's my own true signature.'

We went that afternoon without delay to see the Chief Commissary of Police at the office. He was a gentlemanly Frenchman, much less formal and red-tapey than usual, and he spoke excellent English with an American accent, having acted, in fact, as a detective in New York for about ten years in his early manhood.

'I guess,' he said slowly, after hearing our story, 'you've been victimized right here by Colonel Clay, gentlemen.'

'Who is Colonel Clay?' Sir Charles asked.

'That's just what I want to know,' the Commissary answered, in his curious American-French-English. 'He is a Colonel, because he occasionally gives himself a commission; he is called Colonel Clay, because he appears to possess an india-rubber face, and he can mould it like clay in the hands of the potter. Real name, unknown. Nationality, equally French and English. Address, usually Europe. Profession, former maker of wax figures to the Musée Grevin. Age, what he chooses. Employs his knowledge to mould his own nose and cheeks, with wax additions, to the character he desires to personate. Aquiline this time, you say. *Hein*! Anything like these photographs?'

He rummaged in his desk and handed us two.

'Not in the least,' Sir Charles answered. 'Except, perhaps, as to the neck, everything here is quite unlike him.'

'Then that's the Colonel!' the Commissary answered, with decision, rubbing his hands in glee. 'Look here,' and he took out a pencil and rapidly sketched the outline of one of the two faces—that of a bland-looking young man, with no expression worth mentioning. 'There's the Colonel in his simple disguise. Very good. Now watch me: figure to yourself that he adds here a tiny patch of wax to his nose—an aquiline bridge—just so; well, you have him right there; and the chin, ah, one touch: now, for hair, a wig: for complexion, nothing easier: that's the profile of your rascal, isn't it?'

'Exactly,' we both murmured. By two curves of the pencil, and a shock of false hair, the face was transmuted.

'He had very large eyes, with very big pupils, though,' I objected, looking close; 'and the man in the photograph here has them small and boiled-fishy.'

'That's so,' the Commissary answered. 'A drop of belladonna expands—and produces the Seer; five grains of opium contract—and give a dead-alive, stupidly innocent appearance. Well, you leave this affair to me, gentlemen. I'll see the fun out. I don't say I'll catch him for you; nobody ever yet has caught Colonel Clay; but I'll explain how he did the trick; and that ought to be consolation enough to a man of your means for a trifle of five thousand!'

'You are not the conventional French office holder, M. le Commissaire,' I ventured to interpose.

'You bet!' the Commissary replied, and drew himself up like a captain of infantry. 'Messieurs,' he continued, in French, with the utmost dignity, 'I shall devote the resources of this office to tracing out the crime, and, if possible, to effectuating the arrest of the culpable.'

We telegraphed to London, of course, and we wrote to the bank, with a full description of the suspected person. But I need hardly add that nothing came of it.

Three days later the Commissary called at our hotel. 'Well, gentlemen,' he said, 'I am glad to say I have discovered everything!'

'What? Arrested the Seer?' Sir Charles cried.

The Commissary drew back, almost horrified at the suggestion.

'Arrested Colonel Clay?' he exclaimed. '*Mais*, monsieur, we are only human! Arrested him? No, not quite. But tracked out how he did it. That is already much—to unravel Colonel Clay, gentlemen!'

'Well, what do you make of it?' Sir Charles asked, crestfallen.

The Commissary sat down and gloated over his discovery. It was clear a well-planned crime amused him vastly. 'In the first place, monsieur,' he said, 'disabuse your mind of the idea that when monsieur your secretary went out to fetch Señor Herrera that night, Señor Herrera didn't know to whose rooms he was coming. Quite otherwise, in point of fact. I do not doubt myself that Señor Herrera, or Colonel Clay (call him which you like), came to Nice this winter for no other purpose than just to rob you.'

'But I sent for him,' my brother-in-law interposed.

'Yes; he *meant* you to send for him. He forced a card, so to speak. If he couldn't do that I guess he would be a pretty poor conjuror. He had a lady of his own—his wife, let us say, or his sister—stopping here at this hotel; a certain Madame Picardet. Through her he induced several ladies of your circle to attend his *séances*. She and they spoke to you about him, and aroused your curiosity. You may bet your bottom dollar that when he came to this room he came ready primed and prepared with endless facts about both of you.'

'What fools we have been, Sey,' my brother-in-law exclaimed. 'I see it all now. That designing woman sent round before dinner to say I wanted to meet him; and by the time you got there he was ready for bamboozling me.'

'That's so,' the Commissary answered. 'He had your name ready painted on both his arms; and he had made other preparations of still greater importance.'

'You mean the cheque. Well, how did he get it?'

The Commissary opened the door. 'Come in,' he said. And a young man entered whom he recognized at once as the chief clerk in the Foreign Department of the Crédit Marseillais, the principal bank all along the Riviera.

'State what you know of this cheque,' the Commissary said, showing it to him, for we had handed it over to the police as a piece of evidence.

'About four weeks since—' the clerk began.

'Say ten days before your *séance*,' the Commissary interposed.

'A gentleman with very long hair and an aquiline nose, dark, strange, and handsome, called in at my department and asked if I could tell him the name of Sir Charles Vandrift's London banker. He said he had a sum to pay in to your credit, and asked if we would forward it for him. I told him it was irregular for us to receive the money, as you had no account with us, but that your London bankers were Darby, Drummond, and Rothenberg, Limited.'

'Quite right,' Sir Charles murmured.

'Two days later a lady, Madame Picardet, who was a customer of ours, brought in a good cheque for three hundred pounds, signed by a first-rate name, and asked us to pay it in on her behalf to Darby, Drummond, and Rothenberg's, and to open a London account with them for her. We did so, and received in reply a cheque-book.'

'From which this cheque was taken, as I learn from the number, by telegram from London,' the Commissary put in. 'Also, that on the same day on which your cheque was cashed, Madame Picardet, in London, withdrew her balance.'

'But how did the fellow get me to sign the cheque?' Sir Charles cried. 'How did he manage the card trick?'

The Commissary produced a similar card from his pocket. 'Was that the sort of thing?' he asked.

'Precisely! A facsimile.'

'I thought so. Well, our Colonel, I find, bought a packet of such cards, intended for admission to a religious function, at a shop in the Quai Masséna. He cut out the centre, and see here—' The Commissary turned it over, and showed a piece of paper pasted neatly over the back; this he tore off, and there, concealed behind it, lay a folded cheque, with only the place where the signature should be written showing through on the face which the Seer had presented to us. 'I call that a neat trick,' the Commissary remarked, with professional enjoyment of a really good deception.

'But he burnt the envelope before my eyes,' Sir Charles exclaimed. 'Pooh!' the Commissary answered. 'What would he be worth as a conjuror, anyway, if he couldn't substitute one envelope for another between the table and the fireplace without your noticing it? And Colonel Clay, you must remember, is a prince among conjurors.'

'Well, it's a comfort to know we've identified our man, and the woman who was with him,' Sir Charles said, with a slight sigh of relief. 'The next thing will be, of course, you'll follow them up on these clues in England and arrest them?'

The Commissary shrugged his shoulders. 'Arrest them!' he exclaimed, much amused. 'Ah, monsieur, but you are sanguine! No officer of justice has ever succeeded in arresting le Colonel Caoutchouc, as we call him in French. He is as slippery as an eel, that man. He wriggles through our fingers. Suppose even we caught him, what could we prove? I ask you. Nobody who has seen him once can ever swear to him again in his next impersonation. He is *impayable*, this good Colonel. On the day when I arrest him, I assure you, monsieur, I shall consider myself the smartest police officer in Europe.'

'Well, I shall catch him yet,' Sir Charles answered, and relapsed into silence.

ROBERT BARR · 1850-1912

The Chemistry of Anarchy

It has been said in the London papers that the dissolution of the Soho
Anarchist League was caused by want of funds. This is very far from
being the case. An Anarchist League has no need for funds, and so
long as there is money enough to buy beer the League is sure of
continued existence. The truth about the scattering of the Soho
organization was told me by a young newspaper man who was
chairman at the last meeting.

The young man was not an Anarchist, though he had to pretend to
be one in the interests of his paper, and so joined the Soho League,
where he made some fiery speeches that were much applauded. At
last Anarchist news became a drug in the market, and the editor of
the paper young Marshall Simkins belonged to, told him that he
would now have to turn his attention to Parliamentary work, as he
would print no more Anarchist news in the sheet.

One might think that young Simkins would have been glad to get
rid of his Anarchist work, as he had no love for the cause. He was
glad to get rid of it, but he found some difficulty in sending in his
resignation. The moment he spoke of resigning, the members became
suspicious of him. He had always been rather better dressed than the
others, and, besides, he drank less beer. If a man wishes to be in good
standing in the League he must not be fastidious as to dress, and he
must be constructed to hold at least a gallon of beer at a sitting.
Simkins was merely a 'quart' man, and this would have told against
him all along if it had not been for the extra gunpowder he put in his
speeches. On several occasions seasoned Anarchists had gathered
about him and begged him to give up his designs on the Parliament
buildings.

The older heads claimed that, desirable as was the obliteration of
the Houses of Parliament, the time was not yet ripe for it. England,
they pointed out, was the only place where Anarchists could live and
talk unmolested, so, while they were quite anxious that Simkins
should go and blow up Vienna, Berlin, or Paris, they were not willing

for him to begin on London. Simkins was usually calmed down with much difficulty, and finally, after hissing 'Cowards!' two or three times under his breath, he concluded with, 'Oh, very well, then, you know better than I do—I am only a young recruit; but allow me at least to blow up Waterloo Bridge, or spring a bomb in Fleet Street just to show that we are up and doing.'

But this the Anarchists would not sanction. If he wanted to blow up bridges, he could try his hand on those across the Seine. They had given their word that there would be no explosions in London so long as England afforded them an asylum.

'But look at Trafalgar Square,' cried Simkins angrily; 'we are not allowed to meet there.'

'Who wants to meet there?' said the chairman. 'It is ever so much more comfortable in these rooms, and there is no beer in Trafalgar Square.' 'Yes, yes,' put in several others; 'the time is not yet ripe for it.' Thus was Simkins calmed down, and beer allowed to flow again in tranquillity, while some foreign Anarchist, who was not allowed to set foot in his native country, would get up and harangue the crowd in broken English and tell them what great things would yet be done by dynamite.

But when Simkins sent in his resignation a change came over their feelings towards him, and he saw at once that he was a marked man. The chairman, in a whisper, advised him to withdraw his resignation. So Simkins, who was a shrewd young fellow, understanding the temper of the assembly, arose and said:

'I have no desire to resign, but you do nothing except talk, and I want to belong to an Anarchist Society that acts.' He stayed away from the next meeting, and tried to drop them in that way, but a committee from the League called upon him at his lodgings, and his landlady thought that young Simkins had got into bad ways when he had such evil-looking men visiting him.

Simkins was in a dilemma, and could not make up his mind what to do. The Anarchists apparently were not to be shaken off. He applied to his editor for advice on the situation, but that good man could think of no way out of the trouble.

'You ought to have known better,' he said, 'than to mix up with such people.'

'But how was I to get the news?' asked Simkins, with some indignation. The editor shrugged his shoulders. That was not his part of the business; and if the Anarchists chose to make things uncomfortable for the young man, he could not help it.

Simkins' fellow lodger, a student who was studying chemistry in London, noticed that the reporter was becoming gaunt with anxiety.

'Simkins,' said Sedlitz to him one morning, 'you are haggard and careworn: what is the matter with you? Are you in love, or is it merely debt that is bothering you?'

'Neither,' replied Simkins.

'Then cheer up,' said Sedlitz. 'If one or the other is not interfering with you, anything else is easily remedied.'

'I am not so sure of that,' rejoined Simkins; and then he sat down and told his friend just what was troubling him.

'Ah,' said Sedlitz, 'that accounts for it. There has been an unkempt ruffian marching up and down watching this house. They are on your track, Simkins, my boy, and when they discover that you are a reporter, and therefore necessarily a traitor, you will be nabbed some dark night.'

'Well, that's encouraging,' said Simkins, with his head in his hands.

'Are these Anarchists brave men, and would they risk their lives in any undertaking?' asked Sedlitz.

'Oh, I don't know. They talk enough, but I don't know what they would do. They are quite capable, though, of tripping me up in a dark lane.'

'Look here,' said Sedlitz, 'suppose you let me try a plan. Let me give them a lecture on the Chemistry of Anarchy. It's a fascinating subject.'

'What good would that do?'

'Oh, wait till you have heard the lecture. If I don't make the hair of some of them stand on end, they are braver men than I take them to be. We have a large room in Clement's Inn, where we students meet to try experiments and smoke tobacco. It is half club, and half a lecture room. Now, I propose to get those Anarchists in there, lock the doors, and tell them something about dynamite and other explosives. You give out that I am an Anarchist from America. Tell them that the doors will be locked to prevent police interference, and that there will be a barrel of beer. You can introduce me as a man from America, where they know as much about Anarchism in ten minutes as they do here in ten years. Tell them that I have spent my life in the study of explosives. I will have to make-up a little, but you know that I am a very good amateur actor, and I don't think there will be any trouble about that. At the last you must tell them that you have an appointment and will leave me to amuse them for a couple of hours.'

'But I don't see what good it is all going to do, though I am desperate,' said Simkins, 'and willing to try anything. I have thought some of firing a bomb off myself at an Anarchist meeting.'

When the Friday night of the meeting arrived the large hall in Clement's Inn was filled to the doors. Those assembled there saw a platform at one end of the apartment, and a door that led from it to a room at the back of the hall. A table was on the platform, and boxes, chemical apparatus, and other scientific-looking paraphernalia were on it. At the hour of eight young Simkins appeared before the table alone.

'Fellow Anarchists,' he said, 'you are well aware that I am tired of the great amount of talk we indulge in, and the little action which follows it. I have been fortunate enough to secure the co-operation of an Anarchist from America, who will tell you something of the cause there. We have had the doors locked, and those who keep the keys are now down at the entrance of the Inn, so that if a fire should occur they can quickly come and let us out. There is no great danger of fire, however, but the interruption of the police must be guarded against very carefully. The windows, as you see, are shuttered and barred, and no ray of light can penetrate from this room outside. Until the lecture is over no one can leave the room, and by the same token no one can enter it, which is more the purpose.

'My friend, Professor Josiah P. Slivers, has devoted his life to the Chemistry of Anarchy, which is the title of this lecture. He will tell you of some important discoveries, which are now to be made known for the first time. I regret to say the Professor is not in a very good state of health, because the line of life which he has adopted has its drawbacks. His left eye has been blown away by a premature explosion during his experiments. His right leg is also permanently disabled. His left arm, as you will notice, is in a sling, having been injured by a little disaster in his workshop since he came to London. He is a man, as you will see, devoted body and soul to the cause, so I hope you will listen to him attentively. I regret that I am unable to remain with you tonight, having other duties to perform which are imperative. I will therefore, if you will permit me, leave by the back entrance after I have introduced the Professor to you.'

At this moment the stumping of a wooden leg was heard, and those in the audience saw appear a man on crutches, with one arm in a sling and a bandage over an eye, although he beamed upon them benevolently with the other.

'Fellow Anarchists,' said Simkins, 'allow me to introduce to you Professor Josiah P. Slivers, of the United States.'

The Professor bowed and the audience applauded. As soon as the applause began the Professor held up his unmaimed arm and said, 'Gentlemen, I beg that you will not applaud.'

It seems the fashion in America to address all sorts and conditions of men as 'Gentlemen'. The Professor continued, 'I have here some explosives so sensitive that the slightest vibration will cause them to go off, and I therefore ask you to listen in silence to what I have to say. I must particularly ask you also not to stamp on the floor.'

Before these remarks were concluded Simkins had slipped out by the back entrance, and somehow his desertion seemed to have a depressing effect upon the company, who looked upon the broken-up Professor with eyes of wonder and apprehension.

The Professor drew towards him one of the boxes and opened the lid. He dipped his one useful hand into the box and, holding it aloft, allowed something which looked like wet sawdust to drip through his fingers. 'That, gentlemen,' he said, with an air of the utmost contempt, 'is what is known to the world as dynamite. I have nothing at all to say against dynamite. It has, in its day, been a very powerful medium through which our opinions have been imparted to a listening world, but its day is past. It is what the lumbering stage-coach is to the locomotive, what the letter is to the telegram, what the sailing-vessel is to the steamship. It will be my pleasant duty tonight to exhibit to you an explosive so powerful and deadly that hereafter, having seen what it can accomplish, you will have nothing but derision for such simple and harmless compounds as dynamite and nitro-glycerine.'

The Professor looked with kindly sympathy over his audience as he allowed the yellow mixture to percolate slowly through his fingers back into the box again. Ever and anon he took up a fresh handful and repeated the action.

The Anarchists in the audience exchanged uneasy glances one with the other.

'Yet,' continued the Professor, 'it will be useful for us to consider the substance for a few moments, if but for the purpose of comparison. Here,' he said, diving his hand into another box and bringing up before their gaze a yellow brick, 'is dynamite in a compressed form. There is enough here to wreck all this part of London, were it exploded. This simple brick would lay St Paul's Cathedral in ruins, so, however antiquated dynamite may become, we must always look upon it with respect, just as we look upon reformers of centuries ago who perished for their opinions, even though their opinions were far behind what ours are now. I shall take the liberty of performing some experiments with this block of dynamite.' Saying which the Professor, with his free arm, flung the block of dynamite far down the aisle, where it fell on the floor with a sickening thud. The audience sprang from their seats and tumbled back one over the other. A wild shriek went up into the air, but the Professor gazed placidly on the troubled mob below him with a superior smile on his face. 'I beg you to seat yourselves,' he said, 'and for reasons which I have already explained, I trust that you will not applaud any of my remarks. You have just now portrayed one of the popular superstitions about dynamite, and you show by your actions how necessary a lecture of this sort is in order that you may comprehend thoroughly the substance with which you have to deal. That brick is perfectly harmless, because it is frozen. Dynamite in its frozen state will not explode—a fact well understood by miners and all those who have to work with it, and who, as a rule, generally prefer to blow themselves to pieces trying to thaw the substance before a fire. Will you kindly bring that brick back to me, before it thaws out in the heated atmosphere of this room?'

One of the men stepped gingerly forward and picked up the brick, holding it far from his body, as he tip-toed up to the platform, where he laid it down carefully on the desk before the Professor.

'Thank you,' said the Professor, blandly.

The man drew a long breath of relief as he went back to his seat.

'That is frozen dynamite,' continued the Professor, 'and is, as I have said, practically harmless. Now, it will be my pleasure to perform two startling experiments with the unfrozen substance,' and with that he picked up a handful of the wet sawdust and flung it on a small iron anvil that stood on the table. 'You will enjoy these experiments,' he said, 'because it will show you with what ease dynamite may be handled. It is a popular error that concussion will cause dynamite to explode. There is enough dynamite here to blow up this hall and to send into oblivion every person in it, yet you will see whether or not concussion will explode it.' The Professor seized a hammer and struck the substance on the anvil two or three sharp blows, while those in front of him scrambled wildly back over their comrades, with hair standing on end. The Professor ceased his pounding and gazed reproachfully at them; then something on the anvil appeared to catch his eye. He bent over it and looked critically on the surface of the iron. Drawing himself up to his full height again, he said:

'I was about to reproach you for what might have appeared to any other man as evidence of fear, but I see my mistake. I came very near making a disastrous error. I notice upon the anvil a small spot of grease; if my hammer had happened to strike that spot you would all now be writhing in your death-agonies under the ruins of this building. Nevertheless, the lesson is not without its value. That spot of grease is free nitro-glycerine that has oozed out from the dynamite. Therein rests, perhaps, the only danger in handling dynamite. As I have shown you, you can smash up dynamite on an anvil without danger, but if a hammer happened to strike a spot of free nitro-glycerine it would explode in a moment. I beg to apologize to you for my momentary neglect.'

A man rose up in the middle of the hall, and it was some little time before he could command voice enough to speak, for he was shaking as if from palsy. At last he said, after he had moistened his lips several times:

'Professor, we are quite willing to take your word about the explosive. I think I speak for all my comrades here. We have no doubt at all about your learning, and would much prefer to hear from your own lips what you have to say on the subject, and not have you waste any more valuable time with experiments. I have not consulted with my comrades before speaking, but I think I voice the sense of the meeting.' Cries of 'You do, you do,' came from all parts of the hall. The Professor once more beamed upon them benevolently.

'Your confidence in me is indeed touching,' he said, 'but a chemical lecture without experiments is like a body without a soul. Experiment is the soul of research. In chemistry we must take nothing for granted. I have shown you how many popular errors have arisen regarding the substance with which we are dealing. It would have been impossible for these errors to have arisen if every man had experimented for himself; and although I thank you for the mark of confidence you have bestowed upon me, I cannot bring myself to deprive you of the pleasure which my experiments will afford you. There is another very common error to the effect that fire will explode dynamite. Such, gentlemen, is not the case.'

The Professor struck a match on his trousers' leg and lighted the substance on the anvil. It burnt with a pale bluish flame, and the

Professor gazed around triumphantly at his fellow Anarchists.

While the shuddering audience watched with intense fascination the pale blue flame the Professor suddenly stooped over and blew it out. Straightening himself once more he said, 'Again I must apologize to you, for again I have forgotten the small spot of grease. If the flame had reached the spot of nitro-glycerine it would have exploded, as you all know. When a man has his thoughts concentrated on one subject he is apt to forget something else. I shall make no more experiments with dynamite. Here, John,' he said to the trembling assistant, 'take this box away, and move it carefully, for I see that the nitro-glycerine is oozing out. Put it as tenderly down in the next room as if it were a box of eggs.'

As the box disappeared there was a simultaneous long-drawn sigh of relief from the audience.

'Now, gentlemen,' said the Professor, 'we come to the subject that ought to occupy the minds of all thoughtful men.' He smoothed his hair complacently with the palm of his practicable hand, and smiled genially around him.

'The substance that I am about to tell you of is my own invention, and compares with dynamite as prussic acid does with new milk as a beverage.' The Professor dipped his fingers in his vest pocket and drew out what looked like a box of pills. Taking one pill out he placed it upon the anvil and as he tip-toed back he smiled on it with a smile of infinite tenderness. 'Before I begin on this subject I want to warn you once more that if any man as much as stamps upon the floor, or moves about except on tip-toe this substance will explode and will lay London, from here to Charing Cross, in one mass of indistinguishable ruins. I have spent ten years of my life in completing this invention. And these pills, worth a million a box, will cure all ills to which the flesh is heir.'

'John,' he said, turning to his attendant, 'bring me a basin of water!' The basin of water was placed gingerly upon the table, and the Professor emptied all the pills into it, picking up also the one that was on the anvil and putting it with the others.

'Now,' he said, with a deep sigh, 'we can breathe easier. A man can put one of these pills in a little vial of water, place the vial in his vest-pocket, go to Trafalgar Square, take the pill from the vial, throw it in the middle of the Square, and it will shatter everything within the four-mile radius, he himself having the glorious privilege of suffering instant martyrdom for the cause. People have told me that this is a drawback to my invention, but I am inclined to differ with them. The one who uses this must make up his mind to share the fate of those around him. I claim that this is the crowning glory of my invention. It puts to instant test our interest in the great cause. John, bring in very carefully that machine with the electric-wire attachment from the next room.'

The machine was placed upon the table. 'This,' said the Professor, holding up some invisible object between his thumb and forefinger, 'is the finest cambric needle. I will take upon the point of it an invisible portion of the substance I speak of.' Here he carefully picked out a pill from the basin, and as carefully placed it upon the table, where he detached an infinitesimal atom of it and held it up on the point of the needle. 'This particle,' he said, 'is so small that it cannot be seen except with aid of a microscope. I will now place needle and all on the machine and touch it off with electric current'; and as his hand hovered over the push-button there were cries of 'Stop! stop!' but the finger descended, and instantly there was a terrific explosion. The very foundation seemed shaken, and a dense cloud of smoke rolled over the heads of the audience. As the Professor became visible through the thinning smoke, he looked around his audience. Every man was under the benches, and groans came from all parts of the hall. 'I hope,' said the Professor, in anxious tones, 'that no one has been hurt. I am afraid that I took up too much of the substance on the point of the needle, but it will enable you to imagine the effect of a larger quantity. Pray seat yourselves again. This is my last experiment.'

As the audience again seated itself, another mutual sigh ascended to the roof. The Professor drew the chairman's chair towards him and sat down, wiping his grimy brow.

A man instantly arose and said, 'I move a vote of thanks to Professor Slivers for the interesting—'

The Professor raised his hand. 'One moment,' he said, 'I have not quite finished. I have a proposal to make to you. You see that cloud of smoke hovering over our heads? In twenty minutes that smoke will percolate down through the atmosphere. I have told you but half of the benefits of this terrific explosive. When that smoke mixes with the atmosphere of the room it becomes a deadly poison. We all can live here for the next nineteen minutes in perfect safety, then at the first breath we draw we expire instantly. It is a lovely death. There is no pain, no contortion of the countenance, but we will be found here in the morning stark and stiff in our seats. I propose, gentlemen, that we teach London the great lesson it so much needs. No cause is without its martyrs. Let us be the martyrs of the great religion of Anarchy. I have left in my room papers telling just how and why we died. At midnight these sheets will be distributed to all the newspapers of London, and tomorrow the world will ring with our heroic names. I will now put the motion. All in favour of this signify it by the usual upraising of the right hand.'

The Professor's own right hand was the only one that was raised.

'Now all of a contrary opinion,' said the Professor, and at once very hand in the audience went up.

'The noes have it,' said the Professor, but he did not seem to feel badly about it. 'Gentlemen,' he continued, 'I see that you have guessed my second proposal, as I imagined you would, and though there will be no newspapers in London tomorrow to chronicle the fact, yet the newspapers of the rest of the world will tell of the destruction of this wicked city. I see by your looks that you are with me in this, my second proposal, which is the most striking thing ever planned, and is that we explode the whole of these pills in the basin. To make sure of this, I have sent to an agent in Manchester the full account of how it was done, and the resolutions brought forward at this meeting, and which doubtless you will accept.

'Gentlemen, all in favour of the instant destruction of London signify it in the usual manner.'

'Mr Professor,' said the man who had spoken previously, 'before you put that resolution I would like to move an amendment. This is a very serious proposal, and should not be lightly undertaken. I move as an amendment, therefore, that we adjourn this meeting to our rooms at Soho, and do the exploding there. I have some little business that must be settled before this grand project is put in motion.'

The Professor then said, 'Gentlemen, the amendment takes precedence. It is moved that this meeting be adjourned, so that you may consider the project at your club rooms in Soho.'

'I second that amendment,' said fifteen of the audience rising together to their feet.

'In the absence of the regular chairman,' said the Professor, 'it is my duty to put the amendment. All in favour of the amendment signify it by raising the right hand.'

Every hand was raised. 'The amendment, gentlemen, is carried. I shall be only too pleased to meet you tomorrow night at your club, and I will bring with me a larger quantity of my explosive. John, kindly go round and tell the man to unlock the doors.'

When Simkins and Slivers called round the next night at the regular meeting place of the Anarchists, they found no signs of a gathering, and never since the lecture has the Soho Anarchist League been known to hold a meeting. The Club has mysteriously dissolved.

STEPHEN LEACOCK· 1869-1944

Maddened by Mystery or The Defective Detective

The Great Detective sat in his office. He wore a long green gown and half a dozen secret badges pinned to the outside of it.

Three or four pairs of false whiskers hung on a whisker-stand beside him.

Goggles, blue spectacles, and motor glasses lay within easy reach.

He could completely disguise himself at a second's notice.

Half a bucket of cocaine and a dipper stood on a chair at his elbow.

His face was absolutely impenetrable.

A pile of cryptograms lay on the desk. The Great Detective hastily tore them open one after the other, solved them, and threw them down the cryptogram-chute at his side.

There was a rap at the door.

The Great Detective hurriedly wrapped himself in a pink domino, adjusted a pair of false black whiskers and cried,

'Come in.'

His secretary entered. 'Ha,' said the detective, 'it is you!'

He laid aside his disguise.

'Sir,' said the young man in intense excitement, 'a mystery has been committed!'

'Ha!' said the Great Detective, his eye kindling, 'is it such as to completely baffle the police of the entire continent?'

'They are so completely baffled with it,' said the secretary, 'that they are lying collapsed in heaps; many of them have committed suicide.'

'So,' said the detective, 'and is the mystery one that is absolutely unparalleled in the whole recorded annals of the London police?'

'It is.'

'And I suppose,' said the detective, 'that it involves names which you would scarcely dare to breathe, at least without first using some kind of atomizer or throat-gargle.'

'Exactly.'

'And it is connected, I presume, with the highest diplomatic consequences, so that if we fail to solve it England will be at war with the whole world in sixteen minutes?'

His secretary, still quivering with excitement, again answered yes.

'And finally,' said the Great Detective, 'I presume that it was committed in broad daylight, in some such place as the entrance of the Bank of England, or in the cloakroom of the House of Commons, and under the very eyes of the police?'

'Those,' said the secretary, 'are the very conditions of the mystery.'

'Good,' said the Great Detective, 'now wrap yourself in this disguise, put on these brown whiskers, and tell me what it is.'

The secretary wrapped himself in a blue domino with lace insertions, then, bending over, he whispered in the ear of the Great Detective:

'The Prince of Wurttemberg has been kidnapped.'

The Great Detective bounded from his chair as if he had been kicked from below.

A prince stolen! Evidently a Bourbon! The scion of one of the oldest families in Europe kidnapped. Here was a mystery indeed worthy of his analytical brain.

His mind began to move like lightning.

'Stop!' he said, 'how do you know this?'

The secretary handed him a telegram. It was from the Prefect of Police of Paris. It read: 'The Prince of Wurttemberg stolen. Probably forwarded to London. Must have him here for the opening day of Exhibition. £1,000 reward.'

So! The Prince had been kidnapped out of Paris at the very time when his appearance at the International Exposition would have been a political event of the first magnitude.

With the Great Detective, to think was to act, and to act was to think. Frequently he could do both together.

'Wire to Paris for a description of the Prince.'

The secretary bowed and left.

At the same moment there was a slight scratching at the door.

A visitor entered. He crawled stealthily on his hands and knees. A hearth-rug thrown over his head and shoulders disguised his identity.

He crawled to the middle of the room.

Then he rose.

Great Heaven!

It was the Prime Minister of England.

'You!' said the detective.

'Me,' said the Prime Minister.

'You have come in regard to the kidnapping of the Prince of Wurttemberg?'

The Prime Minister started.

'How do you know?' he said.

The Great Detective smiled his inscrutable smile.

'Yes,' said the Prime Minister. 'I will use no concealment. I am interested, deeply interested. Find the Prince of Wurttemberg, get him safe back to Paris and I will add £500 to the reward already offered. But listen,' he said impressively as he left the room, 'see to it that no attempt is made to alter the marking of the prince, or to clip his tail.'

So! To clip the Prince's tail! The brain of the Great Detective reeled. So! a gang of miscreants had conspired to—but no! the thing was not possible.

There was another rap at the door.

A second visitor was seen. He wormed his way in, lying almost prone upon his stomach, and wriggling across the floor. He was enveloped in a long purple cloak. He stood up and peeped over the top of it.

Great Heaven!

It was the Archbishop of Canterbury!

'Your Grace!' exclaimed the detective in amazement—'pray do not stand, I beg you. Sit down, lie down, anything rather than stand.'

The Archbishop took off his mitre and laid it wearily on the whisker-stand.

'You are here in regard to the Prince of Wurttemberg.'

The Archbishop started and crossed himself. Was the man a magician?

'Yes,' he said, 'much depends on getting him back. But I have only come to say this: my sister is desirous of seeing you. She is coming here. She has been extremely indiscreet and her fortune hangs upon the Prince. Get him back to Paris or I fear she will be ruined.'

The Archbishop regained his mitre, uncrossed himself, wrapped his cloak about him, and crawled stealthily out on his hands and knees, purring like a cat.

The face of the Great Detective showed the most profound sympathy. It ran up and down in furrows. 'So,' he muttered, 'the sister of the Archbishop, the Countess of Dashleigh!' Accustomed as he was to the life of the aristocracy, even the Great Detective felt that there was here intrigue of more than customary complexity.

There was a loud rapping at the door.

There entered the Countess of Dashleigh. She was all in furs.

She was the most beautiful woman in England. She strode imperiously into the room. She seized a chair imperiously and seated herself on it, imperial side up.

She took off her tiara of diamonds and put it on the tiara-holder beside her and uncoiled her boa of pearls and put it on the pearl-stand.

'You have come,' said the Great Detective, 'about the Prince of Wurttemberg.'

'Wretched little pup!' said the Countess of Dashleigh in disgust.

So! A further complication! Far from being in love with the Prince, the Countess denounced the young Bourbon as a pup!

'You are interested in him, I believe.'

'Interested!' said the Countess. 'I should rather say so. Why, I bred him!'

'You which?' gasped the Great Detective, his usually impassive features suffused with a carmine blush.

'I bred him,' said the Countess, 'and I've got £10,000 upon his chances, so no wonder I want him back in Paris. Only listen,' she said, 'if they've got hold of the Prince and cut his tail or spoiled the markings of his stomach it would be far better to have him quietly put out of the way here.'

The Great Detective reeled and leaned up against the side of the room. So! The cold-blooded admission of the beautiful woman for the moment took away his breath! Herself the mother of the young Bourbon, misallied with one of the greatest families of Europe, staking her fortune on a Royalist plot, and yet with so instinctive a knowledge of European politics as to know that any removal of the hereditary birthmarks of the Prince would forfeit for him the sympathy of the French populace.

The Countess resumed her tiara.

She left.

The secretary re-entered.

'I have three telegrams from Paris,' he said. 'They are completely baffling.'

He handed over the first telegram.

It read:

'The Prince of Wurttemberg has a long, wet snout, broad ears, very long body, and short hind legs.'

The Great Detective looked puzzled.

He read the second telegram.

'The Prince of Wurttemberg is easily recognized by his deep bark.'

And then the third.

'The Prince of Wurttemberg can be recognized by the patch of white hair across the centre of his back.'

The two men looked at one another. The mystery was maddening, impenetrable.

The Great Detective spoke.

'Give me my domino,' he said. 'These clues must be followed up,' then pausing, while his quick brain analysed and summed up the evidence before him—'a young man,' he muttered, 'evidently young since described as a "pup", with a long, wet snout (ha! addicted obviously to drinking), a streak of white hair across his back (a first sign of the results of his abandoned life)—yes, yes,' he continued, 'with this clue I shall find him easily.'

The Great Detective rose.

He wrapped himself in a long black cloak with white whiskers and blue spectacles attached.

Completely disguised, he issued forth.

He began the search.

For four days he visited every corner of London.

He entered every saloon in the city. In each of them he drank a glass of rum. In some of them he assumed the disguise of a sailor. In others he entered as a soldier. Into others he penetrated as a clergyman. His disguise was perfect. Nobody paid any attention to him as long as he had the price of a drink.

The search proved fruitless.

Two young men were arrested under suspicion of being the Prince, only to be released.

The identification was incomplete in each case.

One had a long wet snout but no hair on his back.

The other had hair on his back but couldn't bark.

Neither of them was the young Bourbon.

The Great Detective continued his search.

He stopped at nothing.

Secretly, after nightfall, he visited the home of the Prime Minister. He examined it from top to bottom. He measured all the doors and windows. He took up the flooring. He inspected the plumbing. He examined the furniture. He found nothing.

With equal secrecy he penetrated into the palace of the Archbishop.

He examined it from top to bottom. Disguised as a choir-boy he took part in the offices of the church. He found nothing.

Still undismayed, the Great Detective made his way into the home of the Countess of Dashleigh. Disguised as a housemaid, he entered the service of the Countess.

Then at last the clue came which gave him a solution of the mystery.

On the wall of the Countess's boudoir was a large framed engraving.

It was a portrait.

Under it was a printed legend:

THE PRINCE OF WURTTEMBERG

The portrait was that of a Dachshund.

The long body, the broad ears, the unclipped tail, the short hind legs—all was there.

In the fraction of a second the lightning mind of the Great Detective had penetrated the whole mystery.

THE PRINCE WAS A DOG!!!!

Hastily throwing a domino over his housemaid's dress, he rushed to the street. He summoned a passing hansom, and in a few moments was at his house.

'I have it,' he gasped to his secretary. 'The mystery is solved. I have pieced it together. By sheer analysis I have reasoned it out. Listen— hind legs, hair on back, wet snout, pup—eh, what? does that suggest nothing to you?'

'Nothing,' said the secretary; 'it seems perfectly hopeless.'

The Great Detective, now recovered from his excitement, smiled faintly.

'It means simply this, my dear fellow. The Prince of Wurttemberg is a dog, a prize Dachshund. The Countess of Dashleigh bred him, and he is worth some £25,000 in addition to the prize of £10,000 offered at the Paris dog show. Can you wonder that—'

At that moment the Great Detective was interrupted by the scream of a woman.

'Great Heaven!'

The Countess of Dashleigh dashed into the room.

Her face was wild.

Her tiara was in disorder.

Her pearls were dripping all over the place.

She wrung her hands and moaned.

'They have cut his tail,' she gasped, 'and taken all the hair off his back. What can I do? I am undone ! !'

'Madame,' said the Great Detective, calm as bronze, 'do yourself up. I can save you yet.'

'You!'

'Me!'

'How?'

'Listen. This is how. The Prince was to have been shown at Paris.'

The Countess nodded.

'Your fortune was staked on him?'

The Countess nodded again.

'The dog was stolen, carried to London, his tail cut and his marks disfigured.'

Amazed at the quiet penetration of the Great Detective, the Countess kept on nodding and nodding.

'And you are ruined?'

'I am,' she gasped, and sank down on the floor in a heap of pearls.

'Madame,' said the Great Detective, 'all is not lost.'

He straightened himself up to his full height. A look of inflinchable unflexibility flickered over his features.

The honour of England, the fortune of the most beautiful woman in England was at stake.

'I will do it,' he murmured.

'Rise, dear lady,' he continued. 'Fear nothing. I WILL IMPERSONATE THE DOG! ! !'

That night the Great Detective might have been seen on the deck of the Calais packet boat with his secretary. He was on his hands and knees in a long black cloak, and his secretary had him on a short chain.

He barked at the waves exultingly and licked the secretary's hand.

'What a beautiful dog!' said the passengers.

The disguise was absolutely complete.

The Great Detective had been coated over with mucilage to which dog hairs had been applied. The markings on his back were perfect. His tail, adjusted with an automatic coupler, moved up and down responsive to every thought. His deep eyes were full of intelligence.

Next day he was exhibited in the Dachshund class at the International show.

He won all hearts.

'*Quel beau chien!*' cried the French people.

'*Ach! was ein Dog!*' cried the Spanish.

The Great Detective took the first prize!

The fortune of the Countess was saved.

Unfortunately as the Great Detective had neglected to pay the dog tax, he was caught and destroyed by the dog-catchers. But that is, of course, quite outside of the present narrative, and is only mentioned as an odd fact in conclusion.

MARGARET MILLAR · b. 1915

McGowney's Miracle

When I finally found him, it was by accident. He was waiting for a
cable car on Powell Street, a dignified little man about sixty, in a black
topcoat and a grey fedora. He stood apart from the crowd, aloof but
friendly, his hands clasped just below his chest, like a minister about
to bless a batch of heathen. I knew he wasn't a minister.
A sheet of fog hung over San Francisco, blurring the lights and
muffling the clang of the cable cars.
I stepped up behind McGowney and said, 'Good evening.'
There was no recognition in his eyes, no hesitation in his voice.
'Why, good evening, sir.' He turned with a little smile. 'It is kind of
you to greet a stranger so pleasantly.'
For a moment, I was almost ready to believe I'd made a mistake.
There are on record many cases of perfect doubles, and what's more,
I hadn't seen McGowney since the beginning of July. But there was
one important thing McGowney couldn't conceal: his voice still
carried the throaty accents of the funeral parlour.
He tipped his hat and began walking briskly up Powell Street
toward the hill, his topcoat flapping around his skinny legs like
broken wings.

In the middle of the block, he turned to see if I was following him. I
was. He walked on, shaking his head from side to side as if genuinely
puzzled by my interest in him. At the next corner, he stopped in front
of a department store and waited for me, leaning against the window,
his hands in his pockets.
When I approached, he looked up at me frowning. 'I don't know
why you're following me, young man, but—'
'Why don't you ask me, McGowney?'
But he didn't ask. He just repeated his own name, 'McGowney,' in
a surprised voice, as if he hadn't heard it for a long time.
I said, 'I'm Eric Meecham, Mrs Keating's lawyer. We've met before.'
'I've met a great many people. Some I recall, some I do not.'

'I'm sure you recall Mrs Keating. You conducted her funeral last July.'

'Of course, of course. A great lady, a very great lady. Her demise saddened the hearts of all who had the privilege of her acquaintance, all who tasted the sweetness of her smile—'

'Come off it, McGowney. Mrs Keating was a sharp-tongued virago without a friend in this world.'

He turned away from me, but I could see the reflection of his face in the window, strained and anxious.

'You're a long way from home, McGowney.'

'This is my home now.'

'You left Arbana very suddenly.'

'To me it was not sudden. I had been planning to leave for twenty years, and when the time came, I left. It was summer then, but all I could think of was the winter coming on and everything dying. I had had enough of death.'

'Mrs Keating was your last—client?'

'She was.'

'Her coffin was exhumed last week.'

A cable car charged up the hill like a drunken rocking horse, its sides bulging with passengers. Without warning, McGowney darted out into the street and sprinted up the hill after the car. In spite of his age, he could have made it; but the car was so crowded there wasn't a single space for him to get a handhold. He stopped running and stood motionless in the centre of the street, staring after the car as it plunged and reared up the hill. Oblivious to the honks and shouts of motorists, he walked slowly back to the curb where I was waiting.

'You can't run away, McGowney.'

He glanced at me wearily, without speaking. Then he took out a half-soiled handkerchief and wiped the moisture from his forehead.

'The exhumation can't be much of a surprise to you,' I said. 'You wrote me the anonymous letter suggesting it. It was postmarked Berkeley. That's why I'm here in this area.'

'I wrote you no letter,' he said.

'The information it contained could have come only from you.'

'No. Somebody else knew as much about it as I did.'

'Who?'

'My—wife.'

'Your wife.' It was the most unexpected answer he could have given me. Mrs McGowney had died, along with her only daughter, in the flu epidemic after World War I. The story is the kind that still goes the rounds in a town like Arbana, even after thirty-five years: McGowney, unemployed after his discharge from the Army, had had no funds to pay for the double funeral, and when the undertaker offered him an apprenticeship to work off the debt, McGowney accepted. It was common knowledge that after his wife's death he never so much as looked at another woman, except, of course, in line of duty.

I said, 'So you've married again.'

'Yes.'

'When?'

'Six months ago.'

'Right after you left Arbana.'

'Yes.'

'You didn't lose much time starting a new life for yourself.'

'I couldn't afford to. I'm not young.'

'Did you marry a local woman?'

'Yes.'

I didn't realize until later that he had taken 'local' to mean Arbana, not San Francisco as I had intended.

I said, 'You think your wife wrote me that anonymous letter?'

'Yes.'

The street lights went on, and I realized it was getting late and cold. McGowney pulled up his coat collar and put on a pair of ill-fitting white cotton gloves. I had seen him wearing gloves like that before; they were as much a part of his professional equipment as his throaty voice and his vast store of sentimental aphorisms.

He caught me staring at the gloves and said, with a trace of apology, 'Money is a little tight these days. My wife is knitting me a pair of woollen gloves for my birthday.'

'You're not working.'

'No.'

'It shouldn't be hard for a man of your experience to find a job in your particular field.' I was pretty sure he hadn't even applied for one. During the past few days, I had contacted nearly every mortician within the Bay area; McGowney had not been to any of them.

'I don't want a job in my particular field,' McGowney said.

'It's the only thing you're trained for.'

'Yes. But I no longer believe in death.'

He spoke with simple earnestness, as if he had said, I no longer play blackjack, or I no longer eat salted peanuts.

Death, blackjack, or salted peanuts—I was not prepared to argue with McGowney about any of them, so I said, 'My car's in the garage at the Canterbury Hotel. We'll walk over and get it, and I'll drive you home.'

We started toward Sutter Street. The stream of shoppers had been augmented by a flow of white-collar workers, but all the people and the noise and the confusion left McGowney untouched. He moved sedately along beside me, smiling a little to himself, like a man who has developed the faculty of walking out on the world from time to time and going to live on some remote and happy island of his own. I wondered where McGowney's island was and who lived there with him.

I knew only one thing for sure: on McGowney's island there was no death.

He said suddenly, 'It must have been very difficult.'

'What was?'

'The exhumation. The ground gets so hard back East in the wintertime. I presume you didn't attend, Mr Meecham?'

'You presume wrong.'

'My, that's no place for an amateur.'

For my money, it was no place for anyone. The cemetery had been white with snow that had fallen during the night. Dawn had been breaking, if you could call that meagre, grudging light a dawn. The simple granite headstone had read, ELEANOR REGINA KEATING, OCTOBER 3, 1899–JUNE 30, 1953. A BLESSED ONE FROM US IS GONE, A VOICE WE LOVED IS STILL.

The blessed one had been gone, all right. Two hours later, when the coffin was pulled up and opened, the smell that rose from it was not the smell of death, but the smell of newspapers rotted with dampness and stones grey-greened with mildew.

I said, 'You know what we found, don't you, McGowney?'

'Naturally. I directed the funeral.'

'You accept sole responsibility for burying an empty coffin?'

'Not sole responsibility, no.'

'Who was in with you? And why?'

He merely shook his head.

As we waited for a traffic light, I studied McGowney's face, trying to estimate the degree of his sanity. There seemed to be no logic behind his actions. Mrs Keating had died quite unmysteriously of a heart attack and had been buried, according to her instructions to me, in a closed coffin. The doctor who had signed the death certificate was indisputably honest. He had happened to be in Mrs Keating's house at the time, attending to her older daughter, Mary, who had had a cold. He had examined Mrs Keating, pronounced her dead, and sent for McGowney. Two days later I had escorted Mary, still sniffling (whether from grief or the same cold, I don't know), to the funeral. McGowney, as usual, said and did all the correct things.

Except one. He neglected to put Mrs Keating's body in the coffin.

Time had passed. No one had particularly mourned Mrs Keating. She had been an unhappy woman, mentally and morally superior to her husband, who had been killed during a drinking spree in New Orleans, and to her two daughters, who resembled their father. I had been Mrs Keating's lawyer for three years. I had enjoyed talking to her; she had had a quick mind and a sharp sense of humour. But as in the case of many wealthy people who have been cheated of the privilege of work and the satisfactions it brings, she had been a bored and lonely woman who carried despair on her shoulder like a pet parakeet and fed it from time to time on scraps from her bitter memories.

Right after Mrs Keating's funeral, McGowney had sold his business and left town. No one in Arbana had connected the two events until the anonymous letter arrived from Berkeley shortly before Mrs Keating's will was awaiting admission into probate. The letter, addressed to me, had suggested the exhumation and stated the will must be declared invalid since there was no proof of death. I could think of no reason why McGowney's new wife wrote the letter, unless she had tired of him and had chosen a roundabout method of getting rid of him.

The traffic light changed and McGowney and I crossed the street and waited under the hotel marquee while the doorman sent for my car.

I didn't look at McGowney, but I could feel him watching me intently.

'You think I'm mad, eh, Meecham?'

It wasn't a question I was prepared to answer. I tried to look noncommittal.

'I don't pretend to be entirely normal, Meecham. Do you?'

'I try.'

McGowney's hand, in its ill-fitting glove, reached over and touched my arm, and I forced myself not to slap it away. It perched on my coat sleeve like a wounded pigeon. 'But suppose you had an abnormal experience.'

'Like you?'

'Like me. It was a shock, a great shock, even though I had always had the feeling that someday it would happen. I was on the watch for it every time I had a new case. It was always in my mind. You might even say I *willed* it.'

Two trickles of sweat oozed down behind my ears into my collar. 'What did you will, McGowney?'

'I willed her to live again.'

I became aware the doorman was signalling to me. My car was at the curb with the engine running.

I climbed in behind the wheel, and McGowney followed me into the car with obvious reluctance, as if he was already regretting what he'd told me.

'You don't believe me,' he said, as we pulled away from the curb.

'I'm a lawyer. I deal in facts.'

'A fact is what happens, isn't it?'

'Close enough.'

'Well, this happened.'

'She came back to life?'

'Yes.'

'By the power of your will alone?'

He stirred restlessly in the seat beside me. 'I gave her oxygen and adrenalin.'

'Have you done this with other clients of yours?'

'Many times, yes.'

'Is this procedure usual among members of your profession?'

'For me it was usual,' McGowney said earnestly. 'I've always wanted to be a doctor. I was in the Medical Corps during the war, and I picked up a little knowledge here and there.'

'Enough to perform miracles?'

'It was not my knowledge that brought her back to life. It was my will. She had lost the will to live, but I had enough for both of us.'

If it is true only a thin line separates sanity and madness, Mc-Gowney crossed and recrossed that line a dozen times within an hour, jumping over it and back again, like a child skipping rope.

'You understand now, Meecham? She had lost all desire. I saw it happening to her. We never spoke—I doubt she even knew my name—but for years I watched her pass my office on her morning walk. I saw the change come over her, the dullness of her eyes and the way she walked. I knew she was going to die. One day when she was passing by, I went out to tell her, to warn her. But when she saw me, she ran. I think she realized what I was going to say.'

He was telling the truth, according to his lights. Mrs Keating had mentioned the incident to me last spring. I recalled her words: 'A funny thing occurred this morning, Meecham. As I was walking past the undertaking parlour, that odd little man rushed out and almost scared the life out of me. . . .'

In view of what subsequently happened, this was a giant among ironies. As we drove toward the Bay Bridge and Berkeley, McGowney told me his story.

It was midday at the end of June, and the little backroom McGowney used as a lab was hot and humid after a morning rain.

Mrs Keating woke up as if from a long and troubled sleep. Her hands twitched, her mouth moved in distress, a pulse began to beat in her temple. Tears squeezed out from between her closed lids and slithered past the tips of her ears into the folds of her hair.

McGowney bent over her, quivering with excitement. 'Mrs Keating! Mrs Keating, you are alive!'

'Oh—God.'

'A miracle has just happened!'

'Leave me alone. I'm tired.'

'You are alive, you are *alive*!'

Slowly she opened her eyes and looked up at him. 'You officious little wretch, what have you done?'

McGowney stepped back, stunned and shaken. 'But—but you are alive. It's happened. My miracle has happened.'

'Alive. Miracle.' She mouthed the words as if they were lumps of alum. 'You meddling idiot.'

'I—But I—'

'Pour me a glass of water. My throat is parched.'

He was trembling so violently he could hardly get the water out of the cooler. This was his miracle. He had hoped and waited for it all his life, and now it had exploded in his face like an April-fool cigar.

He gave her the water and sat down heavily in a chair, watching her while she drank very slowly, as if in her short recess from life her muscles had already begun to forget their function.

'Why did you do it?' Mrs Keating crushed the paper cup in her fist as if it were McGowney himself. 'Who asked you for a miracle, anyway?'

'But I—Well, the fact is—'

'The fact is, you're a blooming meddler, that's what the fact is, McGowney.'

'Yes, ma'am.'

'Now what are you going to do?'

'Well, I–I hadn't thought.'

'Then you'd better start right now.'

'Yes, ma'am.' He stared down at the floor, his head hot with misery, his limbs cold with disappointment. 'First, I had better call the doctor.'

'You'll call no one, McGowney.'

'But your family—they'll want to know right away that—'

'They are not going to know.'

'But—'

'No one is going to know, McGowney. No one at all. Is that clear?'

'Yes.'

'Now sit down and be quiet.' He had no desire to move or to speak. Never had he felt so futile and depressed.

'I suppose,' Mrs Keating said grimly, 'you expect me to be grateful to you.'

McGowney shook his head.

'If you do, you must be crazy.' She paused and looked at him thoughtfully. 'You *are* a little crazy, aren't you, McGowney?'

'There are those who think so,' he said, with some truth. 'I don't agree.'

'You wouldn't.'

'Can't afford to, ma'am.'

The windows of the room were closed and no street sounds penetrated the heavy frosted glass, but from the corridor outside the door came the sudden tap of footsteps on tile.

McGowney bolted across the room and locked the door and stood against it.

'Mr McGowney? You in there?'

McGowney looked at Mrs Keating. Her face had turned chalky, and she had one hand clasped to her throat.

'Mr McGowney?'

'Yes, Jim.'

'You're wanted on the telephone.'

'I—can't come right now, Jim. Take a message.'

'She wants to talk to you personally. It's the Keating girl, about the time and cost of the funeral arrangements.'

'Tell her I'll call her back later.'

'All right.' There was a pause. 'You feeling okay, Mr McGowney?'

'Yes.'

'You sound kind of funny.'

'I'm fine, Jim. Absolutely first-rate.'

'Okay. Just thought I'd ask.'

The footsteps tapped back down the tile corridor.

'Mary loses no time.' Mrs Keating spoke through dry, stiff lips. 'She wants me safely underground so she can marry her electrician. Well, your duty is clear, McGowney.'

'What is it?'

'Put me there.'

McGowney stood propped against the door like a wooden soldier. 'You mean, b-b-bury you?'

'Me, or a reasonable facsimile.'

'That I couldn't do, Mrs Keating. It wouldn't be ethical.'

'It's every bit as ethical as performing unsolicited miracles.'

'You don't understand the problems.'

'Such as?'

'For one thing, your family and friends. They'll want to see you lying in—What I mean is, it's customary to put the body on view.'

'I can handle that part of it all right.'

'How?'

'Get me a pen and some paper.'

McGowney didn't argue, because he knew he was at fault. It was his miracle; he'd have to take the consequences.

Mrs Keating predated the letter by three weeks, and wrote the following:

To whom it may concern, not that it should concern anybody except myself:

I am giving these instructions to Mr McGowney concerning my funeral arrangements. Inasmuch as I have valued privacy during my life, I want no intrusion on it after my death. I am instructing Mr McGowney to close my coffin immediately and to see it stays closed, in spite of any mawkish pleas from my survivors.

Eleanor Regina Keating

She folded the paper twice and handed it to McGowney. 'You are to show this to Mary and Joan and to Mr Meecham, my lawyer.' She paused, looking very pleased with herself. 'Well. This is getting to be quite exciting, eh, McGowney?'

'Quite,' McGowney said listlessly.

'As a matter of fact, it's given me an appetite. I don't suppose there's a kitchen connected with this place?'

'No.'

'Then you'd better get me something from the corner drugstore. A couple of tuna-salad sandwiches, on wheat, with plenty of coffee. Lunch,' she added with a satiric little smile, 'will have to be on you. I forgot my handbag.'

'Money,' McGowney said. '*Money.*'

'What about it?'

'What will happen to your money?'

'I made a will some time ago.'

'But *you*, what will you live on?'

'Perhaps,' Mrs Keating said dryly, 'you'd better perform another miracle.'

When he returned from the drugstore with her lunch, Mrs Keating ate and drank with obvious enjoyment. She offered McGowney a part of the second sandwich, but he was too disheartened to eat. His miracle, which had started out as a great golden bubble, had turned into an iron ball chained to his leg.

Somehow he got through the day. Leaving Mrs Keating in the lab with some old magazines and a bag of apples, McGowney went about his business. He talked to Mary and Joan Keating in person and to Meecham on the telephone. He gave his assistant, Jim Wagner, the rest of the afternoon off, and when Jim had gone, he filled Mrs Keating's coffin (the de luxe white-and-bronze model Mary had chosen out of the catalogue) with rocks packed in newspapers, until it was precisely the right weight.

McGowney was a small man, unaccustomed to physical exertion, and by the time he had finished, his body was throbbing with weariness.

It was at this point Mary Keating telephoned to say she and Joan had been thinking the matter over, and since Mrs Keating had always inclined toward thrift, it was decided she would never rest at ease in such an ostentatious affair as the white and bronze. The plain grey would be far more appropriate, as well as cheaper.

'You should,' McGowney said coldly, 'have let me know sooner.'

'We just decided a second ago.'

'It's too late to change now.'

'I don't see why.'

'There are—certain technicalities.'

'Well, really, Mr McGowney. If you're not willing to put yourself out a little, maybe we should take our business somewhere else.'

'No! You can't do that—I mean, it wouldn't be proper, Miss Keating.'

'It's a free country.'

'Wait a minute. Suppose I give you a special price on the white and bronze.'

'How special?'

'Say, twenty-five per cent off?'

There was a whispered conference at the other end of the line, and then Mary said, 'It's still a lot of money.'

'Thirty-five?'

'Well, that seems more *like*,' Mary said, and hung up.

The door of McGowney's office opened, and Mrs Keating crossed the room, wearing a grim little smile.

McGowney looked at her helplessly. 'You shouldn't be out here, ma'am. You'd better go back and—'

'I heard the telephone ring, and I thought it might be Mary.'

'It wasn't.'

'Yes, it was, McGowney. I heard every word.'

'Well.' McGowney cleared his throat. 'Well. You shouldn't have listened.'

'Oh, I'm not surprised. Or hurt. You needn't be sorry for me. I haven't felt so good in years. You know why?'

'No, ma'am.'

'Because I don't have to go home. I'm free. Free as a bird.' She reached over and touched his coat sleeve. 'I don't have to go home, do I?'

'I guess not.'

'You'll never tell anyone.'

'No.'

'You're a very good man, McGowney.'

'I have never thought I wasn't,' McGowney said simply.

When darkness fell, McGowney got his car out of the garage and brought it around to the ambulance entrance behind his office.

'You'd better hide in the back seat,' he said, 'until we get out of town.'

'Where are we going?'

'I thought I'd drive you into Detroit, and from there you can catch a bus or a train.'

'To where?'

'To anywhere. You're free as a bird.'

She got into the back seat, shivering in spite of the mildness of the night, and McGowney covered her with a blanket.

'McGowney.'

'Yes, ma'am?'

'I felt freer when I was locked in your little lab.'

'You're a bit frightened now, that's all. Freedom is a mighty big thing.'

He turned the car toward the highway. Half an hour later, when the city's lights had disappeared, he stopped the car and Mrs Keating got into the front seat with the blanket wrapped around her shoulders, Indian style. In the gleam of oncoming headlights, her face looked a little troubled. McGowney felt duty-bound to cheer her up, since he was responsible for her being there in the first place.

'There are,' he said firmly, 'wonderful places to be seen.'

'Are there?'

'California, that's the spot I'd pick. Flowers all year round, never an end to them.' He hesitated. 'I've saved a bit throughout the years. I always thought someday I'd sell the business and retire to California.'

'What's to prevent you?'

'I couldn't face the idea of, well, of being alone out there without friends or a family of some kind. Have you ever been to California?'

'I spent a couple of summers in San Francisco.'

'Did you like it?'

'Very much.'

'I'd like it, too, I'm sure of that.' He cleared his throat. 'Being alone, though, that I wouldn't like. Are you warm enough?'

'Yes, thanks.'

'Birds—well, birds don't have such a happy time of it that I can see.'

'No?'

'All that freedom and not knowing what to do with it except fly around. A life like that wouldn't suit a mature woman like yourself,

Mrs Keating.'

'Perhaps not.'

'What I mean is—'

'I know what you mean, McGowney.'

'You—you do?'

'Of course.'

McGowney flushed. 'It's—well, it's very unexpected, isn't it?'

'Not to me.'

'But I never even thought of it until half an hour ago.'

'I did. Women are more foresighted in these matters.'

McGowney was silent a moment. 'This hasn't been a very romantic proposal. I ought to say something a bit on the sentimental side.'

'Go ahead.'

He gripped the steering wheel hard. 'I think I love you, ma'am.'

'You didn't have to say that,' she replied sharply. 'I'm not a foolish young girl to be taken in by words. At my age, I don't expect love. I don't want to—'

'But you are loved,' McGowney declared.

'I don't believe it.'

'Eventually you will.'

'Is this another of your miracles, McGowney?'

'This is the important one.'

It was the first time in Mrs Keating's life she had been told she was loved. She sat beside McGowney in awed silence, her hands folded on her lap, like a little girl in Sunday school.

McGowney left her at a hotel in Detroit and went home to hold her funeral.

Two weeks later they were married by a justice of the peace in a little town outside Chicago. On the long and leisurely trip West in McGowney's car, neither of them talked much about the past or worried about the future. McGowney had sold his business, but he'd been in too much of a hurry to wait for a decent price, and so his funds were limited. But he never mentioned this to his bride.

By the time they reached San Francisco, they had gone through quite a lot of McGowney's capital. A large portion of the remainder went towards the purchase of the little house in Berkeley.

By late fall, they were almost broke, and McGowney got a job as a shoe clerk in a department store. A week later along with his first pay cheque, he received his notice of dismissal.

That night at dinner, he told Eleanor about it, pretending it was all a joke, and inventing a couple of anecdotes to make her laugh.

She listened, grave and unamused. 'So that's what you've been doing all week. Selling shoes.'

'Yes.'

'You didn't tell me we needed money that badly.'

'We'll be all right, I can easily get another job.'

'Doing what?'

'What I've always done.'

She reached across the table and touched his hand. 'You don't want to be a mortician again.'

'I don't mind.'

'You always hated it.'

'I *don't mind*, I tell you.'

She rose decisively.

'Eleanor, what are you going to do?'

'Write a letter,' she said with a sigh.

'Eleanor, don't do anything drastic.'

'We have had a lot of happiness. It couldn't last forever. Don't be greedy.'

The meaning of her words pierced McGowney's brain. 'You're going to let someone know you're alive?'

'No. I couldn't face that, not just yet. I'm merely going to show them I'm not dead so they can't divide up my estate.'

'But why?'

'As my husband, you're entitled to a share of it if anything happens to me.'

'Nothing will ever happen to you. We agreed about that, didn't we?'

'Yes, McGowney. We agreed.'

'We no longer believe in death.'

'I will address the letter to Meecham,' she said.

'So she wrote the letter.' McGowney's voice was weary. 'For my sake. You know the rest, Meecham.'

'Not quite,' I said.

'What else do you want to know?'

'The ending.'

'The ending.' McGowney stirred in the seat beside me and let out his breath in a sigh. 'I don't believe in endings.'

I turned right at the next traffic light, as McGowney directed. A sign on the lamppost said, LINDEN AVENUE.

Three blocks south was a small green-and-white house, its eaves dripping with fog.

I parked my car in front of it and got out, pleasantly excited at the idea of seeing Mrs Keating again. McGowney sat motionless, staring straight ahead of him, until I opened the car door.

'Come on, McGowney.'

'Eh? Oh. All right. All right.'

He stepped out on the sidewalk so awkwardly he almost fell.

I took his arm. 'Is anything wrong?'

'No.'

We went up the porch steps.

'There are no lights on,' McGowney said. 'Eleanor must be at the store. Or over at the neighbours'. We have some very nice neighbours.'

The front door was not locked. We went inside, and McGowney turned on the lights in the hall and the sitting room to the right.

The woman I had known as Mrs Keating was sitting in a wing chair in front of the fireplace, her head bent forward as if she was in deep thought. Her knitting had fallen on the floor, and I saw it was a half-finished glove in bright colours. McGowney's birthday present.

In silence, McGowney reached down and picked up the glove and put it on a table. Then he touched his wife gently on the forehead. I knew from the way his hand flinched that her skin was as cold as the ashes in the grate.

I said, 'I'll get a doctor.'

'No.'

'She's dead?'

He didn't bother to answer. He was looking down at his wife with a coaxing expression. 'Eleanor dear, you must wake up. We have a visitor.'

'McGowney, for God's sake—'

'I think you'd better leave now, Mr Meecham,' he said in a firm, clear voice. 'I have work to do.'

He took off his coat and rolled up his sleeves.

SARA WOODS · 1922-1985

Every Tale Condemns Me

'Talking of ESP,' said the thin man in the corner diffidently. They hadn't in fact been doing so, but conversation in the first-class compartment had become fairly general, so that he felt it was not an unreasonable way of introducing a change of subject. The stout lady who was sitting diagonally across from him with her back to the engine seemed puzzled and repeated the phrase doubtfully.

'ESP?' she said and looked around for enlightenment. She was a pleasant-looking person with a good fur round her shoulders, a double string of imitation pearls, and an impressive bosom. The Canadian who sat opposite her undertook her instruction.

'Extra-sensory perception,' he said. 'There was an article a week or two back in *Maclean's* . . . I have it sent over. I don't know if you happened to see it.'

There was a murmur of negation. They were too polite to tell him they thought he was talking about toothpaste . . . all of them except for the youngish man on his left, who had once spent a fortnight in Montreal. He added, kindly but misleadingly, 'Seem to have missed that one.' He was a barrister, Antony Maitland by name, and he was travelling back from Arkenshaw after a conference that seemed likely to lead to a brief in the not too distant future.

Perhaps encouraged by this not very convincing show of interest, the elderly man opposite, who looked as though he had spent his whole life climbing the executive ladder to the top of whatever business he was engaged in, added his own comment. 'There has been a good deal of correspondence on the subject in *The Times.*' (An expert in the art of one-upmanship, thought Maitland, amused.)

The clergyman, who had the centre seat with his back to the engine, crowded uncomfortably between the businessman and the woman passenger, nodded his comprehension. There was an air of authority about the businessman's pronouncement, and though he didn't carry a copy of the newspaper he had mentioned it seemed likely that he was one of the Top People. 'Interesting,' said the clergyman. 'Very.'

'Telepathy,' the Canadian was explaining to the stout woman. He was living in England on a salary that was paid in dollars, and had in consequence a sleek and prosperous look, even by contrast with his companions. 'Telepathy, and clairvoyance, and telekinesis—'

'Spiritualism?' she asked hopefully, but with an apologetic look at the clergyman on her right.

He gave a booming laugh and turned back to the thin man. 'Perhaps,' he suggested, 'our friend will explain what aspect of the subject he had in mind.'

'Well . . . clairvoyance,' said the thin man, still sounding diffident if not apologetic.

'Not ghosts,' said Maitland, answering the question in the stout woman's mind though she had not in fact spoken again.

'I knew a chap,' said the businessman helpfully, 'who dreamed he was running in the Grand National and came a cropper at Beechers. Went out and picked a horse called All Fall Down in the three thirty next day. Thought it was an omen you see.'

'Did it win?' asked Antony Maitland.

The businessman shook his head sadly. 'No,' he said. 'That was the funny part about it, don't you see?'

The diffident man spoke again into the silence that followed, while the others were wrestling with the logic of this pronouncement.

'A friend of mine had some very odd experiences.' He looked round him, collecting eyes in a determined way. Only the man who sat opposite him, isolated behind a copy of the *Yorkshire Post*, avoided his glance; and as he hadn't spoken during the hour that had passed since the train came out of the station at Arkenshaw it didn't seem likely that he'd interrupt now. 'It started when we were at school together. We'd been out late one night and were all set to get in by the usual route—'

One of the minor public schools, though the clergyman, eyeing him appraisingly and perhaps a little condescendingly, secure as he was in the knowledge of his own *alma mater*'s undoubted superiority. The stout woman leaned forward and said, 'Boarding school,' helpfully to the Canadian. She was pleased to be able to repay his thoughtfulness, but as she was the only girl in a family of boys and had been well brought up on her brothers' reading matter, disdaining as maudlin stories that were written specifically for the female sex, she was more occupied at the moment in trying to cast the speaker in the role of hero (who broke bounds at night with only the best intentions), or as the depraved boy who went out to drink, or to plead for the time to pay his gambling debts. Unaware of these reflections, the thin man was pursuing his story more confidently now. It crossed Maitland's mind that the diffidence, which he himself knew only too well how to assume on occasion, was no more than a cloak for a determination—or perhaps compulsion wouldn't be too strong a word—to tell the story of his clairvoyant friend.

'There was no question in my mind we'd be all right,' he was saying. 'We'd done the same thing a hundred times . . . well, say, a dozen. But all at once Fred stops and grips my arm. Can't go that way he says, old Manning's waiting for us.'

Because he paused some comment seemed to be called for. 'Awkward,' said Maitland dryly.

'So what did you do?' asked the stout lady, though to Antony at least it was quite obvious he was in no need of encouragement to proceed.

'Well, we argued a bit back and forth,' said the thin man. 'But Fred was always a determined chap, and as there was another way we could take in the end I humoured him. It was rather a long way round and meant going through the chapel,' he added apologetically. The clergyman looked benevolent and sketched a gesture as though absolving him of blame. 'So that's how we got in. But the funny thing was two other fellows got caught using the regular route. Which proved I'd been right to listen to Fred.'

'Well, I never!' said the stout lady comfortably. There was a murmur of approval from the other travellers, though the man with the *Yorkshire Post* remained silent.

'Coincidence, you say,' said the narrator, encouraged. 'And of course if that had been the only thing that happened . . . but it wasn't. After that it was just as if he knew when circumstances were going to be against him. And when the others began to realize that it made him popular, I can tell you. As long as you kept in with him you were all right, he always saw to it that his friends steered clear of trouble.'

'Did he ever dream the winner of the Grand National?' asked the Canadian.

'No, that didn't seem to be the way of it. But he had the most phenomenal luck,' the thin man went on. 'At school, of course, but I told you about that; I really meant later when he joined a firm of stockbrokers in the city, and later got a seat on the exchange. I went into a bank myself,' he added, faintly regretful.

'Precognition,' said Maitland, and smiled at the narrator. 'If I'd been you I'd have stuck to him like glue,' he added.

'Well, of course, I didn't tell you we were cousins, did I? So we were always friends and saw a good deal of each other. But as for your question, there wasn't so much "pre" about it. What I mean is it was more like the inspiration of the moment, and if he'd stopped to tell me it'd have been too late. At least, that's what he always said. If he went racing he'd go up to put on his stake with no idea in the world what he was going to do, and then, bang, down would go his money on the winner. Uncanny it was, I can tell you, and it wasn't just at the races, of course, on the stock market he always seemed to know exactly when to buy and when to sell.'

'Useful,' said the businessman wistfully.

'Yes, but he stopped going to the races quite early,' said the thin man. 'Said it took all the fun out of gambling. Later, after he was married, he'd only back horses his wife picked out for him with a list of runners and a pin.'

There seemed to be some indignation at this, even the clergyman murmuring, 'How very wasteful.'

The thin man took up his tale again rather quickly. 'It didn't really matter from his point of view, though I did wish sometimes he'd tell me . . . but that's water under the bridge now. But when it came to a question of business he'd no objection at all to making use of his gift. Naturally he didn't tell anyone about it, and when I asked him later he just said he'd outgrown it, but I watched him piling up the money and I must say I wondered. But then his sister was getting married and he sent a telegram at the last minute with some lame excuse for not attending the wedding. Two-thirds of the guests went down with food-poisoning, and if you ask me he knew perfectly well something was going to happen.'

'Were you among them?' asked Maitland. 'You said you were cousins,' he explained when the thin man looked at him inquiringly.

'Yes, I was as a matter of fact, and it was a nasty business but we all got over it. All the same, great offence had been taken in the family, and afterwards when I tackled him about it he admitted he had had a feeling . . . just like when we were at school, he said. And he said perhaps it would have been better to take the risk, because after all it didn't happen so often nowadays. I didn't believe him about that, I was quite sure the feelings had been going on all the time and I didn't feel very sorry for him about the estrangement, even when he was cut out of his aunt's will.'

'Did you benefit from that?' asked the clergyman, to the gratitude of all concerned. His cloth, they felt, entitled him to ask questions that would be unsuitable from anyone else.

'Not a bit of it,' said the thin man. 'She was on the other side of his family, you see, and no relation of mine. But I was saying, I couldn't be really sympathetic about it, he'd plenty of money by then, and many's the time I've wished my relations would stop speaking to me.'

'Yes, indeed,' said Maitland. The businessman and the Canadian both sighed sympathetically. The stout lady, however, bristled, as though she thought there might somehow be something insulting in the remark.

The clergyman put the tips of his fingers together and intoned, 'A sad commentary on human nature, my dear sir. Very sad.'

'Oh, I don't know,' said the thin man vaguely. 'Then when he was thinking of getting married himself, it suddenly came to him that he was courting the wrong sister. So he switched to the other one and found she'd had a fortune left to her by her godmother.'

'Are you sure he didn't know about that beforehand?' asked the businessman rather cynically.

'Unless he was lying to me, and I don't think he was. Because then he admitted to me that the inspirations—whatever you like to call them—had never left him, and of course I asked him to help me out a bit, putting me on to a good thing occasionally, but he said the bank wouldn't look very favourably on one of its employees getting involved in the stock market. Well, naturally I didn't leave it there, and he must have known I'd keep on at him so he wouldn't have admitted it unless it was true.'

'And is that the end of the story?' asked the clergyman after there had been a moment's silence.

'No, it isn't. The queerest thing of all happened only a few days ago. He'd made this pile, and his wife had a packet too as I told you, and for some reason they took it into their heads they'd like to live in the country, in the north. Well, money was no object, as I've explained to you, so there was no reason why he shouldn't take an early retirement. Off they went, and found themselves an estate not too far from Arkenshaw and Fred must have enjoyed himself playing the lord of the manor, or the squire, or whatever, because he didn't come south again until our uncle died.'

'An uncle of both of you?' asked the stout lady, who liked to get

anything in connection with family matters quite clear in her mind.
'Yes, this was on Fred's father's side, my father's side too, for that matter. The aunt I spoke of earlier was his mother's sister.'

'The question of his non-attendance at his sister's marriage had been overlooked by the family by now, I suppose,' said the clergyman.

'More or less. Anyway, it was his obvious duty to attend.'

'And this time no premonition prevented him from coming?' asked Maitland, with a little scepticism in his tone.

'Nothing like that.'

'Then perhaps his instinct told him he was about to inherit another fortune,' said the businessman, entering into the spirit of the story.

'If he had one of his feelings about that he didn't tell me,' said the thin man. He paused there, but the expectant eyes of his audience proved too much for him. 'Uncle Michael was nicely off,' he said, 'and he left money half to Fred and half to me. It didn't matter to Fred, of course, but when you've just a bank clerk's salary it meant a good deal to me. Not that I wasn't sorry the old boy had packed it in,' he added. 'He had a stroke, though none of us had expected—'

'Except perhaps Fred?' the Canadian suggested.

'—and he was only about sixty so he should have had a good many years before him. But that wasn't what I was going to tell you.' This time his pause seemed deliberate and he looked round impressively. Obviously the climax of his story had been reached. 'You see he was going to fly back to Yeadon,' he said, 'and I went to Heathrow with him to see him off. And then, just when they called the plane, all of a sudden he got one of his feelings.'

'Now that's something like,' said the Canadian in a pleased tone. 'What I mean, a feeling's of some use if it saves your life.'

'And if it makes you a fortune—'

'Or saves you from getting into trouble at school—'

'Or keeps you from getting food poisoning—'

'Or marrying the wrong girl.'

The man with the *Yorkshire Post* put down his paper suddenly and said in an exasperated way: 'Well, finish your story, man. He went by train instead, and the plane crashed and everyone was killed.'

'Oh no,' said the thin man, 'that wasn't what happened at all. He didn't catch the plane, that's right enough, and we had a bit of an argument about whether he should warn the airline, him saying it was his duty perhaps, and me pointing out they'd just laugh at him. Luckily that time he listened to me, and decided to take the train as you suggested, sir. But he'd be in a bit of a rush to get across town to King's Cross and catch the next one, so he just shoved his airline ticket into my hands to get a refund—he was careful about things like that—and went off to find a taxi.'

'And he caught the train and that crashed,' said the man with the *Yorkshire Post*, who seemed to be of an impatient disposition.

'Not that either,' said the thin man, 'but it was his not taking the plane that did for him all the same. He set off to walk from the station to the house of a friend of his who he thought would drive him out to Yeadon where he'd left his car. If any of you know Arkenshaw you'll know the towpath by the canal. Silly, really, to have gone that way, there's never anyone much about, and the long and the short of it is that he got himself mugged . . . hit over the head and his wallet taken. I'm just on my way back from the funeral.'

Everyone, even the man with the *Yorkshire Post*, had some words of condolence for that. It was left to Maitland, who had vivid memories himself of that particular short cut, to add a question to his expressions of sympathy. 'He was found quite quickly then? If he'd been thrown in the canal I'd have thought—'

'He was just left there, dead on the towpath,' said the thin man. 'But it was queer—wasn't it?—that after all that run of luck it should be a premonition that did for him in the end.'

JOSEF SKVORECKY · b. 1924

An Intimate Business

Lieutenant Boruvka told himself it was conscientiousness that had brought him to the women's prison. When he'd considered the matter in the police car on the way there, he'd been willing to admit that qualms of conscience might also have had something to do with it. But he would have denied with all his heart that it could be the somewhat faded countenance of this fair-haired girl in the coarse prison jacket. He would have denied it because it was the truth.

She sat across from him in the otherwise empty visiting room; the table between them was covered with carved hearts and other, less decent, symbols of love. The lieutenant wondered what miracle had put the carvings there, when conversations at the table were always so closely guarded. But experience had long since shown him that there are truly more things in heaven and earth than can be explained by pure reason. Besides, the table might not always have been here; maybe other girls used to sit around it, and not girls like this one.

Now, looking at her face without the camouflage of makeup, he saw that the years couldn't be denied. Thirty-five? More? Maybe a little less? But she was a slender young woman—under the jacket, apparently made out of rug fabric, he observed a pair of narrow, girlish shoulders—and her grey, widely spaced eyes really knocked him out, although he was of an age where he preferred younger women. Preferred . . . but then, he was vulnerable to beauty of every sort.

She had never confessed at the trial; that was why his conscience kept bothering him. All the evidence had pointed to her, so they'd put her away. But the lieutenant still had the uncomfortable feeling that he'd overlooked something.

Yet everything at the trial had been against her. The autopsy had incontrovertibly indicated the presence of hyoscine, and hyoscine was the poison missing from the stocks of her pharmacist landlady, Mrs Korenac. It had also come out that Mrs Korenac was a serious morphine addict, so that it was no problem for her tenant to obtain something from the chaotic stores in her pharmacy. And the girl did admit to one criminal offence: with the help of her landlady, and occasionally without it, she had supplied her midnight colleagues with benzedrine.

Moreover, she had the classic motive for murder by poison. The words from the transcript of the trial had engraved themselves on the lieutenant's memory:

Prosecutor: Would you kindly tell the court, miss, just what you saw on Tuesday, June 7th at three o'clock in the afternoon, in the corridor by Director Weyr's dressing room?

Witness: I was just coming from the makeup room, and as I was passing the director's door Eve Adam came flying out, her eyes all red from crying.

Prosecutor: Did you hear the defendant say anything on that occasion?

Witness: I did. She turned around in the doorway and she said, or I should say she screeched, 'Just wait, you—' and then she said a terribly bad word. . . .

'It's the truth, lieutenant,' said the girl in the rug-fabric jacket. 'Though I can hardly believe it myself. Even at my relatively young age, I ought to have more sense. But sometimes a woman just doesn't. I could have a brain like a bookkeeper—in fact, I do—but then a rose-coloured cloud settles around me and I act like a crazy young fool. You wouldn't understand.'

The lieutenant wasn't unfamiliar with the condition. He wanted to say something to that effect, but she didn't give him a chance.

'If only I had done it, the rat. If I at least had him on my conscience, like Shura—' She broke off.

'Like who?' the lieutenant asked suspiciously.

'Oh, just somebody I know. She's locked up already, don't worry. She's sort of royalty here in the clink. She doesn't do any work, the gypsy girls do everything for her. They even do her nails, and they give her food from their own rations—she's twice as big as she was when she came in here.'

'For heaven's sake, why?'

'Well, her boyfriend was squealing to the cops. He was sentenced to death by a secret gypsy tribunal and Shura carried out the sentence. Then the gypsies made mincemeat out of him, sewed him up inside a dead horse, and dumped him in the Vah River. Only the horse swelled up—'

'I'm sorry you have to be here in that kind of company,' said the lieutenant. 'In fact, that's why I came.'

'Well, the company isn't all that bad. I have a girlfriend here, her name is Annie Preclikova, and she—' The girl stopped herself again. She had almost yielded to her native volubility and divulged the secret of certain gold items from a certain robbery successfully executed by her friend. They had never got Annie to confess where she'd hidden the gold, and Annie had promised her a share of it when they got out. Fortunately she caught herself in time. She gave the policeman a probing look, and then relaxed at the sight of his round face, his blue eyes, and all the other physiognomical clues to a simple soul: guileless, rather naive, even bordering on dense. How can this chump be a detective, she thought. She scolded herself for talking too much—and started right back in again.

'The thing is, I was gone on him, lieutenant. Completely, head over heels. That's me all over—never do anything by halves. But if I ever get out of here, to hell with love, to hell with emotional attachments! I'll only do it for the sake of my health, only out of calculated self-interest, I swear!'

'I have come to help you,' said the lieutenant, a little pompously and a little out of context. The girl, who was used to thinking the worst, wondered briefly whether this was an immoral proposition in response to her last declaration. But at that moment he looked practically simple-minded, and she squelched the thought.

'That's nice of you,' she said. 'Only it's a shame you didn't think to do it sooner.'

The criminologist reddened. The girl registered this, and straightened a strand of hair that had fallen across her grey eyes. The lieutenant decided it had looked better over her eyes.

'The thing is, I saw him as a god,' she continued. 'Not because . . . not just because he was a famous director and he gave me that bit part. The thing is, I believed in him. He talked a blue streak, I should have recognized his ulterior motive, I'd heard all that often enough over the—I mean, enough guys have tried it,' she went on, and the lieutenant grew sadder. Unlike the girl, who liked to drop literary references now and then, he wasn't very well read, and her mention of some sort of 'motive' aroused his suspicion that she was mixed up in something after all. 'Only I was playing the fool all over again, lieutenant. That's why it really shook me up when I saw him with that little brat. I hate to admit it, but I acted like a darned female, I just blew it.'

'You were startled, were you?' asked the lieutenant, trying to understand.

'Exactly!' She nodded vehemently. 'Imagine me—a crazy young fool sitting on cloud nine, all red hot to do the world a good deed. So I took the stint singing at the lounge at Barrandov film studios, subbing for my friend Lidka, who'd just found out her rich Italian boyfriend was in town. My own gig over at the Lucerna Bar didn't begin until eleven, so I thought I'd do her a favour. And no sooner did I climb up on stage and start singing "Have I got good news for you" than it's to hell with good news—I saw them right there in front of me, at the first table by the dance floor. Rudolf and that nitwit. It was such a shock that it didn't really sink in for about twelve hours. And not only did I have to look at them, not only did my professional position force me to watch Rudolf making time with her—using the same method he'd tried with me, down to every last detail—but I had to keep right on singing that "nobody needs to be alone", because the show must go on, that's the rule in show business, no matter what happens. And I was so wiped out by the whole thing that after I finished singing I just stood there in front of the mike like a pillar of salt, Jarda Strudl had to poke me in the behind with his saxophone, I was that rigid, and then they picked up and left, arm in arm, and Rudolf was murmuring sweet nothings into her silly, eighteen-year-old, piggy little ear—Sorry,' she apologized, and a pink tinge showed through the prison pallor. 'I don't give a darn any more, you know,' she added, unconvincingly. 'It's just that every time I think of that moment I—especially since I recognized that brat from the magazine photo, and realized she's exactly Petr's age, so she could be Rudolf's daughter. And that bast—sorry,' she apologized again, and her grey-eyed gaze touched on the lieutenant's fishy eye.

At that moment the lieutenant wasn't seeing those eyes, but rather the article and the photograph:

Director Weyr has entrusted the roles of the brother and sister to an interesting pair. The brother will be played by Petr Weyr, a student at the Academy of Theatrical Arts and the director's own son, while the part of the sister has been given to a young medical student, Petra Heyduk. The coincidence of the first names has a certain charm, but another circumstance is particularly worthy of note. Although the younger Mr Weyr has the year 1948 on his birth certificate and Miss Heyduk has 1949, they are in fact exactly the same age. Petr Weyr was born several minutes before midnight on New Year's Eve, 1948, while Petra Heyduk first saw the light of day several minutes after midnight on January 1st, 1949. Heaven knows if there isn't a touch of destiny in that. . . .

That, four dots and all, was how the reporter Mrs Malinovska wrote it up in *Vlasta*, a magazine for women—socialist women, but women all the same. The article was accompanied by a photo of two young faces, tilted towards each other more like sweethearts than like siblings. The pose, set up by the reporter, was apparently meant to imply the direction that destiny would take beyond the four dots.

'Petra!' declared the girl with distaste. 'If she had to be a silly little cluck, did she have to have such a silly clucky name too?' she said, with a voice full of poison. 'Sorry. So the next day in his dressing room, I just did my nut.'

'You . . . lost your cool?' the lieutenant prompted her uncertainly, searching in his mind through his daughter Zuzana's vocabulary for any such expression.

'You bet your life I lost my cool,' she retorted. The lieutenant knew from the records of the case that she had started singing in revues back in the year Petr Weyr was born, and had moved to nightclubs later, once they were permitted again—mainly in the border country, in the uranium empire near Jachymov. That was probably where she'd picked up the coarser elements in her language, he thought, and excused her. 'Just like a darned female,' continued the girl. 'So then, in the dressing room, I called him a bastard—sorry—and slammed the door, and that's when that makeup lady saw me. And that was it: I was on my way you know where, flat on my you know what, and I'm still here.'

The lieutenant was all too familiar with the dramatic sequence of events that had followed.

Prosecutor: So, Miss Synkova, you say you worked on Director Weyr's staff as a so-called clapper. Can you tell us what you observed of the victim's behaviour towards the defendant on Wednesday, June 8th? That is, the day after the scene in the corridor as described by the witness Miss Moselova?

Witness: The director had been in a nasty mood ever since he arrived, and the one to catch it the worst was Eve Adam, I mean the defendant. She had the first two scenes that day. And the way he treated her, he didn't yell but he was sarcastic, you know? He kept putting her down. Like he said to her, 'For heaven's sake, if you can't fix it with makeup, would you at least try and *sound* like you're twenty-five?'

Prosecutor: How did the defendant respond to that?

Witness: Normally. She started to cry. She'd been pretty damp in the optical department all day, they had to keep the powder-puff handy, and—

Prosecutor: (Interrupts) I beg your pardon. You said something about some kind of optical department. . . .

The prosecutor's fleeting hope of an espionage or sabotage connection came to nothing. But the girl was found guilty of murder all the same. The lieutenant stared at her pale face and suddenly realized that he kept thinking of her as a girl, although she could have been Zuzana's mother. He couldn't help himself, though. She just wasn't in the same category as Mrs Boruvka, no matter what her age. He recognized the danger of a man of his own age viewing a woman of the prisoner's age as anything so dewy-sounding, shook his head, and urgently tried to recollect the section of the court records that really did refer to optical equipment:

Prosecutor: And you, sir, live in a villa that has a direct view of the victim's home?

Witness: Yes sir, right across the street. I have a telescope on my balcony there. I'm an amateur astronomer—

Prosecutor: What did you see the evening before the murder—that is, on Tuesday—in the second-floor window?

Witness: That's where the movie director's bedroom is—or was. It was dark already, about nine o'clock, when the light suddenly went on in there. I was just looking at the evening star, and I saw that lady over there—

Prosecutor: The defendant?

Witness: That's right. She had her hand on the light switch, but just then the director walked in and turned the light off. Then the curtains were drawn across the window and the light went on again.

Prosecutor: And did you hear anything?

Witness: I did, but that was later. Before eleven. Some woman was having fits over there.

Prosecutor: You mean to say she was shouting?

Witness: That's right, shouting. I could hear it all the way back in my bedroom.

'Anyway,' said the girl, 'I went there to throw that bit part right in his face. I had the crazy idea that I'd make him mad, because he'd have to do those two scenes over with somebody else, and that costs money.'

'Did he accept your resignation?'

'No problem,' said the girl. 'My idea of what it costs to make a movie was kind of naive. And he turned the light out in the bedroom because he noticed that his curtains were open. He was being naive too—he thought nobody knew about him. And then he gave me a lecture. An awful one.'

'About what?'

'I . . . I can't repeat that. He was talking about women, talking as if they were chickens or something, you know? From the point of view of his stupid male superiority. The thing is, he was probably right. Or maybe he wasn't—it's all a matter of what your values are. And your priorities. You understand?'

The lieutenant didn't understand, but he nodded.

'Like falling in love and making a fool of yourself,' she explained. 'Or that coldness of his, like a dog's nose, all brains and meanness.'

The lieutenant nodded again. 'Yes, well . . . you've got something there. It's all a matter of your point of view, as you say. So there was another argument that night, that the neighbour heard?'

'Not an argument, that was when I acted like such an idiot, like I said,' sighed the girl. 'And that neighbour's a fine example of a peeping Tom, repulsive old creep. He's even got a telescope installed for his hobby! Evening star indeed, the old pig!' She almost lost her temper again, but caught herself. 'But never mind that. I was so dumb that the next day I even had second thoughts, wondering if I'd gone off half cocked, quitting the part like that. Not that I regretted it—not a whole lot, that is—but I thought maybe I'd misjudged him, maybe he'd recast Petra's part on account of me and the scene I threw for him on Tuesday in his dressing room, the day the makeup lady saw me. I didn't know he'd recast it before the night I was at his place, he never told me. I didn't find out until the next day that Petra had been replaced. He just let me go ahead and make an ass of myself—sorry— in front of that slob from across the street. Misjudged him? The hell I

did. Heaven knows why he recast her part, but it certainly wasn't on
my account.'

Of course, the lieutenant knew why Director Weyr had decided to
break up that ideal pair of good-looking kids. There was a perfectly
credible story about that in the court records:

I got my hands on that *Vlasta* magazine on Monday. A patient
brought it to my office, asked if I'd seen it, and when I said I
hadn't, she said to take a look. There was the article about how
Weyr cast our Petra in the part opposite his son in the film. But
I couldn't allow anything like that to happen. Why? Listen, the
medical profession is hereditary in our family. My great-
grandfather was a doctor, and my grandfather, and so was my
father. I'm the first one who didn't have a son. I couldn't have
any children, I mean I couldn't have any more children—I suffer
from testicular azoospermia. So Petra had to take up the torch.
But she didn't seem to mind at all. She's wanted to be a doctor
ever since she was a little girl. And she'd done so well in her first
year at medical school. And now, put yourself in her place: girl
like that, pretty, cheerful, an excellent medical student, and
suddenly she finds herself in the movies. There's one important
thing I forgot to tell you: her mother, my late first wife, was an
actress. Not that I put too much stock in heredity, mind you, but
environment means a whole lot. At home Petra always lived in
what I might call a hospital atmosphere, and if she once got a
taste of films and glory—I didn't want to take the chance. So I
set out to see Rudolf. That's right, Weyr. We'd known each other
for years, ever since high school in Brno, and it was my first wife
who introduced Rudolf to his wife. We used to get together for
a few years after they married. We played tennis, went to the
cottage, you know how it is. But naturally, a film director hasn't
got much of a future out in Brno, and Rudolf got a job in
Prague—his father-in-law was head of some production group
at the Barrandov studios there. So we stopped seeing each other.
Later on I was transferred closer to Prague, to Pardubice. But
there just wasn't enough time. I met Rudolf once or twice when
I came to Prague on business, but that was all. The kids practically didn't know each other. So when I saw that article, I went
to see him. It turned out he'd cast Petra in that role just to please
me. When I explained how worried I was, how Petra might turn
out to be a lousy movie star when she could have been an

excellent physician, he admitted that I was probably right. No, I didn't tell Petra. Rudolf promised me he wouldn't tell her either, he'd blame it on screen tests or something. He'd say Petra wasn't photogenic. No, I know she is, I know it all too well. She's my daughter, but maybe I can say it and it won't sound like boasting. If she weren't my daughter, and if I were a quarter of a century younger.... That's another thing. Petr is an attractive young man. And studying medicine is hard enough without having other things on your mind, not to mention a baby under foot. No, no, I want Petra to be a doctor, and it will be a whole lot better for her to be able to diagnose a case of appendicitis than to play walk-ons in the movies or wait on a movie-star husband. I explained all this to Rudolf, and he heard me out, and followed through.

And a few more sentences from the flustered testimony of Petra Heyduk, medical student:

The truth is that I wondered why he took the part away from me. As for the screen tests being bad, he can save that for his dumb extras from the Film Club. I thought he was mad at me because I slapped him.

Prosecutor: Slapped him?

Witness: I slapped his face in the taxi on the way down from Barrandov. He was really after me, and with no encouragement, either. So I said to myself, it's probably true what they say about film directors and the casting couch, you know what I mean?

Prosecutor: I don't want you to hold anything back, now.

Witness: I haven't got anything to hold back. That little part wasn't worth it to me. So I gave up on the fame and glory of the silver screen. Besides, I was having problems in histology on account of it, and my dad would have been awfully unhappy if I'd flunked the exam. So I never gave another thought to why they took the part away from me. But. . . .

Prosecutor: Go on, please!

Witness: Well, when he cast that phoney little twit in the part. . . . I do wonder, now. Maybe she went along with him. In fact—

Prosecutor: Thank you, miss, that will suffice.

'No way, he didn't recast it because of that,' sighed the grey-eyed girl. 'But it's a mystery why he did. Did you see the Lastovicka girl that he had time to cast in the part before, as you say, I did him in?'

'I don't say you did him in, miss,' the lieutenant declared, offended. 'If I thought that, I wouldn't be sitting here today. I believe you are innocent. But we need evidence.'

'If the evidence you need to get me out of here is as flimsy as what it took to put me in—' She waved a hand. 'I don't have any illusions. That's the way it goes, it's always a lot easier to get into trouble than it is to get out of it. But did you see that Lastovicka girl?'

'I did,' admitted the lieutenant. 'She still has the part. The film is being completed with Burdych as director, and she, Miss Lastovicka, well. . . .'

And he recalled the testimony of the assistant director:

He phoned me up, that would have been on Tuesday, the day before the murder. It was about eight in the evening. That reporter, Mrs Malinovska, was just over at my place, so she had it in the paper the very next day. He wanted me to get hold of Miss Lastovicka right away, that night, and tell her she'd be taking over the part from Petra Heyduk. I wanted to object, but he said Petra's father had forbidden her to do it and that was that, and he hung up on me. The next day it was all over the papers, thanks to Mrs Malinovska: that Petra Heyduk gave up the part on the wishes of her father. 'Allegedly,' it said, 'so that work in motion pictures not interfere with her studies. But who knows. . . ?'

'It boggles the mind, doesn't it? A girl like Lastovicka!' She was indignant. 'He boots out a cute little thing like that silly Heyduk girl, and hires a mug you can only shoot from behind, if you don't want to scare everybody in the movie house. Explain that to me, will you?' She was really quite upset, and an almost rosy colour glowed through her pallor. She was a very dynamic girl, the lieutenant thought. All the sadder that she had to be in prison. And again he felt a pang of conscience for not having been as diligent in this case as he might have been.

'Though, to be perfectly honest,' she added, brushing a strand of fair hair out of her beautiful eyes again, 'no matter what she looks like, I kind of like the Lastovicka girl better beside young Weyr than I did Petra. I don't know how come, but the two of them . . . I just couldn't see them together.'

'No?' The lieutenant was genuinely puzzled. He took a photograph out of his breast pocket, the one he'd clipped out of *Vlasta.* Those two little heads tilted towards each other in a pretty pose. He passed the picture to the girl.

'No way,' said the prisoner. 'They just don't go together. Don't you see what I mean?'

The picture travelled back to the lieutenant. He saw nothing odd about the picture, except that any two young people should be so attractive. He thought of a similar picture, a snapshot that immortalized himself and his sister when they were about the same age as these two. The photographer hadn't even put it in his show window. He and his sister had looked a lot alike, and the only thing that could be said about the lieutenant's appearance at the age of eighteen was that he was a dead ringer for an amiable but somewhat dull Simple Simon.

'Really?' He cleared his throat. 'I don't know what's off about them. I think they seem like an ideal couple, I mean for a movie. Don't you?'

And the photograph travelled back across the table. The girl bent over it and furrowed her blonde brows. A little wrinkle formed between them; the lieutenant's eyes rested on it, the girl noticed, and the wrinkle vanished.

'An ideal pair of lovers, maybe,' she said slowly. 'But in this film they were supposed to play brother and sister.'

She thought a moment. 'It's probably just female intuition, an advantage we chickens occasionally have over you lords of creation. Or do you ever have intuitions yourself, lieutenant?'

'No, I don't,' he said sadly. 'I work purely by deduction. And occasionally'—he turned slightly pink—'I get a little help from coincidence.'

'If only you could get some help from coincidence in my case,' sighed the girl.

'I wish I could,' declared the lieutenant, and he flushed bright red. The girl looked at him and her intuition suggested something to her. Unfortunately it wasn't anything that would prove that on the night of Wednesday, June eighth, she hadn't murdered Rudolf Weyr.

On the contrary, everything still pointed to her. The lieutenant realized it again and again that evening as he pored over her file, plugging his ears so as not to hear his progeny, eighteen-year-old Zuzana and thirteen-year-old Joey, indulging in their devotion to the music known as rock. The clapper the director had sent to pick up his medication on Tuesday, the day before the murder, might have had the opportunity to substitute a capsule of hyoscine for one of his regular ones, but in her case there was a conspicuous absence of any sort of motive, let alone access to the poison.

And the capsules were something special. The director suffered terrible migraines, and common run-of-the-mill painkillers didn't work for him. His capsules were prescribed for him by his brother, head of the Pharmacological Research Institute, who was in fact personal physician and health adviser to the entire Weyr family. True, he had a profound interest in toxicology, but—like the clapper—he had no motive. Besides, the batch of capsules that included the fatal one had been made up at an ordinary pharmacy. Weyr carried them in a silver pillbox in his hip pocket except at night, when he put the box on his night table within reach of the bed. Whoever smuggled the poisoned capsule into it must have been very close to him. Hyoscine acts mercifully but definitively, by putting one to sleep, and according to the coroner death had occurred shortly before midnight.

It was abundantly clear that the clapper hadn't planted the hyoscine. True, Weyr had given her a lift on the day of the murder, but the only important thing about that ride was her testimony that he took one capsule from the silver pillbox in the car, and complained of especially severe pain. He also voiced his doubt that a single capsule would be enough, stating that before he went to sleep he would have to take another dose of 'this poison'. He surely didn't mean anything by the metaphor. He didn't know it wasn't a metaphor.

He let the clapper out on Wenceslas Square and around half past seven arrived at his own villa. The astronomer across the street had set himself up on the balcony for his observations, just as he had the previous evening when he glimpsed the girl in the director's bedroom. When he saw that the director had arrived, he went inside to have his dinner. He returned to his post at eight o'clock and remained there, in spite of a consistently cloudy sky, until eleven. The lights in the director's study were on all that time, but the blinds were drawn. At about half past ten the light came on for a while in the bedroom, and a female silhouette crossed in front of the curtained window. She stood for a moment—as if in hesitation—and then went back and switched off the light. Because there were no interesting shadows to enliven the blinds in the study, thanks to a poorly placed lamp, the witness got bored around eleven and went to bed. At a quarter past eleven Weyr phoned his assistant to say that he didn't feel well and that it was entirely possible he wouldn't be coming in the next day. He gave him instructions to direct the shooting of several detail shots without any actors. He said he had pains in his left side and was having trouble breathing. Probably the flu, even though it was June. . . .

The expert medical witness of course recognized the pains as typical symptoms of early hyoscine poisoning, just preceding the critical moment when the victim falls into a deep sleep.

Naturally the prosecutor wanted to know who the female silhouette was. Weyr and his son had lived alone in the house for the whole month of June, and his son hadn't returned home that night until late, so it couldn't have been any ladyfriend of his. Apparently between 7:30 and 8:00, while the witness was at dinner, some woman had come to the house and Weyr had let her in—unless of course she had come in the back way, in which case it could have been earlier or later. Maybe she always came in the back way: Weyr would have been afraid of her presence being discovered. Be that as it might, the defendant had no alibi for the time in question—she claimed she'd been at home, but she had no witnesses—and so it could very well be her silhouette that was observed by the astronomer behind the drawn curtains. According to the prosecutor, it probably was. Around half past ten, he postulated, an argument ensued and Weyr sent the defendant to the bedroom to bring him a capsule from the pillbox on the night stand. The accused was just waiting for an opportunity like that. She walked into the bedroom and turned on the light, but she didn't go over to the night stand at all. She didn't have to. She had the capsule with the hyoscine all ready. She waited a moment—which appeared to the witness to be a 'hesitation'—and then returned to the study and handed the capsule to Weyr. Weyr swallowed it and the defendant left soon thereafter. It could have been after 11:00, when the witness had already gone to bed. The coroner testified that by midnight, precisely according to hyoscine's schedule, Weyr was dead.

The defendant of course denied all this, maintaining that the prosecutor's hypothetical reconstruction was based on a total unfamiliarity with psychology, at least that of the female of the species. Having got into a violent argument with Weyr earlier, she would have never have allowed him to make an errand girl out of her that same evening. She insisted on her innocence, the prosecutor insisted on his reconstruction. As is usually the case in Czechoslovakia, the judge was inclined towards the side of authority. . . .

The lieutenant looked up from the file. In the whole dark room the lamp with the green shade illuminated only his face—a face that kinder people compared to the moon, and more malicious ones to a pancake. The orgy of noise in the next room was escalating, a bleating voice from the television set was singing something that seemed to be about St Vitus Cathedral bringing somebody down—no, it must be something else, how would a cathedral get into a rock song? All the same, the lieutenant got up and opened the door a crack. He saw Zuzana staring wide-eyed at the screen, where a sleazy-looking youth writhed repulsively and twanged on a guitar. Sure enough, the great cathedral of St Vitus rose in the background.

Sighing, the lieutenant shut the door and sat down in an armchair. The aesthetic ideals of his daughter's generation mystified him. He would have understood it if Zuzana had been infatuated with, say, young Weyr. But when he had brought home the picture of that sweet young couple, Zuzana had remarked to a friend of hers, 'She's all right, but that pretty boy—I don't think I've ever seen a slicker, creepier guy in my whole life. Have you?' And the friend had agreed.

An infinitesimal hope began to dawn in the lieutenant's breast: after all, he himself certainly didn't belong to the category of pretty boys. . . . But the hope died as he realized that the girl in jail didn't belong to his daughter's peculiar generation.

He closed his eyes, and in his memory he returned to the thin, eager, but desperate face, bare of makeup or any other artifice. 'Look at me,' the face said urgently. 'Would I be capable of that? I was bewildered for a while, I was crazy over him and that's the truth; if you'd found him strangled in his bed, then it could have been me who did it. But I always get over things in an awful hurry. You know what I told you, about how I behaved at his place the night before? Well, I was already feeling uncomfortable about that on the way home, and in the morning I almost went and apologized to him, but then I read about the Lastovicka girl and it occurred to me that he'd recast that horror in the part on account of me. Lieutenant, I could have strangled him in the throes of emotion, he was a fine example of a womanizing bast—sorry. But could the throes of emotion last long enough for me to steal the hyoscine, steal an empty capsule, put them together, and then carry that seed of death around with me day and night? I had no idea there was such a thing as hyoscine. If I'd have wanted to poison somebody, I'd probably have gone hunting for toadstools. They didn't pay much attention to natural sciences at the classical lyceum I went to.'

'You went to a classical lyceum?' asked the lieutenant, amazed.

'I did. A bishop's lyceum, at that,' said the girl. 'That's why I sing in dives.'

The lieutenant almost asked her to explain, but then he recalled a period when graduates of religious high schools had a lot of difficulty continuing their studies at universities. She must have been graduating just about then.

'Well, what do you say, lieutenant? Would the throes of emotion last long enough for me to go dig up a book on toxicology? For that matter, these little fingers could easily have handled that whoring old throat of his—sorry!'

'Don't mention it,' said the lieutenant. 'Anyway—ahem—there have been such cases. I mean, of intense emotion lasting over an extended period. With such—ahem—erotically motivated murders, things happen that are truly incredible. For instance, did you ever read about the case of the security guard in Komarno?'

The girl shook her head. 'Did he use hyoscine, too?'

'No,' said the lieutenant. 'A pistol. But that's not the point. The security guard, you see, was a particularly short man—'

'Inferiority complex.'

'As a matter of fact, you're right. And when he was passing a garden on his way home from work one Saturday afternoon, he saw a young machinist he knew by sight from the plant. He was sitting there—ahem—with a very pretty girl. You understand: he knew the young man only by sight and he didn't know the girl at all. But that was enough.

'Did he shoot them?'

'Not them,' said the lieutenant. 'By virtue, as you so cleverly remarked, of his inferiority complex, he found himself in the throes of emotion, ran back to the plant—it was almost three kilometres—broke into a locker, grabbed a pistol, and returned on foot to the garden.'

'You're kidding!'

'It seems improbable, but that is what he did,' said the lieutenant sadly. 'The two of them weren't sitting in the garden any more so the guard broke into the house, but they weren't there either and so, out of accumulated envy, he shot the young man's parents and two brothers. The throes of emotion lasted,' concluded the criminologist, 'all of three hours.'

'Well, now you've wiped me out,' declared the girl. 'Nobody's going to believe me after that. It just shows that in cases like this, anything's possible.' She had no idea how true her words were—or how often she would prove this to herself during the next two years. The lieutenant turned a page in the file and started rereading the testimony of the director's son. It made matters even worse:

Yeah, I heard some kind of argument. Just vaguely. I have an attic room and I'm not interested in my father's girlfriends. Some woman was screeching there, I don't know if it was the defendant. Screeching women all sound the same. Yeah, that was on Tuesday. On Wednesday I made a late night of it, I didn't get in till after midnight. The house was quiet by then. And in the morning I went to wake up Dad, because Mom had been in Podebrady for treatment for more than a month. We were supposed to go to the studio together early that morning, but he just lay there and he was—sort of—done for. I can take a whole lot—but when I realized Dad was stone cold, I felt sick. I nearly passed out.

Of course, he didn't pass out. He called the police instead. And when the lieutenant got that far in his reminiscences, he suddenly seemed to revive. He jumped out of the armchair, staring into the darkness of the room. Before him, approximately where the framed certificate naming him as exemplary public servant hung on the wall, he visualized the face of young Weyr, the face that Zuzana accused of slick prettiness. And beside it, in his mind's eye, he saw the face of the doctor's daughter, permanently and somewhat overly wide-eyed, saying, When he cast that phoney little twit in the part. . . . I actually do wonder, now, why they took the part away from me. . . . And then the two faces vanished, and the girl in the jacket made of rug fabric reappeared. She wasn't sitting behind the table any more, she was standing, shaking his hand in her callused palm, torturing him with her grey eyes, and then she thought of something. 'Lieutenant—show me that picture again! The one of those two charmers.' When he brought out the magazine clipping, she stared at it and declared, 'Sure, I know what's odd about those two. It's perfectly obvious! They look too much alike!' And he had gaped, finally seeing it—a delicate, subtle resemblance, as if the face of the doctor's daughter had somehow penetrated into the features of the director's son.

The lieutenant rubbed his forehead and looked around his study with his mouth open. Then he stumbled over to the bookshelf, searched for a while, and pulled out a fat volume, a reference book. He brought it over to his desk and with impatient fingers flipped it open at the end of the letter A. He soon found the reference:

AZOOSPERMIA, TESTICULAR—the absence of sperm in the ejaculate. It is to be assumed that the original sex cells did not travel to the embryonic gland when it was forming in the 6th-7th week of intrauterine life. Prognosis very poor, and no substantial improvement can be expected from any course of treatment.

The lieutenant rested his gaze on a point in the distance, smiled a little, and quickly grew sad again.

Now you are in possession of enough clues to name the murderer and the motive. But which of Father Knox's commandments has been violated? Remember, it's all a question of deduction!

She sat opposite him again, and there was still a table between them, but this time it was a marble table in the art deco Paris Café. The grey eyes were bordered with the monstrous but beautifully professional makeup that was all the rage. Now her face disclosed only about two-thirds of her actual age, and the lieutenant was stewing in the juices of suppressed emotion. But there was nothing to be done about that.

In an alto voice which confirmed that she was a singer, the girl said with admiration, 'Lieutenant, it's even more incredible than the story of the security guard!'

'I mentioned that—ahem—under the influence of the erotic, nothing is impossible,' he said. 'She had long since come to terms with his mistresses, as well as with the knowledge that he didn't love her any more. What she couldn't accept was the realization that he had never ever loved her—not even right after the wedding, when she was totally convinced of his feelings for her. She couldn't bear the fact he hadn't married her for love, but because her father could advance his career.'

'And all it took was the photo?'

'That was all. She noticed it just the way you did. In short, woman's intuition. I could use some of that.' The lieutenant gave her an aching glance. 'For instance, if you were in my investigation unit. . . .' He added hesitantly, 'One comrade policewoman just got married, I don't know if she intends to stay with us, but you have your high school diploma, you could take a course and—'

The girl shook her head.

'I couldn't,' she said. 'Don't be angry, lieutenant, but I've had enough of murder for a lifetime. I just signed a contract with Pragokoncert, to work abroad.'

The lieutenant's face did what they describe in novels. It fell.

'Abroad?' His voice registered profound disappointment.

'That's the way it is,' sighed the girl. 'The fact is that they cleared my name—rehabilitated me, as they say—but you know people, nobody will ever altogether forget it, especially with a woman in a case like this. Heaven knows what actually happened, they'll say, some sort of nightclub singer, we know her type! All she has to do is make eyes at the judge—he's just a man, after all. . . . You know how people are, lieutenant, I don't have to tell you anything.' The lieutenant turned pink, taking this differently from the way she meant it. 'So I'll just be an export nightclub singer in all the bars of the world. Pragokoncert will get a percentage of my income in foreign currency, so our beloved socialist state gets something to make up for the shame I'll bring down on it by my behaviour in all those bars. I can get away with it there because nobody will know me. They won't know that I was supposed to have poisoned a guy and that I only got off because I slept with three prosecutors and one senile judge.' Her voice was bitter.

'It wouldn't be all that bad,' the lieutenant tried to suggest, but the singer just waved a hand and took a deep drag on the Philip Morris cigarette he'd given her. He'd bought the package for her. He didn't smoke, except for an occasional stogie when there were no young girls around.

'Never mind that, all right? Just finish telling me what happened. So she noticed the resemblance too?'

'She did, and to top it off, she read in the magazine the interesting detail about their dates of birth, December 31, 1948 and January 1, 1949. And in the second article she found out that the Heyduk girl had turned down the part on the wishes of her father. Then all it took was for her to remember how close her husband had been to the Heyduks in Brno, back when they were in the process of getting married, and for a while thereafter, before they moved to Prague. She didn't even need to know about the doctor's ailment. She guessed intuitively why Dr Heyduk was dead set against his daughter getting too closely acquainted with young Weyr.'

'And the poison?'

'Weyr's brother is a famous toxicologist, and she had free access to his office. His apartment, too.'

The girl shook her head and said, illogically, 'Poor Mrs Korenac.

How much time do you think they'll give her?'

'A lot, I'm afraid,' said the lieutenant.

'And she's innocent.'

'Well—'

'I mean, in the case of Weyr's murder.'

'In that case she is,' agreed the lieutenant. 'Of course, she had a mess in her pharmaceuticals and her prescriptions. She claimed she'd used the hyoscine for a medication that someone brought her a prescription for, but she couldn't find the prescription and she couldn't remember the patient.' The lieutenant paused. 'It took Mrs Weyr a little over an hour to come by car to Prague from Podebrady, where she was in a sanitarium for medical treatment. She climbed out of a window after lights-out—she had a private room on the ground floor—and was in Prague by half past nine. She entered the villa by the back door, so the astronomer didn't see her arrive. Incidentally, he got probation for voyeurism,' said the lieutenant.

'Serves him right, the old scarecrow. Amateur astronomer my foot! They needn't have bothered with probation.'

'They couldn't help that. He had a clean bill of health otherwise. Anyway, Mrs Weyr found her husband with a terrible headache. She explained that she'd come to pick up some things, they bickered back and forth for a while, and at half past ten her husband sent her upstairs for a capsule. By midnight she was back in her room in Podebrady.'

The old criminologist fell silent. The art deco café was pleasantly bathed by the dusky evening light so conspicuously absent in the public places of the plastic era, and it buzzed with the conversations of old women over their teacups. The girl was silent too. Old-fashioned brass buttons gleamed on the front of her stylish blue blazer. She went to a lot of trouble to keep up with fashion, and Lieutenant Boruvka was somehow moved by that. Maybe because it was probably a little too late. . . .

He suppressed those four dots in his mind and said, 'It is in fact a case full of—ahem—eroticism. Dr Heyduk wasn't so much afraid that his daughter would drop out of medical school but that she might—'

'Might sleep with her own brother. Or maybe even with her own daddy,' the girl said matter-of-factly. 'A lovely little Oedipus story. She and Petr didn't have the faintest idea that they were related?'

'No. The late Mrs Heyduk had never told anyone, and the doctor didn't figure it out for himself until after he married a second time.

They couldn't have children so he had himself checked out. Testicular azoospermia is congenital.'

'Oh, what the hell,' said the girl, which seemed a little cynical to the lieutenant. But he quickly excused her—he remembered all those low nightclubs in the mining district. 'They could have had some fun, those kids,' she said. 'In this decadent day and age, it wouldn't be the most degenerate thing going on.'

'Well, maybe not,' admitted the lieutenant, unprofessionally. 'But I don't think it would have happened anyway.'

'Oh, come on, it happens almost every day,' the girl said cheerfully.

'I know. But young Weyr is—you might say—too good-looking. Today's young girls—at least if I can judge by my daughter—like ugly men better. Like Mickey Rooney,' he said. 'Don't you like Mickey Rooney?'

The girl shook her head. 'Personally, I like Gérard Philipe,' she mused. 'And after him, not anybody, really.'

The lieutenant grew sad again. Then a faint hope arose.

'They're playing one of his old films, Fanfan the Tulip. Would you—' he cleared his throat predictably, unaware of the adolescent cliché he was acting out, 'some evening, if you could find the time. . . .'

The girl looked over at him with her grey eyes. She didn't need intuition to see it any more, it was written all over his face. Only she was just three days out of prison, and she'd had enough. For a long time. Or she thought she had, at least at that moment. She wasn't thinking about the fact that she owed her freedom to the lieutenant; girls are always ungrateful. And she shook her head even before the lieutenant finished asking.

Translated by Kaka Polackova Henley.

ERIC WRIGHT · b. 1929

Twins

'I want to get it right,' he said. 'After making the mistake in the last book about how long it takes to get from Toronto to Detroit, I want this one to be water-tight. So just go along with me until I'm sure that it'll work.'

They were standing on the edge of an old mine shaft about ten miles north of Sudbury. The shaft had been sunk in the thirties and they had had to claw their way through dense scrub pine to reach it, and pick the locks on two chain link fences that guarded the hole. At least it was too late in the year for mosquitoes. She wondered how he had found this place.

He seemed to hear what was in her mind. 'I found it two years ago,' he said. 'I came up here hunting with Art. Someone told us we might find a bear along at the garbage dump but we missed the road and came to this place.'

He was a writer of detective stories. As far as he could, he liked to 'walk the course' of his plots until he was sure they would work. She always went along as a primary test that the story was possible. The stories often took them to some pleasant places, so it was like getting a second holiday, but this time she had come because she needed to know what was in his mind. Sudbury in October is not a popular vacation spot. 'Tell me again,' she said. 'How does he get her to come this far? I wouldn't.'

'You just did,' he pointed out.

'That was research. Unless you make your villain a writer, you're going to have trouble. What is he, by the way?'

'I haven't decided yet. It's not important. I want to make sure this works, then I can flesh it out.'

'Yes, but it doesn't work if the reader can't believe she would stumble through a quarter mile of bush in this godforsaken landscape. You've got to find a good reason.'

'I'll find one. Let's get the plot straight, shall we?'

'This isn't the way you usually work. Usually you get the characters first, then let the plot grow out of them. So you say, anyway.'

'Yeah, but this plot is ingenious. I mean, the villain thinks it is, so I want to test it before I spend my time creating his world. Okay?'

'Okay, so now he kills her. Right? And drops the body down there.' She kicked a small rock over the edge of the hole and listened hard, but there was no 'ploomp' or rattle of the sound of the rock reaching bottom. It must go down hundreds of metres.

'That's right. He throws the gun in after her; he's made sure it's untraceable. Then he drives south to the motel in Parry Sound where they have a reservation. When he gets there it's dark.' He looked at the sky turning pink in the west. 'He registers as her.'

'Where did you get this idea?'

'From us. People are always saying we look alike, as if we're a couple of gerbils.'

'Where does he change his clothes?'

'In the car, on a side road, probably the Pickerel River road, somewhere quiet. He doesn't actually have to change much: just put on a blonde wig, lipstick, glasses.' He looked down at himself to show what he meant. Both of them were dressed in sneakers, blue jeans, and heavy bush jackets that came well below the waist. 'Then he checks in at the motel, as her, saying "her" husband is turning the car around or picking up beer or something. The point is the motel people have seen "her" and believe that he is there, too. An hour later, he goes to the motel office, as himself, to ask for a wakeup call, so now the motel people have seen "her" and him. Then, around midnight, the fighting starts. The people in the units on either side hear a hell of a row going on, sounds of someone being smacked around, and it goes on so long they complain to the desk, and the night clerk phones over and asks them to pipe down.'

'The row is on tape, right?'

'Right. Then early in the morning the row starts again and there's a lot of door-banging and the neighbours see "her" leaving, walking away. At breakfast time, he checks out leaving a message in case his wife returns. He tells the clerk she walked out on him during the night. She's probably gone to another motel. His message is that he's not going to wait around; he's gone home.'

'So he left the motel in the blonde wig, then came back quietly as himself a bit later. Wasn't he taking a chance?'

'Not really. If anyone saw him, he could always say he had tried to follow his wife, but she disappeared. And that's that. He goes home and when his wife doesn't appear that day he reports it to the police. But in circumstances like these it looks likely that the wife has simply gone off somewhere. It's a few weeks before he can get the police seriously interested.'

'And when they do take it seriously, do they find her?' There was not much light left now. In the east the sky was almost black.

'I don't know. It doesn't matter. A few weeks is as good as six months.'

'They'll suspect him. After the row.'

'But they won't be able to prove anything. When he leaves the motel after breakfast, he checks in with the Ontario Provincial Police in Parry Sound, in case "she" has checked in with them, and he does the same thing all the way down to Toronto, establishing a solid time trail with no gaps for him to drive back up to Sudbury. Then it's easy to make sure he's covered for the next week in Toronto.'

'It might work,' she said. 'Have you figured out how you are going to solve it? How Porter will, I mean.' Gib Porter was the writer's hero.

'Not yet.'

'You could start with a hunch. You could find out what time he left Sudbury and why it took him five hours to get to Parry Sound. Did anyone see his car parked along the highway, stuff like that?'

'Why would anyone be suspicious?'

She pondered. 'Her father. He never liked the man she married, never trusted him, so he hires Gib Porter.' Now it was close to dark. 'What about the car? Someone might have seen their car parked along the highway.'

'It's rented. Perfectly ordinary rented car. If anyone sees it they won't memorize the licence plate. They'll just assume that it's a couple of hunters. But I haven't seen anyone around, have you?'

'No, I haven't. Who would be wandering around this moonscape?' She had to admit that he seemed to have everything covered. 'One last thing,' she asked. 'Why? What's the reason?'

'Motive, you mean?' He shrugged. 'Another woman, I guess.'

'Come on. This is 1990. That was a motive back when you had to wait seven years for a divorce. People change around all the time now.'

'Not if she refuses. The other lady, I mean. This guy has fallen in love with someone who refuses to see him until he is free. She was raised in the Brethren. She loves him, but she believes in the sanctity of marriage.'

'Does she, indeed. It isn't his wife's fault, then.' She turned her back on him and walked towards the road. She needed to know one more thing. 'In the meantime, old buddy-boy,' she said over her shoulder, 'we'd better be getting back.'

He reached inside his jacket and pulled out the little handgun he had bought in Detroit. 'Don't turn round Lucy,' he said. She turned and saw that her last question was answered. It wasn't a game. She said, 'It isn't going to work.'

'It'll work, all right. It's going to work.' He pulled the trigger once, twice, three times.

Everything else went smoothly. His wife had often criticized his plots for being too complicated, but this one worked. Two hours later the night clerk at the Sturgeon Motel in Parry Sound signed in Mrs Harry Coates, a blonde lady with sun-glasses (though it was quite dark), while her husband unloaded the car. During the night the clerk had to call them twice to ask them to pipe down because they were fighting and arguing so loudly that the guests on either side had called to complain. The rowing ended in the early morning with a lot of door-crashing, then Mrs Coates came to the desk to check out. She still had sun-glasses on, but now the clerk thought they were probably covering up a black eye. Her husband, she said, had left her, taken a train or bus back to Toronto, maybe even hitch-hiked—she didn't know or care. She left a message for him in case he called. He never did, though.

She drove home and waited for two days for him to return, then she called the police. They made some routine enquiries, but they weren't very interested. The story of the night in the motel was clear, and the guy was almost certainly putting a scare into her by taking off for as long as his money held out, but pretty soon he would use a charge card or something like that, then they would be able to reel him in. They did establish that he had a girl-friend tucked away in a condominium on Sherbourne Street, and they kept an eye on her place but she was as mystified as they were, and he certainly never showed up. Nor did he try to call her. A month later the police assumed foul play and sent out a serious enquiry, and she began the process of establishing her legal position if he should have disappeared for good. When the first snow fell she knew they wouldn't find him until the spring at the earliest, and then what would they find? A body, with no money in the wallet, and the gun that had killed him. (She had thrown *his* gun, from which she had removed the ammunition the night before they started their trip, when she realized what he was planning, into the French River on her way to Parry Sound.) And what would they conclude? That he had been picked up hitch-hiking, robbed and killed and dumped into the mineshaft by a local thug. There was still the very slight risk that someone had seen them when they went into the bush that evening, but it was a chance *he* was prepared to take, so it was pretty small. Since the chance of finding the body in the first place was about ten thousand to one, the further remote chance that someone saw them near the mineshaft was an acceptable risk. All she had to do was nurse her grief for the few weeks while the police made their enquiries.

The plan had been perfect, or pretty good. If she had not long known about the lady in the condominium, and if she had not come across his fishing tackle box with the loaded gun, the wig, and the make-up kit, packed ready to go, while she was searching for a pair of pliers, she would never have wondered what he was up to. After that it was just a matter of getting hold of a gun herself, and giving him every chance to prove her guess was wrong. The rest went exactly as he had planned.

TIMOTHY FINDLEY · b. 1930

Memorial Day

Tuesday, 29th May, 1990,
Cambridge, Massachusetts.

Dear Nadine,

Enclosed you will find the most recent entries from my journal. I went down this morning and had them xeroxed in one of those copy shops the students use in Harvard Square.

Please don't be alarmed. What they reveal is locked inside me, secure forever. What a monstrous story it is. It tells of brutalities I have known myself—though not to the same degree as you. And not, by any means, to the same degree as your mother.

Yes. I know it was you at the window. But I could not bring myself to wave. Perhaps that is why I am sending you these pages now. They will tell you what I know. I hope they will also serve as an embrace.

Please believe me,
Yours in friendship,
Nessa V.H.

Friday, 25th May, 1990: Cambridge, Mass.

And so, another benchmark in the year's unfolding has begun. *Memorial Day Weekend.* Out with the flags and in with the gardens!

I am staying here with Lettie Woods, my cousin, in the grand old house on Biddle Street. This is the house I remember with such a mixture of joy and fear from childhood. It was here that mother used to bring me when my father went away and mother was in need of family comfort. Back in those days before the war, 51 Biddle Street was a house of women, lorded over by an absent master.

Bochner Woods, my grandfather, lived out most of his adult life in that ugly suite of rooms at the old Adelphi on Park Avenue. Grandmother Mary came up here to Cambridge, Massachusetts and established residence in 1904. She did this in order to preserve her sanity and to protect her children from their father's outbursts of rage.

Later on, in the 1920s and 1930s, mother, her sister Sarah, and Uncle Bertram's widow, Aurelia, would gather here on the screened-in porches—looking out at the fading light over Biddle Street—dreaming of safety yet to come, which never came. Of all those women, only my mother did not fear her husband. Only her father.

They made a loving and cohesive group, these women, and under Grandmother Mary's tutelage, they set their female course for survival in a world that, for them, was all too male. One of the principal terrors of that world was my grandfather, Bochner Woods—Wall Street manipulator, coal and oil baron, woman hater. It could be said that his hatred lived in an annex to this house. When he came here, Grandmother Mary enticed him out of her bedroom into the summer-house out back. It offered him male privacy. Also, the status of a place apart where other men could come and visit him without the impediment of what he called 'female excesses'—meaning female needs and points of view. At night, as my grandfather drank with his friends, Grandmother Mary quietly went about with her keys and locked all the doors of number 51. Thank God that time is past.

I am here because I have been commissioned by Peter Hamilton to landscape *Shingles*, his family's estate on Plymouth Bay. I accepted the job with a mixture of fascination and apprehension. Peter is a dear, enthusiastic lad and, though naive, he has a kind of charming wilfulness that is irresistible. He seems to have made his way past all his family's turmoil with the same blind perseverance that children show who cannot imagine death. I like him very much, though I sense that by entering that family's life again, I am placing young Peter's optimism in jeopardy. I could not bear to be the cause of his disillusion. Perhaps it will not happen. I have tried to put the Hamiltons altogether out of my mind. That was some years ago. Now, they are back.

Lettie gave a dinner party tonight to celebrate my return to Biddle Street. Being Lettie, she even sent out handwritten, formal invitations: *You are invited to meet my dear cousin, Ms Vanessa Van Horne, etc. . . .*

Peter Hamilton came with his wife. Ten years ago, he married the Lowell-Adams girl from Quincy. Bethany Lowell-Adams betrays not one whit of her ancestry. Nothing but sweetness and sunny smiles. She wears her fair hair long and loose and spent the whole meal brushing it back from her plate.

Bethany is little-girlish in an unbecoming way. She affects a childlike voice and tilts her head towards her shoulder every time she speaks. This manner makes me feel, with every word she says and every smile she bestows, that I am being condescended to—a feeling I cannot abide. The back goes straight up, hard against my chair—as if I must prove that I am actually older and taller than this woman who pretends to be sixteen. Thank God—Peter took her away before the meal was over. They—with some of the other guests—had to attend some event at the Fogg Museum to which the rest of us had not been invited.

The rest of us consisted of Andrew Cornell, who teaches American History at Radcliffe—Nan and Kenneth German from the School of Architecture at M.I.T. and a man called William Teachers—or Teacher Williams, I don't know which. His names seemed interchangeable when it came to how the others addressed him—and, since he was a stranger to me before we met this evening, I ended up addressing him as 'sir'. He is greatly old—so 'sir' was quite appropriate and seemed to please him.

At table, before they departed, Peter and Bethany told one and all that I had been hired *because I had gone to school with Peter's mother, Nadine.* I had rather hoped I might have been hired because of my reputation. After all, I have some status amongst the landscape architects of North America. Partly, I fully recognize, because I am a woman in a man's field—but mostly, I like to think, because of my work restoring the parks of New York, Boston, and Philadelphia. My work with various civic governments has also extended to providing suitable grounds for museums of art and other public buildings. Besides which, I have dissuaded many private owners from subdividing their estates in ways that would be harmful to the ecologies of their various neighbourhoods. I am proud of this. But, no. I have been hired by Peter Hamilton because I went to school with his mother.

I wonder if Peter knows that, if my mother had achieved her ambition for me, I might have ended up married to his father. The war, however, prevented that. It stepped between us—and the sophomore from Smith College who went to visit her parents in the Dutch East Indies in 1941 ended up in Bandung Prison, where she spent the war, and returned to America to find that Gardner Hamilton was engaged to Nadine Rylands. My mother, God rest her, was devastated. But—*the best laid plans of mice and women oft gang astray.* . . .

What Peter wants—what Bethany has insisted I achieve—is a complete reworking of the gardens facing the Bay. I am to remove the famous Hamilton Folly and replace it with a terraced swimming pool and bath-house pavilions.

'But you *can't* remove the Hamilton Folly!' said Kenneth German. 'It's a masterpiece!'

He said this with such vehemence that Bethany Hamilton threw back her girlish head and gave a girlish laugh.

'Oh, *Mister* German!' she said. 'A masterpiece? It's the ugliest thing I have ever laid eyes on!'

'That,' said Kenneth German, 'is the point, Mrs Hamilton. It is a masterpiece of bad taste.'

'Well—whatever it is—I would prefer my swimming pool to having such a monstrosity staring me in the face every time I step out through the library doors,' said Bethany.

I had to use my napkin to hide my smile. The thought of Bethany Hamilton emerging from the library was impossible to countenance. What might she do in there? Perhaps rearrange the books according to their colours. . . .

'Maybe Miss Van Horne could incorporate the Folly into some other vista,' said Teacher Williams.

'I might, sir,' I said. 'But I doubt it. Memory tells me it is rather large.'

'What is it, in fact?' Cousin Lettie asked. She had never seen the Hamilton Folly.

'A belvedere,' said Nan German.

'And what is a belvedere?' Lettie asked.

'A place from which you can look out over an attractive view,' said Nan. 'Sometimes, it's a tower. More often, it's a sort of summer-house—a gazebo, even, sitting on a hill.'

'It means *beautiful vista*,' said William Teachers.

'*Belle*, yes. French, isn't it?'

'Well,' said Bethany, 'whatever it means—in whatever language—the Hamilton Folly is history. I absolutely hate it and insist that it be removed.'

Peter attempted to be diplomatic. 'Perhaps Vanessa can make it work somewhere else. I don't really mind the idea of that, so long as we get our swimming pool and our pavilion.'

Soon after that, the Hamiltons left with the other people invited to the Fogg. I will be seeing both the Hamiltons tomorrow. Peter is coming to drive me down to *Shingles* in the morning, so that I can make my initial assessment. Of course, the highlight of the visit—so far as I'm concerned—is the chance it gives me to say goodbye to Gardner Hamilton, the man I might have married. He lies there—dying, now, of a stroke. Peter says, however, you can read his eyes.

Mid-May nights in Cambridge, Massachusetts, it is customary to go out walking after dinner. Since I live in New York—where you cannot go out walking with impunity after dark—these Cambridge ambles and meanders are a source of unique delight for me. Whole dinner parties rise from table—eight or ten people—throw down their napkins and carry their conversations out into the streets. It is a charming exercise.

I think perhaps the charm must have to do with all the yards beyond the rows of white picket fences and all the trees that make of almost every street an avenue. And in May, of course, towards the time of Memorial Day, the lilacs are in bloom and the evening air is filled with their scent. Doors and windows all stand open beyond their screens and the lamps inside throw a golden light that increases as the darkness falls across the lawns.

We took such a walk this evening. Six of us, altogether, after the others had departed—the men in linen suits—the women in silk and cotton dresses—drifting like moths beneath the honey locusts and the chestnut trees.

Cantabrigians take great pleasure in their various neighbourhoods. Harvard and Radcliffe are natural enclaves and the proximity of Boston across the Charles offers the comfort of historical lineage. *This is us,* the neighbourhoods seem to say, *and we are here to stay forever.* For those of us who live and try to breathe in New York City, there is no such comfort. We wake every morning to find yet one more relic of our past has fallen in the night and is tumbled at our doorstep.

I am here to destroy such a relic. Expressly. 'You must convince my father,' Peter Hamilton said to me on the 'phone the other day, 'with the brilliance of your designs, Vanessa—that the time has come to be rid of the Hamilton Folly. Forever.'

Forever.

Andrew Cornell, from Radcliffe, seems to agree with that assessment. 'Even as a Folly, it's a failure,' he said as we walked along. 'I dare say, if anyone stands before it amazed, their amazement rests on the fact that it ever escaped from the draughting board.'

'Who did design it,' Lettie wondered. 'Does anyone know?'

'Richard Morris Hunt,' said Teacher Williams—who was bringing up the rear.

'That's right,' said Kenneth German.

Kenneth and Nan were walking out in the road, loving and in love after forty years of marriage. They were walking arm in arm. I could hardly bear to watch them. My father was killed before my mother's eyes in the camp at Bandung. Shot. I saw it, too. But what I mourn is the loss of the years they might have had together. There, tonight, in the image of Nan and Kenneth German, I caught the vile reminder of how little love there is that lasts. Which is why my father's death was tragic. He and my mother were in love the way the Germans are—they look like that, in my mind's eye picture of the years together they never had. While the dread of Bochner Woods, who terrorized his wife and children, went on until he dropped from a standing position in his nineties. . . .

Nan said, 'There's an interesting story about the Hamilton Folly and Richard Morris Hunt. You know that he was the architect who gave us over half of Newport, the Vanderbilt Mausoleum, and most of the gothic palaces on Fifth Avenue?'

'Yes,' I said. I had lived in one of them.

'He was Vanderbilt's toady,' said William Teachers. 'A toady and a tart.'

Nan laughed. We all did.

Nan went on. 'John North Hamilton was a contemporary of Cornelius Vanderbilt—and there was something of a rivalry between them. When it came to raising houses, every time Cornelius Vanderbilt moved a stone, John North Hamilton had to move one, too. Around the time *The Breakers* was being completed for Cornelius at Newport, John North tried to entice Hunt, Vanderbilt's architect, away from him with a larger fee. The idea was that Hunt would erect an even greater summer palace for Hamilton, down on Plymouth Bay. But, no dice. So John North took up an architect of his own—Arthur Little, of Boston. What Richard Morris Hunt created in stone and marble—Arthur Little created in wood and shingles. The shingle style caught on—and a few of Boston's finest—even a few of New York's finest—began to commission their summer houses from Little instead of Hunt.'

'Isn't it extraordinary,' said Andrew Cornell, 'that a whole school of architecture evolved because two men could not abide one another. Perhaps a useful lesson. I mean, if hatred could be solved on a draughting board. . . .'

'Ah, yes,' said Nan. 'But Hunt had his revenge on Little. In fact, he nearly ruined Little's reputation.'

'Which is where the Folly comes in,' I said.

'Which is where the Folly comes in.' Nan and Kenneth came up onto the sidewalk and we turned, at that moment, homeward.

'Knowing that John North Hamilton could not refuse such a coup—he offered to make a contribution to the Hamilton estate. And, of course, what he offered was that Folly . . .'

'Right smack dab in the middle of the south lawn, facing Plymouth Bay!' said Kenneth. 'Right smack dab in the middle of the lawn!'

Ever over-serious, Andrew Cornell could not perceive the humour of this wickedness. 'What a dreadful thing to do,' he said. 'To ruin such a beautiful piece of architecture as *Shingles*. It's an aesthetic crime!'

William Teachers, now in the dark somewhere ahead of us, called back, 'The crime was, John North Hamilton paid him for it.'

'Yes,' I said. 'And loved it.' I had seen the Folly, myself, years ago and remember vividly how fond the Hamiltons had become of it. John North died revering it, in 1922—and Gardner has carried on the reverence, so I understand, to this very day. Or, at least until the stroke came along and felled him. Now, who knows what he thinks—unless his eyes can tell you.

Saturday, 26th May, 1990: *Shingles*

Nadine Rylands, Peter's mother, suffered all her early life from chronic unpopularity. I went to school with her at Miss Hale's Academy in Philadelphia, where even the teachers referred to her as 'poor Nadine Rylands'. It was her father's fault—not hers.

V.S. Rylands. Well—we all remember him. Two steps down from the devil, as they used to say. I was in prison during his heyday. War profiteering, racketeering, and union-busting brought him a fortune bigger than J.P. Morgan's—another hated man of whom even Grandfather Woods was afraid.

V.S. Rylands died—or rather, he disappeared in 1953.

No one has ever been able to prove what happened. Many have tried and failed—even in spite of the obvious. He vanished shortly after having scored a victory against the Sub-Committee that had been investigating his involvement in union-busting. The prosecution's key witness had been silenced in classic fashion. Cement.

Enough said.

Rylands walked out of the hearings a free man. One week later—he disappeared.

Everyone, of course, was properly mystified. But they also cheered—some cheered out loud and some in whispers. The residue of fear has not quite been dispelled even now.

I have the most vivid memories of V.S. Rylands. No one knows what the 'V' stood for, but the 'S' was for Samuel—a name he never used. Perhaps it was just too formal—perhaps too biblical—and perhaps, he was afraid of the subsequent connotations. 'Sam', on the other hand, would not have raised images of violence if 'Rylands' itself had not become a synonym for hobnailed confrontations—men beating other men with baseball bats and Sub-Committee meetings dominated by Rylands' snarling, shark-skinned lawyers and Sam's own leering face with its dark-lensed glasses and yellow teeth.

He used to come to Miss Hale's Academy—driven there with his wife by a man of spectacular height who stood, both hands in the pockets of his jacket, smiling inexplicably, ten feet off to the left of Mrs Rylands' elbow.

Mrs Rylands, Nadine's mother, had been a Hollywood actress. Not a star and not a starlet—but an actress who could read her lines with some intelligence. Her name, back then, had been Rita Mae Hoople which, for the movies, they had shortened to Rita Mae. Sam once said of her—as quoted in the press—*I don't know where she gets off thinking she has a right to speak on her own. She made her name real well by doing what she was told to do—and that's the way I like it* . . . This was said at the time—the one and only time—that Rita Mae had speculated in a public place on the future of the labour move-ment—*now my husband's got a hold of it.* She stopped making films that very same year. Rylands bought her contract. It was 1939. *I want to devote my life to my daughter, Nadine,* she was quoted as saying.

Her devotion ran to standing off to one side as Sam raised hell at Miss Hale's—complaining that his daughter *had a right to a private room in what, after all, was a private school*—or some such thing. Rita Mae Rylands watched her husband serenely through a veil. I remember her eyes behind that veil—black as jet and cold as marbles. And her lips, sealed tight except to admit the tip of her cigarette.

She was dressed by Adrian of Hollywood, whose most famous client had been Norma Shearer—blonde and elegant—almost aris-tocratic. Rita Mae Rylands had surmised that if Adrian could turn a middle class Canadian from Montreal into an upper class Park Avenue American, then surely he could do the same for her. The essence of her attitude, I guess, was her need to put the rest of the world in its place before the rest of the world put her in hers.

The whole world stopped in 1946 when Peter's father, Gardner Hamilton, said he was going to marry *poor little Naddie Rylands.* He might as well have said he was going to marry Hester Prynne—scarlet letter and all. Not that such things do not happen outside of novels. I'm sure they do—but not to Gardner Hamilton. As an alliance of fortunes, it was breathtaking; as an alliance of persons—inconceivable.

Mother and I had only just returned from Java, where we had spent four years as prisoners of the Japanese. Our health was in a shambles; my father had died; we no longer knew who we were and our sense of reason was already harried to the breaking point. Our forays into society were tentative and often alarming.

This, of course, was in New York, which had gone through a violent surge of energizing during the war and had been transformed into a place where light itself was noise. It was there, one evening at a party, that Gardner Hamilton, whom I had known since we were little children, stepped towards me and said, *I want you to meet my fiancée.*

I knew her, of course, but I didn't recognize her at first. All the transformations her mother had attempted to achieve for herself had, somehow, transpired in Nadine. The plain, bewildered girl who had been so afraid of speech her voice could hardly be heard, now spoke my name with all the assurance of Eliza Doolittle. *Dear Vanessa,* she said—our roles completely reversed—*how good it is to see you and how sad and sorry I am to hear the news about your father.*

Sad and sorry, indeed. I turned away—and back again, and struck her in the face. After that I went away and wept. One year later—after her marriage—we became friends—and have remained so ever since.

So here I am in the house that Nadine Rylands has turned into a hospice—only sorry that I shall not see her. Exhausted by Gardner's ordeal, she apparently has slipped away somewhere into seclusion. Seven nurses have taken her place. No one has said so, but I suspect she has gone to the Betty Ford. The atmosphere here at *Shingles* is as tense as the atmosphere in a falling plane. No one cries out—but someone will.

I have been promised a visit with Gardner later. The head nurse tells me he is resting, now—that euphemism for fear which is always used by everyone but the patient himself. The urge to cry for help is palpable in the air around his rooms.

I took a pill when I went upstairs. I haven't felt my heart was in jeopardy till now—but the place itself and Gardner's proximity have begun to tell. And I've only been here for three short hours.

At first, we refreshed ourselves and took a short walk. If Bethany persists in riding on my heels every step I take while I am here, I shall have to speak. She thinks of me as old—touching my elbow constantly with little maddening finger-tips. I want to hit her hand away—or, better, bite it off. Maybe she's afraid that, if I'm left alone with Peter, I'll convince him not to destroy the Folly.

Certainly, the Folly is a failure as a folly. Andrew Cornell was right about that.

It is, indeed, a belvedere—but not as large as I had remembered. None of its porches gives much room for standing, let alone sitting. The porticoes have so little width that a person of any breadth would not get through. It is neither large nor small—it is simply there and grey and in the way. It serves no purpose where it stands because it affords no view of anything except the rising slope at the top of which it should have been sited. Looking out between its pillars past its gargoyles—all you have is a 'view' of grass. Yes. It should be removed. There can be no doubt.

Lunch was Bethany from start to finish. Boring. As I came upstairs to write in this book, I overheard with the greatest relief her plans to visit the shops in Quincy this afternoon. *The children will want some flags for Memorial Day.*

Other towns are nearer—*but the Quincy flags are best.* Unquote.

Peter went off this afternoon to sail with a friend. I was turned loose with my camera to photograph the lay of the land.

It has good lines and I can work with it. To the east and to the south, from the top of the rise, you can see Plymouth Bay, but I think I will suggest some trees on the right, in order to fudge the view of smoke stacks there. Not too intrusive—but visible—and best if I could obscure them partially. The rise itself drops down from a short plateau to the stony beach below. Once the Folly is gone, my job will be more or less a case of getting the modulations right for the terracing effect.

As I was coming back towards the house, admiring the great wide sweeps of its shingled wings, I saw a woman watching me from one of the upper windows. Not Bethany, I knew for certain. On the other hand, not one of the nurses, either. Not in uniform—but in what appeared to be night attire.

At once, I wondered if it could be Nadine. Perhaps she had not gone away into seclusion, after all—but was ill and resting somewhere in the house and giving out the excuse of being absent only in order not to have to confront some confounded guest like me.

I almost waved, but thought better of it. If whoever it was—Nadine or not—had wanted to acknowledge me, all she had to do was open the window and call down *hello.* I looked away and pretended I hadn't seen her.

Once I achieved the library, I rang the bell and when the house boy came I asked him to bring some brandy and some water. I hate it when they bring a drink that's mixed. Unless, of course, it's a cocktail.

The room was large and, though Victorian in fact, would now be called Edwardian because of all the windows and the sense of space. The bookshelves ramble instead of climbing. The highest is barely seven feet from the floor—and they're interspersed with little walls of various widths on which a myriad of photographs in frames is on display.

There were the Hamiltons, circa 1895, playing croquet on the lawns in windy weather. John North Hamilton looked like Teddy Roosevelt—all done up in khaki clothes and a tip-brimmed hat. He wore a moustache, carried a stick, and looked so fierce you might be excused for thinking he had captured all the members of his family and was standing guard in order to ensure they did not escape. I must assume he was relatively young, back then—roughly thirty years before my birth and twenty-odd years before the birth of his own last son, who is now upstairs on his death-bed.

John North must have had a second wife, for the woman leaning there against a tree in the photograph could not have been Gardner's mother. She looked to be in her thirties, at least. Old before her time—and dead before his.

At first, I failed altogether to identify the lawns as being the ones I had walked across just now—the lawns I could see by turning round and looking out the window. I failed, because I could see no Folly there in the photograph—whereas, in reality, there it was, intruding—*smack dab in the middle of the lawn*—as Kenneth had said it would be. Had someone brushed it away in developing the film?

Certainly the Folly had been built by 1895—but since that time, it must have been moved. No one had mentioned that. Where had it been?

I tried to remember where it had sat when I'd come here as a child. But I couldn't place it. Yes, I had seen it—that was definite. But where—which prospect?

I wondered when Kenneth had seen it first—before or after me.

I looked at the other photographs to see if they would tell me. I was engaged in this when the boy returned with my drinks. He was not alone.

A woman spoke from somewhere close behind me. I had heard the boy come in, but was so engrossed in my search I had not turned around.

'You're looking for the Folly, aren't you,' this woman said.

She came and stood beside me. I could see that she was a good deal more than middle aged, but not yet sixty.

'Are you Miss Vanessa Van Horne?' she asked. She was civil, proper, and self-possessed. I told her that I was.

'I'm Mrs Brady,' she said. 'I run the house.'

She had a sturdy build and a round, sea-reddened face.

'Ah, yes,' I said. 'How do you do?'

I moved towards the brandy decanter.

Mrs Brady stayed near the photographs.

Once I had poured an inch of brandy and three of water, I turned back and faced her. 'It is a puzzle,' I said. 'About the Folly, I mean.'

'It was moved to its present location in 1953,' said Mrs Brady.

'Oh?' I said. 'Why?'

I sat down.

Mrs Brady continued where she was—a formal distance, but not unfriendly.

'It used to sit up there beyond the rise and somewhat down the other side,' she said. 'It faced the sea. But, 1953, there was that hurricane. The one they called *The Witch*. . . .'

'Oh, yes!' I smiled. I remembered it with relish. I had taken some of my prize-winning photographs, then, of the destruction. *Hurricane Norma* was its real name. October 30th and 31st. On Hallowe'en. Which is why we called it *The Witch*.

'Yes. And it caused a great deal of damage around these parts,' Mrs Brady said.

At last, she had begun to move—and nervously, I thought. The memory must have disturbed and agitated her. She picked up ash trays and put them down again—straightened some photographs and ran a piece of Kleenex from her pocket along the backs of some chairs.

'Were you here, then?' I asked.

'Yes.' She nodded. 'Just a girl of twenty. I was a day maid in 1953.'

'A day maid?'

'Yes. I lived in town and came out days. Now, I live here, you see.' She paused in her activity.

There was a sound above us of someone hurrying down the upper hall.

Nurses.

Mrs Brady acknowledged the sound and then she said, 'The whole shoreline was took up and brought down. There was a lot of water damage. Half the hill went down into the sea. Dreadful. And we almost lost the belvedere altogether. After that, it was moved. To preserve it. Mister Gardner Hamilton loves that thing beyond all reason. It's almost unnatural.' She smiled. It was a lovely smile—warm and honest—not a trace of practice in it.

'They want me to remove the belvedere, you know,' I said. I was beginning to feel some guilt about my quick decision to have it torn away. I had forgotten how affectionate Gardner's feeling for it was.

'And will you?' Mrs Brady asked. 'Have it removed, Miss Van Horne?'

I looked out the windows—shifting in my seat so I could see where the Folly stood. 'I don't know,' I said. 'I haven't made up my mind.' I looked back then at Mrs Brady and I said, 'Would you be offended if I asked you to stay a moment—sit down and talk with me?'

She said it would not offend her at all—and sat down opposite me in a Morris chair. I was seated in a sofa.

'Did they move it right away?' I asked. 'It interests me. If I have to have it moved again, instead of destroyed, I want to know what that will entail. Do you remember?'

'Yes. Very well,' she said. 'Brady himself was involved in it, you see.'

'Your husband?'

'Dead now, but nineteen, then. I came here because of him. Brady was Gardner's stable boy and we were mad in love. Even in spite of the differences in our ages.'

'But that was only a year or two.'

'Yes. But I was older. And it wasn't done, to be older, then, if you were the girl. They called it cradle-snatching!'

Both of us laughed.

Mrs Brady said, 'Brady and a dozen other men worked through the latter part of the hurricane, shoring up the belvedere where the sea had torn away its earth. I watched a bit of that—but got afraid and came back in. There was people here that week. Mister Rylands—he was here. And his wife. People like that and a few Hamiltons. A family affair. I can't remember. Thirty-seven years ago. Maybe a wedding, though I can't think whose. Mister Gardner and Mister Peter were both in residence then, as now—though Mister Peter was only a child. Of course, he moved out later, after he married Miss Lowell-Adams. Then he came back, when Mister Gardner took ill. . . .'

I cut her off. I didn't want to hear the Hamilton family history. I knew it all too well.

'1953,' I said. 'You say Mister Rylands was here.'

'And his wife,' said Mrs Brady.

'And his wife,' I repeated. 'I knew his wife. Rita Mae.'

'Yes,' said Mrs Brady. All at once, she seemed uncomfortable.

'I went to school with Mrs Gardner, you know,' I said. 'Nadine Rylands.'

'Yes, ma'am.' The discomfort grew.

I pressed my luck.

'Whatever became of Mrs Rylands, Mrs Brady? Do you know? After Mister Rylands died, I mean.'

There was the briefest pause.

Mrs Brady got up quickly out of the Morris chair and adjusted its position on the floor. A rug had been disturbed and she had to flatten it back in place with the toe of her shoe. She looked like an animal, tamping down the earth where it had buried something. Carefully, carefully, tamp, tamp, tamp. Except that an animal does it with its nose. Mrs Brady did it with a small-sized *Sportable* walking shoe. Brown.

'I think she died,' she said—meaning Rita Mae. 'Went back to Hollywood and drank herself to death.'

'Oh.' I hadn't known that.

'I'm sorry Mrs Gardner isn't here right now,' I said. 'I was looking forward to seeing her.'

'Yes,' said Mrs Brady.

She was reverting to her monosyllabic communication mode. I

could tell she wanted to leave the room—but I couldn't let her go before I had a few more answers.

'Mrs Brady—memory tells me that Mister Rylands died in the fall of 1953. Died or disappeared. Isn't that so?'

'I don't really know, Miss Van Horne. I only know he was here that week. Something was being celebrated.'

'Do you think he might have disappeared in Hurricane Norma? Maybe helping Brady and Mister Gardner save the belvedere?'

'I couldn't answer that. I do remember he had a fight with his wife. But I don't remember when he disappeared.'

But she did. She did remember and she couldn't hide it. That's why she was so anxious to escape from me. If I kept asking questions, she was going to answer them. Honesty was in her nature and she knew she could not lie with conviction. But why did she have to lie? Surely, it couldn't matter less to her whatever became of V.S. Rylands.

'Mrs Brady—before you go . . .' I said. She sighed with relief. The ordeal was nearly over.

'Yes, ma'am?'

'I heard a story once . . .'

'Yes?'

'Mrs Gardner—Nadine told me, when we were in school. It was about her father. She said he did the most terrible things to Rita Mae—her mother. Terrible things like broken bones—disfiguration. I didn't believe her then—but I have good reason, now . . .'

I looked beyond the windows at the belvedere. The Folly.

'You say that something happened here that week—the week of Hurricane Norma. Was it something dreadful?'

Mrs Brady looked away. She bit her lip and trembled. Then she put one hand against the back of her neck and looked very hard at the floor. Her voice, when she spoke, was gentle—but undermined by rage.

'Yes. It was. I suppose you know it was. But, oh—I wish . . .'

I waited.

'I wish that all such things as men with fists would disappear from the world forever.' She looked up hard at me, then, with utter candour—not even blinking. 'Not one soul,' she said, 'who was present here that week was sorry to think he might be dead. He was gone and that was all that mattered.'

'Yes,' I said. 'I believe it.'

Mrs Brady looked at the floor again.

'He beat her something awful. With a stick. I didn't see it, but others did. She wouldn't have a doctor and she wouldn't have police. This was before the hurricane. There was rain and all—but it was before the hurricane. Mister Gardner had a fight with him—and locked him in a room. He tried to get her out of the house. Mrs Rylands, I mean—and his own wife, too.'

'Nadine.'

'But they wouldn't leave. They would not leave. And then the hurricane came—and after that a person *couldn't* leave.'

'Who else was here? Can you remember names?'

'I can't. There was children. Mister Peter was a boy back then, of course. And there was other children, too. With parents—Mister Gardner's sister was here—Mrs Royale and her husband . . .'

'Lawyers, yes. I knew them both.'

'Others—I really don't remember.'

'And you don't remember exactly when you saw Mister Rylands last?'

'No.' She said it firmly enough.

'Was it before the storm?' I said. 'The hurricane.'

'Maybe. I don't remember. The fight was before, that's all I know.'

That was the last of what she had to say—but not, I assume, the last of what she knew.

When she had gone, I got up carefully—I don't know why—but I rose as if I was afraid of disturbing something—someone. Then I poured myself a second brandy and water and went outside and stared for a long hard while at the belvedere. Maybe it wasn't a folly, after all.

Sunday, 27th May, 1990: *Shingles*

(I write this before I sleep. Early Sunday morning.)

Half-an-hour later, I came inside and lay down on my bed. They've put me in a splendid room. It overlooks a garden filled with flowering shrubs and roses. Two of my windows were open and I could smell the cherry blossoms and the sea. Someone must have cut the grass this morning. Sweetgrass and thyme. I thought of what I do—my profession—that all these wonders—flowers and herbs and trees and earth are the tools with which I work. And when I think a line, I cannot think of anything but form—form, formality, breaks, and divisions. Everything I use must reach the spirit through the eye.

The eye.

And I thought of the belvedere—the famous Folly—and I thought, by every aesthetic rule I know and every instinct, too—my eye cannot abide its presence where it is. But if I pull it down . . .

I sat up.

I left the bed and went across the room to the door.

The only person who knew the answer was lying across the hall, immobilized. But Peter had said you could read his eyes.

I went.

I didn't knock. I just went in.

A nurse I hadn't met was sitting in a chair. A book lay open in her lap—but she was looking out a window.

'I am Vanessa Van Horne,' I said. 'I have come to say goodbye to Mister Hamilton.'

The nurse—maybe twenty-five or six with honey-coloured hair and skin—stood up and set her book aside and led me further into the room. She didn't say a word until she said: 'Mister Hamilton? Your friend, Miss Van Horne, is here to see you.'

Then she went away—and sat again in her chair.

'Gardner. . . ?' I said.

He was lying, bundled up with a towel across his forehead. His hands, the fingers very slightly crooked, were resting on the coverlet. White—both coverlet and hands. A million tubes and wires were feeding him and draining him. I had to move up very close before I could see his eyes.

'Hello,' I said.

I touched his lips with my fingers.

'It's Vanessa, Gardner—and I've come to ask you a question.'

His eyes said *yes*—that he understood.

I said that Peter had hired me to redesign the gardens—telling him all about the terraced swimming pools and bathing pavilions. He listened without alarm at first—but when I said that the belvedere would have to be moved, a look of panic appeared in his eyes that was so intense it frightened me.

But I had to know at least a little more than I had guessed.

'1953,' I said. 'October, 1953.'

I could see that he wanted desperately to speak. All I could think was that I had to speak for him, somehow.

'Hurricane Norma, Gardner. You and the belvedere. You moved it, didn't you. Had it moved.'

Yes.

'But you didn't have to move it, did you. Not to save it. Did you. You could have left it where it was and it would have been all right . . .'

He wavered over this. He couldn't tell what I was up to. His eyes shifted—left me and then returned. But they held no answer.

'Be honest with me, Gardner. Trust me. For God's sake—it's me, Vanessa. Trust me.'

He waited. The eyes, at last, were calm.

'You didn't have to move it, did you. Not to save it.'

No.

I smiled.

'I'm glad,' I said. 'You cannot know how glad I am.'

I was almost weeping—but I didn't do that. I tried to laugh, instead.

'It proves you have good taste, you see.'

His eyes said *what?*

I said, 'Well, Gardner, if you'd had to move it to *save* it, at least you would have chosen somewhere appropriate to put it. Wouldn't you. But seeing it ended up where it did, I figured maybe something else had entered into your decision.' His eyes began to panic.

Then I said, 'Someone else's taste, perhaps?'

His eyes relaxed again.

'So,' I said. And I held his hand. 'Maybe for Nadine's sake—seeing it's where *she* wants it—maybe we should leave it where it is.'

I waited for a moment.

His eyes were locked on mine. I smiled.

'Don't worry, my dear,' I said. 'The Folly is at rest.'

His eyes filled up with tears.

I said goodbye.

I will never—it is certain—see him again. But I am happy. Now he, too, can rest.

Monday, 28th May, 1990: Memorial Day: at Lettie's.

This will call for every ounce of ingenuity I can muster. Somehow, Peter and the dreadful Bethany must be convinced to leave the Folly where it is. And only I can do that.

How?

For myself, I will raise it as a monument to 'poor Naddie Rylands', who surely stared at me from a window down at *Shingles* some time Saturday afternoon. And to her mother, Rita Mae, who suffered all those years from Rylands' tyranny. And—yes—I will raise it, too, like a fist at grandfather Bochner Woods—for my grandmother's sake—and all her kind.

HOWARD ENGEL · b. 1931

The Three Wise Guys

The visions of sugarplums dancing in my head stopped dancing and disappeared into the graveyard of interrupted dreams when the telephone rang.

'Hello?'

'Benny? I hope I didn't get you up?'

'Martha? What time is it?'

'How am I supposed to know? I haven't worn a timepiece since I lost the one my wicked old stepmother left me. I just phoned to wish you a merry Christmas, Cooperman.' Martha sounded like she was on a tear and I was one of the people she shared the knowledge with by telephone. She knew I was no boozer, so I usually heard about her exploits after the fact.

'Merry Christmas yourself, Martha. Have you been up all night? I'm assuming that that grey stuff outside my dirty window is day.'

'Oh, Benny, you can't be cross with me, not on Christmas. You're the only person in town I know who won't be up to his knees in wrapping paper and squalling brats this morning. Jews don't celebrate Christmas, they just started it.'

'Martha, it sounds like you've been doing enough celebrating for Christian and Jew alike. Answer my question: have you been up all night?'

'Of course I have. I decided not to go down to my sister's in Bermuda. My brothers have all kicked the bucket except for Francis, and she, that wife of his, phoned to say that they were having an intimate inner-family celebration this year. Just sixty or seventy of her dearest and closest friends, but not her own husband's sister. There are getting to be fewer and fewer Tracys in the phone book, I said to her. He, Francis, wouldn't even talk to me. But I don't care, Benny. May the good Lord keep them childless, that's all. I'm not interrupting anything, am I, Benny?' Martha paused here and I looked at the unslept-in half of my bed. It was as flat, clean, and un-mussed as it usually is.

'Nothing particular,' I said.

'Good! I was just thinkin' about you, you little devil, and so I thought I'd give you a call.'

'And so you just picked up the phone and called me at the break of day.'

'Benny, it's broken, long ago. And I didn't see any russet mantle on yon high eastward hill either. Too many condos going up in Grantham, Benny. It's a bloody crime.'

'Martha, who have you been celebrating with?' That stopped her for long enough for me to find my jacket with my cigarettes and get a Player's alight without actually touching a foot to bare linoleum. The fact that I upset a pile of paperbacks while doing it was only a minor catastrophe. Any day that began with a call from Martha was already separated from its fellows.

'Celebrating with?' she said, beginning to catch up with the drop in tempo. That was the only kind of drop that she would allow to escape her when she was flying high, as she obviously was this morning. I'd met Martha Tracy in 1980. She was working for a real estate tycoon, local variety, who had apparently just shot himself with a target pistol. That was when I still thought of myself as a specialist in divorce work. I guess that back then the penny still hadn't dropped that there was no more money to be made transom-gazing or standing under leaky eavestroughs getting evidence of marital infractions for divorce lawyers. Don't get me wrong. When there was a buck to be made in divorce work, I was all for it. Nowadays I take what comes along and wait until it comes along, searching titles in the registry office for my cousin, Melvyn. Since our first meeting, Martha had helped me out in a few investigations. A couple of times she had put up a witness for me in her house over on Western Hill. Once she put me up when some heavies were looking for me.

Martha was almost as good on the phone as she was in person. Face to face, you saw the firm, Churchillian jaw and the solid, no-nonsense figure. At this hour in the morning, she was almost realer than real. This wasn't the first time she'd got me out of bed, it is true, but I had to remember the times when the shoe was on the other foot.

'I was celebrating with the celebrated Martha B. Tracy, that's who. I closed up the stores along St Andrew Street and I had a little celebration that started at the Golf Club and I ended up where I always do, at midnight mass at St Mary's, because it's just around the corner from my place.'

'You caused quite a stir, I'll bet.'

'It's not what your twisted little mind's thinking, Benny. I got caught in a fight with some young punks.'

'During the service?'

'Sure. I hadn't gone to confession so I couldn't join in the line for Holy Communion. I was just sitting there next to the column with the poor box attached, over the left-hand side as you face the altar. Hell, you wouldn't know anyway. Have you ever been in St Mary's?'

'Martha, I've even rung the bells.' She didn't believe me, but I didn't want to slow down her story, if that's what it was planning to be. 'Tell me what happened.'

'I was sitting there, minding my own business, when three young punks came along and tried to grope me.'

'They were after your maiden treasure, were they?'

'Don't be condescending. They were rude and violent, although in the end they ran away out the door in the transept.'

'Seriously, were you hurt, Martha?'

'I'll last. I'll lay you out, Cooperman. You'll see. To be honest, they weren't after me, they were after a package wrapped in newspaper that was wedged into the corner of the pew I was in. Their interest in me was in removing an obstruction. But, Benny, how was I to know? They didn't say "Move over", they just started beating me up. That's what I thought they were doing. I thought they'd mistaken me for a drunk and were trying to roll me, get my purse.'

'What happened to the package?'

'That's what I'm calling you about. What's the matter with your hearing? The package was full of plastic bags of a white powder, Benny. I think I scored a kilo and a half.'

'You didn't score anything. They don't even say that on TV any more, Martha. Let me think. Ahnnn.'

'Well?'

'I'm thinking. I'm thinking.'

'You and Jack Benny. You're going to tell me to take it to the cop shop, right?'

'It might make it easier to go to confession.'

'I thought of that, when I thought about it, that's what I thought. But, cops and those young punks, Benny. They're just high school kids. Why send for the howitzers when we haven't even tried small-arms fire yet?'

'What am I in this, a BB gun? Martha, you have to tell the cops. See if you can talk to Sergeants Savas and Staziak. They won't thump those punks any more than is coming to them. Okay?'

'Now I'm thinking. It's hard, Benny, when you've been through what I've been through.'

'Did anybody follow you when you left St Mary's?'

'Yes . . . no. No, everybody'd left by the time I got up. I may have passed out from the shock of it all.' There was another of her reflective pauses. 'I think the service was over a good little while before I left the church. The altar candles had all been put out and there wasn't anybody hanging around the doors.'

'Did anybody try to mess with you on your way home?'

'A couple of kids asked if I had any spare change. You know the way they do nowadays. They're all at it. But nobody tried to get the package from me.'

'Martha, I've known you a long time, right?'

'A few summers. Yes. Why?'

'There's a part of this you won't tell me. Come on, why don't you want to go to the cops? This is Benny, remember? Tell Benny.'

'Aw, Benny, it's because I think I know the kids who did it. I've watched them grow up. They used to shovel the snow off my sidewalk and sell me chocolate bars I didn't need for their basketball teams. There has to be a gentler way than going for the heavy artillery.'

'They could have cut your throat in church, Martha, and you're worried about getting somebody new to do your sidewalk. Come on!'

'Jason Abbott was always a nice kid. So was Lester Garvey and that other one, that Larry, whatever-his-name-is: Storchuck, I think. I think they were surprised to see me there, Benny. What am I going to do? You're the private detective.'

'Private investigator. I'm not a detective. Look, Martha. This is a big drug drop. This isn't nickel and dime stuff. Those kids were making a big connection. Unless you were exaggerating about the size of that package.'

'Well, I didn't actually weigh it. Maybe it's closer to a dozen ounces or so. Benny, if you'd seen their faces when they ran away—'

'You're breaking my heart, Martha. Tell me about the Little Match Girl.'

'Tell me when you ever rang the bells at St Mary's on St Andrew Street West? That's not your local synagogue, is it?'

'I'll make this brief. Just long enough for me to check the number for Chris Savas at Niagara Regional Police. When we lived at 40 Monck Street, our neighbour, Jim O'Reilly, was a butcher until he retired.

After that he was a bellringer at St Mary's. When I was three or four, we were great pals. He used to take me on his shoulder into the church tower and I'd help him with the ropes.'

'And I've lived in that parish all my life and I didn't know that, Benny. I guess the poet didn't go far enough when he said, "Never send to know for whom the bell tolls, it tolls for thee." '

'You can always toll a bell, Martha, but you can't tell it much. Let's get back to your problem. The solution is in calling Chris Savas at 555-6000.' I repeated the number and she grudgingly wrote it down. I ended the conversation by telling her that I'd come over in about an hour. She was getting stubborn and fractious at her end of the line. She didn't want me sitting in her kitchen, she wanted the package of dope out of her house without having to send a couple of kids to jail on Christmas Day. But she agreed at last and I rolled out of bed, showered, shaved, and did all the things I didn't think I was going to do on Christmas, beginning with stepping out into the freezing world.

St Mary's Church on St Andrew Street West was cool and dim, the way churches should be. There was some light coming through tall pointed windows, glazed with small panes of window glass. The stained glass would come after the roof had been fixed and the steeple had been raised up to the height the architect had had in mind. There wasn't much light coming off the frozen streets anyway; even the best stained glass would have failed to inspire much in this light.

I found the column with the poor-box on the left-hand side of the church and checked the pew where Martha had been sitting. Somebody had carved a small recess in the angle of the seat, where it met the supporting plank. Long sermons and idle hands, I thought. As I was coming out, three teenagers were on their way in. They checked me out by pretending to show a keen interest in a statue of the virgin in a candle-lit side chapel. They looked about sixteen years old, maybe younger. The boy in the middle was a light-skinned black with his hair shaved close to his head up the sides. He wore it longer at the crown. The other two boys had similar cuts, except that one of them, the dark-haired one, had chevron-like cuts all the way up the skull, where the barber had cut closer to the scalp than elsewhere. They were all wearing black leather jackets and chewing gum. I stood behind them watching them and the elevated statue. As soon as I stopped, their attention was divided.

'What do you want?' asked the black kid.

'That was a royal screw-up. We heard what happened.' I was trying on a part I rarely play. It might get me some information, it might get me shoved into the altar rail. 'We're very cross with the three of you,' I said with deliberate understatement. 'What are you planning on doing about it?'

'The broad was starting to shout. We had to get away!' said the kid with the chevron haircut, who was now looking a little younger than the other two.

'You let that old bag make a monkey out of you! You know who she is at least?'

'She's—' began the black kid, then he stopped himself. 'She's just somebody came to hear mass, is all. We don't know her from nobody.'

'She was kicking up and making a racket. You gotta see it from our side,' said the boy who'd been silent until now.

'We thought you kids could handle this.'

'We told you we never done nothin' like this before. Nothin' this big.'

'You never saw me before in your life and you better remember that.'

'He means that's what we told Eddie Manion.'

'Eddie didn't tell you to give the stuff away to women who get a little high on Christmas Eve.'

'Look, mister, we didn't even want to take the stuff from Eddie.'

'That's right, he twisted our arms. Said he'd tell Father Daeninckx on us if we didn't play along.'

'And what did he tell you to do with it?'

'Just hold it over the long weekend and then give it back to the Dittrick Hotel.'

'That's right. Now what are you going to do? Eddie's got a long memory and a short temper.'

'Maybe you could explain . . .' The black kid let the words die on his tongue. The two others looked at him.

'You could do hard time getting mixed up with Eddie Manion in this.'

'Yeah, we've been talkin' about that all night.'

'Hey, who are you working for anyway, mister? Are you with Manion in this or what?'

'Listen you three. Manion is finished. He's all washed up, hung out to dry, and you've just had the escape of your lives if it happens. That's a big if, I'm tellin' you. You've been playing Russian roulette with an automatic and you don't even know it.'

'What the hell can we do about it?'

'If I were the three of you, I'd bury myself in homework over the holidays and forget about the street action for about six months for a start.'

'Are you a nark or a cop or what?'

'Listen up, the three of you. The cops know who you are. You've been identified. Which one of you is Lester?' The two white boys fingered their black pal. 'Everything depends on what you do from now on.'

'Okay, okay, mister, we'll be cool, right?' The other two agreed with Lester and began backing away from me.

'Just a minute! Where can I get news to you if something should come up? I may need to get in touch over the weekend.' The three huddled and when they came up for air one of them gave me the Storchuck phone number. I wrote it down and let the boys casually retreat down the aisle of the nave and through the felt-covered doors in the permanently temporary baffle that surrounded the front doors. In a moment, I heard the muffled slam of one of the three big front doors. On my own way out, I was tempted to set alight all the candles that had gone out overnight, but I decided not to meddle in which prayers got answered and which were put on hold. I also avoided dipping my fingers into the scallop shell of holy water that stood near the entrance. I'd just spent more time in church than my whole family for the last thousand years.

When I got to Martha's, I could see that she was nursing an impressive hangover. On top of that, she seemed nervous. She reported that she had talked to Corporal Harrow on the phone. From her face, I could see she hadn't been happy with the conversation. 'Some cops ask you questions that make you feel that it's your own fault for being robbed, Benny, like you'd drawn a target on yourself and aimed the gun.'

'Is he coming over?'

'That's what the man said.'

'What's bothering you, Martha?'

'Does it show? I must be getting old, Benny.' She was puttering about in her kitchen, wiping the perfectly clean counter with a blue cloth again and again. In the end, I managed to out-wait her and she told me about her doubts. 'That Harrow fellow is convinced that the boys are part of a gang of dope peddlers.'

'Well, if that package was full of dope . . .'

'I know, I know,' she said, rinsing out the blue cloth. 'But, Benny, he talked like they were the kingpins of the drug market. He said he'd get them if it cost him his badge.'

'Excessive zeal, is that what you're complaining about?'

'Benny, look. Harrow scared me more than the kids did.'

'Did you give him their names?'

Martha avoided my face. 'They slipped my mind. That corporal is very intimidating. And I didn't want to get them in any more trouble than they're already in. You know what I mean?'

'Yeah,' I said, watching Martha make a couple of cups of her specialty, instant tap-water coffee. 'The corporal used to be a sergeant until he lost his spurs trying a fast one. I guess it's still eating him.' Martha gave me a look with one of the cups. 'We go back a long way together,' I explained. 'As a matter of fact, I don't think it will do those kids any good if Harrow finds out that I've been involved in this. I'll check back with you in a couple of hours. Okay?'

'M'yeah, I guess. Bring some pizza if you can find a place open. This town's got no consideration for single people.'

I left, avoiding the broken front step, and went back home. Half an hour later, Martha called; 'Benny, is it you?'

'No, it's Donner and Blitzen. What happened?'

'Well, he came over and grilled me about the whole thing, and managed to get me to give their names. Damn it, I knew I would under pressure. It's the way I'm made, Benny.'

'Well, that settles their hash, I guess. Christmas in the cells. Hark the herald from the basement of the cop shop.'

'It may not be as simple as that, Benny.'

'You mean he still has to get you to pick them out of a lineup?'

'More than that. I opened the package before Harrow got here.'

'And?'

'And I made up another package with the same sort of freezer bags. And I gave that to Harrow.' Martha's voice was trailing off so that I could hardly hear her.

'What did you put in the bags, Martha?'

'Talcum,' she whispered.

'Talcum!'

'Well, I had an extra supply from the time I had athlete's foot a year ago.'

Martha never ceased amazing me, but I didn't tell her and I didn't bore her about tampering with evidence either. I was too busy with a scheme that was coming together in my own head. Over the phone

I gave Martha the Storchuck boy's phone number. I briefed her on what to say to him. She mumbled agreement that with Martha often means the opposite and I went out to track down a very special pizza.

In the end, I had to settle for a run of the loom model that looked like it had collected the anchovies from at least fifty earlier jobs. When I got it to Martha's place, I checked the landscape for patrol cars. The coast was as clear as the night that was beginning to fall. I could count sharp, untwinkling stars overhead between the wisps of clouds. Lack of cloud cover lets the cold in, or at least that's what I've always been told.

The broken step nearly undid my sore back, but I managed to get to her door without further injury. I could hear her coming before I laid a glove on the door. 'Pizza!' I announced and handed in the cardboard box, which was beginning to sag. Martha carried it to the porcelain-topped old-fashioned kitchen table and opened the lid.

'Perfect,' she said. 'Help yourself to beer in the icebox.' A lot of people in Grantham still say icebox even though they've never seen one. Martha had, so I made allowances as I took the tops off two ales. Martha hated what she called the 'play-beer' that was advertised on television.

Martha and I toasted one another and helped ourselves to the first of the gooey wedges of dripping cheese and pastry. Martha was drinking her second beer by now, and telling me, as she often did, about the time she came to her senses next to a provincial cabinet minister in a roadhouse outside Fredericton, New Brunswick, staring down into the remains of a congealed pizza. It must have been the sad story of her life judging by the number of times she recounted the tale.

'Do you think your scheme will work, Benny?'

'We won't know until we hear about it on TV or read about it in the paper on the day after Boxing Day,' I said. 'I can even see the headline, Martha: DRUG KINGPIN NAILED WITH KILO OF COKE.'

'Manion will be the most surprised guilty party the cops ever pulled in in a raid,' said Martha. 'It took a twisted mind like yours to think up such a diabolical plot.'

'Martha, you did most of it when you made the fake package of talcum. I mean the talcum was real, only—'

'I can read your mind. Don't bother to finish.'

'Manion wanted the stuff out of his place, the Dittrick Hotel, until after the long weekend. That meant he'd been tipped off that the hotel was going to be raided.'

'What better time than Christmas?'

'When it happens, he's going to get the surprise of his life. The kid will know where to hide the stuff where even a dumb cop can't miss it.'

'And the three kids? Don't forget Harrow is hot on their trail.'

'Yes, and when he catches them, he can arrest them for possession.'

'No he can't. They are not in possession.'

'Well, he could get them on conspiring to commit an indictable offence. Only, once the lab checks it out, Harrow will find his case against the guys has exploded in a puff of talcum powder.'

'Even if they'd been caught with a ton of it, there's no law that says you can't own as much talcum as you want.' Here Martha's face fell. If I hadn't been almost nose to nose with her across the table, I might have missed it.

'What is it, Martha?'

'I was just trying to remember. No. I'm *sure* it was the talcum I gave him. I'm eighty per cent sure of it.'

ALICE MUNRO · b. 1931

Fits

The two people who died were in their early sixties. They were both tall and well built, and carried a few pounds of extra weight. He was grey-haired, with a square, rather flat face. A broad nose kept him from looking perfectly dignified and handsome. Her hair was blond, a silvery blond that does not strike you as artificial any more—though you know it is not natural—because so many women of that age have acquired it. On Boxing Day, when they dropped over to have a drink with Peg and Robert, she wore a pale-grey dress with a fine, shiny stripe in it, grey stockings, and grey shoes. She drank gin-and-tonic. He wore brown slacks and a cream-coloured sweater, and drank rye-and-water. They had recently come back from a trip to Mexico. He had tried parachute-riding. She hadn't wanted to. They had gone to see a place in Yucatan—it looked like a well—where virgins were supposed to have been flung down, in the hope of good harvests.

'Actually, though, that's just a nineteenth-century notion,' she said. 'That's just the nineteenth-century notion of being so preoccupied with virginity. The truth probably is that they threw people down sort of indiscriminately. Girls or men or old people or whoever they could get their hands on. So not being a virgin would be no guarantee of safety!'

Across the room, Peg's two sons—the older one, Clayton, who was a virgin, and the younger one, Kevin, who was not—watched this breezy-talking silvery-blond woman with stern, bored expressions. She had said that she used to be a high-school English teacher. Clayton remarked afterward that he knew the type.

Robert and Peg have been married for nearly five years. Robert was never married before, but Peg married for the first time when she was eighteen. Her two boys were born while she and her husband lived with his parents on a farm. Her husband had a job driving trucks of livestock to the Canada Packers Abattoir in Toronto. Other truck-driving jobs followed, taking him farther and farther away. Peg and the boys moved to Gilmore, and she got a job working in Kuiper's store, which was called the Gilmore Arcade. Her husband ended up in the Arctic, driving trucks to oil rigs across the frozen Beaufort Sea. She got a divorce.

Robert's family owned the Gilmore Arcade but had never lived in Gilmore. His mother and sisters would not have believed you could survive a week in such a place. Robert's father had bought the store, and two other stores in nearby towns, shortly after the Second World War. He hired local managers, and drove up from Toronto a few times during the year to see how things were getting on.

For a long time, Robert did not take much interest in his father's various businesses. He took a degree in civil engineering, and had some idea of doing work in underdeveloped countries. He got a job in Peru, travelled through South America, gave up engineering for a while to work on a ranch in British Columbia. When his father became ill, it was necessary for him to come back to Toronto. He worked for the Provincial Department of Highways, in an engineering job that was not a very good one for a man of his age. He was thinking of getting a teaching degree and maybe going up North to teach Indians, changing his life completely, once his father died. He was getting close to forty then, and having his third major affair with a married woman.

Now and then, he drove up to Gilmore and the other towns to keep an eye on the stores. Once, he brought Lee with him, his third—and, as it turned out, his last—married woman. She brought a picnic lunch, drank Pimm's Number I in the car, and treated the whole trip as a merry excursion, a foray into hillbilly country. She had counted on making love in the open fields, and was incensed to find they were all full of cattle or uncomfortable cornstalks.

Robert's father died, and Robert did change his life, but instead of becoming a teacher and heading for the wilderness, he came to live in Gilmore to manage the stores himself. He married Peg.

It was entirely by accident that Peg was the one who found them.

On Sunday evening, the farm woman who sold the Kuipers their eggs knocked on the door.

'I hope you don't mind me bringing these tonight instead of tomorrow morning,' she said. 'I have to take my daughter-in-law to Kitchener to have her ultrasound. I brought the Weebles theirs, too, but I guess they're not home. I wonder if you'd mind if I left them here with you? I have to leave early in the morning. She was going to drive herself but I didn't think that was such a good idea. She's nearly five months but still vomiting. Tell them they can just pay me next time.'

'No problem,' said Robert. 'No trouble at all. We can just run over with them in the morning. No problem at all!' Robert is a stocky, athletic-looking man, with curly, greying hair and bright brown eyes. His friendliness and obligingness are often emphatic, so that people might get the feeling of being buffeted from all sides. This is a manner that serves him well in Gilmore, where assurances are supposed to be repeated, and in fact much of conversation is repetition, a sort of dance of good intentions, without surprises. Just occasionally, talking to people, he feels something else, an obstruction, and isn't sure what it is (malice, stubbornness?) but it's like a rock at the bottom of a river when you're swimming—the clear water lifts you over it.

For a Gilmore person, Peg is reserved. She came up to the woman and relieved her of the eggs she was holding, while Robert went on assuring her it was no trouble and asking about the daughter-in-law's pregnancy. Peg smiled as she would smile in the store when she gave you your change—a quick transactional smile, nothing personal. She is a small slim woman with a cap of soft brown hair, freckles, and a scrubbed, youthful look. She wears pleated skirts, fresh neat blouses buttoned to the throat, pale sweaters, sometimes a black ribbon tie. She moves gracefully and makes very little noise. Robert once told her he had never met anyone so self-contained as she was. (His women have usually been talkative, stylishly effective, though careless about some of the details, tense, lively, 'interesting'.)

Peg said she didn't know what he meant.

He started to explain what a self-contained person was like. At that time, he had a very faulty comprehension of Gilmore vocabulary—he could still make mistakes about it—and he took too seriously the limits that were usually observed in daily exchanges.

'I know what the words mean,' Peg said, smiling. 'I just don't understand how you meant it about me.'

Of course she knew what the words meant. Peg took courses, a different course each winter, choosing from what was offered at the local high school. She took a course on the History of Art, one on

Great Civilizations of the East, one on Discoveries and Explorations Through the Ages. She went to class one night a week, even if she was very tired or had a cold. She wrote tests and prepared papers. Sometimes Robert would find a page covered with her small neat handwriting on top of the refrigerator or the dresser in their room.

Therefore we see that the importance of Prince Henry the Navigator was in the inspiration and encouragement of other explorers for Portugal, even though he did not go on voyages himself.

He was moved by her earnest statements, her painfully careful small handwriting, and angry that she never got more than a B-plus for these papers she worked so hard at.

'I don't do it for the marks,' Peg said. Her cheekbones reddened under the freckles, as if she was making some kind of personal confession. 'I do it for the enjoyment.'

Robert was up before dawn on Monday morning, standing at the kitchen counter drinking his coffee, looking out at the fields covered with snow. The sky was clear, and the temperatures had dropped. It was going to be one of the bright, cold, hard January days that come after weeks of west wind, of blowing and falling snow. Creeks, rivers, ponds frozen over. Lake Huron frozen over as far as you could see. Perhaps all the way this year. That had happened, though rarely.

He had to drive to Keneally, to the Kuiper store there. Ice on the roof was causing water underneath to back up and leak through the ceiling. He would have to chop up the ice and get the roof clear. It would take him at least half the day.

All the repair work and upkeep on the store and on this house is done by Robert himself. He has learned to do plumbing and wiring. He enjoys the feeling that he can manage it. He enjoys the difficulty, and the difficulty of winter, here. Not much more than a hundred miles from Toronto, it is a different country. The snow-belt. Coming up here to live was not unlike heading into the wilderness, after all. Blizzards still isolate the towns and villages. Winter comes down hard on the country, settles down just the way the two-mile-high ice did thousands of years ago. People live within the winter in a way outsiders do not understand. They are watchful, provident, fatigued, exhilarated.

A thing he likes about this house is the back view, over the open country. That makes up for the straggling dead-end street without trees or sidewalks. The street was opened up after the war, when it was taken for granted that everybody would be using cars, not walking anywhere. And so they did. The houses are fairly close to the street and to each other, and when everybody who lives in the houses is home, cars take up nearly all the space where sidewalks, boulevards, shade trees might have been.

Robert, of course, was willing to buy another house. He assumed they would do that. There were—there are—fine old houses for sale in Gilmore, at prices that are a joke, by city standards. Peg said she couldn't see herself living in those places. He offered to build her a new house in the subdivision on the other side of town. She didn't want that either. She wanted to stay in this house, which was the first house she and the boys had lived in on their own. So Robert bought it—she was only renting—and built on the master bedroom and another bathroom, and made a television room in the basement. He got some help from Kevin, less from Clayton. The house still looked, from the street, like the house he had parked in front of the first time he drove Peg home from work. One and a half storeys high, with a steep roof and a living-room window divided into square panes like the window on a Christmas card. White aluminum siding, narrow black shutters, black trim. Back in Toronto, he had thought of Peg living in this house. He had thought of her patterned, limited, serious, and desirable life.

He noticed the Weebles' eggs sitting on the counter. He thought of taking them over. But it was too early. The door would be locked. He didn't want to wake them. Peg could take the eggs when she left to open up the store. He took the Magic Marker that was sitting on the ledge under her reminder pad, and wrote on a paper towel, *Don't forget the eggs to W's. Love, Robert.* These eggs were no cheaper than the ones you bought at the supermarket. It was just that Robert liked getting them from a farm. And they were brown. Peg said city people all had a thing about brown eggs—they thought brown eggs were more natural somehow, like brown sugar.

When he backed his car out, he saw that the Weebles' car was in their carport. So they were home from wherever they had been last night. Then he saw that the snow thrown up across the front of their driveway by the town snowplow had not been cleared. The plow must have gone by during the night. But he himself hadn't had to shovel any snow; there hadn't been any fresh snow overnight and the plow hadn't been out. The snow was from yesterday. They couldn't have been out last night. Unless they were walking. The sidewalks were not cleared, except along the main street and the school streets, and it was difficult to walk along the narrowed streets with their banks of snow, but, being new to town, they might have set out not realizing that.

He didn't look closely enough to see if there were footprints.

He pictured what happened. First from the constable's report, then from Peg's.

Peg came out of the house at about twenty after eight. Clayton had already gone off to school, and Kevin, getting over an ear infection, was down in the basement room playing a Billy Idol tape and watching a game show on television. Peg had not forgotten the eggs. She got into her car and turned on the engine to warm it up, then walked out to the street, stepped over the Weebles' uncleared snow, and went up their driveway to the side door. She was wearing her white knitted scarf and tam and her lilac-coloured, down-filled coat. Those coats made most of the women in Gilmore look like barrels, but Peg looked all right, being so slender.

The houses on the street were originally of only three designs. But by now most of them had been so altered, with new windows, porches, wings, and decks, that it was hard to find true mates any more. The Weebles' house had been built as a mirror image of the Kuipers', but the front window had been changed, its Christmas-card panes taken out, and the roof had been lifted, so that there was a large upstairs window overlooking the street. The siding was pale green and the trim white, and there were no shutters.

The side door opened into a utility room, just as Peg's door did at home. She knocked lightly at first, thinking that they would be in the kitchen, which was only a few steps up from the utility room. She had noticed the car, of course, and wondered if they had got home late and were sleeping in. (She hadn't thought yet about the snow's not having been shovelled, and the fact that the plow hadn't been past in the night. That was something that occurred to her later on when she got into her own car and backed it out.) She knocked louder and louder. Her face was stinging already in the bright cold. She tried the door and found that it wasn't locked. She opened it and stepped into shelter and called.

The little room was dark. There was no light to speak of coming down from the kitchen, and there was a bamboo curtain over the side door. She set the eggs on the clothes dryer, and was going to leave them there. Then she thought she had better take them up into the kitchen, in case the Weebles wanted eggs for breakfast and had run out. They wouldn't think of looking in the utility room.

(This, in fact, was Robert's explanation to himself. She didn't say all that, but he forgot she didn't. She just said, 'I thought I might as well take them up to the kitchen.')

The kitchen had those same bamboo curtains over the sink window and over the breakfast-nook windows, which meant that though the room faced east, like the Kuipers' kitchen, and though the sun was fully up by this time, not much light could get in. The day hadn't begun here.

But the house was warm. Perhaps they'd got up a while ago and turned up the thermostat, then gone back to bed. Perhaps they left it up all night—though they had seemed to Peg to be thriftier than that. She set the eggs on the counter by the sink. The layout of the kitchen was almost exactly the same as her own. She noticed a few dishes stacked, rinsed, but not washed, as if they'd had something to eat before they went to bed.

She called again from the living-room doorway.

The living room was perfectly tidy. It looked to Peg somehow too perfectly tidy, but that—as she said to Robert—was probably the way the living room of a retired couple was bound to look to a woman used to having children around. Peg had never in her life had quite as much tidiness around her as she might have liked, having gone from a family home where there were six children to her in-laws' crowded farmhouse, which she crowded further with her own babies. She had told Robert a story about once asking for a beautiful bar of soap for Christmas, pink soap with a raised design of roses on it. She got it, and she used to hide it after every use so that it wouldn't get cracked and mouldy in the cracks, the way soap always did in that house. She was grown up at that time, or thought she was.

She had stamped the snow off her boots in the utility room. Nevertheless she hesitated to walk across the clean, pale-beige living-room carpet. She called again. She used the Weebles' first names, which she barely knew. Walter and Nora. They had moved in last April, and since then they had been away on two trips, so she didn't feel she knew them at all well, but it seemed silly to be calling, 'Mr and Mrs Weeble. Are you up yet, Mr and Mrs Weeble?'

No answer.

They had an open staircase going up from the living room, just as Peg and Robert did. Peg walked now across the clean, pale carpet to the foot of the stairs, which were carpeted in the same material. She started to climb. She did not call again.

She must have known then or she would have called. It would be the normal thing to do, to keep calling the closer you got to where people might be sleeping. To warn them. They might be deeply asleep. Drunk. That wasn't the custom of the Weebles, so far as anybody knew, but nobody knew them that well. Retired people. Early retirement. He had been an accountant; she had been a teacher. They had lived in Hamilton. They had chosen Gilmore because Walter Weeble used to have an aunt and uncle here, whom he visited as a child. Both dead now, the aunt and uncle, but the place must have held pleasant memories for him. And it was cheap; this was surely a cheaper house than they could have afforded. They meant to spend their money travelling. No children.

She didn't call; she didn't halt again. She climbed the stairs and didn't look around as she came up; she faced straight ahead. Ahead was the bathroom, with the door open. It was clean and empty.

She turned at the top of the stairs toward the Weebles' bedroom. She had never been upstairs in this house before, but she knew where that would be. It would be the extended room at the front, with the wide window overlooking the street.

The door of that room was open.

Peg came downstairs and left the house by the kitchen, the utility room, the side door. Her footprints showed on the carpet and on the linoleum tiles, and outside on the snow. She closed the door after herself. Her car had been running all this time and was sitting in its own little cloud of steam. She got in and backed out and drove to the police station in the Town Hall.

'It's a bitter cold morning, Peg,' the constable said.

'Yes, it is.'

'So what can I do for you?'

• • •

Robert got more, from Karen.

Karen Adams was the clerk in the Gilmore Arcade. She was a young married woman, solidly built, usually good-humoured, alert without particularly seeming to be so, efficient without a lot of bustle. She got along well with the customers; she got along with Peg and Robert. She had known Peg longer, of course. She defended her against those people who said Peg had got her nose in the air since she married rich. Karen said Peg hadn't changed from what she always was. But after today she said, 'I always believed Peg and me to be friends, but now I'm not so sure.'

Karen started work at ten. She arrived a little before that and asked if there had been customers in yet, and Peg said no, nobody.

'I don't wonder,' Karen said. 'It's too cold. If there was any wind, it'd be murder.'

Peg had made coffee. They had a new coffee maker, Robert's Christmas present to the store. They used to have to get take-outs from the bakery up the street.

'Isn't this thing marvellous?' Karen said as she got her coffee.

Peg said yes. She was wiping up some marks on the floor.

'Oh-oh,' said Karen. 'Was that me or you?'

'I think it was me,' Peg said.

'So I didn't think anything of it,' Karen said later. 'I thought she must've tracked in some mud. I didn't stop to think, Where would you get down to mud with all this snow on the ground?'

After a while, a customer came in, and it was Celia Simms, and she had heard. Karen was at the cash, and Peg was at the back checking some invoices. Celia told Karen. She didn't know much; she didn't know how it had been done or that Peg was involved.

Karen shouted to the back of the store. 'Peg! Peg! Something terrible has happened, and it's your next-door neighbours!'

Peg called back, 'I know.'

Celia lifted her eyebrows at Karen—she was one of those who didn't like Peg's attitude—and Karen loyally turned aside and waited till Celia went out of the store. Then she hurried to the back, making the hangers jingle on the racks.

'Both the Weebles are shot dead, Peg. Did you know that?'

Peg said, 'Yes. I found them.'

'You did! When did you?'

'This morning, just before I came in to work.'

'They were murdered!'

'It was a murder-suicide,' Peg said. 'He shot her and then he shot himself. That's what happened.'

'When she told me that,' Karen said, 'I started to shake. I shook all over and I couldn't stop myself.' Telling Robert this, she shook again, to demonstrate, and pushed her hands up inside the sleeves of her blue plush jogging suit.

'So I said, "What did you do when you found them," and she said, "I went and told the police." I said, "Did you scream, or what?" I said didn't her legs buckle, because I know mine would've. I can't imagine how I would've got myself out of there. She said she didn't remember much about getting out, but she did remember closing the door, the outside door, and thinking, Make sure that's closed in case some dog could get in. Isn't that awful? She was right, but it's awful to think of. Do you think she's in shock?'

'No,' Robert said. 'I think she's all right.'

This conversation was taking place at the back of the store in the afternoon, when Peg had gone out to get a sandwich.

'She had not said one word to me. Nothing. I said, "How come you never said a word about this, Peg," and she said, "I knew you'd find out pretty soon." I said yes, but she could've told me. "I'm sorry," she says. "I'm sorry." Just like she's apologizing for some little thing like using my coffee mug. Only, Peg would never do that.'

Robert had finished what he was doing at the Keneally store around noon, and decided to drive back to Gilmore before getting anything to eat. There was a highway diner just outside of town, on the way in from Keneally, and he thought that he would stop there. A few truckers and travellers were usually eating in the diner, but most of the trade was local—farmers on the way home, business and working men who had driven out from town. Robert liked this place, and he had entered it today with a feeling of buoyant expectation. He was hungry from his work in the cold air, and aware of the brilliance of the day, with the snow on the fields looking sculpted, dazzling, as permanent as marble. He had the sense he had fairly often in Gilmore, the sense of walking onto an informal stage, where a rambling, agreeable play was in progress. And he knew his lines—or knew, at least, that his improvisations would not fail. His whole life in Gilmore sometimes seemed to have this quality, but if he ever tried to describe it that way, it would sound as if it was an artificial life, something contrived, not entirely serious. And the very opposite was true. So when he met somebody from his old life, as he sometimes did when he went to Toronto, and was asked how he liked living in Gilmore, he would say, 'I can't tell you how much I like it!' which was exactly the truth.

'Why didn't you get in touch with me?'

'You were up on the roof.'

'You could have called the store and told Ellie. She would have told me.'

'What good would that have done?'

'I could at least have come home.'

He had come straight from the diner to the store, without eating what he had ordered. He did not think he would find Peg in any state of collapse—he knew her well enough for that—but he did think she would want to go home, let him fix her a drink, spend some time telling him about it.

She didn't want that. She wanted to go up the street to the bakery to get her usual lunch—a roll with ham and cheese.

'I let Karen go out to eat, but I haven't had time. Should I bring one back for you? If you didn't eat at the diner, I might as well.'

When she brought him the sandwich, he sat and ate it at the desk where she had been doing invoices. She put fresh coffee and water into the coffee maker.

'I can't imagine how we got along without this thing.'

He looked at Peg's lilac-coloured coat hanging beside Karen's red coat on the washroom door. On the lilac coat there was a long crusty smear of reddish-brown paint, down to the hemline.

Of course that wasn't paint. But on her coat? How did she get blood on her coat? She must have brushed up against them in that room. She must have got close.

Then he remembered the talk in the diner, and realized she wouldn't have needed to get that close. She could have got blood from the door frame. The constable had been in the diner, and he said there was blood everywhere, and not just blood.

'He shouldn't ever have used a shotgun for that kind of business,' one of the men at the diner said.

Somebody else said, 'Maybe a shotgun was all he had.'

It was busy in the store most of the afternoon. People on the street, in the bakery and the café and the bank and the post office, talking. People wanted to talk face to face. They had to get out and do it, in spite of the cold. Talking on the phone was not enough.

What had gone on at first, Robert gathered, was that people had got on the phone, just phoned anybody they could think of who might not have heard. Karen had phoned her friend Shirley, who was at home in bed with the flu, and her mother, who was in the hospital with a broken hip. It turned out her mother knew already—the whole hospital knew. And Shirley said, 'My sister beat you to it.'

It was true that people valued and looked forward to the moment of breaking the news—Karen was annoyed at Shirley's sister, who didn't work and could get to the phone whenever she wanted to—but there was real kindness and consideration behind this impulse, as well. Robert thought so. 'I knew she wouldn't want not to know,' Karen said, and that was true. Nobody would want not to know. To go out into the street, not knowing. To go around doing all the usual daily things, not knowing. He himself felt troubled, even slightly humiliated, to think that he hadn't known; Peg hadn't let him know.

Talk ran backward from the events of the morning. Where were the Weebles seen, and in what harmlessness and innocence, and how close to the moment when everything was changed?

She had stood in line at the Bank of Montreal on Friday afternoon.

He had got a haircut on Saturday morning.

They were together, buying groceries, in the IGA on Friday evening at about eight o'clock.

What did they buy? A good supply? Specials, advertised bargains, more than enough to last for a couple of days?

More than enough. A bag of potatoes, for one thing.

Then reasons. The talk turned to reasons. Naturally. There had been no theories put forward in the diner. Nobody knew the reason, nobody could imagine. But by the end of the afternoon there were too many explanations to choose from.

Financial problems. He had been mixed up in some bad investment scheme in Hamilton. Some wild money-making deal that had fallen through. All their money was gone and they would have to live out the rest of their lives on the old-age pension.

They had owed money on their income taxes. Being an accountant, he thought he know how to fix things, but he had been found out. He would be exposed, perhaps charged, shamed publicly, left poor. Even if it was only cheating the government, it would still be a disgrace when that kind of thing came out.

Was it a lot of money?

Certainly. A lot.

It was not money at all. They were ill. One of them or both of them. Cancer. Crippling arthritis. Alzheimer's disease. Recurrent mental problems. It was health, not money. It was suffering and helplessness they feared, not poverty. A division of opinion became evident between men and women. It was nearly always the men who believed and insisted that the trouble had been money, and it was the women who talked of illness. Who would kill themselves just because they were poor, said some women scornfully. Or even because they might go to jail? It was always a woman, too, who suggested unhappiness in the marriage, who hinted at the drama of a discovered infidelity or the memory of an old one.

Robert listened to all these explanations but did not believe any of them. Loss of money, cancer, Alzheimer's disease. Equally plausible, these seemed to him, equally hollow and useless. What happened was that he believed each of them for about five minutes, no longer. If he could have believed one of them, hung on to it, it would have been as if something had taken its claws out of his chest and permitted him to breathe.

('They weren't Gilmore people, not really,' a woman said to him in the bank. Then she looked embarrassed. 'I don't mean like you.')

Peg kept busy getting some children's sweaters, mitts, snowsuits ready for the January sale. People came up to her when she was marking the tags, and she said, 'Can I help you,' so that they were placed right away in the position of being customers, and had to say that there was something they were looking for. The Arcade carried ladies' and children's clothes, sheets, towels, knitting wool, kitchenware, bulk candy, magazines, mugs, artificial flowers, and plenty of other things besides, so it was not hard to think of something.

What was it they were really looking for? Surely not much in the way of details, description. Very few people actually want that, or will admit they do, in a greedy and straightforward way. They want it, they don't want it. They start asking, they stop themselves. They listen and they back away. Perhaps they wanted from Peg just some kind of acknowledgement, some word or look that would send them away, saying, 'Peg Kuiper is absolutely shattered.' 'I saw Peg Kuiper. She didn't say much but you could tell she was absolutely shattered.'

Some people tried to talk to her, anyway.

'Wasn't that terrible what happened down by you?'

'Yes, it was.'

'You must have known them a little bit, living next door.'

'Not really. We hardly knew them at all.'

'You never noticed anything that would've led you to think this could've happened?'

'We never noticed anything at all.'

Robert pictured the Weebles getting into and out of their car in the driveway. That was where he had most often seen them. He recalled their Boxing Day visit. Her grey legs made him think of a nun. Her mention of virginity had embarrassed Peg and the boys. She reminded Robert a little of the kind of women he used to know. Her husband was less talkative, though not shy. They talked about Mexican food, which it seemed the husband had not liked. He did not like eating in restaurants.

Peg had said, 'Oh, men never do!'

That surprised Robert, who asked her afterward did that mean she wanted to eat out more often?

'I just said that to take her side. I thought he was glaring at her a bit.'

Was he glaring? Robert had not noticed. The man seemed too self-controlled to glare at his wife in public. Too well disposed, on the whole, perhaps in some way too indolent, to glare at anybody anywhere.

But it wasn't like Peg to exaggerate.

Bits of information kept arriving. The maiden name of Nora Weeble. Driscoll. Nora Driscoll. Someone knew a woman who had taught at the same school with her in Hamilton. Well-liked as a teacher, a fashionable dresser, she had some trouble keeping order. She had taken a French Conversation course, and a course in French cooking.

Some women here had asked her if she'd be interested in starting a book club, and she had said yes.

He had been more of a joiner in Hamilton than he was here. The Rotary Club. The Lions Club. Perhaps it had been for business reasons.

They were not churchgoers, as far as anybody knew, not in either place.

(Robert was right about the reasons. In Gilmore everything becomes known, sooner or later. Secrecy and confidentiality are seen to be against the public interest. There is a network of people who are married to or related to the people who work in the offices where all the records are kept.

There was no investment scheme, in Hamilton or anywhere else. No income-tax investigation. No problem about money. No cancer, tricky heart, high blood pressure. She had consulted the doctor about headaches, but the doctor did not think they were migraines, or anything serious.

At the funeral on Thursday, the United Church minister, who usually took up the slack in the cases of no known affiliation, spoke about the pressures and tensions of modern life but gave no more specific clues. Some people were disappointed, as if they expected him to do that—or thought that he might at least mention the dangers of falling away from faith and church membership, the sin of despair. Other people thought that saying anything more than he did say would have been in bad taste.)

Another person who thought Peg should have let him know was Kevin. He was waiting for them when they got home. He was still wearing his pajamas.

Why hadn't she come back to the house instead of driving to the police station? Why hadn't she called to him? She could have come back and phoned. Kevin could have phoned. At the very least, she could have called him from the store.

He had been down in the basement all morning, watching television. He hadn't heard the police come; he hadn't seen them go in or out. He had not known anything about what was going on until his girlfriend, Shanna, phoned him from school at lunch hour.

'She said they took the bodies out in garbage bags.'

'How would she know?' said Clayton. 'I thought she was at school.'

'Somebody told her.'

'She got that from television.'

'She *said* they took them out in garbage bags.'

'Shanna is a cretin. She is only good for one thing.'

'Some people aren't good for anything.'

Clayton was sixteen, Kevin fourteen. Two years apart in age but three years apart in school, because Clayton was accelerated and Kevin was not.

'Cut it out,' Peg said. She had brought up some spaghetti sauce from the freezer and was thawing it in the double boiler. 'Clayton. Kevin. Get busy and make me some salad.'

Kevin said, 'I'm sick. I might contaminate it.'

He picked up the tablecloth and wrapped it around his shoulders like a shawl.

'Do we have to eat off that?' Clayton said. 'Now he's got his crud on it?'

Peg said to Robert, 'Are we having wine?'

Saturday and Sunday nights they usually had wine, but tonight Robert had not thought about it. He went down to the basement to get it. When he came back, Peg was sliding spaghetti into the cooker and Kevin had discarded the tablecloth. Clayton was making the salad. Clayton was small-boned, like his mother, and fiercely driven. A star runner, a demon examination writer.

Kevin was prowling around the kitchen, getting in the way, talking to Peg. Kevin was taller already than Clayton or Peg, perhaps taller than Robert. He had large shoulders and skinny legs and black hair that he wore in the nearest thing he dared to a Mohawk cut—Shanna cut it for him. His pale skin often broke out in pimples. Girls didn't seem to mind.

'So was there?' Kevin said. 'Was the blood and guck all over?'

'Ghoul,' said Clayton.

'Those were human beings, Kevin,' Robert said.

'Were,' said Kevin. 'I know they *were* human beings. I mixed their drinks on Boxing Day. She drank gin and he drank rye. They were human beings then, but all they are now is chemicals. Mom? What did you see first? Shanna said there was blood and guck even out in the hallway.'

'He's brutalized from all the TV he watches,' Clayton said. 'He thinks it was some video. He can't tell real blood from video blood.'

'Mom? Was it splashed?'

Robert has a rule about letting Peg deal with her sons unless she asks for his help. But this time he said, 'Kevin, you know it's about time you shut up.'

'He can't help it,' Clayton said. 'Being ghoulish.'

'You, too, Clayton. You, too.'

But after a moment Clayton said, 'Mom? Did you scream?'

'No,' said Peg thoughtfully. 'I didn't. I guess because there wasn't anybody to hear me. So I didn't.'

'I might have heard you,' said Kevin, cautiously trying a comeback.
'You had the television on.'

'I didn't have the sound on. I had my tape on. I might have heard
you through the tape if you screamed loud enough.'

Peg lifted a strand of the spaghetti to try it. Robert was watching her,
from time to time. He would have said he was watching to see if she
was in any kind of trouble, if she seemed numb, or strange, or showed
a quiver, if she dropped things or made the pots clatter. But in fact he
was watching her just because there was no sign of such difficulty and
because he knew there wouldn't be. She was preparing an ordinary
meal, listening to the boys in her usual mildly censorious but unruffled
way. The only thing more apparent than usual to Robert was her
gracefulness, lightness, quickness, and ease around the kitchen.

Her tone to her sons, under its severity, seemed shockingly serene.

'Kevin, go and get some clothes on, if you want to eat at the table.'

'I can eat in my pajamas.'

'No.'

'I can eat in bed.'

'Not spaghetti, you can't.'

While they were washing up the pots and pans together—Clayton
had gone for his run and Kevin was talking to Shanna on the
phone—Peg told Robert her part of the story. He didn't ask her to, in
so many words. He started off with 'So when you went over, the door
wasn't locked?' and she began to tell him.

'You don't mind talking about it?' Robert said.

'I knew you'd want to know.'

She told him she knew what was wrong—at least, she knew that
something was terribly wrong—before she started up the stairs.

'Were you frightened?'

'No. I didn't think about it like that—being frightened.'

'There could have been somebody up there with a gun.'

'No. I knew there wasn't. I knew there wasn't anybody but me alive
in the house. Then I saw his leg, I saw his leg stretched out into the
hall, and I knew then, but I had to go on in and make sure.'

Robert said, 'I understand that.'

'It wasn't the foot he had taken the shoe off that was out there. He
took the shoe off his other foot, so he could use that foot to pull the
trigger when he shot himself. That was how he did it.'

Robert knew all about that already, from the talk in the diner.

'So,' said Peg. 'That's really about all.'

She shook dishwater from her hands, dried them, and, with a critical look, began rubbing in lotion.

Clayton came in at the side door. He stamped the snow from his shoes and ran up the steps.

'You should see the cars,' he said. 'Stupid cars all crawling along this street. Then they have to turn around at the end and crawl back. I wish they'd get stuck. I stood out there and gave them dirty looks, but I started to freeze so I had to come in.'

'It's natural,' Robert said. 'It seems stupid but it's natural. They can't believe it, so they want to see where it happened.'

'I don't see their problem,' Clayton said. 'I don't see why they can't believe it. Mom could believe it all right. Mom wasn't surprised.'

'Well, of course I was,' Peg said, and this was the first time Robert had noticed any sort of edge to her voice. 'Of course I was surprised, Clayton. Just because I didn't break out screaming.'

'You weren't surprised they could do it.'

'I hardly knew them. We hardly knew the Weebles.'

'I guess they had a fight,' said Clayton.

'We don't know that,' Peg said, stubbornly working the lotion into her skin. 'We don't know if they had a fight, or what.'

'When you and Dad used to have those fights?' Clayton said. 'Remember, after we first moved to town? When he would be home? Over by the car wash? When you used to have those fights, you know what I used to think? I used to think one of you was going to come and kill me with a knife.'

'That's not true,' said Peg.

'It is true. I did.'

Peg sat down at the table and covered her mouth with her hands. Clayton's mouth twitched. He couldn't seem to stop it, so he turned it into a little, taunting, twitching smile.

'That's what I used to lie in bed and think.'

'Clayton. We would never either one of us ever have hurt you.'

Robert believed it was time that he said something.

'What this is like,' he said, 'it's like an earthquake or a volcano. It's that kind of happening. It's a kind of fit. People can take a fit like the earth takes a fit. But it only happens once in a long while. It's a freak occurrence.'

'Earthquakes and volcanoes aren't freaks,' said Clayton, with a certain dry pleasure. 'If you want to call that a fit, you'd have to call it a periodic fit. Such as people have, married people have.'

'We don't,' said Robert. He looked at Peg as if waiting for her to agree with him.

But Peg was looking at Clayton. She who always seemed pale and silky and assenting, but hard to follow as a watermark in fine paper, looked dried out, chalky, her outlines fixed in steady, helpless, unapologetic pain.

'No,' said Clayton. 'No, not you.'

Robert told them that he was going for a walk. When he got outside, he saw that Clayton was right. There were cars nosing along the street, turning at the end, nosing their way back again. Getting a look. Inside those cars were just the same people, probably the very same people, he had been talking to during the afternoon. But now they seemed joined to their cars, making some new kind of monster that came poking around in a brutally curious way.

To avoid them, he went down a short dead-end street that branched off theirs. No houses had ever been built on this street, so it was not plowed. But the snow was hard, and easy to walk on. He didn't notice how easy it was to walk on until he realized that he had gone beyond the end of the street and up a slope, which was not a slope of the land at all, but a drift of snow. The drift neatly covered the fence that usually separated the street from the field. He had walked over the fence without knowing what he was doing. The snow was that hard.

He walked here and there, testing. The crust took his weight without a whisper or a crack. It was the same everywhere. You could walk over the snowy fields as if you were walking on cement. (This morning, looking at the snow, hadn't he thought of marble?) But this paving was not flat. It rose and dipped in a way that had not much to do with the contours of the ground underneath. The snow created its own landscape, which was sweeping, in a grand and arbitrary style.

Instead of walking around on the plowed streets of town, he could walk over the fields. He could cut across to the diner on the highway, which stayed open until midnight. He would have a cup of coffee there, turn around, and walk home.

One night, about six months before Robert married Peg, he and Lee were sitting drinking in his apartment. They were having an argument about whether it was permissible, or sickening, to have your family initial on your silverware. All of a sudden, the argument split open— Robert couldn't remember how, but it split open, and they found themselves saying the cruellest things to each other that they could imagine. Their voices changed from the raised pitch and speed of argument, and they spoke quietly with a subtle loathing.

'You always make me think of a dog,' Lee said. 'You always make me think of one of those dogs that push up on people and paw them, with their big disgusting tongues hanging out. You're so eager. All your friendliness and eagerness—that's really aggression. I'm not the only one who thinks this about you. A lot of people avoid you. They can't stand you. You'd be surprised. You push and paw in that eager pathetic way, but you have a calculating look. That's why I don't care if I hurt you.'

'Maybe I should tell you one of the things I don't like, then,' said Robert reasonably. 'It's the way you laugh. On the phone particularly. You laugh at the end of practically every sentence. I used to think it was a nervous tic, but it always really annoyed me. And I've figured out why. You're always telling somebody about what a raw deal you're getting somewhere or some unkind thing a person said to you—that's about two-thirds of your horrendously boring self-centred conversation. And then you laugh. Ha-ha, you can take it, you don't expect anything better. That laugh is sick.'

After some more of this, they started to laugh themselves, Robert and Lee, but it was not the laughter of a breakthrough into reconciliation; they did not fall upon each other in relief, crying, 'What rot, I didn't mean it, did you mean it?' ('No, of course not, of course I didn't mean it.') They laughed in recognition of their extremity, just as they might have laughed at another time, in the middle of quite different, astoundingly tender declarations. They trembled with murderous pleasure, with the excitement of saying what could never be retracted; they exulted in wounds inflicted but also in wounds received, and one or the other said at some point, 'This is the first time we've spoken the truth since we've known each other!' For even things that came to them more or less on the spur of the moment seemed the most urgent truths that had been hardening for a long time and pushing to get out.

It wasn't so far from laughing to making love, which they did, all with no retraction. Robert made barking noises, as a dog should, and nuzzled Lee in a bruising way, snapping with real appetite at her flesh.

Afterward they were enormously and finally sick of each other but no longer disposed to blame.

'There are things I just absolutely and eternally want to forget about,' Robert had told Peg. He talked to her about cutting his losses, abandoning old bad habits, old deceptions and self-deceptions, mistaken notions about life, and about himself. He said that he had been an emotional spendthrift, and had thrown himself into hopeless and painful entanglements as a way of avoiding anything that had normal possibilities. That was all experiment and posturing, rejection of the ordinary, decent contracts of life. So he said to her. Errors of avoidance, when he had thought he was running risks and getting intense experiences.

'Errors of avoidance that I mistook for errors of passion,' he said, then thought that he sounded pretentious when he was actually sweating with sincerity, with the effort and the relief.

In return, Peg gave him facts.

We lived with Dave's parents. There was never enough hot water for the baby's wash. Finally we got out and came to town and we lived beside the car wash. Dave was only with us weekends then. It was very noisy, especially at night. Then Dave got another job, he went up North, and I rented this place.

Errors of avoidance, errors of passion. She didn't say.

Dave had a kidney problem when he was little and he was out of school a whole winter. He read a book about the Arctic. It was probably the only book he ever read that he didn't have to. Anyway, he always dreamed about it; he wanted to go there. So finally he did.

A man doesn't just drive farther and farther away in his trucks until he disappears from his wife's view. Not even if he has always dreamed of the Arctic. Things happen before he goes. Marriage knots aren't going to slip apart painlessly, with the pull of distance. There's got to be some wrenching and slashing. But she didn't say, and he didn't ask, or even think much about that, till now.

He walked very quickly over the snow crust, and when he reached the diner he found that he didn't want to go in yet. He would cross the highway and walk a little farther, then go into the diner to get warmed up on his way home.

By the time he was on his way home, the police car that was parked at the diner ought to be gone. The night constable was in there now, taking his break. This was not the same man Robert had seen and listened to when he dropped in on his way home from Keneally. This man would not have seen anything at first hand. He hadn't talked to Peg. Nevertheless he would be talking about it; everybody in the diner would be talking about it, going over the same scene and the same questions, the possibilities. No blame to them.

When they saw Robert, they would want to know how Peg was.

There was one thing he was going to ask her, just before Clayton came in. At least, he was turning the question over in his mind, wondering if it would be all right to ask her. A discrepancy, a detail, in the midst of so many abominable details.

And now he knew it wouldn't be all right; it would never be all right. It had nothing to do with him. One discrepancy, one detail— one lie—that would never have anything to do with him.

Walking on this magic surface, he did not grow tired. He grew lighter, if anything. He was taking himself farther and farther away from town, although for a while he didn't realize this. In the clear air, the lights of Gilmore were so bright they seemed only half a field away, instead of half a mile, then a mile and a half, then two miles. Very fine flakes of snow, fine as dust, and glittering, lay on the crust that held him. There was a glitter, too, around the branches of the trees and bushes that he was getting closer to. It wasn't like the casing around twigs and delicate branches that an ice storm leaves. It was as if the wood itself had altered and begun to sparkle.

This is the very weather in which noses and fingers are frozen. But nothing felt cold.

He was getting quite close to a large woodlot. He was crossing a long slanting shelf of snow, with the trees ahead and to one side of him. Over there, to the side, something caught his eye. There was a new kind of glitter under the trees. A congestion of shapes, up to the lower branches of the trees. He headed toward these shapes, but whatever they were did not become clear. They did not look like anything he knew. They did not look like anything, except perhaps a bit like armed giants half collapsed, frozen in combat, or like the jumbled towers of a crazy small-scale city—a space-age, small-scale city. He kept waiting for an explanation, and not getting one, until he got very close. He was so close he could almost have touched one of these monstrosities before he saw that they were just old cars. Old cars and trucks and even a school bus that had been pushed in under the trees and left. Some were completely overturned, and some were tipped over one another at odd angles. They were partly filled, partly covered, with snow. The black holes were their gutted insides. Twisted bits of chrome, fragments of headlights, were glittering.

He thought of himself telling Peg about this—how close he had to get before he saw that what amazed him and bewildered him so was nothing but old wrecks, and how he then felt disappointed, but also like laughing. They needed some new thing to talk about. Now he felt more like going home.

At noon, when the constable in the diner was giving his account, he had described how the force of the shot threw Walter Weeble backward. 'It blasted him partway out of the room. His head was laying out in the hall. What was left of it was laying out in the hall.'

Not a leg. Not the indicative leg, whole and decent in its trousers, the shod foot. That was not what anybody turning at the top of the stairs would see and would have to step over, step through, in order to go into the bedroom and look at the rest of what was there.

EDWARD O. PHILLIPS · b. 1931

Solstice

'And if that weren't enough, the s.o.b. has asked for a divorce,' said Gillian Jordan.

'Don't worry,' replied Laura Thompson. 'He can always be made to change his mind. Perhaps it's time to try a little suicide. A suicide attempt always bring them back with their tail between their legs, if you'll pardon the expression.'

'But, Laura, I don't know the first thing about suicide, or suicide attempts for that matter. If I crawled out onto a ledge of the Sun Life Building or one of the girders of the Jacques Cartier Bridge I'd probably fall, from sheer vertigo.'

'Good God, Gillian, I'm not suggesting anything half so melo-dramatic. No guns, no knives, no standing on a kitchen chair with a rope around your neck. What I have in mind are pills, darling. Everyone has sleeping pills. Flush them down the toilet and leave the bottle on the night table. Play Sleeping Beauty. I remember you used to act with the Players' Club at college. Just before he bundles you off to Emergency to have your stomach pumped out, you will wake up and give him the shock of his life. He'll be so relieved he'll beg your forgiveness. And hold out for a sable coat. Even secretaries are wearing mink these days.'

The woman addressed as Laura returned to toying with her crab salad and Chablis. Her business card read 'Art Consultant', but her true vocation in life was to remain thin. Two successful divorces had allowed her to dress with expensive taste, but she wore the hard, lacquered look of a woman, no longer young, making an uneasy pact with middle age.

Her lunch companion looked less like a sister than a clone. The resemblance came more from shared style and attitudes than similarity of feature. Gillian was softer, rounder, more pliant than her lunch companion, with beautifully cut blond hair of a shade never seen in nature. Aside from having been friends in college, both women wore and carried the insignia of affluence: Italian shoes, broad gold bracelets, sleek handbags, and watches whose number-less faces were of lapis lazuli and malachite.

'A sable coat would be nice,' admitted Gillian, spearing the last caper on her plate; 'but I really wonder whether staying married to Bob is worth those pelts. It's not as if he hasn't had affairs before. I've spent so much time looking the other way I'll swear I've damaged a disc. Up to now they've been nonentities, nothing more than com-pliant little bimbos. He even wanted his *cinq à sept* from *quatre à six* as he likes to eat his supper at 6:30. It's almost as if he were playing squash. One cannot feel seriously threatened by that sort of punch-the-clock carrying on. But this one must be serious. He claims he's in love. And this is the first time he's mentioned divorce.'

'Whether or not you decide to give him one is your decision. But take my advice, darling; hire a detective and get the goods on him. I know it sounds low and mean, but you have to feather your nest. Those Teddy Bear romantics like Bob are not to be trusted. Love may make their whatnots get hard, but their brains go all soft. Love becomes its own categorical imperative, and they can become quite ruthless towards anyone standing between them and the love object. Cover your ass, Gillian. And now I must dash.'

Gillian did not reply, but sat, thoughtfully, while Laura repaired her mouth with a lipstick whose case unfolded into a tiny mirror. As she replaced the tube in her handbag she spoke.

'Let me have a word with my lawyer. When it comes to divorce he's the best. I know he has more clients than he can handle, but he may take you on as a favour to me. I'll speak to him and get back to you. Thanks for lunch, darling. Next time on me.' Laura Thompson walked from the restaurant as if down a ramp.

Gillian Jordan paid the lunch cheque and left the restaurant with no apparent destination. Marriage had enabled her to stop working. In fact, being able to quit her job had been one of the principal blandishments of marriage in the first place. That, and having just ended a long love affair whose severance left her emotionally beached, like a dolphin on a sand bar. She had not married for love but because marriage seemed the best option at the time. Although legally a contract marriage is really a series of bargains and com-parisons, so Gillian had come to learn.

She paused, irresolute, on Sherbrooke Street, uncertain of how to spend the rest of this splendid June afternoon. Somehow the prospect of divorce, with its inevitable complement of splitting up possessions, took the bloom off shopping. She was surprised by the warmth of the sun on her back. Nearly two thirds of the month had already slipped past, but Gillian had been too preoccupied with domestic difficulties to notice.

When she first met Bob Jordan he was a man in need of a wife. An earlier marriage had ended in divorce after his wife went stridently feminist and turned into a liability for a man shouldering his way up the corporate ladder. He needed a woman who was a class act, to use an expression of which he was fond, someone whose presence as helpmeet and hostess would enhance his image and bolster his prestige.

Had Gillian's mother been alive, she would have accused her daughter of marrying 'beneath her'. Her father had been less censorious, realizing that underneath the 'diamond in the rough' Bob Jordan was definitely 'a man on the go'. If Bob understood he was an unpolished diamond, it was with the self-satisfied awareness of someone cheerfully admitting to a tin ear for music or of knowing nothing whatsoever about art, yet quite certain of what he liked. But a smart and soignée wife (a classy broad) would be a definite asset. If she could not polish the rough edges, she could at least deflect the light from picking out their jagged contours.

At first the combination of novelty and vanity had persuaded Gillian she was happy, or at least content. A new man had come into her life at a time when her self-esteem had taken a beating; moreover, he wanted to marry her. A vigorous if unsubtle sex life supplemented by an immense diamond solitaire convinced Gillian she had made the right decision, and that her compromises would be well worth the rewards. The compromises turned out to be many: supper at six-thirty instead of dinner at eight, a slab of steak charred on the gas barbecue instead of Tournedos Rossini or Beef Wellington. After eating, Bob regularly fell asleep in his Ezeboy recliner, a can of Coors at his elbow. If he had to snore away his supper, Gillian would have preferred him in a wing chair, his feet on the matching footstool, a glass of port on the occasional table. Besides, the recliner had gouged a hole in her vertically striped living room wallpaper, and its plaid plush clashed violently with her starkly contemporary Italian furniture. He wore a baseball cap with plastic mesh around the back to do his weekend chores. Once he realized she disliked the cap he took to wearing it indoors.

She began to wince at his 'Hi, Honey, I'm home!' called out if he had been away for several days on a business trip, or merely to Mac's Milk for a paper. Gillian disliked the easy familiarity of nicknames, Sugar, Sweetie, Kiddo, and, worst of all, Cuddle Bumps, as his hand slid under her nightgown. Gillian did not fight back in the conventional sense; she did not shout, threaten, throw things. Instead she withdrew, either physically by leaving the room, or by folding in on herself, like a desert flower in time lapse photography.

At first she withdrew sporadically, at hockey games, at the bowling alley, when Bob's sister came down from Thunder Bay and breast fed her baby at the kitchen table. These withdrawals usually took place when others were around, their presence rushing in to fill the vacuum left by Gillian's silent refusal to participate. Gradually, however, Gillian began to close in on herself when alone with Bob. And even though not the most sensitive of men, he could not fail to notice.

He began to see other women. Contrary to the dictum that the wife is the last to know, Gillian discovered there were any number of dear friends only too anxious to relate, for her own good naturally, that Bob had been seen lunching with a pneumatic brunette at a little French restaurant just enough out of the way to be out of the way. Gillian felt she ought to have minded more than she did. Using his snoring as an excuse she moved into the spare bedroom. He did not object. But in public she continued to fulfil her side of the bargain. She gave elegant dinners, went out on her husband's arm, greeted his friends and business associates as though she really were glad to see them, and presented a façade without cracks to the world. The scuttlebutt had it that Bob Jordan was headed for politics.

On a sudden impulse Gillian ducked into a phone booth. Fishing a morocco-bound directory from her handbag, she dialled her doctor's office and asked if she might be squeezed in for five minutes sometime this afternoon. A timely cancellation gave her an appointment within the hour. Gillian walked the short distance to the medical building and spend half an hour thumbing through back issues of *Time* and *Newsweek.*

Her mind wandered elsewhere. It was difficult to think of the marriage as being over when there had been no real marriage to begin with. It had been a partnership, however, with affection and respect on both sides, at least initially. And now Bob wanted to dissolve this partnership unilaterally so he could, presumably, embark on a new marriage based on love, not expediency.

As she sat, idly flipping pages, Gillian considered her options. She had reached an age when children were no longer possible. Even should she become pregnant she was unwilling to contemplate the disruption in her life a child would entail. Her father, for whom she used to keep house, had been incarcerated in a nursing home, his roomy apartment sublet. Gillian did not relish the idea of going back to work, but to be a divorced or separated woman, even with adequate alimony, would leave her with a succession of days to fill. There was always the possibility of lovers, or a lover; Gillian preferred to think in the singular. But true passion, once experienced, is difficult to recapture. Also passion did not arrive alone but with retainers: jealousy, suspicion, recrimination, and the rest of those exhausting accomplices that turned one's life into chaos. Like many in her age group, Gillian recoiled from change, preferring the understood problem to its untried solution.

Further speculation was interrupted by a crisp 'The doctor will see you now'. Gillian entered the office, smiled, shook the doctor's hand. She had always preferred male doctors, finding in the sexual difference an invisible but real barrier between herself and the enforced intimacy of the examination. The doctor listened attentively, studying her above the half lens of his reading glasses while she spoke diffidently of marital problems keeping her awake. Whatever it was would surely pass, only a bad patch at the moment. Could he give her a prescription to make her sleep? A couple of good nights would help greatly to put things into perspective. Gillian gave a good performance, a measure of reticence, a dash of pathos, a shot of self-reliance, skilfully blending the ingredients to give the illusion of a woman no longer able to read herself to sleep.

After the customary caveats about careful use and only when necessary the doctor wrote out a prescription for Dalmane. Gillian tucked the folded slip into her purse, thanked him, and left.

There being nothing she wanted to buy, and not feeling suitably contemplative to undertake the galleries, Gillian walked home along Sherbrooke Street. She did not mind walking in high heels if she did not have to hurry. Home, if such it could be called, was a penthouse condominium commanding a spectacular view of both the mountain and the river. In spite of vistas, to ride thirteen floors on an elevator for a carton of milk or a newspaper went against nature. She and Bob had started married life in a town house with a small but pleasant garden, which Gillian missed. Bob had decided a condo was more up-market, better for the image than a house below Sherbrooke Street. If they separated, Bob could certainly keep the condominium. That is, if they separated.

To fake suicide is a malicious practical joke, the cruellest. But graded on a scale of one to ten is it any more cruel than informing your wife of eight years, without prelude or preamble, that she has become superfluous in your life and could she leave, the sooner the better? Having at first dismissed Laura Thompson's suicide suggestion as no more than a bitter joke, Gillian was beginning to wonder if it wouldn't be quite wickedly amusing to give Bob the fright of his life. Why else had she made an impromptu appointment with her doctor, to request a prescription she did not need? Heretofore, her way of dealing with Bob had been to withdraw, to remove herself both physically and mentally from his aura, another term he was given to using. Was not suicide the ultimate withdrawal? The very logic and consistency of the plan made Gillian smile inside. As if to underline her resolve, she made a detour to her pharmacist, choosing imported soap while he counted out the capsules.

And maybe, just maybe, the charade would convince Bob that he wanted the marriage to continue. Gillian herself had not slammed the door. She had already made enough compromises that one or two more wouldn't matter. Nor could she honestly fault her husband for having fallen in love. Gillian still loved the man who had left her for a well-paid job in Saudi Arabia. She preferred to think of herself as abandoned. It helped to gloss over the truth, that she had, in the last resort, been unwilling to give up her comfortable life and move to a country whose customs, religion, attitudes towards women, she did not, would not understand. Then there had been her father; who would look after him?

The parting had been quietly bitter, full of unspoken recrimination. But even though she understood she would probably never see her lover again, the love endured. She wished it didn't; she could not bear to let it go. Gillian found herself quite prepared to accept her husband's affair, provided the situation did not disrupt her life. To her natural indolent nature it somehow seemed easier to ride out the present contretemps than to flounce into uncertainty.

On this particular evening she knew Bob would be in for dinner, at seven-thirty. One of the concessions Gillian had won in exchange for moving to the penthouse was to push the evening meal ahead one hour. With the new constraint in their relationship she was at least spared his 'Hi, Honey, I'm home'. Instead, he had taken to calling her Gillian, which she liked to be called and on which she would insist were they to survive the storm.

As she began to prepare dinner, Gillian resisted the urge to make a pot of tea. If she really was going 'to roll over and play dead', as her father used to command his immense, smelly sheepdog, then she must restrict her fluid intake. Nothing destroys the illusion of coma faster than a quick sprint to the toilet.

Her preparations were brief. An excellent and sophisticated cook, Gillian had long ago given up on trying to raise Bob's appreciation of food. Just so long as she put meat and potatoes onto the table, followed by a baked dessert, he was content. Gillian felt like an underused resource, her one domestic skill being exploited only when she entertained. Tonight's meal was to be dense and heavy: pork, potatoes, apple pie with chocolate ripple ice cream, food guaranteed to weigh heavily on the stomach and send him to sleep in the recliner while she set the scene for her suicide scenario. The more she thought about the plan, the better she liked it.

Bob let himself into the apartment. His 'Good evening, Gillian', sounded pompous and stiff, coming as it did from a mouth far more comfortable with 'Hi, Honey!' Bob Jordan wore his flashy good looks with the easy assurance that his high voltage smile and firm hand-shake would continue to open doors. Easy living had begun to thicken his waist, flesh out his jaw, heighten his colour; but the still faint signs of decay only added to his appeal, suggesting, as they did, a life lived without stint. He dressed with expensive taste; but, as far as Gillian was concerned, he still managed to give the impression he would be more comfortable at the race track than in the boardroom.

'Good evening, Robert,' she replied as he pulled off his jacket, tugged at his tie, undid the top button of his shirt. 'Drink?' she added, meaning should she pull the tab on a can of beer. Most of the time Bob couldn't be bothered with a glass, and Gillian found the aluminum can less offensive than a brown glass bottle.

'Scotch,' he ordered, to her faint surprise as he seldom drank liquor before eating.

'I'll join you,' she volunteered, going into the kitchen to pour drinks.

She could tell from the hunched way he sat on the armless leather chair that there was something on his mind. After putting down his drink she made herself at ease on the sofa, evening pants and a

loosely fitting sweater embroidered in sequins being more comfortable for simulated suicide than a dress.

'You can eat any time you like.'

He went right to the point. 'Honey—Gillian, I wonder if we couldn't
get this thing cleared up. If you give me the divorce I promise to see
you're well taken care of. You know that. And we can't go on this
way much longer.'

'Which is to say you can't.'

'If you won't divorce me I'll move out anyway.'

'You already have, to all intents and purposes. Perhaps you should,
for a while. Live with your doxy on a day to day basis. Perhaps you'll
learn a casa chica lacks the charm of a penthouse.'

Bob paused, baffled. Unfamiliar with the word 'doxy', he still
understood it to be a slur. And he spoke no Spanish.

'Do you really want to wait out three years for a divorce? You may
want to get married again. You're a very attractive woman, for your
age.'

Knowing her rival, if such a melodramatic term could be used, was
ten years her junior, Gillian shrugged. She would not let her husband
see that in a crude attempt to be courteous he had managed to flick
the lash. Bob was six months younger than Gillian. And she minded
growing older, hated the first intimations of crepe at the throat, the
faint delta of lines around the eyes. What she disliked most of all was
the fact she allowed it to bother her. Only by a slight widening of her
large hazel eyes, always her best feature, did she betray how deeply
she had been insulted.

'You could well be right. Tell you what. Let me sleep on it one more
night, and I'll give you an answer tomorrow, without fail. Now
perhaps you should think about eating before everything dries out in
the oven.'

Emotional stress did not put Bob off his food. If anything, his wife's
procrastination propelled him into second helpings, including an
extra scoop of ice cream, the last in the container, so as to avoid waste.
Nor did anxiety contrive to keep him awake, and soon the digestive
process had him ambling over to his Ezeboy, which he pushed back
to the third, almost horizontal position. In doing so he managed to
shave the wallpaper.

Gillian knew she had well over an hour to prepare her scenario.
She cleared the table, loaded the dishwasher, put away the food. Her
first impulse had been to leave the fallout from dinner. Does anyone

about to shuffle off this mortal coil really worry about the roasting pan? However, Gillian did not want to face it, cold and congealed, when, like Lazarus, she returned from the grave.

Having dealt with the kitchen, Gillian went into the bedroom to set the scene. She toyed briefly with the idea of placing herself prone on the living sofa. But since it was the kind of furniture designed to seduce the eye rather than accommodate itself to mere human contours, she decided she would be more comfortable on her own bed. She lay down and proceeded to try out a variety of positions, arms at her sides, tucked under her head, legs variously crossed, until she found one she felt she could sustain for that length of time between Bob's finding her and the strategic moment when she revealed the fraud.

Having decided on the physical *mise-en-scène*, she turned her attention to props: a little whisky in the tumbler she had toyed with before dinner, her lipstick still on the rim. She carried it to the night table and set it down beside the empty bottle of Dalmane, whose red and yellow contents had been flushed down the toilet. She turned off the overhead light, leaving only the lamp on the night table with its flesh-coloured bulb to cast the most flattering light on the scene. After freshening her makeup—she intended to be a beautiful corpse—Gillian made one final trip to the toilet, running the tap to help her expel all excess fluid. Then she sat and read a detective story until a creak from the living room announced Bob had wakened and shifted his chair into the upright position.

For one panic stricken second Gillian felt her resolution falter, as she was swept with a realization of the unpleasantness of the deception she was about to enact. She had almost decided to hide the bottle, spill the scotch into the handbasin, put on the light, and agree to the divorce, when she remembered Bob's observation that she was still an attractive woman, for her age, one who might well find herself another man. Even though she did not love her husband in a passionate, physical way, he was still her property. She was prepared to lend out, not relinquish. Furthermore, to be left for a younger female puts any woman's vanity on the block. He must be made to smart. With renewed resolve she stretched out on the bed, legs crossed at the ankles, hands folded across her abdomen, her expensively flaxen head on a pillow turned away from the light.

She heard Bob, still groggy from sleep, call her name, 'Honey? Gillian? Are you there?'

She had to force herself not to answer, remembering that she was presently in coma. Footsteps came down the passageway. Gillian clamped her eyes shut and willed herself not to move.

Bob entered the bedroom. 'Gillian?' He crossed to stand beside the bed. She heard him suddenly expel breath, followed by a small, sharp sound as he replaced the empty pill bottle on the glass-topped table. During the pause that followed, Gillian prepared herself to act as if limp and unconscious when he shook her, the next action in the drama. But he failed to touch her, anywhere. Nor did he pick up the telephone. Instead he left the room and went into the kitchen, now silent as the dishwasher had completed its cycle.

Judging from the sounds coming down the passageway, Gillian could have suspected, had she not known better, that he was pouring himself a drink. She barely had time to recompose herself when Bob returned to the bedroom and seated himself in the rocking chair where she ordinarily sat and read whenever the urge to withdraw overcame her. The chair creaked slightly under his weight, followed by a soft tinkle, as if ice cubes were striking the side of a tumbler. Then silence.

It took Gillian a handful of what seemed like very long seconds to realize Bob was sitting in her chair, drinking a highball, and waiting for her to die. Caught up, as she had been, in the gleeful malice of her charade, she had not even considered how neatly she had apparently provided a solution to his problem. With Gillian dead he would be at liberty to marry his current bimbo. Instead of the pleasant anticipated agony of remorse and orgy of self-recrimination, Gillian was faced with the unpalatable, unflattering realization that her husband wanted her out of the way badly enough to let her die. Too late she remembered Laura Thompson's caveat over lunch, that she had best beware of Teddy Bear romantics, especially when thwarted.

There remained the immediate problem of what to do next. Was she to sit bolt upright and accuse him of wanting her dead, an accusation he would glibly deny? Or should she wait it out for a few minutes more, giving him the benefit of the doubt and pretending he was too shocked and startled to know how to react.

Lying there, under his silent scrutiny, she found her body screaming to shift position. The left nostril seemed to detach itself from the rest of her face; it developed a rebellious itch which took every volt of her concentrated willpower not to scratch. Relief came as Bob went to pee in her bathroom. He did not bother to close the door, adding insult to outrage, but his brief absence afforded her a chance to scratch the offending nostril and wriggle her body without changing position. The comfortable pose she had chosen began to constrain her like a straitjacket.

Gillian had heard, as who has not, that a drowning man sees his life flash before his eyes. The same did not hold true for a make-believe suicide, but Gillian still found herself wondering how and why she had come to a point in her life where an ugly practical joke on the man she had married was blowing up in her face like a homemade terrorist bomb. If ever her vanity had taken a pasting it was now, as she lay on her own bed, pretending to be in a self-induced coma, while her husband sat watching her, drinking a highball, and waiting for her to die; or, more likely, holding out until he knew she was too far gone to be revived in Emergency.

Was she being punished for having played the ultimate practical joke? The prone Gillian dismissed the idea at once. She did not believe all that claptrap about divine retribution and universal justice. His eye might well be on the sparrow, but it was certainly not fixed on Gillian Jordan, who had shown the poor judgement to marry a bad apple. She had made her bed and now must lie in it, immobile, playing dead and dying to move, while her left ankle began to tingle and her right ear to itch. She had fought back by not fighting back, by feigning withdrawal into the ultimate silence of coma and death. And Bob was quite simply letting her go, beating her at her own game. For possibly the first time since she married her husband, Gillian longed to yell, scream, throw things, slap his face, lay waste. All those words she had been trained as a girl to quell came churning to the surface of her consciousness as she lay rigid, trapped in her own deception, power-less to move until enough time had elapsed to convince her beyond all reasonable doubt Bob wanted her dead.

The telephone rang; its familiar sound made strange by the present setting almost tripped her into a spasm of movement. Bob crossed to answer, standing so close to the bed she could feel heat from his body. 'Yes?'

'Bob, it's Laura. May I have a word with Gillian?'

'Not at the moment, Laura. She's asleep.'

'Asleep! I thought you were the one who took naps after dinner.'

From where she lay Gillian could hear Laura's voice, distant but distinct.

'I guess she must have been tired, Laura. We both dozed off after supper, but Gill hasn't waked up yet. Do you want her to call you when she does?'

'No, that won't be necessary. I'll speak to her tomorrow.'

'Fine, I'll tell her you called. Good night, Laura.' Bob's voice came out so corn-syrup smooth, coupled with that old con-artist trick of repeating the person's name, that Gillian could have rolled over and sunk her teeth into his leg. Her pulse raced furiously. For a terrified moment she feared he might reach down and lift her limp arm to feel the pulse she knew would give her away. But Bob did not reach for her wrist. Once on his feet, however, he left the room and returned to the kitchen, giving Gillian a welcome chance to wriggle, stretch, and recompose herself before he returned to sit in the rocking chair. Through slitted eyes Gillian could see he was carrying a fresh high-ball. Fortunately she had taken the precaution to empty her kidneys, so for a while anyway she could continue to play along.

By immobilizing the body and playing dead, she had left her mind free to roam. Gillian tried to recall incidents in her marriage which would have so alienated her husband he would wish her dead. She could not bring herself to believe adulterous passion the sole motive. That kind of deadly liaison was the stuff of fiction, of film, of daytime serials watched by housewives who had briefly known desire as teenagers in the back seat of a car. To marry without love is not a crime, even less so when in all respects she had been a model wife. Or had she? Ought she to have, at least once, shouted, slapped, smashed china? Should she have let him know he had the power to penetrate the veneer and stir the woman below the surface? She had responded to him sexually, but that had been her choice. Yet to withdraw from the ordinary, to skirt the com-monplace and avoid, whenever possible, the banal, was all this—in the most trite of television phrases—to die for? But there sat her husband, drinking whiskey, something he rarely did in the evening, waiting, watching, doing nothing while she pretended to sink inexorably deeper into the coma from which it would soon be impossible to rouse her.

Gillian wondered whether it was time to end the play, to yawn, stretch, rub her eyes, pantomime waking up. She would blithely admit to having thrown out the prescription the doctor insisted on prescribing. The scotch before dinner at the end of a long day had made her drowsy. Had there been any calls? She would also agree to granting him a divorce, but only after she had hired a detective, a lawyer, and whomever else it took to grab every last cent he had, and then some.

The telephone startled her into immobility. Still holding his drink, the ice cubes gently clicking, Bob crossed to answer.

'Bob, it's Laura again. Is Gill awake yet?'

'No, she's not.'

'Is she all right?'

'I don't see why not.'

'She didn't take a sleeping pill or anything?'

'Not to my knowledge.' His voice went liquid with sincerity. 'Of course I was asleep when she lay down.'

Still prone, Gillian heard a pause on the telephone line.

'Well, I think I'll come over. I'd like to have a word with her, and she may be awake when I get there.'

Gillian could hear her husband trying to control his voice. 'Don't bother, Laura. It's getting late. I plan to turn in early, and if Gillian's tired why not just let her sleep it out?'

'What I have to tell her is worth waking up for. I'll be there in fifteen minutes.'

Gillian could hear the click as her friend hung up.

'Shit!' hissed Bob as he slammed down the receiver. Here was a development he hadn't counted on, Laura bustling in, all angular efficiency, to discover Gillian in coma. And why hadn't he done anything? Laura would corroborate Gillian's story, if Gillian decided to tell it. Using great self-control the recumbent Gillian managed not to smile.

Bob strode out to the kitchen and splashed whisky into his glass. At least that's how it sounded to Gillian. Returning to the bedroom he crossed to the bed and put down the tumbler with a click on the night table. Realizing he would now be forced to take some kind of action, she braced herself to act pliant under his hands.

Not too gently, he wrapped her studiously limp body in the quilt lying folded at the foot of the bed. Pausing for one, last, hefty swallow of scotch, which Gillian could now smell on his breath, he lifted her easily from the bed and carried her out to the elevator. The corridor stood empty, as did the elevator itself, which they rode down to the garage. With her head resting on his shoulder, Gillian sneaked a squint, enough to see the garage stood deserted. Bob carried her to the car, unlocked the door, and dumped her without ceremony into the front seat. In doing so he managed to bang her head smartly on the door frame. Only by bearing down on her lower lip with her top teeth did she manage to refrain from crying out.

Without bothering to buckle her seat belt, Bob closed the passenger door and climbed into the driver's seat. As luck would have it, Gillian's head was turned away from the driver, which allowed her the occasional circumspect glance out the window. The car left the garage, drove two blocks, then turned west onto Sherbrooke Street. Obviously he was taking her to the Emergency entrance at Queen Elizabeth Hospital. It was Gillian's plan to wait until he had driven up to the Emergency exit and pulled to a stop. Then she would clamber out of her side of the car and confront him across the hood.

She could recognize the major intersections by the traffic lights: Clarke, Metcalfe, Lansdowne, Grosvenor, Victoria, Claremont. Gillian contrived to keep the eye nearest the driver closed while her right eye registered their progress towards the hospital, almost as if her face were twisted into a permanent wink. Bob drove with the exaggerated care of one who has been drinking, slowing down well in advance of a red light, flashing his directional signals before changing lanes (something he never did when sober) and keeping well within the speed limit.

It was only after the car had passed the Queen Elizabeth Hospital and edged itself into the right lane for access onto the Decarie Expressway that Gillian realized Bob had no intention of taking her to Emergency, at least not until they had driven around for a while so the Dalmane could fully work its magic spell. Laura would arrive at the condo to find nobody home, while Bob was driving Gillian along the Trans-Canada Highway with no apparent destination.

Suddenly Gillian could contain herself no longer. A flood of rage, scalding and incandescent, gripped her like a spasm of pain.

'You goddamn sonofabitch!' she yelled at her husband, uttering the first profanity she had ever used with him since the wedding. At the same time she fought her way free of the enveloping quilt as though clawing her way from quicksand.

'You're awake—you were faking it. You bitch!'

Alcoholic astonishment caused Bob Jordan to look at his wife and take his eyes from the road. At the same time a corner of the quilt fell across the steering wheel. Bob pushed it violently away, and with that gesture lost momentary control of the car. The vehicle veered sharply to the left, directly into the path of an *Urgences Santé* ambulance travelling east along Sherbrooke Street well in excess of the speed limit. The driver of the ambulance was taken to the Queen Elizabeth Hospital with two broken legs and concussion. The occupants of the automobile died on impact.

One year later, during that part of June when the sun hangs unmoving in the sky, Laura Thompson carrying freesias rode a taxi to the Mount Royal Cemetery. While the cab waited she stood for a few moments in front of the double grave capped by a single stone. For those few moments Laura Thompson tried to think appropriate thoughts, with limited success. Then, bending down, she placed her freesias on Gillian's side of the grave. Touched by her own gesture, she paused for yet another pensive second until, mindful of the meter, she returned to the taxi and drove away.

GILLES ARCHAMBAULT · b. 1933

Mother Love

It's always been my fate to please. On her deathbed, my mother told me I was handsome and always had been. Poor thing, she didn't know that this natural charm of mine has prevented me from succeeding in life. How do you develop a taste for work when women put all the money you need at your disposal? These reflections come to me while I sit drinking a planter's punch outside a large New Orleans hotel whose name I must not reveal. I've come to this city on a special mission. The woman who sent me, Camille Bolduc, is very fond of young men in their thirties. I'm not the first she's supported, and I won't be the last. Some have laughed at her. Not me. I even perform little services for Camille, like collecting her rents, having her villa at Saint-Sauveur redecorated, or occasionally acting as her chauffeur. Out of modesty, I won't mention my exploits in bed. If Camille found out I was indiscreet, it would distress her. How much younger she's grown since I came into her life! She wants to make love all the time. I'm the one who has to pretend to have a migraine, just to get some rest! I won't say she's fat, but she's large. Still, the face is pleasant, brown eyes, a light complexion.

I know she's sixty. If she doesn't look it, that's because of the many hours she spends at the beautician's. Her taste for the innocent pleasures of late afternoon is sometimes clouded by her husband's illness. Sometimes she wonders, as she caresses me, if she has the right to deceive him. I'm glad she has these scruples. As if our old family inheritance of morality could protect me.

In fact, I owe this all-expenses-paid vacation to the old man's illness. Camille is afraid he'll die without seeing his son again. She can't bear it when things don't proceed in an orderly fashion, she insists that traditions be respected. I'm not at all sure Bolduc is still conscious; nor do I think he's that keen to see his son. The kid took off four years ago with twenty thousand dollars' worth of jewels. Camille's heart knows no bounds. Her bank account, which I prefer not to think about too much, is equally generous. Ah, may I live a long, long time with my Camille! Well, three or four years. Sometimes I imagine her dying, whispering to me that I've brightened her last years. Then she'd leave me a nice little inheritance and I'd make it grow.

I'm only thirty, but already I'm thinking of a golden retirement somewhere around Cape Cod. I'm not all that partial to hot countries. Above all, I can't stand humidity. Don't talk to me about New Orleans! They can boast all they like about the French Quarter and the birthplace of jazz. For music, all I like is Bach. And Bourbon Street's just a hangout for drunks, prostitutes, and tourists who don't know how to behave. The dixieland you hear everywhere, without even going into the bars, is coming out my ears. The street stinks of sperm and alcohol. It makes me sick. Only a mother's anguish could push me to come here. Because the runaway son works on this very street. Camille thinks he's a maître d' in a French restaurant; last night I learned he clears the tables. The humiliation she'd feel if . . . ! But there's worse. The cashier at the restaurant is very talkative. Especially after making love, when I popped the cork on the Dom Pérignon. The titillating details I found out about Antoine. Humiliated isn't all Camille would be!

Is it really desirable that he up and leave the banks of the Mississippi? Aren't the muddy yellow waters of this river better suited to his nature? Especially if he confessed all his crimes to his mother? Wouldn't she push her feelings of guilt to the point of devoting herself exclusively to the memory of her husband and the presence of her long-lost son? Always look twice, don't rush things. And this planter's punch is too sweet. Bring me a gin fizz instead. Where did the waitress learn to smile like that? You'd swear women's lib had never existed. Do I really have to meet Antoine tonight? The old man won't croak for another week, anyway.

Surely women's lib allows its members to smile. At my first hint, the waitress took offence. So I'm walking down Royal Street one more time, stopping in front of the antique-shop windows. Maybe I'll find a charm for Camille's bracelet. After all, it's her money. At Toulouse Street I turn resolutely towards Bourbon. Why put it off till tomorrow? I've never seen Antoine. He took off long before I entered Camille's life. I've got a picture of him. He's fat. Not surprising, considering his parents. The cancer has eaten away all Bolduc senior's flesh, but his wife must weigh one sixty-five, easily. To justify it, she says her plumpness prevents premature wrinkles. She's always eating, and drinks more than she should. Mind you, it doesn't bother me. Since we never go out together, because of the gossip. How she resents the people who prevent her from flaunting herself with her boyfriend. Sometimes we take a little trip in Vermont. Then she can hardly control herself. People look at us, judge us. I don't like that. But I should concentrate on Antoine. What she's told me about him. Don't make any mistakes. The rest, what's been added to the picture since last night, I'll find a way of revealing.

A sign on the restaurant door announces that dinner is served after 5:30. Americans! I was wondering if it wouldn't be better to wait until the official opening time than to knock on the door, when the latter opened to let out an enormous boy with a broom in his hand. I'd never have believed he could be so fat!

'Antoine?'

No reaction. Like talking to a brick wall.

'Are you Antoine?'

'What?'

'Antoine, I'm here on behalf of your mother.'

'Sorry, I don't . . .'

'Listen, I don't mean you any harm. I just want to talk to you.'

'I told you . . .'

'Maybe you'd rather I put the drug squad on your tail?'

Even Camille, in her moments of ecstasy, never had such a profound expression. The mastodon looked at me as if I were Maigret come back from retirement. Any more, and I'd be reassuring him. Don't cry, old man, and all that. Anything to keep him from drawing attention to us.

'Follow me. But wait till we're alone before you talk. There's a couple from Marseilles working here. Husband and wife.'

What if I told him I'd spent the night with the wife—even if she is a cashier from Marseilles?

He took me into a little room next to the kitchen where cases of food were stored. At first I was afraid there'd be a rat, but my anxiety didn't last long.

'What's the matter with her, getting interested in me all of a sudden?'

'She's so fond of jewels. She was telling me just last week she lost three of them, four years ago. They'd have to be worth fifty thousand dollars now. Canadian dollars, obviously. You wouldn't have them by any chance, would you, kid?'

'What do you mean? And don't call me "kid"!'

'Listen, fat man, maybe you aren't familiar with American law. You know pushing is serious? Especially in Louisiana. If I were you . . .'

'Mind your own business.'

'What did you do with the jewels?'

'It's a long time since I had them.'

'So you admit it? And there's your poor mother, wondering if she didn't just lose them. Your mother has such a big heart.'

'Baby, if you really knew her, you'd wouldn't say that.'

'Now you're the one being familiar.'

'Fuck off! The old bitch never loved me. Too busy with men to care about me. The psychiatrist told me it's her fault I'm . . .'

'You're a pansy? Say it, if it makes you feel better.'

'She told you?'

'Oh no. But it's obvious.'

'She was always talking to me about girls.'

'If you only knew how she loves you.'

'What do you know about it?'

'She wants you to go back to Montreal.'

'She'd better not count on it. I like it here.'

'Your father's dying, Antoine.'

'Who cares? As far as I'm concerned, he can go any time. He's never existed. All he was good for was making money. His wife understood that soon enough! My father's a slot machine. But what have you got to do with it?'

'Let's say I'm a friend of the family.'

'Don't make me laugh! She's getting them younger all the time. What are you, thirty?'

'That's not the issue!'

'What is the issue?'

'Your dying father. It seems he's asking for you.'

'Give me some time to think. The restaurant opens in fifteen minutes; the tables aren't ready. I'll get shit.'

'Especially since you don't have a work permit.'

'Mind your own business!'

'Naughty boy!'

'Look out. If I get angry . . .'

'You can't get angry, fat man. Use your head. But don't take too long. I'll be back tomorrow night.'

'If you want to talk to me, don't start making threats!'

A distressing commotion had arisen in the immense mass of flesh. Fat drops of sweat stood out on his prematurely wrinkled forehead.

His white shirt was already wet in the armpits.

'What do you do when you get really angry? Eat three chickens? Or jerk off?'

I admit, as soon as I'd said it I was sorry I'd been so cruel. Such vulgarity isn't like me. Camille would never understand such a slip of the tongue, she who never speaks of 'fucking' but asks me to come and 'lie down' beside her, she who so wishes me to have class.

'You're disgusting!' replied Antoine, who had gained at least six pounds since the start of our conversation. Fear made him swell up like a balloon.

'Tomorrow, nine o'clock. Remember, I'm not patient!'

Imagine you're reading a police thriller right now. You certainly wouldn't be very happy if the narrator revealed the key to the mystery too soon. That's why I won't tell you right away what went on in my head as I was drinking a beer that night at a bar on that endless Bourbon Street. More than three hours on a plane, to end up getting to know just one place! I can't tell you how I detest this narrow street, which at the moment is filled with strollers whose distinguishing features are obesity, loud voices, heavy drinking, and body odour. They've opened the shutters on the windows so that people will stop to listen to the singer-pianist, whose name is Al Broussard and who never stops laughing, as if he were already in paradise. Maybe it's blues he's playing. At least that's what Alice, my Marseillaise, claims as she snuggles up to me in spite of the heat. Absorbed by thoughts along lines that lead in the direction of Cape Cod, I'm not thinking about music much anyway. If I'm smiling broadly at my companion, it's not that I find her as beautiful as I pretend, but that I know I'm a little less anxious to take Antoine back home to his mommy.

You couldn't say there's a crowd at the restaurant tonight. Half of the thirty tables are occupied. Eating in silence, or almost. Not much wine, but they keep their cocktails throughout the meal. When I came in, Alice smiled at me. She cuts a fine figure behind the bar. Almost beautiful. My time with her wasn't wasted. Three hours after we met she was in my bed, telling me all about Antoine. Damn Antoine! To see him racing around filling water glasses, clearing and setting tables, you really wouldn't think he'll soon be an heir. But he's coming towards me, and he looks alarmed. I thought he'd keep me in suspense for a while, just as a matter of form.

'I'd rather we didn't talk here.'

'Where do you want to go? Preservation Hall, or the Cathedral?'

'Don't be stupid. No, you're coming to my place.'

'Is it far?'

'In the suburbs. Half an hour by car. Does Chef Menteur Highway mean anything to you?'

'Not a thing. What time do you finish work?'

'I don't know. It's never the same.'

'Listen, fat man, I'll wait for you at my hotel. The Hyatt.'

'And if I don't show?'

'I'll go looking for you. Or the police. I just found out you've already had trouble with the morality squad. That worries me.'

'One time. Anyway, they let me go.'

'For lack of proof. But I've got the proof.'

'Tabarnac!'

'Watch it, Antoine, most of the customers think you're French. I'm broad-minded, it doesn't bother me if you lend your house to prostitutes and take minors there yourself. Your mother . . .'

'Don't bother.'

'Imagine the worst. For instance, suppose I couldn't help telling the police that the teenager whose body was found by the Saint Louis cemetery was once your boyfriend. That his name was Kim. There was Manuel too, and Ian.'

'I've never heard of them.'

'Those are just their first names, big guy. I've got the last names too. Don't talk so loud. You've got a thin little voice, but you don't control it well.'

'Anyway, I don't know those boys. I can't support anyone on what I make.'

'You know very well why you keep on working here. Contacts. I love to see a little guy from back home succeed in the States. Like my brother—he's got a motel in Fort Lauderdale.'

'Asshole. What do you want? For me to go and see my father before he dies? No way. I'll phone him if you like. That's all. My life is here now.'

'What do I want? I'm going to tell you, later. Room 326. Wait, I'll write down the number. Be sure you come alone. I'm scared of your friends. They're not from my type. I bought a little silencer. American cities are so unsafe, you never know who you're going to run into. So, ask the waiter to bring me the cheque. Now that I think about it, I'm not really hungry.'

'Ask him yourself.'

'Antoine! That hurt!'

As soon as the fat boy disappeared to the kitchen, I stood up, leaving a few bills on the table. More than necessary. What did it matter? Camille, who pays the bills, doesn't skimp on the details of my accounts. Alice looked at me lovingly as I passed. I smiled at her discreetly. I walked to the hotel, cursing bloody Bourbon Street one more time. The tourists looked even more obese. I wanted to deflate them. It wasn't possible that those enormous skins could be filled with nothing but fat. A trombonist was playing 'When the Saints Go Marching In', a young black in hobnailed boots was dancing in the middle of the road, a street vendor was selling hot dogs, and I was thinking of the next symphony season, to which I'd have to accompany Camille. Maybe 'accompany' isn't the word, since I have to sit ten rows away from her. For me the torture isn't to be separated from Camille, but to listen to the music without moving a muscle. I'm not sure she enjoys the experience all that much, even if she does claim to love everything cultural. She says beautiful music gives her a rest. From what? I ask you.

I readily admit that blackmail is a wicked thing. If the practice were too widespread, it would be a threat to social order. But handled tactfully, where underhanded characters are concerned, it can prove entirely moral. I'm basically honest. For instance, if I let Camille support me, it's because I know it does her enormous good. It's thanks to young people like me that ladies past their first bloom can experience the ecstasy of love a little longer. We bring them the elixir of youth. She drinks my youthful blood, as she put it in a poem she read at a society gathering that, for reasons of propriety, I didn't attend. It's obvious that I do more for her than her rotten son. So it's easy for me to admit Antoine is a small-minded toad I can exploit as I wish.

He turned up at my hotel room as promised. To gain his trust, I received him in pyjamas. The gorgeous pale blue silk ones Camille gave me at Easter. With his faded T-shirt and pants worn out at the knees, Antoine looked like what he was: a fat boy who clears tables in a restaurant. He refused the cognac I offered. I never touch drugs.

'Does it bother you to work so late at night?' I asked, to add a touch of civility.

'What's it to you?'

'Don't be cross, little guy!' I said, sorry to humiliate him like that. Just because I'm good-looking doesn't mean I'm entitled to take advantage. As Camille says, what God gives, he can take away.

'I haven't got any time to waste. Exactly what do you want?'

'I came to New Orleans to take a son back to his mother.'

'I've told you what I think of that.'

'Let me finish. God, you're impatient! I wanted to take you back. Not any more.'

'So what do you want?'

'To get you to sign a few papers.'

'What kind of papers?'

'For instance, notes admitting that you owe me some poker debts.'

'I've never played cards.'

'Neither have I. But you've done some pretty rotten things. All I'd have to do is get talkative. The little bags of heroin, the prostitutes, the transvestites. Not very nice. To think that your mother gave you everything.'

'You aren't ashamed to blackmail me? I've told you, I haven't got any money.'

'But you will. And it won't be long coming.'

'Do you know what's in my father's will?'

'Do I know! A friend of mine drew it up. You're going to inherit about five hundred thousand dollars. Give me half and I'll get out of your life.'

Antoine looked at me as if I was the Messiah come to reward all the world's lard-asses. His round, hairless face had never looked so ugly.

'You're sure?'

'I told you, the lawyer's a friend of mine.'

'If I don't sign your papers, you lose a lot of money too.'

'But I'm not risking the electric chair.'

'I never killed anyone. Jesus!'

'Such language! Maybe you didn't kill anyone, but when things are messy, judges don't go to a lot of trouble to get positive proof. Especially when the people in front of them are in an illegal situation. If I called the police right now, your father could still change his will. Camille, I mean your mother, won't be very hard to convince. Not when her son abandoned her in such a cowardly fashion.'

'So I've got no choice. Either I inherit or you turn me in?'

'Brilliant deduction.'

'Can I think it over?'

'No. I don't want my expenses to run too high. I've got some decency.'

'You have to be kidding!'

'You're going to sit down at that little table over there. I've got paper. Good vellum. And a pen. You're going to write what I tell you. Set your mind to it. This is important. How's your spelling? I hate mistakes. I think I'd almost rather give up my share . . . well, almost!'

Now that everything's fallen apart, all I have left is the memory of a city I detest. The French Quarter! I'm going to do some advertising for the New Orleans State and City Tourist Center. Antoine got his revenge all right. He wasn't as stupid as I thought. He slipped a word about me to his friends—nice thugs who worked me over right in my hotel room. A knock at the door, I think it's my breakfast, and it turns out to be some giant who gives me a knee in the stomach. What happened next I have to imagine. I'd hidden the paper in the lining of my jacket, but they tore everything apart. They even went to the trouble of planting enough bags of cocaine and syringes in my room for me to be accused of trafficking. The complaint I laid against Antoine went nowhere, since he'd quit his job. Two weeks later his enormous corpse was floating in the Mississippi, near the port. Thinking it over, maybe my fate is preferable. Under lock and key, to reflect on the mistakes I've made. Never underestimate fat people. But why doesn't Camille write? Who's taken my place at her side? Deep down, I don't miss her that much. She had too much flesh on her, after all. And Alice is so nice on visiting days. She says I can work at the restaurant when I get out in five years. That helps me put up with the prison food. . . .

Translated by Sally Livingston

ERIC McCORMACK · b. 1938

Eckhardt at a Window

The dusty wooden frame of the window holds nine double-glazed panes of glass, three levels of three panes on top of each other. If Inspector Eckhardt stands on tiptoe on the threadbare carpet, the top panes are at his eye level. The middle row is comfortably situated for him, for he is a man of medium height. He has to stoop slightly, however, his chin on the sill, to look through the bottom row. If he stands a few feet away, the window is all one greater window, the panes look symmetrical, crystalline, even identical. But from close up, at nose distance, which he prefers, each pane is individual, unique, each discloses new worlds to Inspector Eckhardt's eye. A bevel in the double glass here, a warp there, reveal the reflections of twin, overlapping grotesque faces in two grotesque rooms, Chinese boxes that do not quite fit. As for what he sees on the outside—a warp in the pane, a bubble, a bevel, invent a city he can scarcely recognize of monstrous trees and nightmare houses reshaping themselves constantly as he moves his grey head, a landscape of plastic writhing forever in an inferno.

Inspector Eckhardt is thinking about the deaths, one year ago, of a woman and a man. He remembers the tall, beautiful, fair-haired woman he first met on that dull, November day, in this northern city. She was shivering, wearing a thin dress under a short coat. Her face was oval, a noticeable nose, green, green eyes. The lower lids were convex, half-eclipsing those two green worlds.

Inspector Eckhardt, a widower without children, a meditative man, liked the look of her right away, her voice, an innocence about her. She was long-legged, long-striding in spite of her grief—she had come to the old police station to report a death. In her deep, surprising voice, she wanted to tell him about the ludicrous accident that had happened less than an hour before. Her strange eyelids could not stop the tears from spilling out.

She was apologetic, but not about her grief. She was sorry for this: that in her confusion, she hadn't paid much attention to the location of the house where the accident had happened. It had no telephone, so she ran outside, along the street till she found a taxi, and asked for the nearest police station. And now, where was the house with the dead body? She was sure of one thing only: it was on a tree-lined street, maybe a mile or two away.

The Inspector smiled at her insistence on this fact. He did not tell her that the entire district for miles around the station was full of tree-lined streets, that it was a forest masquerading as a city. People who lived here a long time knew their way around, knew how to see the differences between one street of trees and another. His new men often lost their way the first few times out.

Darkness was sinking in as she talked, sitting in the wooden chair in front of his desk. Through the window behind her, Inspector Eckhardt could see those very streets beginning to fade into night. It was a cold November darkness, and the lamps would hardly illumine those streets, making it useless to go looking for the house. She didn't know, in fact she said she'd never known, even the number of the house, or the name of the street. He told her, as kindly as he could, that it didn't matter much. Her friend, being dead, would be content to wait till the morning.

She shuddered. Yet she wanted to talk, and he wanted to listen to her, to watch the movement of those strange eyes, as much because of the pleasure it gave him as to help her ease herself of her burden of sorrow. He told her a formal statement could wait till the morning, but that he'd like to hear all about her friend. She should just relax and say whatever came to mind.

'A little spout of blood.' She used that phrase several times. She said this little spout of blood, just a drop or two, used to spurt from her friend's forehead right between his eyebrows at least once a day. Surely that would be remarkable in anyone. The blood would trickle down his face, and he'd wipe it with a Kleenex, nervously, a horse flicking at flies. She wasn't long up from the country, and had been sitting in a bar, when he picked her up a month ago. She liked the look of him, and said nothing even when she first saw the blood spout. It used to frighten her, and it would fill him with a devastating sadness. But she said nothing.

She found out, eventually, why the blood made him so sad. One day they were sitting, talking. He was stroking, as usual, the crystal of his digital watch as he talked, intent on the nervous transformations of the little figures under the glass. He looked up and stared into her eyes. He was afraid, he said, that the blood that spouted out of his forehead wasn't his own. It was the blood of all the people he'd killed gushing back out of him.

Killings. He saw how shocked she was, and so he began telling her about them.

When he used to kill, he said, he felt as though he was watching someone else do it, a creature who looked like him, but who was on the other side of a two-way mirror. Years ago, when he was a child, he used to think it must be some other child who looked like him burying cats alive or setting them alight with gasoline, watching them try to leap out of their pain, living Catherine wheels. Then, years later, surely that was some other young boy who just happened to look like him, pushing another lonely boy into a disused canal, standing there, fascinated by the muddy gurgles, and the eventual brown calm. Or shoulder-charging an old man, light as a feather, down the dark stairwell of an apartment building and watching him crumple silently at the bottom, a broken butterfly with blood at the mouth. And even now, he could hardly admit that this killer was no one else but himself, this brown-bearded man who killed for hire and showed no pity for any of those he destroyed with his gun, his knife, his car, by fire, by water, or by other necessary means.

But one night as he was getting ready for bed, the blood gushed, for the first time, out of his head. He was undressing in front of the mirror, trying to comprehend the man on the other side of the glass, when it erupted. He quickly wiped it away, already fearful, and saw that there was no sign of a cut, not even a burst pimple, only the smooth forehead of a killer.

It wasn't long after, one night in a bar, that he met her, and they became lovers, he loving someone, and that, too, for the first time in his life.

He told her he felt he was divided once more into separate parts by meeting her. She'd somehow built a transparent wall around him, so that now his past life was someone else's, an unloved man he hardly knew.

He wanted to dedicate himself now to loving, the way he had before to killing. He wondered if love could cancel out, somehow, all of the deaths. So he began taking her to the places where he'd done his murders over the years, and they made love standing up in alleys and hallways, lying down in city parks and seedy basements, in daytime and in the night. Always, in spite of everything, the blood came.

Then, just that day, they went to a house in a tree-lined street. He'd phoned her early in the afternoon, and they'd taken a taxi to the house.

They went straight upstairs, she hardly noticing the creaky stairs, the faded prints in their cracked frames on the walls, to a dusty room with some shabby chairs and a rusted wall-mirror. In the middle of the bare floor stood a metal-framed coffee-table with a glass top.

They made love in front of the mirror. She watched his hands move under her clothing in the reflection: the image of the two lovers in the mirror before her, and the feel of his hands on her flesh doubled her pleasure.

After the love-making, he'd sent her downstairs to the kitchen to make coffee. She was standing by the stove when she heard a crash upstairs. She called up to him from the hall to ask if anything was wrong. She thought he called back that it was okay, so she went into the kitchen again.

After a few minutes, a drip fell past her head onto the chipped white stove, a reddish splotch. And another. For a moment she didn't understand. She looked up at the ceiling where a reddish-brown drip was gathering. She knew then what it was.

Terrified, she ran out of the kitchen and up the stairs, her feet hollow on the worn linoleum, hardly noticing the faded prints of hunting scenes behind broken glass. She reached the landing and looked through the open living-room door.

The bearded man is spread-eagled across the frame of a low coffee-table whose glass top has collapsed. He himself is impaled upon a sliver of green glass about eighteen inches long. It has pierced his back, travelling on through his body inside the left shoulder-blade, driven by his weight, slicing through his heart like a butcher's knife.

The point of the glass protrudes through his chest without tearing his green silk shirt, but far enough to make an obscene bosom. His eyes are open and he looks surprised. In the middle of his forehead, a little ruby of wet blood is forming.

She runs to him, sobbing. He is quite, quite dead.

He must have sat right down on the glass-topped table, making it cave in, explode at the weight of him. It was meant to take a vase of flowers, or a glossy picture book, never a man's weight. He must have fallen backward into the empty frame, crucifying himself, skewered by a long sliver wedged against the floor, his body making new lips to suck in the glass.

Inspector Eckhardt felt sorry for her. Her green eyes were full of tears, this tall, fair-haired woman, occasionally touching his arm as she talked. She still couldn't believe what had happened. For so long she too had been alone, sad. Then she met the bearded man and her life was full of meaning, love became a barricade against an unbearable past. And now the barrier had been demolished.

She looked tired now. The Inspector nodded in sympathy. He didn't even know her name, but that could wait. Nor did she call the bearded man any name at all. Always it was 'he', with a little emphasis. Inspector Eckhardt wondered if she even knew the man's name, but he didn't ask. He'd enjoyed listening to her, and he could get all the details from her tomorrow morning.

He told her she could go home now and come back in the morning early to make a statement and help them find the house. Again, her strange green eyes filled. She said she'd no place to go, she'd given up her apartment just that day, so that she could move in with the bearded man.

Inspector Eckhardt looked at her, liking the looks of her, tall and warm. He liked the way she would reach out across the desk and touch his arm quite unselfconsciously, trusting him.

It was no problem, he said. She could stay in the station's little night-shift room. He'd ask the duty sergeant to get her a cup of coffee and a sandwich. She should try to sleep, even though it was early, because next morning she'd have to help them find the house with the body of her dead lover.

After she left with the sergeant, the Inspector sat for a while, thinking about her, and the strange accident she'd come to report. He thought, too, about his own mood of contentment, that he'd be seeing her again in the morning. He couldn't help feeling that in some way he wasn't yet sure of, this was a remarkable day for him.

Inspector Eckhardt did indeed see her very early the next morning. The fair-haired woman must have slipped out of the station during the night, and when he saw her in the early morning, there was a great change in her condition.

Dawn is just breaking, a frosty November dawn in the city. The sky is a heavy sheet of opaque glass with fissures prised apart by wedges of sunlight.

On a piece of waste ground stands a huddle of men, their breath silently trumpeting in front of them. A car pulls up on the nearby street, the engine throbbing, and a grey-haired older man in a heavy winter coat picks his way through the sparkling weeds towards the men.

'Over here, Inspector Eckhardt.'

The Inspector nods to the men, and leans forward to look at the shape lying on the iron ground. He can see that it is the frozen body of a long-legged young woman in a skimpy dress, her clothes, her fair hair sculpted in hoar-frost, a sparkling Christmas bundle. She is sprawled on her back. Her eyes are the eyes of a statue, completely whitened in the frost of this November morning.

Inspector Eckhardt also sees, glittering in the occasional sunshine, the long splinter of frosted glass protruding from her belly, a lethal banner which she grips in her two frozen hands.

Inspector Eckhardt was too shocked by this death, too saddened by the thought that he'd never see the woman again. He knew he must work, and work, and work. The investigation of her death wasn't in his hands; it was his job to find the body of the bearded man, and he'd waste no time that day in getting on with it.

He and his team knocked on door after door, peered through dozens of dusty windows, examined every house that seemed unoccupied in those tree-lined streets. In vain. Some of Inspector Eckhardt's men wondered out loud whether, perhaps, her story was just a bit far-fetched. Late in the afternoon, he himself began to probe the fringes of that possibility: that there was no body, that she had made up an insane lie.

Then, just before dusk, news came in that the body had been found.

The house is on one of those tree-lined streets in the maze of tree-lined streets surrounding the station. The streets are mirror images of each other. Only a bump on the road here, an oddity in architecture there makes the difference to those who know.

The grey-haired man steps out of the cruiser and walks up the pathway of a small, run-down house. The door opens, and staleness makes a brief raid on the sharp, colder outside air. He notes the creaky steps, the faded prints on the wall, the worn linoleum. On the dim landing, he glimpses three rooms: a bathroom with a chipped sink, an empty bedroom with a cracked mirror on the wall. Then the living-room, with another smell, one he knows only too well.

'Right in here, Inspector Eckhardt.'

Through the parasitic fuss of photographers and detectives, the Inspector sees, by the light of a bare ceiling bulb, the dead man, crucified on a rectangular metal frame, broken glass all around him, his eyes wide open. His face is bearded, a thin brown beard on a thin face, his hairline receding. It is the face of a young man who has never been young. His cheeks are lined with experience and sadness.

But two things are ominously wrong. No gush of blood stains the dead forehead, one of the last things she had told him. The bearded man's brow is smooth and unmarked. But more disturbing still, he has not been pierced through his back. Instead, Inspector Eckhardt can see, as can all the others, the broad end of a long sliver of glass protruding sickly from between his legs, an obscene phallus coated in blood and excrement.

That was all a year ago, a year in which no resolution to the mystery of the deaths had appeared. Inspector Eckhardt had made sure the investigation of the fair-haired woman's death was pursued without slacking. But no witness could be found, no motive appeared. Her past was a blank, no one claimed her or identified her. The investigators dealt with her death as a murder, but they did concede that it was just possible she might have stabbed herself with the shard of glass—a very unpleasant way to commit suicide.

As for the bearded man impaled on the glass, nothing could be discovered about him except that he had just recently paid a year's rent on the old house on the tree-lined street.

Inspector Eckhardt remembered how she said they'd always make love on the scene of former killings. So, day after day he wearied his eyes with the dust and faded type of old files. He even began having nightmares about seedy crimes camouflaged by the trees of those street. But he could find no record of a killing in that house. It belonged to an old couple who had retired and migrated to the South.

Soon the entire case of the fair-haired woman and the bearded man was interred, in its turn, in a filing cabinet. Inspector Eckhardt's superiors told him plainly that the two deaths, no matter how strange, of an apprentice hooker and a presumed lover-cum-hired-killer were of minor importance in the general scheme of things.

But Inspector Eckhardt did not forget, could not forget. For him, he didn't quite know why, the case was of major importance in his 'general scheme of things'. He'd stand for hours looking out of his window, a juggler with too many rubber balls, trying just once to put it all together. He was beginning to consider that his career up to that point had been a time of innocence, a novitiate. He felt that he too had walked right through a mirror, and everything was changed.

The case, he had to admit to himself, delighted him as much as it puzzled him with its possibilities, its enigmas. Yes, she was dead. But now he was high priest of his own private religion, and must create a theology around the mysteries. Part of his ritual was to meditate daily upon the fair-haired woman, at times his goddess, at times a demon. Why had the description she'd given of the death of the bearded man been so accurate yet so wrong? How could the dead man have answered her call from the kitchen? Why had she left the police station during the night? What had made her go to the waste ground to die?

Daily, he invents ingenious resolutions to the mystery. For example, he theorizes, keeping the details sketchy, that it could be a murder-suicide. The essence is this: the fair-haired woman must murder the bearded man by somehow (this is one of the very vague parts) forcing him to sit on the fragment of glass in the old house, then she must slip away to the waste ground to stab herself in the stomach.

Or, in another version, it is the bearded man who must be the murderer. He must go to the waste ground to meet the fair-haired woman, stab her in the stomach with the piece of glass, then return to that musty house and sit down, quite deliberately, on the sliver of glass.

Naturally, in this second version of the murder-suicide theory, the order of the deaths is reversed. But then, neither first nor second version accounts for her visit to the police station, nor for her determination to tell her story. Yet the Inspector finds something satisfying in both versions, maybe the suggestion of a doomed, perverted love, maybe the symbolism of the glass. Or maybe, it's just the enigma of which of the two is the murderer, which the suicide.

Inspector Eckhardt is also gently nursing a double-murder theory. It goes like this: someone wants to kill the fair-haired woman and the bearded man, perhaps to avenge one of his paid killings—the motive is unclear. The murderer somehow forces the bearded man to sit on the sliver of glass (again, the Inspector is unhappy with this part), somehow terrifies the fair-haired woman into lying convincingly to the police (slightly less difficult for the Inspector to imagine), and then into leaving the station in the middle of the night for the waste ground, to meet her own murderer (tricky, this part too, the Inspector admits).

Sometimes the Inspector even proposes two separate murderers, one for the bearded man, one for the girl, perhaps acting in collusion, perhaps not, although the use of the glass is so unusual it suggests a conspiracy. The flexibility of the two-murderer theory, however, is its main appeal: the permutations of which-killer-kills-whom-and-why are expanded marvellously by this simple ploy.

Inspector Eckhardt likes all variations of the double-murder theory for another reason. They exonerate the fair-haired woman, making her perhaps the tragic victim of her love for a felon. Besides, the slaying of the bearded man, an admitted assassin, is reassuring for the Inspector: justice, no matter how rough, still prowls the streets of the city.

But one thing always bothers him. Why, he constantly asks himself, did the fair-haired woman come to the station and lie? That, he still finds hardest of all to take.

For a year, Inspector Eckhardt speculated and speculated, enjoyed speculating, standing there by his window. He never lost patience at the incompleteness of his theories, for he felt confident that, in time, the whorls, the distortions, the bumps would disappear, and the clear, inevitable truth would stand forth.

Then, just that morning, almost a year to the day after the deaths, he was obliged to look at the whole matter differently. Not a mile from the station, a crew of hydro-company men had been making routine inspections of the lines. They had been checking out an old house when they found something grisly.

The grey-haired man, stocky in his winter coat, swings his legs out of the cruiser. He walks along the path to the door of the house where some men in hard hats stand smoking and talking. It's a small house, paint peeling from the clapboard. This house would be hard to distinguish from most of the others in the tree-lined street.

He pushes open the creaky door, ducking past a brief ambush by the stale air, and walks along the hallway to the staircase—he can hear the sounds of voices upstairs. He climbs the creaking staircase with its worn linoleum, his shoes echoing. He notes the faded prints on the walls. He stops on the landing, where the smell is even mustier. In a room with an open door, a few men are scuttling around, maggots in uniform.

'Come in, Inspector Eckhardt,' one of them says, without turning. And he sees what occupies their attention.

The fully-clothed body of a man lies on its back in the metal frame of a glass-topped coffee-table surrounded by broken glass. The body has lain there a long time. The Inspector can see that the face and the exposed parts of the flesh have turned a mottled blue. The cheeks have partly decomposed, exposing the bone. The eyes have dried up to raisins. The clothing and the floor beneath the skeletal frame of the table are heavily stained by the leakage of body fluids.

The cause of death is very clear: the body has been pierced through the back by a long sliver of glass, wedged against the floor. The glass has penetrated so deeply that the point, a deadly nipple, sticks out of the chest through the material of what was once a light green shirt.

Lying on the button band of the shirt, a rag of brown hair has peeled away from the chin. A scalp of long brown hair hangs from the back of the lolling head like a trophy. The ends of the fingers had decomposed, exposing bone, but on the mottled blue left wrist, a digital watch dangles. The angular numbers are still prowling agitatedly under their glass cover.

Inspector Eckhardt, back in his office in the station, stands by his window, late in the afternoon. He is thinking of the fair-haired girl, the bearded men, and the possibility of faceless, shadowy avengers. In the window panes, he fancies he sees them, playing a variety of parts, here stabbing themselves, there stabbing each other, or each being stabbed by all the others in a frenzy of glass.

The Inspector sighs. The darkness outside is deepening, and soon he will see with cockroach eyes the multiple images of himself reflected more distinctly in the window. Vaguely, through the double glaze, the nightscape of the city will emerge on this November afternoon, creating itself in light, the beginnings of a miraculous painting-by-numbers.

Inspector Eckhardt, standing by his window, is not discontented with the way things have worked out. He knows now that he has no wish ever to solve his mystery (he feels sure that it *is* his, meant for him alone), only to contemplate it, to delight in its complexities.

He walks slowly back to his desk marvelling again at the discovery of the second bearded man's body. Behind him, nine, or is it eighteen, other misshapen Inspector Eckhardts slide, hobble, somersault back to their separate desks. They sit down in unison. After a moment's pause, as on a signal given, all of them, with the most convoluted motions, reach for pencils, find them with an impossible accuracy, and begin to write.

ELLEN GODFREY · b. 1942

Common or Garden Murder

Neighbours. They're great when you need them, but it's better not to get too involved with them. Especially when you've got kids, and they don't; sooner or later there'll be trouble, and there's no escape from a neighbour. They're always there; and you can end up sneaking out of your own house, hoping not to be seen by a neighbour you're in trouble with.

Of course it's ridiculous to be a prisoner in your own house, but it's the kind of thing that happens to me. My curiosity tricks me into going too far, and then I'm not clever enough to get out of trouble. Trying only makes things worse; I ought to know better by now. At forty, quite the worse for wear, I'd like to think I've learned some common sense for my sins, but the signs all point in the opposite direction.

When I moved into my new house by the sea the first thing I decided not to do was get too involved with my next-door neighbour. I was going to keep my curiosity under control. Even now I'm not sure how it happened, how I got mixed up with my neighbour, Tory Barton. I look back to try to understand how it all happened and to see where I went wrong. I really want to know.

It was his garden that interested me, not him. It was too beautiful for me to resist. And who would ever dream that a beautiful garden could draw in a person too far, draw in a person until she was involved in murder?

There really was something very special about the effect that garden had on me. It seemed almost to be promising me something, something that I wanted, something that was very important to me.

In that first autumn after I moved in, I would walk over the rocky bit of ground that separated his property from mine, just to look at it. Standing there and looking down, I would think that the sunshine was more mellow in Barton's garden than anywhere else. Apple and pear trees, their branches so heavy with fruit that they leaned upon their stakes, cast soft restful shadows on the smooth green lawn. The leaves of the trees were full and heavy with sunshine, holding and reflecting the light. Beyond the fruit trees, the runner beans climbed vigorously on the white-painted trellis. Hedges of colourful dahlias separated the rows of dark green cabbages; there were prickly red currant bushes under their netting, and squash, cucumber, and tomatoes, each without a blemish, without a mite, the soil turned and worked and weedless around every plant, vine, and stake.

Barton's crowning glory grew on the slope on the seaward side of the garden. There, sheltered from the sea breeze, warmed by the sunlight reflected off the rocks, and thick on their vines, grew the dark luscious fredonia grapes which Barton was so proud of. Still, who could argue when Barton boasted, 'Have you ever seen a vine like it? Does anyone else on this coast have grapes like this?' You had to agree. I had read in the gardening column of our newspaper that the climate was too harsh for grapes . . . and yet, there was Barton's vine, a masterwork.

I had quickly learned that I had to be careful not to be caught looking at the garden. But it was hard to resist, especially when I was having a rough day with the kids, and the damned dog, and the house getting to be just a bit too much, and most likely the van on the fritz again. Even though I knew that the last thing I needed on days like that was to have Barton making a pass at me. And that's all it seemed to take—just seeing me looking at his garden was enough to give him the idea that I was longing for a little fun and games.

Women in my position are vulnerable, and we are supposed to be careful. I know it, and I knew right from the start I might have trouble when I rented a house next to a divorced single man. In fact, when I heard about him I even wondered if I ought to go ahead and take the house. But the old two-storey tudor-style place, with its big windows and funny nooks and crannies, was too perfect to pass up. The house was just run-down enough for me to afford, yet it was big enough and had a sea view. Down behind, there were lots of neat places for the kids to wander. I thought the funny old house might help make up to the kids for what they had lost by me making a hash of my marriage and losing them their father in the process. I know I'm not supposed to put it that way—everyone says it takes two to break up a marriage—but I tried my hardest and still my husband left me for someone else. Whose fault could that be, if not mine?

Anyway, a lecherous neighbour is no reason for the kids not to live in the kind of house they had always wanted. I told myself he'd probably take one look at me driving by in the big yellow van with my hair every which way and the tailpipe (which I've been meaning to get fixed and *still* haven't) tied on with rope, and not even bother to try anything.

Of course I was very lonely and pretty unhappy. I was trying not to think about my husband, Marcus, and his new posting in Paris, and his pretty new girlfriend. I don't know, it might even be that, without realizing it, I was hoping to like Tory Barton. Maybe that is why I accepted so easily his invitation to come in and have a glass of wine, the first time he caught sight of me, on the rocky spit of land that divided our properties, feasting my eyes on his wonderful garden.

'Well, I'm not sure,' I said, thinking of my dusty, ratty jeans and feeling not really up to his smoothness. I knew right away, as soon as I saw him, that he was one of the 'perfect' people. He was wearing sharply creased khakis, and a blue cotton crew-neck sweater that matched his pale blue eyes.

I'm sure my looks will be enough to put any flirtatious thoughts out of his mind, I told myself as we walked along his spotless marble foyer (how *do* other people keep the entryway carpets of their houses from going all grungy?) and along a thickly carpeted hall into a perfect kitchen, like an illustration in *Western Living* magazine. It was easy to see that appearances meant a lot to him, and in that department a woman like me, surely, would not be a very worthwhile conquest. Turning forty, ten pounds overweight, too many sad lines in her face and the general falling of everything that can fall after four children—I didn't belong in that shiny, spotless kitchen.

But Tory Barton did not seem to notice how uncomfortable I felt, sitting awkwardly on the spindly barstool at his gleaming kitchen counter, while he poured wine into large, long-stemmed glasses.

'I have, quite literally, the best view in this city, don't you think?' Tory had asked, turning to look out of his kitchen window and to show me his perfect profile, his thick, silvery grey hair, blow-dried in the latest style, sweeping away elegantly from his temples.

'Yes, yes it certainly is,' I said, for the view over the straits was magnificent. The architect had set the house and placed the windows along the seaward side, to show a wonderful sweep of coast that made the viewer feel he was a lord, high up in his castle, surveying an isolated, uninhabited, perfect realm.

'Naturally I had to pay plenty for it,' said Tory. 'But it was well worth it. What else is money for? To buy beauty. That's what I always say.'

Again I agreed. With four children to feed on a fixed monthly alimony it was an idea I really didn't have to worry about one way or the other.

'And you, Sylvia,' he said, pausing over my name almost like a dog positioning a bone between its paws, 'how do you find that old house you rented? Pretty creaky I bet. Not much spent on maintenance over there, as far as I can tell.' He didn't wait for me to answer. 'It's nice for me, having a single woman living next door; I hope we can get to know one another better. Not that I'm lonely, of course—I'm never lonely—but you . . . tied down with all those boys . . . I'm sure you could use. . . .' His voice tailed off into a knowing smile. 'You must find it . . . very. . . .'

'Not at all,' I said hurriedly, wondering what was wrong with me, that I would let the conversation start to go wrong when I had only been in his kitchen for a few minutes. I knew already that I didn't like Tory Barton very much, although I felt, for some reason, a little sorry for him, maybe because he did seem kind of lonely. Still, I wished I was almost anywhere but alone with him, drinking his wine, and not knowing how to get out of what I could see was coming.

'One of my wives was a movie star,' he told me with pride in his voice. 'Sara Blixen.'

I said, without thinking, that I had never heard of her.

'You're kidding.' He mentioned some movies I had never heard of. 'And she's on "Hollywood Squares" a lot.'

I wasn't sure about 'Hollywood Squares' either. Was it a TV show or a kind of filmstar-world drug? I could see it would be better not to admit my ignorance and seem even more a fool.

'I used to rub her back when she was under pressure,' he told me, 'but she turned out to be as heartless as the other three, no matter what I did for her.'

I knew it wasn't a good idea to let a man tell you about his bad luck with women, so I tried to change the subject, but Tory had the conversation under his control and I didn't have a chance. I found myself listening to him going on about how he had done 'everything' for his wives, but how he found out they were only interested in one thing, money. He said sadly that nothing would satisfy them.

When he wasn't talking about his past he was prying into mine. He wanted to know how much my husband had earned a year, and what stocks and property he had, and how much alimony I got. When I told him—I couldn't figure out how not to—he told me firmly that I had been badly treated.

'Royally screwed, in my opinion. I could have got you more, if you had known me then; I would have helped you. I've helped a lot of my friends whose marriages broke up. And what is really good about it is, both of them—the husband and the wife—thanked me afterwards. Now *that's* unusual, but, to tell you the truth, I could have been a professional negotiator. It's a knack I have. . . .'

I interrupted. 'But I didn't want more.' Somehow it seemed important to me not to be lumped in with the actress on 'Hollywood Squares'. 'Marcus worked really hard for his money and *he* earned it. I have to admit it, I was just not very good at helping him. And I didn't want to, either, so why should he owe me anything? The kids, yes, and he's doing that; but me, I don't see it. I wanted to stay out of that life at External, all the entertaining and that kind of thing. I just wanted to have babies and take care of them. As it turns out, now I'm unemployable, but, after all, whose fault is that?'

He smiled at me, and I could see he thought I was trying to prove to him that I wasn't one of those women who were only after a man for his money. And although he knew that that was all women wanted, he liked me for lying to him about it. He expected it and felt good to have things work out the way he expected. His smile suddenly revolted me.

'Look,' I said, trying to explain, 'wives in External are supposed to be elegant, and charming, and good at running a house, and they're supposed to entertain beautifully. It's part of the job. Marcus's new girlfriend is French; she's perfect at that stuff. But I just never did it the way Marcus wanted. I wasn't a help; I was a hindrance.' I didn't say, although I thought about it as I spoke, how Marcus complained that the kids got in the way of his 'professional obligations' and how he wanted to send them away to boarding school. I didn't see things the way Marcus did; how could anybody send little boys of five and seven and nine away? Even the oldest, at twelve . . . you only had them such a short time, surely it wasn't right? Marcus said that if I wanted to keep the kids around I should be able to manage the way other External wives did.

'I just gave up trying,' I told Tory Barton. 'I just didn't want to try any more. Nothing I did was done the way he wanted. So what does he owe me for?'

'You handled it very badly, in my opinion. But it isn't your fault. Women like you need good lawyers and friends who rally round in time of trouble.' He gave me that awful smile again.

'I have to be going now,' I said gulping down my wine. 'The children will be coming home from school any minute and. . . .'

'But I wanted to show you around my house,' he said, his smile fading.

'Maybe some other time,' I said weakly, cursing myself as soon as the words were out of my mouth.

He brightened a little. 'You're such an attractive woman, a desirable woman. . . . I feel that somehow, you and I. . . .'

It had turned into a farce. I got myself away as quickly as I could. I decided after that afternoon that Tory Barton was a phoney (expecting me to take him seriously when he said he found me 'attractive', 'desirable'; it was really pretty insulting) and the only thing he had going for him was his garden. I know it was an over-reaction, but I think I was still quite easily hurt then, and it did hurt that I had seemed to him so easy, so vulnerable, and so dumb that I would believe such a feeble line.

After Tory Barton got over being annoyed about the rude way I had 'run out of the house in the middle of a friendly drink', he used to talk to me about whatever was obsessing him at the time, if he could catch me when I was walking the dog, or when he came over to borrow something. So it wasn't long after his trouble with Kieran began that I got all the details from him first hand.

And then, after Kieran was killed and I had made up my mind to forget all about his death because it really had nothing to do with me, I still kept thinking about Tory Barton, and his garden, and his grapevine, and the perfection of his house and his life . . . compared to the slap-dash, screwed-up life the kids and I led in the big old house, looking over his garden. And I kept seeing the image of old Kieran lying dead between the two houses, like a symbol of unfinished business.

The municipal trucks were the first sign of trouble. I heard the thrum thrum of their motors early one morning as I hustled around the kitchen making breakfast. The noise distracted me from my usual morning hassles: reminding the kids not to forget their homework, checking on who had soccer practice and who needed a dental excuse and doing all the other last-minute stuff other mothers probably have made careful lists of the night before. When all four of them were off, and I had made sure that no one had forgotten his knapsack, I sat down with that most blessed cup of coffee and cigarette of the day. Then I heard the sound of earth rolling down the rock slopes and workmen calling to one another. I stuck my bare feet into a pair of wellingtons, buttoned a heavy sweater over my bathrobe, and ventured out.

Carefully skirting the eucalyptus hedge that shielded our front yard from the lane, I peered around without letting myself be seen. Two bright yellow municipal trucks were dumping fill on the rock out-cropping between our house and Barton's. This was peculiar because that narrow rocky spit was the property of the municipality. I had been told that when I moved in. It was dedicated as a 'sea access' and no one could put a house on it. My landlord's assurances of this had surprised me, because the lot was a funny triangle. The point at the road was no more than fifteen feet wide, widening out towards the sea to a sharply sloping rocky coast of about a hundred and fifty feet. No one could or would want to build on this triangular piece of rock, high on my side, but sloping sharply downwards towards Barton's. Now, as I watched, peering out from behind the eucalyptus, the contours of the rock were disappearing under torrents of earth.

Forgetting my unmade-up face and my bathrobe hanging out below my sweater I approached one of the workmen.

'Hey, what's up? What're you guys doing?'

'Dumping fill.'

'But why?'

'How should I know?' the workman said, looking around for his mate. 'Hey, Rick, the lady wants to know why we're dumping fill,' he called out, his voice just audible above the sound of the engine and the fill falling out of the dump truck onto the rocks.

The second workman approached. 'No idea, lady, nothing to do with us. Call the municipality if you wanna know anything.'

Just then I saw Kieran coming towards us along the lane. The old man was a figure of fun to my kids. He walked down to the end of our road every day, slightly stooped over, wearing a dirty tweed cap and an old worn plaid jacket with several layers of shirts under it, each of a different colour. The kids had told me that old Kieran had once owned half of the land in the neighbourhood. They were probably right; he must have become a millionaire many times over as he sold it off, parcel by parcel, over the years. The main road was called Kieran Road. I had heard stories of his peculiar tastes in houses and had sometimes seen him on a tractor, or a bulldozer, working a piece of wasteland, which soon after was subdivided, given a cute name, and then built up with fancy, ugly houses.

Now he shuffled towards me and gestured towards his cap. 'Morning,' he said in a surprisingly strong, young voice. As he got closer, I could see that he was really very old and frail-looking, despite the voice; well into his eighties, I thought, with bits of white whiskers poking out of the crevices round his sunken mouth, and his small eyes vague and bleared over.

'Good morning,' I said. 'You're Mr Kieran?'

'That's right, and you're the lady that rented the Morris place last September, around there, eh?'

I nodded, 'What's going on here, Mr Kieran?'

'It's to be a fine house for my sainted sister, God rest her soul. In her memory. I'll rent it out, just by the month, you know. Because I might decide to live in it myself. Haven't quite made up my mind.'

'But I thought this land belonged to the city. That's what they told me when I rented my house.'

He laughed, showing a row of perfect, white teeth. 'Bound to say that, but it doesn't mean a thing. This land is mine. Has been for fifty years. So was the land your house is on, and Mr Barton's there. All of it my land once. Mine and my sister Mary's. This is the last piece left along here, and I'm going to build some house here, you'll see.'

'But the lot's so small, and all rocky.'

'For the moment. Just for the moment. A course we got to pass the percolation test, so the municipality's dumping the fill here for me. It'll all be just fine. Architect's got it all worked out—you'll see. No problem. Amazing what you can do these days to make land fit your plans.'

'But look, the dirt is sliding over into Mr Barton's garden onto his grapevine.'

'We'll clean it up later,' Kieran said without much interest. 'Building things is always messy. Right now we got this work to do. Clean up's the last step.'

He turned away from me and began shuffling back towards the workmen. Remembering my bathrobe and my morning coffee, and the chance that Barton might look out his window and see me, I took off for home.

It was an unusually warm day, and by noon it was hot enough to leave the front door open, so I could hear the kids coming towards the house, fighting and arguing in the distance. Timmy was threatening to tell Mommy on Jackie if Jackie didn't let Timmy ride his ten- speed. The screen door banged, and they came rushing in, leaving muddy footprints on the carpet, each anxious to be the first to get his side of the story across. There was no point in listening, really. As they talked, Jackie's cheeks flushed with indignation, and Timmy hopped from foot to foot in his excitement, dropping clods of mud on the kitchen floor with each hop.

It was perfectly obvious what had happened. Jackie's breath smelled unmistakably of peanut butter and chocolate; he must have stopped on the way home, contrary to standing orders, and bought a candy bar. It was clear from Timmy's manner that he hadn't gotten any, and the oval smudge of fresh mud on his pants' leg was where Jackie had kicked him when he argued for his share of the booty. When the candy was gone, Timmy had tried blackmail, seeing if at least he could barter his knowledge of Jackie's forbidden behaviour for a ride on the coveted ten-speed. The oldest, Mark, was smirking in the background. At thirteen he felt himself beyond such arguments, unless he had started them. The littlest, Robert, was waiting breathlessly to see what I would do.

Knowing what had happened ought to have helped me to know what to do, but it didn't. I usually *did* know what had happened behind my back. That was one thing Marcus had eventually hated about me, even though he had loved it at first. He called me a witch and said that I could see right through him. When that stopped feeling like love to him, it started being very unpleasant indeed.

I can understand that. Knowing what people want to keep secret doesn't give you a clue what to do about it. Should I let Jackie know I knew he had disobeyed my rule about candy between meals? I couldn't enforce it, obviously. Yet telling him I knew would only prove to him that I wasn't serious when I forbade something.

Then, knock on wood, when he was tempted towards something serious like drugs, he'd already have the habit of sneaking, of going against my will. Or did he have it already. . . .

'Oh be quiet all of you, you're giving me a headache! And look, mud all over the rug and kitchen floor. Haven't I told you and told you to take off your shoes before you come screaming in here? Now just sit down and eat your lunch and don't say a word.'

'But he hit me. . . .' 'No he started it. . . .' 'No, he's a tattleface. . . .'

'Well he said. . . .'

'SHUT UP!'

Luckily lunch was clam chowder, and for a few minutes there was no sound but the clinking of spoons, and the crunching of crackers, and the spilling of milk—as it did at least once each meal-time.

When I had mopped up, I asked the boys if they knew what was going on next door. They knew of course. Where curiosity was concerned they took after their mother.

'Old Kieran's going to build a humungous house next door,' Mark told me.

'It seems impossible, there's just rock there. The city won't allow it.'

'Yes, but I heard at school that Kieran can do whatever he wants, Mommy. They say the city is afraid of him because he's so rich and he has so many houses and so much land—all that stuff. So if anybody doesn't like it, they all say it's just too bad on them. Is that true, Mommy? Is it?' Mark was worried. 'I don't think it's fair.'

'*I* think it sucks,' said Robert, not wanting to be left out.

'A new house on that little bit of rock? Totally awesome,' said Timmy, who was always hoping for a friend to move in nearby, a friend to help him gang up on Jackie.

I said, 'Well, what does Mr Barton think? If they build up the land next to him, his garden will be in a hole.'

'The old creep was out there screaming at the workmen when we came home for lunch today,' Mark said. He had always hated Tory Barton.

'The old fart,' said Robert.

We had a brief discussion about language, and the kids rushed off, back to school. In the echoing silence left behind I could hear the municipal trucks and the sound of fill pouring onto the rock, and the new 'lot' being created between my house and Tory's. When I thought of Tory, who always had everything under control, and Kieran, who seemed always to get his way, I felt a chill, and I wondered how it would all come out.

This was my kind of mess, but this time it was happening to one of the 'perfect' people.

There was never any doubt about who killed Kieran. But then, *that* wasn't the point. Tory admitted it, and I myself was a witness.

There had been a party at the house of Dr Mills, an orthodontist whom I knew rather too well (two of the boys were already under his very expensive care). Most of us in the neighbourhood were invited. I put on my dress-up outfit and went over. I didn't intend to stay too long, since Mark was 'babysitting' as usual and I wanted to limit the damage. I went to the party for the same reason I always go to parties: I was hoping I would meet a rich and tender man who could hardly wait to sweep into my life, hire me a housekeeper, and take me away to Hawaii for a long holiday. This fantasy always made me look forward to going out. After half an hour or so, when I realized that once again the dream man hadn't shown up, I tended to drink too much and go home early.

The first person I saw when I got there was Tory Barton, looking a bit pissed, leaning warmly over the cigarette of a young woman I had never seen before. I avoided him and found myself talking to another stranger, a man who turned out to be a very nice person. Maybe I wouldn't have liked him so much if we'd met in other circumstances, but in the din of the party, and after the first two drinks (which I tend to drink very quickly when I arrive in a crowd of people alone), we seemed to get along as if we'd known each other for a long time. Nothing particularly exciting, and he certainly wasn't going to sweep me off my feet and rush me off to Hawaii, but still. . . .

He looked to be in his late forties, with a wrinkled face, as if life had dealt rather harshly with him and he had accepted that. He laughed easily and had a sweet smile which made me smile back no matter what the point and feel happy inside. His name was Rob MacNally and he practised law in town. It sounded boring to me, mostly real estate and business law, but he said he liked it. He saw how people acted when money was at stake. He said they were worse than he thought people would be when he was young, but as he got older he expected a hell of a lot less, so he was more and more often pleasantly surprised when they acted better than he had expected. I liked that. We laughed a lot, and when I apologized for talking too much he looked at me and said he hadn't enjoyed himself this much at a party in a long time.

I didn't believe him. But I liked him for saying so, and more for the way he said it: sort of gentle and relaxed, his eyes looking out of that worn face as if to say that I too had delivered more than he had expected, and that was good enough. He was just easy with himself, and I felt more comfortable with him than I had with anyone—and that includes myself—for a long time.

But it was a party and I knew I had to circulate. So I spent quite a long time talking to Mrs Mills. We compared the 'woes' of a rich orthodontist's wife to the 'joys' of being a single parent. She had a lot more problems than I had, or at least so she said, and I found the idea comforting.

I didn't notice until later than I should have that, as usual, I had drunk too much and that it was getting towards the time the porno movies started on TV, and I had to get home, to be sure the kids weren't watching them.

Tory saw me leaving. 'Hey Sylvia, going so soon? Worried you'll turn into a pumpkin at eleven? Ha, ha.'

It was obvious that he was even more pissed than I, and I edged away from him.

'I noticed, you always leave before the fun. . . . What are you afraid of?'

'I'm walking, I really have to be going, and I left the boys without a babysitter.'

'No problem, no problem. I'll just zip you home in my MG—you've never ridden in it anyway, and now's your chance. Chance of a lifetime.' He smiled at the young woman next to him, and she smiled back.

But I had no intention of going with Tory Barton, particularly when he was so pissed, and I made excuses and hurried out the door before he could catch me and insist. I wondered if everyone in the world thought I left parties early because I was afraid of something, and I didn't like the idea. Still there wasn't much I could do about it. When you marry young and stay with one man for twenty years and think of no one else, you often find yourself acting like a prude. The problem is, the choice usually seems to be between being a prude or letting yourself go completely.

It was a very dark night. The wind was high, off the sea, and the trees shook and groaned and leaned over me as I walked through the blackness. I didn't mind. It wasn't cold, and the fresh air felt good and clean after the fug of the party. There were no sidewalks most of the way, and the streetlights shed barely any light in their unequal struggle with the moist dark night air. Around each was a soft misty halo of light, and I could hear some of them humming like noisy insects hidden in the night air.

Always cautious, I walked against the traffic, and when I saw a car approaching (there weren't many at that time of night, it was past eleven), its headlights dim blurs until it was almost upon me, I walked far onto the shoulder until the car had passed. My sweater and hat were dark, and I knew that I must be practically invisible.

As I turned into our lane, I heard a car coming from behind me, very fast. As it approached, the headlights wavered. Thinking that someone might have had too much, and possibly be tight enough to drive over the middle, I stepped off onto the shoulder and looked back and 'saw' the whole thing. The headlights of the car wavered again, there was a thud, and a screeching of brakes. The car door opened, and by its light I saw that it was Tory Barton's snazzy little MG. We both ran towards the dark patch on the road, he unsteadily, I, fully alert, sobered by my half-mile walk in the wind and by the shock of what had just happened.

'I didn't see him. Nobody could have seen him. He was invisible, just invisible,' Tory was saying in a high, frightened voice. We both came upon the figure at the same time and saw him, lying thrown onto the soft muddy shoulder. It was Kieran, and he was dead.

So that was all there was to it, it appeared. I testified at the inquest; Tory was given a scolding by the coroner, and the city came and took away the fill on the land next door, at Tory's expense.

Yet, even after I got over the shock of what had happened, I found I couldn't stop thinking about it, going round and round, worrying over it. Sometimes I was craven enough to think that if, just for once, I had remembered to get the van looked after, I would have *driven* and been home half an hour earlier and missed the whole thing. Then, at least, I would not have been a witness to death.

But the van was parked at the end of the lane, in front of Tory's, useless that night, and I *had* walked, and I *had* seen it all. If I had had less to drink, would I have seen Kieran as I came walking towards him and told him to walk on the shoulder? If I had taken the ride with Tory, would he have left earlier and so not been at the wrong place at the wrong time?

Pointless thoughts; at the time, the best thing seemed to be to try not to think about it at all. I told myself, over and over—as I had testified at the inquest—that it was no one's fault. Even if Tory hadn't been drinking, he very well might not have seen Kieran. I hadn't seen him. I knew the best thing would be to try to forget about it as soon as possible.

The morning after the accident, when I was walking the dog, I saw the rubber marks on the road, and the fine sparkling crumbs of broken glass. Saw, but did not look at; I did not want to look at the bloodstains on the edge of the road and the depression on the soft shoulder where the body had come to rest. I didn't want those images to go into that place in my mind where all the other sad things collect, the ones that I can't help or do anything about. Things like Marcus not wanting me and the kids, and how my life seems always to be more than I can handle.

After all, whose fault is it if an unloved, unlovable, frail old man, a neighbourhood laughing-stock, and a developer of eyesores, gets run down accidentally late at night? And what was he doing there, anyway, after 11:00, on a Saturday night?

The morning after the inquest was a beautiful one, warm and sunny. I knew I ought to get out and do some gardening, so I put on a pair of gardening jeans, looked for my gardening gloves with no success, then collected what tools I could find and went out into the yard.

But I didn't get much done. Instead I found myself, drawn by the soft warm air and the sunshine, out of my weed-filled yard and over towards Tory Barton's. I moved cautiously around the hedge and lurked behind a tree, checking to be sure he too wasn't out, directing his gardeners, or working himself. But no, the garden was peaceful and silent in the morning light. I approached over the rocks between, now stripped of the loads of fill but still muddy and slippery, and looked down into Tory Barton's little Eden.

The spring blossoms had fallen from the apples and pears and been replaced by clouds of tiny pearly green leaves, the grass was already very lush, and shoots of vegetables showed up in their rows, rising out of the neatly tilled soil. But Tory Barton's garden did not look beautiful to me that morning. It looked rigid, lifeless, and sinister. I was astonished. It was as if you had unexpectedly come too close to a painted backdrop. Scenery once full of splendour was revealed to be coarsely painted smears of colour, meaningless and flat. I backed away and hurried home.

At lunch, the children seemed to sense my mood. They were subdued as they ate. All except Robert, who said suddenly, as he reached for the last of the Sara Lee brownies (I had meant to bake that morning, but somehow had not gotten around to it), 'Mom, why did Mr Barton kill Kieran?'

The question hung in the air, and I shrank back from it, hating it, wishing it unsaid, and feeling, at the same time, the awakening of that stupid curiosity of mine that makes me find out what I would be oh so much better off not knowing.

'It was an accident, Robert,' I said. 'Wipe the crumbs off your mouth please. Not with the tablecloth, for God's sake.'

'What's the difference, Mommy?'

'Oh, be serious,' Timmy said. 'Even babies know what an accident is. Even teeny tiny tots.'

'So then tell him yourself, smartass,' said Jackie.

We had the usual talk about language, and then when the kids went back to school I sat for a long time at the table, finishing off the brownies, looking out the window, and smoking, thinking about everything. My thoughts went around and around and I felt worse and worse, until I knew I couldn't stand to let things stay the way they were.

Then the doorbell rang, and it was Rob MacNally. He had been at the inquest the day before, sitting among the spectators, in the back row, watching everything. It had surprised me to see him there, surprised me even more that seeing him made me feel happy, and made the whole experience more bearable for me.

He had come up to me afterwards and we had talked a bit, but I had been in a hurry to get back before the kids came home for lunch and hadn't been able to stay. Although we didn't talk long, I had felt his sympathy, felt that he knew how hard I found the whole thing. So that, when he said he might come by to talk about it with me when I wasn't so rushed, I hadn't made the kind of excuses I usually do. I'd just looked at him and said, 'Yes, thank you, I'd like that.' Then he'd smiled without replying, and I thought, oh dear, I probably fouled it up again by being too pushy when he was just being polite. But now, here he was, and I would have been more glad to see him if I hadn't been still in my grimy jeans, with soil under my fingernails, and no brownies left to offer him.

But we had a cup of tea together, before the kids got back, and we talked about the inquest, and about old Kieran.

'He had everything the way he wanted in this city, you know,' MacNally said. 'It's a pretty corrupt place; most of the aldermen are in real estate or are lawyers heavily dependent upon it. They won't cross a man like Kieran.'

'I know. It doesn't seem right, but somehow I can't believe God knocked him off because he contributed to the corruption around here.'

MacNally smiled. 'I know what you mean. His death does seem just a tad too neat.'

I felt very comfortable with MacNally. Maybe that's why I could tell him about what was worrying me without feeling foolish. 'That's just it. It's all so neat . . . too neat. I can't stop worrying about it. I knew Kieran was wrecking Tory Barton's garden. It's awful of me, but I think, maybe Tory . . . but I know that can't be right. I was there that night, and it was so dark you couldn't see your hand in front of your face. There was no way in God's green earth that Tory Barton could have known that Kieran would walk down the street at that time, and there was no way, even in the last minute before the accident, that Barton could have seen that he was about to hit him.'

'That makes sense.'

'So why do I keep worrying about it? It's not my fault, what happened. It's not my responsibility.'

'Well, what do you think?'

'I wish I knew. Something about it is really bothering me. More than just the sad death of an old man, I mean.' I found myself boasting a little. 'I've always been good at figuring things out, putting the pieces together, you know? And somehow these pieces don't fit.'

MacNally looked thoughtful. 'Maybe you don't have all the pieces, maybe that's the problem.'

'My husband always said that about me,' I said, feeling my face go hot as I wondered if MacNally was laughing at me. 'He used to say, "You can't manage what's on your own plate; you shouldn't keep wanting to explain what's on other people's."'

'He sounds like kind of a jerk to me,' MacNally said mildly.

'No, not at all,' I said. 'He is actually a very fine man. Very highly respected in External. Everyone says so. It's amazing how fast he's moved up. I just wasn't the right wife for him.'

'Or he wasn't the right husband for you.' MacNally looked around, noticing the shabbiness of the house, and the fact that there really wasn't quite enough furniture. 'For a guy in External he doesn't seem to have looked after you as well as he might.'

'That's what Tory Barton said. Do you think so too?' For some reason I felt I had to defend Marcus. It made it all worse somehow, if he too was at fault. 'Why should he, if he doesn't want to? It's up to him, isn't it?'

'It's not just a measure of love,' MacNally said. 'It's also a measure of responsibility. But anyway, this isn't my business. I'm sorry if I seem to be pushing in.' He smiled. 'Just the lawyer's habit, I guess, seeing everything in an adversarial light, with winners and losers. Please excuse me.'

'Oh no, that's all right. But maybe you're right about Kieran. Maybe

I don't have all the pieces.'

'I'm pretty sure you don't,' MacNally said. He was looking out the window as he spoke, not at me.

'Maybe I'll try to find a few more.'

'I think you should. I think that would be a good idea. And will you let me know what you find out?'

'Do you want me to? You really don't think it's silly?'

'Not at all. I think it's eminently sensible.'

'I'll do my best then.'

He looked right at me this time not smiling. 'Yes, please do. Let's keep in touch.'

'Sorry you're so upset.' Tory's face was all concern. He grasped my arm and drew me solicitously into the top level of his living room. There were big soft chairs and a sofa full of cushions positioned around the window. There was also a low glass table with a gold cigarette case, a big crystal bowl of cashews, and a silver wine bucket, sweating, with a bottle of French wine in it. Syrupy music with a heavy beat was playing, coming out of very large speakers.

'I'm upset too; I think it would do us both good to talk it over,' he said.

I nodded, and tried to suppress my nervousness. How could I have been so stupid, I thought. Of course he would think my request to 'talk over what had happened' meant I wanted him to make love to me. I ought to be used to awkward situations like this, but I'm not.

I sat down in a chair and ate some cashews. Luckily there wasn't any problem making conversation with Tory Barton.

He lounged back into the sofa. 'I wake up in the night and feel the thud and see it all pass before my eyes,' he said. 'Poor old man. I bet he didn't even know what hit him.'

'What I can't understand is,' I said, through the cashews, while he gracefully poured me a glass of wine, 'what the old man was doing out at that time of night.'

'I can't understand it either,' said Tory. 'It's a total mystery to me. I just never would have expected it, not in a million years. A person would think that if he wanted to go down there to see how his building site was coming he would go in the daytime. Or drive his car, or at least be walking around with a flashlight, for God's sake!' His voice rose.

The very words 'building site' seemed to cause his face to redden.

'Did you see it? Did you see what he was doing?'

'Yes, I—'

'What he was doing was, it was inexcusable! The fill was falling over onto my grapevine and wrecking it! And cutting off the view of my garden!'

'I can't understand how the city—'

'I called our alderwoman. I said to her, "I'm a taxpayer and something has to be done. Has to. This is a travesty! Doesn't a man have the right to enjoy his property in peace? Isn't your home still your castle, even in this day and age? But there's more to it than that," I said to her. "Do you know that I paid over twenty thousand dollars extra for the view rights? Do you know that? I'll fight this," I told her, "and I can afford to. I'll get an injunction. But that the city should be a party to it! It's unconscionable. Why do you do his bidding? The city—at his beck and call! Make no mistake about it"—I told her quite, quite clearly, believe me—"make no mistake about it. I'll sue the pants off him, and I'll sue the pants off the city."'

'And what did she say?'

'Oh, she was upset. Mind you, aldermen don't have as much say as they used to; it's all planners nowadays. But she said she'd get right on it. Yes, I have to give her credit for that, at least. She called the municipality and this Mr MacDonald came around and talked to me personally. But the long and the short of it was that they were going to go on loading up the fill until the damn site passed the percolation tests.'

'And so, what did you do?'

He had forgotten me, forgotten to offer me another drink, a cigarette, forgotten to look meaningfully into my eyes.

'I have my contacts, you know. I got a look at the plans for the house. And I couldn't believe my eyes.'

'What do you mean?'

Tory stood up and began walking around the room. 'A monstrosity!' he cried out, waving his arm, indicating a large, shapeless something or other. 'The house was an unbelievable abortion. A concrete bunker, a huge block of a thing which would shut out my view, shut out the sun from the entire east side of my garden. You know they had already just about killed my grapevine. I honestly thought that was the worst thing I had to face. But when I saw those plans I couldn't believe it. I called MacNally, my lawyer, as soon as I got home.'

'What did he say?'

'What's that got to do with it? You don't ask your lawyer what to do. You *tell* him what to do, and if he won't do it, you get another one. I've had lots of lawyers and I know how to deal with them. That's what I was trying to explain to you when you told me about your divorce. You have to remember that lawyers are just hired help. I simply gave MacNally the outline of the case myself, and told him we had to get on to it at once.'

At the sound of MacNally's name my heart made a sudden and surprising bang inside my chest. If he were involved why hadn't he said anything? If he were Tory Barton's lawyer it would explain why he was at the inquest. What else did it explain? I didn't have time to work it out, Tory Barton was in full flight.

'Of course, I had to warn him about running up costs. Lawyers think nothing of charging you every time they sneeze; you have to keep control. So naturally, I warned him I had no intention of paying for his ignorance. If he didn't know the law on this kind of thing I'd find someone who did, I told him straight out.'

I felt suddenly that I was fed to the teeth with Tory Barton's obsession with money. Everything seemed to come down to that in the end. I guess my expression showed my disgust, because he became a bit defensive.

'Well, these lawyers, they'll charge you for their own research if you're not careful. After all, what other profession makes you pay when they have to look up information they should have learned in school or kept up on? Anyway, I told him, if he didn't know the law on this I'd find someone else who did. But, not to worry, he knows me and there was no problem. After all, we're old friends, MacNally and me. He knows how I think. Why a couple of times he's told me I ought to have been a lawyer myself. I've got the legal mind, you see. But then. . . .'

His voice sank, the pride went out of it, he sounded almost disappointed as he went on, '. . . for once, luck was on my side. Oh, I don't mean that the way it sounds. God knows, I wouldn't wish what happened on anybody. But there's no point in being a hypocrite . . . and I have to admit, that, at least . . . about the garden. . . .'

In the awkward pause that followed, I tried to lead the conversation back to the night of the accident. I tried to get a clear description of what happened. But Tory wandered off, first talking about his garden, obsessively, then trying again to see if I would confess that I was lonely and wanted his comforting embrace.

'Oh no, not lonely, not at all,' I said with as much conviction as I could. 'What with the kids . . . and the housework. . . .'

I thought 'housework' would be a good word. I never knew a man who didn't find the very word off-putting. It's guaranteed to break up the kind of steamy atmosphere he was trying to create by talking about our loneliness, our need for comfort, and by pouring on the wine. I recognized the spacey feeling I get when I have drunk a little too much, and I noticed Tory's words were moving by in a kind of smooth rhythm, making a lot more sense than they should have, without really meaning anything. He was talking now about his loneliness, his need for someone understanding, about how two people. . . .

I got up and began looking for my purse.

'But why are you leaving? It's so nice, talking to you like this, I thought maybe we could. . . .' He came up to me and took my hand between his and stroked it gently. He was standing very close to me, looking into my eyes. The smell of his aftershave was overpowering.

I was angry and frightened. I pulled my hand out from his, stepped backward, and stumbled against the coffee table. He grabbed me and pulled me close, and I tensed at his touch. He didn't notice and I had to wrench free. His passionate expression changed to anger.

'What are you playing at anyway? *I* didn't ask you to come here, you know. God, how I hate women who tease.'

'But . . . I just . . . a talk between friends . . . awfully upset about Kieran. . . .' I hurried towards the door with Tory right at my heels, talking angrily, his face red.

'I suppose you won't be happy unless you have the whole game: expensive restaurants, presents, flowers. . . . I thought we were both too old and too sensible for those silly games. And frankly,' he went on, his voice spiteful, 'you're lucky to get the chance. God, why do all women have to dance around beforehand. Jesus, it really pisses me off. We both know. . . .'

By then I was at the door, and I opened it gratefully. 'No, I'm sorry, Tory. Really. I'm sorry I gave you the wrong impression.' Hating myself for apologizing to him, I hurried away, leaving him standing angrily in the doorway.

I turned back to look at him, and to wave apologetically, despite myself. He did not wave back. His face was dark red and his expression was spiteful and vindictive.

The kids were late coming home from school that day, and I was glad. I still wasn't over what had happened at Tory's house. Had I really led him on? Was it 'asking for it' even to suggest to a neighbour that you were worried over the death of someone and needed to talk about it? It had seemed like a harmless way to get more of the 'pieces' Rob MacNally and I had discussed.

But I had been kidding myself and I should have known better. The stupid scene was all my fault. Probably it could have been handled properly—but it was too late for that now.

Only the two youngest, Timmy and Robert, were due back that afternoon. The other two had soccer practice. When they came in, Timmy was bleeding from a long cut on his shinbone. I bandaged it, worrying about whether I ought to take him to Emergency and get it stitched up. I never know for sure which cuts need stitches and which don't. But the thought of waiting in Emergency for an hour or two while the other two kids came back to an empty house decided me to take the chance this one would be okay.

'What happened?' I asked, when the tears were dry, the comforting done, and the bandage securely in place. There was a long silence. Robert looked stricken. 'I won't scold you, Robert,' I said. 'I'm sure it was an accident.'

'Oh it was, Mommy, it was,' he said eagerly, running up to me and butting his little head in my lap, where I knelt, gathering up Band-aid wrappers from the bathroom floor. 'I didn't mean to do it; it was an accident. Truly. Cross my heart and hope to die, stick a needle in my eye.'

I shuddered at the image. 'Don't say that.' I took him in my arms and his tears soaked into my shirt

'I didn't mean to knock him off his bike and he fell in front of a car and almost got killed like Mr Kieran and it really was an accident. You said, Mommy. Like that. But I don't get it. How come, if Timmy got out of the way and got his bike out of the way, how come Mr Kieran didn't?'

I sat down in the wicker chair in the bathroom, feeling very weak, suddenly, and seeing, in that instant, the headlights of Tory's car wavering the instant before the impact, as if the car had turned towards the road edge. I held Robert tightly in my lap with one arm and reached out and drew Timmy close with the other. With the boys held close, I listened to all the details of the boys' near accident.

'Let's forget all these horrible things.' I hugged the boys. 'But what *I* don't understand,' I said, half to myself, 'is what Mr Kieran was *doing* that night.'

'Oh, Mommy. I'm surprised at you,' crowed Timmy, mimicking my favourite phrase of reproach. 'You're supposed to know everything and be a witch like Daddy said.'

'Yes Mommy, I'm surprised at you too,' Robert said happily. 'Cause *we* know all about it.'

'I give up,' I said.

'Mr Kieran went every night, exactly at eleven, to the place where they were putting the dirt, Mommy,' Robert told me.

'Yes, and he stayed for half an hour *precisely*,' Timmy added, using Jack Webster's voice.

'How do you guys know that?' I wanted to know. 'You're supposed to be asleep at 11:00.' But it was obvious. They must be sneaking out of their room at night to watch the smelt fishermen. I had noticed wet running shoes the last few mornings and sand on the kitchen floor when I swept up after breakfast.

The boys gave each other meaningful looks. Robert said, 'It was Mark's idea. But once we saw that old Kieran out in the middle of the night, we kind of spied on him. It was neat; Mark said you could set a watch by the old bugger.'

Ignoring Robert's language I said, 'But why? What did he do there?'

'He just sat on the big rock, there, you know, and sort of talked to himself,' Timmy said.

'You didn't happen to hear what he said?'

But I had already realized what Kieran was doing there. I understood why he came, in the night, to sit alone and look at his new building site that meant so much to him. He was dreaming of the fitting tribute he would build for his sister, Mary.

I had heard people talking about his devotion to her, or maybe his obsession would be a better way of putting it. He came to sit there and commune with Mary, and to discuss the house with her. Promising that nothing and no one would stop the project which would store up glory in heaven for her, and give him honour in her eyes.

I had a talk with the boys about their sneaking out at night, and later, I knew, I would have to ground Mark who, it appeared, was the ringleader. Probably have to ground all of them. They knew they were forbidden to go out at night, and most especially forbidden to go near the water. How do you get kids to obey? I wish I knew.

Finally I asked the question whose answer I feared. I asked it of Mark that night, just before the goodnight kiss. 'Mark,' I said hesitantly, 'do you think Mr Barton knew about Kieran coming down here every night?'

I waited for the answer. Mark took after me. He had the habit of making leaps from small details to the explanation of what had happened, and he, too, usually turned out to be right. It was a quality which his father had never liked in him; Marcus would shout at him and call him a know-it-all. That was one of the reasons I didn't miss Marcus as much as I might have.

'Yes, Mommy,' said Mark. He was drowsy. The long scolding, the tears, the hot bath, and now the goodnight kiss, warm and relaxing. He was half asleep. 'I've been worrying about it anyway, after the accident. Mr Barton used to stand in his kitchen window and watch Mr Kieran sitting there. I saw it, Mommy. Just before eleven, just before old Kieran came along, Mr Barton would turn off his kitchen lights. But you could still see him, if you knew he was there, sort of a faint shadow. And he'd stand there, in the dark, and look, and watch old Kieran. And old Kieran would sit on that big rock, and smoke that stinky pipe, and talk to himself out loud. Sometimes he'd look up at the house where Barton was standing but I don't think he could see him. *I* wouldn't have known Mr Barton was there if I hadn't seen him turn off his lights so he could look out into the dark. Anyway, Kieran sat under the streetlight at the end of the road; it kind of shines on that rock, you know? He was easy to see. They were in a fight, it seemed like, sort of looking at each other and figuring out their plans. Something like a game. But not knowing the other knew he was there, you know what I mean?'

His voice was getting fainter. 'The whole thing made me feel yucky. They were both real losers, Mommy. I wish somebody else besides Mr Barton had that awesome garden. . . .'

So Tory had lied. He knew Kieran came down to his plot of land at the end of the lane every night. He knew then. And if he watched as Mark described he must know everything about it. Where on the road Kieran walked, what time he arrived, what time he left—everything.

Was Tory Barton clever enough, and mean enough . . . or was the word, evil? Was Tory Barton clever enough and evil enough to plan to kill a helpless old man and then to carry through the plan in such risky circumstances?

And if it were true, what I feared, what was my part in it? Was I partly at fault? I realized I had been frightened all along that somehow

I was part of the bad thing that had happened.

I struggled with the idea of Tory doing this thing; and I found I couldn't believe it. He was one of the 'perfect' people, one of those people who are always in control, with his neat, orderly, elegant house, and his neat, orderly, elegant garden. How could such a man take such a risk: trusting in his position in the community to escape blame, and using a neighbour as a witness, to run down a frail old man?

I didn't want to think about my part in this little play.

Had Tory Barton been sizing me up all along? Casting me for a part in his terrible drama? I remembered his remark at the party about my 'turning into a pumpkin at eleven'. Because he knew that, he might have been able to time the accident. If I had agreed to accept a ride with him, he could have delayed our departure until the time was right. But he hadn't worried. He had known that because I always left before the 11:00 porno movies, he could count on my being on that long stretch of the road at the right time one way or the other. And, remembering his surprise and angry face when I ran from his house that last time it was easy to believe he had thought I was completely foolish and controllable until that moment.

The plan itself—that was easier to deal with. It was hard to escape the idea that there was no simpler way to kill someone in Canada right now and get away with it. Pretend to be a bit drunk, pretend it was an accident. Even if you were tried and sentenced—and that hadn't happened to Tory; the police hadn't pressed charges—if you were rich and had good lawyers you could keep appealing and eventually get off with a fine. But the most likely outcome was what had happened to Tory—nothing. He had only to pick a night of a neighbourhood party and find a fool for a witness. He had succeeded in doing both.

But then, I told myself, I was making something from nothing, blowing it all up out of proportion. After all, Tory himself had told me that he could stop Kieran's building legally; and that he had been going to do it.

But he had lied when he said he didn't know what Kieran was doing, walking down the lane that night. Lied that he didn't expect to see him. Maybe there was another lie in the story about his conversation with his lawyer.

I remembered, suddenly, the way MacNally had looked when we had discussed the accident. I knew now that he had known more than he had been able to say. Why had he come to see me the day after the inquest and encouraged me to find the 'missing pieces'? He surely hadn't been drawn by my beauty.

No, even in my misery I knew that wasn't fair. MacNally liked me, and had been concerned about me. It was a surprise to me to realize that I was sure of that; sure that the friendship we felt for each other didn't have something nasty lurking behind it too. But even so, even with that understood, I realized for the first time that MacNally had some other purpose as well. Lawyers had their professional ethics; there were things about their clients they couldn't say. But something must have happened to make him suspicious. What if MacNally thought Tory had a motive, but knew he couldn't talk about it unless he was sure enough of the other things—that Tory *knew* Kieran would be down there, and when he would be down there?

I felt sick inside. My head ached, and I wanted to escape into some fresh air, but the pressure was inside me. It looked as if I would have to bear up under it until I knew the whole story. I reached for the phone to call MacNally and tell him I had got hold of some pieces, the picture was taking shape, and he had better come over and see if, now, any of *his* pieces looked like they belonged in the puzzle.

'I came to the inquest because I had reason to be worried about that accident,' Rob MacNally told me.

We were sitting at the kitchen table the next morning. The kids were gone, the house was quiet and peaceful, with the sounds of the waves on the rocks coming in quietly through the open window. I felt sickish and dragged out. I had not slept the night before, even when Rob said he would come over first thing next morning. Hearing what I had learned he had promised to tell me everything he knew, explaining that he had not wanted to talk about it before because of lawyer-client privilege. Now, he said, things had gone beyond that. We agreed we had to thrash the whole thing out right away. The more I talked to Rob MacNally, the more I liked him; and it ought to have been comforting to have him on my side. But when I remembered how I stood there and watched as the car struck the old man I felt so bad that it seemed as if nothing could help.

Still, in the morning, after several cups of coffee, I had my wits about me a little more than I had the night before, and I was starting to get used to what then had seemed unthinkable. 'And the inquest put your mind at rest, did it?' I asked Rob.

'Yes, at first. Just as you said yourself, there seemed no way that Tory could be criminally involved. My problem was that knowing him, as I do, and knowing how he felt about that old man and his house, I couldn't stop worrying about it.'

I understood that. 'He consulted you about the house, I know. But he told me he was going to sue, so I thought that side of things was all under control. He said there was no problem.'

I noticed the rims of Rob's ears go pink as I spoke. 'Well, he lied. I told him as I would tell you, or anybody that asked me, that it was impossible in this city to succeed in stopping a man like Kieran from building a house on his own property—"right to enjoyment of the view" clauses or easements notwithstanding. That's a reality around here, and a man as experienced as Tory Barton would know that as well as you or I would.'

'But if he still wanted to fight, why would you object?'

'You don't take on a case when you haven't a chance of winning. It's against legal ethics. Sometimes we lawyers try to talk a client out of something because we know the chances of success are slight, and we want to be sure the client is really keen enough to go on to the finish. I've had conversations like that with Tory and with plenty of other clients. I make it a principle never to let a client sue on principle. But if, after they calm down, they still want to sue, and there's any possibility of winning, and they know that it's going to cost, then well, of course, I'll give it my best shot.

'But when it's absolutely hopeless I say so. I have to. And I have to refuse the case. That's how I do business. Tory simply had to accept it when I explained to him that this was not a case he could win, and this was a case I was not prepared to fight for him.'

He smiled. 'You know Tory. Do you think he would have paid my fees after I spent time and money fighting a case we were bound to lose?'

'What did he say? Did he accept it, that he couldn't take Kieran to court?'

'Not at first,' Rob said. 'But we went at it a bit, and eventually he seemed to get the idea.'

'How did he take it?'

'Just as you'd expect. He told me he'd get a lawyer who had more balls, that he'd fly down to Vancouver to find the best, and that obviously I was only good for the small-town stuff.'

I felt hurt for Rob. I could accept Tory's meanness more easily when it was directed at me than when it was directed at Rob. I could feel myself flushing.

'Don't let it get to you,' Rob said gently. 'People like Tory Barton always know where to stick the knife. They specialize in going after what they sense are your weak points. But Tory tended to miss the mark with me. A remark like that might have hurt me when I was younger, but believe me, I've heard worse. It just rolls right off me now. No, *that's* not what's got me upset. It was worrying about what had really happened with that accident.'

We talked a while longer, and then Rob called the police, right from the kitchen phone. He said he knew a few people there, and it would be easier for him. I sat at the kitchen table, smoking, watching him, but only listening from time to time. I was thinking about Tory Barton, and what kind of man he was, and what he had done. I was finally accepting the truth about it; and it wasn't easy. From the bits of conversation I did take in, I could tell that Rob was getting his point across. The police would reopen the matter of Kieran's death.

And I was responsible for that. I started to use the word 'fault', to think 'that's my fault' but I stopped myself. When I looked back on the events since the coroner's inquest I was surprised to realize that I was not sorry about what had happened. I knew, and somehow it made me feel good knowing it, that I could not have done anything else than what I had done and that it had been the right thing to do. The fact that Rob MacNally felt the same way was a help, but it wasn't the whole story.

Now that Tory Barton has gone, the garden, under its new owners, is slowly growing wilder and more ordinary. I can enjoy looking at it to my heart's content. Even though it has lost some of its strange seductive magic, I find it, if possible, even more beautiful. I take a little responsibility for that, for the garden's new beauty. Maybe that's why living here now, in the big old house, with the kids and the dog doesn't seem as hard as it used to.

ANDRÉ MAJOR · b. 1942

A Questionable Case

I

It was the slack time of the afternoon and he was sitting alone outside a café on Rue Saint-Denis, drinking the syrupy coffee that you could take for espresso if you've never set foot in Italy. He crumpled the empty Philip Morris package and took another from the pocket of the tweed jacket folded over the back of the chair beside him. He lit a cigarette, slipped a five-dollar bill with the cheque under the Cinzano ashtray, and stood up, the jacket over his shoulders like a cape. Sweat made his shirt stick to his chest.

He walked up Saint-Denis as far as Sherbrooke, his shoulders slumping. When he saw his reflection in the window of a vegetarian restaurant, he straightened up, but a moment later he was stooped again. Once inside the lobby of an old apartment building that had been freshly renovated, he caught his breath and pressed one of the thirteen fake ivory buttons. A woman's voice asked who it was; he answered curtly, 'It's me,' and pushed open the door as soon as the buzzer pierced his ears.

She had left the door ajar. He closed it behind him, struck by an unusual odour of river sludge, a swampy stench. Then he saw her in the doorway of the bathroom, covered from head to foot in what appeared to be a uniform of mud, her hair knotted on top of her head. 'What are you doing?' he asked, his arms hanging uselessly at his sides. She tried to speak, but the words were distorted by her dried mask, across which spread a network of cracks. 'Another one of her fads,' he said, as if addressing some third party. And he placed his jacket on the arm of a white rattan chair while looking around for an ashtray. Finally he had to stub out his butt in a pot where a scraggy flowerless stem with a couple of leaves was subsisting. 'Will you be long?' he asked. She let out a raucous noise that infuriated him. He took his jacket and left. Outside it was still stifling, without a hint of a breeze. He waved down a taxi heading east and asked the driver to take him to the corner of Boulevard Saint-Joseph and Avenue de Parc. There he paid and got out, his jacket over his arm. He hesitated for a moment in front of a copper plaque riveted decades before into the grey stone of the building whose door he finally pushed open, noticing on the left the dermatologist's waiting room, and quickly walked up the dark staircase. He stopped in front of the oak door with a minuscule yellowed rectangle where he made out the name of the tenant. At that moment the door of the apartment beside opened and an old man appeared, looking anxious.

'No answer,' he said.

'That's odd, because there was a big racket going on in there. I thought Monsieur Gadbois must be moving,' added the old man, whose trousers floated around his waist, held up by narrow suspenders.

'I just got here,' he answered, 'I didn't hear anything.'

'Did you buzz?'

'Did I buzz?' he said, hesitantly. 'I think so.'

'Because if you don't buzz, M. Gadbois won't answer.'

'Oh.'

They fell silent, and the old man pressed his ear against the door. 'I can't hear anything now. It's strange. A while ago, like I said, there was a lot of noise. Knock and see, you never know . . .'

But they heard footsteps coming faster and faster up the stairs. Two men soon emerged from the shadows. The taller, with a strong scent of aftershave, passed between them and tried the door, which opened easily. 'You,' he said to his friend, who was wearing a straw hat that was too tight, and breathing with difficulty, 'stay with these two.' Then they heard him dial the phone and speak in a staccato voice, but too low to grasp anything. Sweat was running down his armpits, and the wool of his jacket irritated his skin. The assistant had planted himself in front of the door, where he could watch what was going on in the apartment. Suddenly the silence was broken by a groan, which modulated into low moaning. Awkwardly he extracted a cigarette from his package, offered it to the assistant who waved it away, then to the old man who took it because he was probably incapable of refusing anything, and lit another with trembling hands. Time stood still; the old man kept sighing apprehensively, repeating, 'I knew it, I knew there was something strange going on . . . ' He'd stuck the cigarette behind his ear.

A siren wailed plaintively, then footsteps echoed downstairs in the lobby. Two stretcher-bearers went by without seeing them. The assistant opened the door wide. This time things moved quickly: the stretcher-bearers left without his seeing anything, the policeman having positioned himself between him and them. As soon as they had disappeared into the darkness, the policeman relit the cigar he'd been absent-mindedly chewing on. 'All right, you two, what do you have to say?' he asked without looking at either of them, apparently fascinated by what he'd seen in the apartment. 'I heard a racket at one point . . . ' said the old man.

'When?' cut in the policeman.

'Oh I don't know, an hour ago, maybe a little longer. . .'

'And you, young fellow, what were you doing here?'

'I came to have a word with the boss, we had a meeting.'

'You work for that rag of a paper too?'

'Well . . . '

'Exactly what did you hear?'

'Nothing, I just got here when . . . '

'I wasn't asking you,' the policeman broke in, looking at the end of his cigar, which had gone out.

'Hard to say. I was just listening to the baseball game when all of a sudden it sounded like someone was moving furniture, like something falling.'

'Voices?'

'Couldn't say so, no. Monsieur Gadbois lives alone. I've never heard anything except the radio or the TV.'

'You weren't tempted to go and see what was happening?'

'No sir. I don't stick my nose in my neighbours' business.'

'You can go back to your baseball, Monsieur——?'

'Crépeau. Ed Crépeau. Keep me posted. After all, he's been my neighbour for almost ten years.'

'You can count on it.'

The old man slipped away, visibly disappointed to return to his dull everyday life.

'You're coming with me,' said the policeman, entering the apartment. 'And don't touch anything.'

'You're acting as if Gadbois was dead.'

'He could easily die on the way.'

'What happened?'

'What did you have against him?' cut in the policeman, scratching his neck where a large vein pulsed.

'Frankly, we had an argument yesterday, and I wanted to clear the air.'

'At his place? Why not at the office?'

'Listen . . . '

'I'm listening, buddy, but if your boss dies, anything you say can backfire on you.'

At that moment he realized the assistant had disappeared. 'If I'd been mixed up in this, you certainly wouldn't have found me here at his door, waiting for you.'

'Let me see your papers.'

He handed him a wallet as damp as his palms.

Sitting on the arm of the chair, the policeman examined the papers and made notes in a small black book. Everything about him was out of proportion—his hands, his ears, his feet. Although of medium size, he was endowed with over-developed extremities. He had a long broken nose and breathed noisily. 'Getting back to that argument,' he said, finally, handing over the wallet, 'what happened?'

'An article hit him where it hurt, and he fired me.'

'But you weren't new at the paper. . . . And you came to see him so you could beg him to take you back, is that it?'

'If you like.'

'You're not in the union?'

'I never wanted to be.'

'And in your opinion, if you could have seen him in private, you'd have worked it out, he'd have had you back at work tomorrow morning?'

'How should I know?' he said in an irritated tone.

The policeman kept running a knobby hand over his knee, as if that soothed him, while staring fixedly at the lamp upset in the middle of the room and the white leather divan that had clearly been moved. 'He'd have taken you back?' the policeman asked again, as if he couldn't remember the other's answer.

'Probably.'

'What makes you think so?'

'He's a little quick-tempered, but I've been there ten years and that counts with him.'

'What department?'

'Entertainment.'

'The private lives of the stars. Who's screwing who, and all that?'

'Why not?'

The policeman sighed as he stood up. 'You're still at the same address?'

'Yes.'

'Don't go too far away. We may need to talk to you—seriously.'

The other nodded and left the apartment after vainly looking for some place to put his butt. He stamped it out on the landing and went down, his jacket over his arm.

It was just as stifling as before. He passed some Hassids, in their black hats and coats, apparently oblivious to this oppressive late afternoon. The traffic was heavy, punctuated with blasts from car horns. He lit a cigarette while waiting for a telephone booth in which a fat woman was having trouble with change. In the end she extricated herself with her load of parcels. She muttered something in Greek, and he shrugged his shoulders. She must have broken the phone; nothing worked. He headed east as far as boulevard Saint-Laurent, where finally, in the lobby of a restaurant advertising foods from around the world, he found a phone in working order. But there was no answer at the number he dialled, and he swore as he hung up.

II

He went down the few steps that led to a bottle-green basement door, took out a key that he put back in his pocket after a few moments' hesitation, and pressed the button once, then twice again, very quickly. She opened the door sullenly. He tried to smile at her, but she asked abruptly, 'Did you forget something?'

'No, nothing. But I'm in trouble, Ghyslaine. No joke.'

She stood back to let him into an ill-lit room littered with dirty dishes and cheap magazines. Everything seemed to have been lying around for days. He didn't dare to sit down, watching her stuff herself straight from the peanut butter jar, more naked in her out-dated baby dolls than if she'd worn nothing at all. The heat made her short red hair curl.

'I was going to bed,' she said morosely. 'I've been up since six this morning.'

'Listen, Ghyslaine, I'm going to ask you to do one more thing for me. It's nothing for you, but for me it's very important. If anyone asks you if I was here this afternoon, around two, two-thirty, say yes.'

'I wasn't even here! How can you expect me to say something like that?'

'You can say you called me from the restaurant.'

'Why should I say that?'

He sighed as if she was asking too much, and took out his cigarettes, which he examined at length until she renewed her attack:

'I've got a right to know why.'

'What difference does it make?'

'I don't want to get mixed up in your lies. Get your actress to do it.'

'We're finished.'

'Already?' she asked in mock surprise.

He had lowered his eyes, as if still in shock. 'It's not true,' she went on. 'You left me here to go and live with her—a lot of good it did you. Because let me tell you, I'm not going to mend your broken heart. Oh no.'

'Listen, Ghyslaine . . . '

'No, don't start again, I know your story by heart. We're not from the same world—I understood that a long time ago. And I don't want to be your stand-in ever again, is that clear?'

'Can I stay here tonight?'

'I'd rather you didn't.'

'All right. I'll go, but can I count on you about the phone call?'

She was silent, gnawing on a biscuit, and he could see her leg swinging under the table. 'If you won't do it, I won't hold it against you. I've been a bastard often enough....' Her leg swung even more quickly. 'Okay!' she cried, 'but get out of here, now—and stay out!' He took his leave, looking pathetic, and moved heavily toward the door. Suddenly she stood up and, as if in spite of herself, asked: 'What's going on?'

'Serious trouble, that's all I can say.'

'Worse than the other time?'

'Worse than ever,' he laughed self-consciously.

She tore his jacket from his arm and threw it onto the chair. 'You can stay here tonight, but don't talk about her, all right?'

'It's over, I told you.'

'What does that mean with you, "over"?'

She didn't even wait for the answer, but poured a large glass of milk and drank it in one long gulp. 'I'm taking a shower and going to bed.' As soon as he heard the water running in the bathroom, he dialled a number and said quickly: 'Yes, it's me . . . I'm sorry about this afternoon, but I was nervous. Gadbois gave me the sack . . . ' He was silent for a moment, then his voice betrayed irritation. 'What? You knew that already? Speak more clearly. There's someone there? Okay, all right. I'll meet you around midnight, in front of the theatre.' Sweating profusely, he unbuttoned his shirt and took it off, along with his trousers, shoes, and damp socks. He drew the flowered curtain aside and joined her under the shower. She went on soaping herself vigorously. When he tried to caress her, she pushed him away and got out of the tub. He stayed under the water for a moment, rubbed himself down quickly, and got out too, aroused. He dried himself, then went to the cramped room where she was already lying down, apparently asleep. But he hesitated to go in, as if fascinated by the floury whiteness of her body. He jumped: a heavy rain was starting. Freshness penetrated between the half-closed shutters. Moving stealthily, as if to surprise her, he knelt at the foot of the bed. She didn't move, even when he began licking the sole of her foot, then each toe, at length, without managing to extract the slightest sigh of encouragement. His tongue slowly moved up to the goosepimpled thigh. She had spread her legs and drawn one knee up to her stomach, offering him not only her open sex but the dark orifice of finely striated flesh into which he sank his tongue several times before hearing a groan from deep in her belly. Then, squeezing her clitoris between his lips, he ejaculated. She had clutched his hair to hold him against her until the final tremors of her flesh subsided. But she hadn't opened her mouth.

He got up and looked at the clock on the bedside table. She curled herself around the pillow. He left the room and dressed in silence. No doubt she'd fallen asleep. When he called her, she didn't answer.

III

There was no one else in front of the theatre where he'd been pacing back and forth for almost an hour, a newspaper under his arm. 'What's she doing?' he asked out loud, not realizing that a car had pulled up along the sidewalk, its headlights off, close by him. As he turned, hearing a door slam, he found himself facing the policeman from that afternoon, this time chewing on a new cigar. 'Well, young fellow, you gave me a good run.'

'Me?'

'I've got an update, and it's not good for you.'

He took the time to light his cigar, take a drag, and blow it absent-mindedly in his face. 'Your boss just died,' he said. The other laughed nervously. 'You're kidding.'

'Not at all.'

'Do you expect me to cry?'

'I don't expect anything. I could arrest you right now as an important witness, but I always make it a rule to give a guy a chance.'

He had spaghetti sauce in the corner of his mouth. 'Go ahead and arrest me—you already know everything I can tell you.'

'Still, it's strange you haven't thought about it since this afternoon. You could have remembered certain things—like what you were doing in the middle of the afternoon. Around two o'clock, let's say.'

'I was at a friend's place, on Rue Wolfe—1623 Wolfe.'

'Let's say you were there at two. But after that, at three, three-thirty?'

'I had something to eat on Saint-Denis, then I went to see a friend. I was just waiting for her now. And she can confirm it.'

'You must mean Elisa. I just saw her. Still shaken by the news. I had the impression it was a real blow for her. From what I gathered, it was sort of on her account that Gadbois couldn't stand the sight of you any more.'

'What do you mean by that?'

'Your Elisa. Elisa who, again?'

'Trottier.'

'Yes, that's it, Trottier. Well, from what she's told us, she was fond of Gadbois—that's one way of putting it—and you took it badly. Very badly.'

'You're making this up!'

'Elisa Trottier is ready to make a formal statement, all we have to do is go and get her. I'm telling you this to fill you in. To save us some time.'

The policeman had placed one foot on the car's bumper, a mocking smile on his lips. 'You get an idea of how things go, after fifteen years on the job: you sniff around here and there and you're bound to find something. Sometimes it's not very convincing. But frankly, in your case I was lucky. You had phoned the paper about seeing Gadbois, around ten this morning. The secretary told you the boss had stayed home because he was sick.'

'So?'

'You're right, that doesn't prove anything. It's not much of a trail. And if you did have something to do with this, you wouldn't have turned up at Gadbois's door an hour later, would you?'

He signalled with his hand and the assistant got out of the car, the brim of his ill-fitting hat like a halo around his head. 'Luc, tell him what kind of evidence we have against him.'

'It comes to the same thing,' the assistant laughed. 'The dead man had time to talk, and I was there.'

'Wounded, you mean,' the chief corrected.

'Yeah, wounded. The ambulance crew were there too.'

'You see,' said the policeman. 'You could have got it off your chest. We've wasted a lot of time for nothing.'

'It doesn't stand up,' he said, 'it can't.'

'Why?'

'I have the right not to talk.'

'Sure you do. You can talk later. Here.'

And he offered him a light. The cigarette trembled between his lips. His shirt was soaking. 'You say it's impossible,' the policeman continued, 'because you hit him from behind and he didn't see you, is that it?' He was silent, as if too exhausted to react. 'How about we go to Rue Wolfe?' the policeman suggested. The assistant drove. The streets were deserted, the tires hissed softly on the road. 'I hope your alibi is good, because when the court hears the ambulance crew's version . . .'

'A police ambulance crew,' he said.

'Their word has to be as good as yours, don't you think? A garbage writer like you? When I think that my wife reads your trash . . . ' he sighed.

'End of the line,' said the assistant.

'Wait here, this won't take long.'

Ghyslaine took forever to answer. She was blinking and trying to cover herself with a sheet. 'Excuse us,' said the policeman. 'We have just one thing to ask you, if you don't mind.' And he went inside, hiding the cigar in his hand. She remained standing, didn't invite them to sit down. 'You spent the day here today? Oh—I forgot to ask if you know this fellow.'

'Yes, a little.'

'You were at home today?'

'Well, I left for work about seven. I must have got back—I don't know for sure, but before five o'clock, anyway.'

'Your friend spent the day here, you say?'

'It's hard to tell . . . '

'Seeing as you weren't here, yes, I can understand that. So what did you mean?'

'I called him around two o'clock. I can't say exactly when. Between two and three.'

'I see. You're sure about that? It's strange, because another friend of his—maybe you know her, a certain Elisa—she claims this gentleman went to see her then.'

Now she looked wide awake, her face crimson. The policeman

watched the two of them. 'Think carefully before you say anything. This is very important. Your friend could be charged with murder. Maybe if you think hard you'll remember exactly what happened— for instance, if he was the one that phoned, not you.'

'That Elisa must be right,' she said, biting into the words. 'Because now that I think about it, it wasn't today I spoke to him on the phone, it was yesterday.'

'Would you be prepared to repeat that in court?'

'If you ask me to, yes.'

There was an embarrassing silence; all three seemed rooted to the spot, waiting for some kind of conclusion. It was the policeman who took the initiative: 'That won't be necessary. Our friend is beginning to understand, isn't he?'

'Understand what?' he asked, almost plaintively.

'Well, good night, Mademoiselle, and sorry for disturbing you,' said the policeman as he headed for the door. Ghyslaine turned her back without saying goodbye. Outside, the policeman took out his lighter and relit his cigar. The other took the opportunity to find his cigarettes and light one.

'Hey,' said the policeman, taking his arm, 'Philip Morris. That's strange . . . '

'Why?'

'They found a Philip Morris butt on the balcony, at Gadbois's.'

'A butt?' he asked, lost, his shoulders more slumped than ever.

The policeman took his arm and led him firmly towards the car. The door slammed with a dull thud. 'Let's go, Luc. I've had enough, how about you?' The assistant grunted in agreement. Hands on his belly, the third man bent over and vomited between his legs. 'That's really a lousy thing to do. In a brand new car . . . ' Then he lowered the window. The assistant was driving at an easy pace. To see them, you could have thought they were tourists, enjoying the fresh night air.

Translated by Sally Livingston

LAURENCE GOUGH · b. 1944

Big Time

It all started about quarter to five on a scorcher Saturday afternoon in August. Roy and I were playing pool at Ace Billiards, in the new mall on the north side of town, over there by the tracks. Roy had just racked the balls when all of a sudden, for no particular reason, the lights seemed to go dim. I glanced up and saw this phenomenon had been caused by an armoured car that had straddled the sidewalk in front of the big picture window overlooking the parking lot.

Roy caught me staring at the armoured car, grinned. We were both working part-time down at the gas station by the highway. Neither of us was making a whole lot of money.

I chalked my cue, settled into a comfortable crouch, and took my shot. The balls exploded, raced clattering around the smooth green felt. Roy and I watched the five ball crawl towards a corner pocket, hang trembling on the lip. I willed it to drop, but it ignored me.

Roy lit a cigarette, studied the table.

The armoured car's rear door swung open, and a guy in a natty silvery-grey uniform jumped out. I noticed he wore a chrome-plated revolver on his right hip, but couldn't tell what colour his eyes were.

Someone in the truck handed down a metal dolly and maybe a dozen empty canvas bags. One of the bags fell off and the guard crouched to pick it up. Another guy came out of the back of the truck. This one was armed with a pump-action shotgun. Turning, he slammed shut the door and followed his buddy around to the front of the truck and across the road to the supermarket. I watched them disappear inside and then turned back to the table.

We were playing eight-ball. Roy had sunk everything but the black. Then, as always, he'd choked up.

I ran my side of the table, picking the balls off one by one, in numerical order. Roy was quiet, kept busy smoking a cigarette down to his fingers. I knocked off the seven and lined up the eight. I could've ended the game real easy by drilling that sucker straight into a side pocket, but instead decided to try a long, tricky double bank into the far end.

Roy picked up the rack, getting ready to start a new game. You got to understand that he wasn't in a hurry to lose—only that deep down inside he knew he didn't have any choice.

The eight ball dropped with a dull thud, right on schedule. Roy sighed. I went over to the window, which smelled of industrial-strength cleaning agents and dead flies. Inside the cab of the armoured car I could dimly see the driver hunched over the wheel, his uniform stained black by the green-tinted bulletproof glass. He turned and looked towards me, right at me. I lit a smoke, shielded my face with my hands.

Now why did I bother to do that? Instinct? Was I planning something already, before I was even aware of it?

Across the road, the door to the supermarket swung open and the guard with the shotgun sauntered out onto the sidewalk. The other guy pushed the dolly outside. The empty canvas bags had been exchanged for full ones. Had to be the weekend receipts in there. Forty, maybe fifty grand.

I winced as something small and round pressed into the small of my back. Reflexively, I started to raise my hands.

'You were thinking evil thoughts, weren't you?' said Roy.

I put my hands back in my pockets, kept my eyes on those two guards and all that money.

Lucky thing, too. They were halfway across the road when a young woman stepped off the curb, moving towards them. I got no idea what was on her mind, but I do know she wasn't paying much attention to where she was going. The armoured car guys saw that they were on a collision course, and slowed to let her pass in front of them. The one with the shotgun said something that made his partner laugh. The girl glanced up, gave them a big smile. The guy with the shotgun smiled right back at her, and then the guy pushing the dolly joined in. Now they were all three of them smiling—it was like they were having a smile contest.

The girl continued towards the parking lot. Now that she knew she had an audience, she put a little extra zip into her walk.

Roy and I and the smiling guards watched her cross to a dusty old Ford. Getting into the car, she flashed more leg than you'd find on the average ladder. The shotgun whistled appreciatively, and got another smile to add to his collection. The dolly-pusher tilted his hat back on his head at a rakish angle and those two suddenly happy fellas continued on their way across the road and around to the back of the truck.

The guy with the scattergun tapped the end of the barrel against the door, which immediately swung open. The money and dolly and guards vanished into the maw of the armoured car. A moment later the vehicle drove ponderously away, its transmission grinding almost as loud as my teeth.

Roy squinted across the table at me. 'What're you thinking, Jack?'

'You and LaVerne going out tonight?'

He nodded. 'I'm supposed to pick her up at seven. Gonna enjoy some delicious Chinese Cuisine and then take in a movie.'

'LaVerne still working at the lingerie shop?'

'Sure is. Girl's got ambition. Intends to stick with it until somebody discovers her and she becomes a rich and famous model.'

'She's a looker. Bound to happen any minute now.'

Roy nodded, and then frowned. 'Why'd you want to know if I was seeing her tonight?'

I rested an arm on his shoulder. 'Listen real careful,' I said, 'because I'm only gonna repeat this twice.'

It wasn't easy, but I made myself wait until LaVerne had polished off the last eggroll, *and* stopped chewing, before I banged my fork against the side of an empty beer bottle. When I had as much of the lady's attention as anyone was ever going to get, I gave her my pitch. I talked fast, because of her limited attention span. When I'd finished my little speech she stared at me for a moment as if totally awestruck.

Then she said, and these are more or less her exact words, 'Jack, that idea smells so darn bad, I wouldn't use it to wrap a dead fish!'

I gave Roy a wink, leaned back in my chair, and ate a fortune cookie, fortune and all.

LaVerne examined herself in a little mirror attached to a gold chain around her waist. Her tongue flicked out, fastened on a wayward grain of rice. 'I have no desire whatsoever to be a member of the criminal element. I yearn to be a famous model. One of these days people will look back and say mine was the face that launched a thousand subscriptions to *Vogue.*'

'No doubt about it,' I said. But candidly, in my opinion LaVerne's major assets are located somewhat lower than her chin. If you catch my drift.

Roy looked at his watch. I had a feeling that they were going to have to leave right away or be late for the movie, and that I was going to get stuck with the bill.

I was right.

At three o'clock in the morning the telephone started ringing. I took a big bite of my liverwurst and tomato on rye, picked up and said howdy. It was Roy, all right. I could hear LaVerne breathing fast over his shoulder, the fragile tinkling of ice in a glass. It'd taken her even longer than I'd expected, but she'd finally worked out that a purse full of money would buy her out of this one-mall town and into the model's paradise of New York City, or Edmonton, whatever.

I said, 'So how was the movie?'

Roy chuckled. 'Better than the chop suey, Jack.'

'That why you called, to compare Sylvester Stallone with a bowl of wet noodles?'

'Not exactly.'

'Then maybe you better meet me in the lane behind Culver's Sporting Goods in exactly twenty-four hours.'

'Yeah, okay.'

'Be sober, Roy. Wear dark clothes and bring your sledgehammer.'

'Okay!' said Roy.

I hung up, and went over to the kitchen counter to make myself another sandwich.

Culver's is on the south side of town, near the river, in an area of small businesses and light industry. At 3:30 in the morning, the streets were darn near as empty as LaVerne's head. I parked my Chevy in the lane right behind Roy's candy-apple DeSoto. The driver's door swung open and Roy climbed out, the sledgehammer swinging loosely at his side. On the DeSoto's radio, a cowboy was singing about the sad state of his stock portfolio.

'You oughtta turn that off,' I said. 'You'll wear down your battery and your intellect all at the same time, listening to that stuff.'

'Thought it might drown out the racket of the sledge.'

'Doubt most people could tell the difference, Roy.'

I went over to the DeSoto and peered inside. There she was, curled up on the back seat in her yellow baby-doll jammies. There was a cigarette clutched in one of her dainty little hands, a half-empty bottle of vodka clutched in the other. Her hair wasn't up in curlers, mind you. But then, nobody's perfect.

'Hello, LaVerne,' I said. 'Real cute outfit.'

She ignored me. 'Shut the door,' she said to Roy. 'You're letting in a draft.'

Roy shut the door. We strolled across the alley to Mr Culver's back door. It was made of heavy-gauge plate steel. Roy wasn't at all fazed. He wound up and gave it a tremendous whack. Sparks lit up his pale blue eyes and the sound of the blow echoes back and forth across the narrow confines of the alley, causing LaVerne to crank up the volume of the radio.

'She's always been a girl who liked her music,' Roy observed.

I said, 'Let's try the window. Glass might prove more fragile.'

The window was protected by a grillwork of one-inch welded steel bars running in vertical and horizontal rows set about six inches apart. A formidable obstacle—or at least it would've been, if the bolts securing the grill to the building hadn't been more rust than metal.

Five hours and a dozen blisters and a thousand curses later, we were inside.

While Roy fiddled with an army surplus bazooka Culver had on special, I used a hacksaw to severely abbreviate the barrels on a couple of twelve-bore shotguns. I then helped myself to a pair of .357 Magnums for each of us, and stuffed as much ammunition as I decently could into the pockets of my jeans. Not that we planned to shoot anybody, you understand. As any professional thief can tell you, the whole idea of packing large quantities of lethal firepower is to intimidate people so badly you are not required to actually pull the trigger.

I was in the middle of the difficult task of choosing the best model Swiss Army Knife to suit my purposes when I heard the unwelcome sound of a key scratching in the front lock. Roy stared at me. I stared at his watch.

It was nine o'clock sharp.

Mr Culver was about to open up for business, and a whole lot more.

It was well known around town that Mr Culver always packed a pistol, and that it was his personal inclination not to start asking questions until he'd run out of bullets.

I raised both hands high in the air in the universal pose of abject failure.

Roy, on the other hand, chose that moment to learn how to fire a bazooka.

There was a thin plywood wall between the front of the store and the storage area where Roy and I had been busy arming ourselves to the teeth. The bazooka's muzzle blast knocked the wall flat, and we were blessed with a quick glimpse of Mr Culver looking astounded. Then the roof fell in, and he was buried under quite a large amount of lath and plaster.

Out in the alley, we found LaVerne snoring in the back seat and the DeSoto's battery even deader than I expected Mr Culver to be.

I started the Chevy and gave him a push, got him moving fast enough to jump start his antique. Fifteen minutes later, we met in the parking lot behind LaVerne's apartment. Roy was in such a good mood that he let me carry LaVerne's good end up all three flights of stairs.

As soon as we'd tucked his sweetie into bed, Roy and I divided up the guns and ammo, and I went home. At high noon I stopped practising my fast draw long enough to tune in the news on the radio. Apparently the explosion and resulting fire at Culver's had levelled the entire block—every square inch of which happened to be owned by Mr Culver. Fortunately, the only serious injury resulting from the catastrophe had been a self-inflicted head wound suffered by Mr Culver's insurance agent.

During all the rest of that week, LaVerne and Roy and I went over my simple plan time and time again, until I was finally satisfied that they both knew exactly what to do and exactly when to do it.

The next Saturday morning, I was so excited that I woke up real early, before the alarm could go off. The sky was clear, and even though it was barely eleven o'clock, the temperature was already in the low eighties.

I made myself a pot of coffee and drank it down to the grounds. The phone rang. Roy had thought it over, and decided he wasn't cut out to be an armed robber after all. Time for a pep talk. I reminded him he was guilty of attempted murder and warned him of the possibility of someone sending an anonymous letter to the cops, should he try to duck out on me now.

At quarter to five, right on schedule, the armoured car pulled up in front of Ace Billiards. Only this time Roy and I weren't inside playing a harmless game of pool. This time, we were crouched down low in a stolen lime-green Pontiac cabriolet with guns in our hands, dollar signs in our eyes, and our hearts in our mouths. As it turned out, the Pontiac belonged to Culver's insurance agent. But that was pure coincidence, despite anything you might've read to the contrary. *And we had no idea that the poor guy was LaVerne's father!*

The routine hadn't changed one little bit. The rear door swung open and the guard jumped out, followed by the metal dolly and empty bags, the shotgun. Roy and I kept real low as the two guards crossed the road and vanished inside the supermarket. I peered at Roy's watch. The guards and money were due back outside in just under five minutes. Timing was crucial to the success of my plan.

Roy gave me a weak smile. He shoved a shotgun shell in his mouth and tried to light up his Bic.

I said, 'You ought to give those up. Supposed to be bad for your health.'

I sank a little lower in my seat. The hands of Roy's watch trudged reluctantly around the dial, like convicts in a prison yard in an old black and white movie. At the three minute mark, Roy popped open the Pontiac's glove compartment and hauled out the pair of nylon stockings LaVerne had sold him at a staff discount. He unfolded a stocking and pulled it over his head.

I said, 'That the first time you've ever done that? If so, you sure are good at it.'

I pulled on my stocking, and was relieved to find there was plenty of room to spare.

Roy said, 'Just about time.'

'Then where in heck is that girl LaVerne?'

The supermarket doors flew open. The guards came out in single file. The dolly was loaded high with fat canvas bags, thirteen of them.

Roy punched me on the arm. 'There she is!'

There she was, all right.

She was dressed, if that's the word, in a strapless black silk evening gown she must surely have eased into one thread at a time. Her long and shapely legs were encased in fine mesh stockings with bright little sparks of silver in them, that flashed provocatively, like a trout in a stream, with every step she took.

On her dainty feet, she wore a pair of black patent leather shoes with six-inch heels. She'd had her hair attended to, and her thick blond tresses were piled high up on her head, beehive style, all fluffy and shining in the light. Her skin was a flawless, creamy white. Her eyes were as blue as Paul Newman's, almost.

She was smiling as if she would never stop, and to top it all off, she wasn't wearing her braces.

It was plain for all to see that the girl believed she was poised on the edge of the Big Time, and was more than ready to step on over to the other side.

Roy and I climbed out of the lime-green Pontiac and moved in on the guards. They didn't pay us the slightest attention. As expected, they only had eyes for LaVerne.

'Freeze!' Roy shouted jealously.

The one pushing the dolly wiped a trace of drool from his chin.

'Freeze!' Roy shouted again.

I relieved those two poor stricken love-puppies of their weapons. Roy pushed the dolly towards the getaway car. LaVerne's eyes followed the progress of the cash, but the rest of her didn't move an inch.

Inside the armoured car, the driver was shouting into a microphone. Roy had already managed to stuff eight of the bags into the Pontiac's back seat. On the sidewalk, LaVerne arranged her lips in a pout, and languidly ran her fingers through her hair.

'LaVerne!' Roy shouted, 'C'mon, let's go!'

The girl tilted her upper body, bent a leg, thrust out a hip and blew him a kiss.

Roy's shotgun went off, the sudden explosion as shocking as a slap in the face.

LaVerne brought her hands to her mouth and fluttered her eyelashes.

I turned around just in time to see Roy and most of the Pontiac disappear under a seething mass of dark blue uniforms. More cops were moving in on me, their mouths set, eyes gleaming in cruel anticipation. I dropped the sawed-off shotgun I'd borrowed from Mr Culver, exchanged the .357 Magnums and my Swiss Army Knife for a pair of handcuffs. The nylon stocking was ripped unceremoniously from my face.

Someone in the crowd gasped, and observed as how I was the polite young fella worked down at the gas station by the highway. 'Not any more, he don't,' said one of the cops. I stepped on his foot, to give myself a little more elevation, and a clearer view of LaVerne.

She was surrounded by television cameras and out-thrust

microphones, and in a voice even lower than her neckline or personal code of moral conduct, was detailing her lifelong ambition to travel to New York City, and magazine racks all over the whole darn world. Flashbulbs popped like champagne corks.

Then a paddy wagon arrived and they bundled Roy and me inside.

What a monstrous turn of events.

As the wagon pushed slowly through the crowd, Roy peered out the wire-reinforced window in a vain attempt to catch one last glimpse of the local girl who was about to make good. The wagon turned a corner, and LaVerne was lost forever, and Roy turned towards me.

'Know something, Jack?'

'What's that, Roy?'

'I went over to the library yesterday, and looked up the crime of armed robbery. In our neighbourhood, the penalty is usually twenty years to life.'

'Well,' I said, 'didn't I tell you we were going to hit the Big Time?'

'Not just us. LaVerne, too.' Roy smiled a sad and somewhat wistful smile. 'Fact is, things couldn't have worked out better for her if she'd planned it this way.'

'No kidding.'

Roy's eyes got very small, his forehead corrugated up like a set of venetian blinds, and his skin turned the approximate colour of an eggplant. 'Are you telling me,' he said, 'that LaVerne might've had something to do with us getting caught?'

I managed a hollow laugh. 'Why, heck no! Of course not!'

Roy's forehead slowly unfurled. He stuck his fists back in his pockets, and I sighed with relief. I imagine that sometime during the next twenty-odd years of heavily enforced idleness, Roy'll figure out that LaVerne isn't answering his postcards 'cause she done him wrong.

All I can say is that I hope I'm not in the same cell with him when it happens.

TIM WYNNE-JONES · b. 1948

The Imposture

Leslie was lying in the graveyard the night of the imposture. He had stretched out on his favourite spot, a rise just off Heavenly Way and in back of Golden Trumpet Path. It was a warm Saturday night. If he strained his ears he could hear the sound of baseball drifting down Milkweed Creek from Tressourville. Tressourville was out of sight, around the bend. The Loonies were at home to the Winchester Bandits. Leslie didn't strain his ears. He concentrated on the buzzing quietness of twilight and let the summer in the trees lull him. He became part of the buzzing quietness. He fell asleep.

Ting, ting. He awoke to the sound of chisel on stone; ting, ting. It was not an annoying sound. Still rummaging around in the basement of his unconscious, he tried guessing at the letters. It was almost as much fun as guessing the numbers being dialled on a phone. Ting, ting. Leslie took an elevator ride up to the next level of consciousness: accounts payable. He opened his eyes. It was dark. In the dark, *ting, ting* didn't sound so pleasant any more. He looked down the bank of gravestones to the willows by the marsh. Nothing moved. He raised himself on his elbows. The hammering came from some distance behind him. It stopped. Leslie found his feet. He crossed over the rise, the thick grass soaking up his footsteps. Peeking out from behind the Glassbeak Mausoleum, he glanced down the sweep of Heavenly Way to the gates of Tranquil-lity Square. A shadowy figure glided towards the gates, swerved past the gate-house, and followed the line of the fence into the trees and out of sight. Leslie followed.

In a copse of alders, where the underbrush was thick and the fence missing teeth, Leslie found a cap in the low branches of a tree. He reached up, removed it, and put it in his pocket.

Charlie Metford was out walking his dog when Leslie bicycled by him minutes later on his way home.

'Evening,' said Charlie.

'Evening,' said Leslie, not stopping to talk.

Leslie didn't go to church the next morning with Mother. He rode his bike back out to Paradise. Fletcher Spigott, the groundskeeper, would be at the cemetery early. Sunday was his busy day. Leslie took his camera.

Fletcher had already found the desecration when Leslie arrived. So had Mrs David Dunton Thornwhip Small. She was shaking a bunch of cornflowers at Fletcher. Blue, purple, pink, and white. She was giving him a piece of her mind. Fletcher was flailing his arms around in the same jerky, incomprehending way he did when Leslie was thrashing him in a game of Spite & Malice.

'We got ourselves a problem here,' groaned Fletcher, seeing his friend approaching.

'We?' said Mrs Small, regarding Leslie suspiciously.

'Good morning,' said Leslie.

Mrs Small adjusted her stole.

Leslie joined the groundskeeper and Mrs Small at the foot of a large plot, surrounded by an ankle-high wrought-iron fence and over-shadowed by a tomb of chocolate-coloured stone, as generous as the headboard of a double bed. Amidst the rough tracery of celtic vines two smooth rectangles, one to either side of a tangled cross, bore the inscriptions:

R.I.P.

David Dunton Thornwhip Small

1917-1984

and

R.I.P.

Mrs David Dunton Thornwhip Small

1920-1985

The '1985' wasn't all that bad for something carved in the dark.

'I know what this means,' said Mrs Small, pointedly.

'Sorry,' said Leslie. 'I hadn't even heard you were sick.'

'Don't be an ass!' said Mrs Small. She glared at him. The eyes on her stole glared at him too, for good measure. Mrs Small's gaze took in the camera hanging around Leslie's neck.

'Sightseeing?' she asked.

'Leslie spends a lot of time out this way,' chirped Fletcher. He was smiling, glad to be relieved of Mrs Small's sole attention.

'How very irregular,' said Mrs Small.

Leslie didn't like the look in his inquisitor's eyes nor the trend in the conversation. 'It might be the VOICE people,' he suggested. Mrs Small's face clouded.

'The voice people?' muttered Fletcher. His smile drooped.

'The Voice of Intelligence, Conscience, and the Environment,' snapped Mrs Small. She flung the cornflowers on her husband's grave. 'The rally was one thing. The petitions another. But this!'

'It's awful,' said Fletcher.

'It's wishful thinking,' said Mrs Small, fixing Leslie with a glare, daring him to comment. Leslie shook his head. He sighed.

'People feel pretty strongly about the Tritrac company coming to town,' he said. It was his finest moment. He instantly regretted it.

'They do, do they!' boomed Mrs Small. 'Tritrac will bring this community three hundred jobs,' she said. 'Tressourville is a depressed area.'

'That's true,' said Leslie, cowering a bit.

'Besides, I don't own the company,' said Mrs Small. 'Do you think I get any pleasure chasing after my late husband's Ottawa connections just so they'll think to throw a crumb or two our way? Do you suspect I get some kind of a kick-back?'

'I don't suspect anything of the kind,' said Leslie, trying to keep his voice from breaking. But temerity got the better of him once again. 'What VOICE thinks is that Tritrac makes digital switcher systems for the American military.'

'Oh,' said Fletcher. He was having trouble following the conversation.

'Haven't I seen you somewhere before?' said Mrs Small. Leslie began to shrink back to his normal size.

'Ah, yes,' said Mrs Small. 'The Tressourville *Times.* You're the little man who sells advertising.' Her thin lips had been quivering. They stopped. 'You're probably counting on the country club's annual four-page spread for the tournament.'

'The Small Cup,' said Fletcher triumphantly. He did follow golf.

'It was your late husband's custom,' said Leslie, trying to sound contrite. 'I had a talk with Mrs Clooney. We looked at some mock-ups.'

'Oh?' enquired Small. 'Recently?'

'Before she passed away,' said Leslie.

Mrs Small laid her gloved hand on her breast in a pretence of relief. 'Have you heard that I'm planning on taking over the management of Rivercrest?' she said.

'There was a rumour,' said Leslie timidly.

'Well, I suspect we will be seeing you in the next little while,' said Mrs Small. An unpleasant smile flickered across her stony face. 'We'll take another look at your mock-ups.' She looked once more at Fletcher, at Leslie, at the graffiti on her gravestone. An equation registered in her eyes.

'Well,' she said. 'There's nothing left to do here but call the authorities.'

'There's a phone in the gatehouse,' said Fletcher. He was going to offer to phone himself but Mrs Small brushed past him with a curt nod and headed towards the stone hut. Her stole bounced on her narrow shoulders, laughing silently at the two men. Suddenly Fletcher gasped. He threw Leslie a look of sheer misery, and then ran after Mrs Small. He had remembered the calendar hanging on the back of the gatehouse door.

Leslie took a photo of the vandalized stone. From his pocket he drew a little black notebook in which he began to write up the incident for the *Times*. Randy Downes was the paper's reporter, but he was upriver for the weekend. Leslie could give him the facts. He chewed distractedly on the end of his pen. But which facts?

'I remember Small when he was the district school inspector,' said Mr Jackson.

'Keep still,' said Dorothy Neil, Leslie's mother. She was cutting Mr Jackson's hair, what there was of it. It was their little arrangement. In return he brought her windfalls and sour milk for baking. He was perched on a chair in the middle of the kitchen floor. There were old editions of the Tressourville *Times* scattered optimistically at his feet. He held the latest edition in his chubby, mottled hands. Leslie was standing at the kitchen window eating an apple and watching clouds gather over the garden.

'Oh, he was a real rakehell in those days,' said Mr Jackson. 'Gadding about. Dirty weekends down in Brockville.' This notion tickled Mr Jackson. He chuckled. 'The Board of Ed was paying him to drive all over visiting the country schools, and he was spending half of the time talking poor farmers out of river frontage and rights-of-way, that kind of thing. Oh, did he have an eye for the market.' Leslie's apple crunched. Dorothy's scissors snipped at the air. Low thunder rumbled in the distance. Mr Jackson cracked the back of the paper. 'Shrewd bugger,' he said. This made him shake with silent laughter. Dorothy waited for the fit to pass.

'Remember all the rumours, Dorothy?' he said.

'I was almost one of them,' said Dorothy.

'What do you make of that, Les?' said Mr Jackson, shaking and wheezing.

'Mom's a real caution,' said Leslie.

Mr Jackson shook and wheezed and coughed. Dorothy took the opportunity to borrow his newspaper. 'They sure made a mess of it,' she said, clucking. 'Look how the grass is all chewed up in the corner here.' Leslie left the window and regarded the picture on the front page. It was the one he had taken Sunday morning. A lot of mess, he thought, for one shadowy figure.

'Will you look at that?' said Dorothy. She read: 'Out of three hundred employees at the new plant, Tritrac has hired only twenty-three from Tressourville. The rest were transferred or hired through an agency in Ottawa.'

'Still,' said Mr Jackson. Recovered now, he took back his newspaper from Dorothy's hands. 'There's no need to pull a stunt like that one at Paradise Gardens.'

'There's nothing here says VOICE is responsible,' said Dorothy. Leslie returned to the window.

'Protesters,' sighed Mr Jackson. He settled back into his chair. The scissors snipped again. 'You'd think they could find something better to do with their time,' he said. Suddenly he leaped from his chair cupping his ear. 'Oww!'

'Sorry,' said Dorothy. 'My arthritis.' Mr Jackson sat down again reluctantly. Leslie smiled to himself.

'Well, at least they could find something better to protest,' said Mr Jackson. He winced, fearing another attack.

The thunder rumbled closer. Leslie watched the line of shadow drawing nearer. He watched the first rain bend the carpet of leaves in the garden.

A protest, he thought. A solitary protest.

It rained all the next day. It was still raining when Leslie drove out to the Rivercrest Country Club. Mrs Small had left a message at the *Times* office. Leslie put off the visit as long as he could. It wasn't a good day for golf. Wind gusted up the fairways, shaking the trees at the side of the driveways and raising the nap on the closely cropped grass. Small flags shivered on abandoned greens. Puddles shimmered and danced on the pavement. There was only a handful of cars in the parking lot. Leslie caught a glimpse of members lounging around the copper-chimneyed fireplace in the clubhouse. They were drinking long drinks. Leslie parked his Beetle around back, as close to the office as he could get. With his briefcase over his head he negotiated a path through the rockery garden. Linda Woolnough saw him coming up the path and greeted him at the door.

'She's with the members in the lounge,' Linda said as she closed the door behind him. 'I'll get you a coffee,' she said. Leslie thought he saw a look of pity pass across her face: the new lamb for the slaughter.

She retired to her inner office while Leslie hung up his coat in an alcove by the door.

The office was fine from the waist up. There were glass bookshelves with leather-bound volumes, and trophies. There were framed photographs of golfers and happy, scrubbed people in whites and blazers who liked golf or maybe just liked having their picture taken. Below the wainscot, at the working level, a different story was unfolding. The office was in a turmoil. There were file folders and ledgers everywhere. The black mahogany desk was piled high with correspondence. A purple-coloured poodle had risen from his nap in the desk's swivel chair when Leslie had entered. He surveyed the room groggily, then tried to get back to sleep. He turned and turned again. Leslie turned his attention to the picture window. It framed the rockery garden like a painting. It was a wild, tangled but beautiful garden full of cornflowers. It did not fit the Rivercrest decorum at all. Beyond it, across the yard, the doors of the workshed were open. Duane Clooney was working on the gang-mowers. He bent down, file in hand, his broad back striped with sweat.

'He hasn't been the same since his mother died,' said Linda, re-entering the room with a tray. She looked around for a place to put it. She sighed. 'Nothing has been the same,' she said.

'I don't think your new manager is much good,' said Leslie. He allowed Linda a moment of shock before nodding towards the desk where the purple poodle was snoring. Linda smiled complicitly while Leslie whitened his coffee. 'The bunkers are in better shape,' she said.

'Surely it'll all come together once you learn the ropes,' said Leslie. Linda shook her head. 'I worked for Fern Clooney six years. She wasn't a person who let out much rope. She prided herself on her independence. Her efficiency. I don't think even Mr Small knew much about how she managed this place. It was her secret.'

The door of the inner office opened and Mrs Small entered. She was wearing an expensive suit and a silk scarf to hide her wizened neck.

'I'll get the mock-ups,' said Linda and hurried back to her office, squeezing past Mrs Small on the way.

'Good afternoon, Mr Neil,' said Mrs Small. She swept up the poodle from her chair and took its place behind the desk. Linda returned with several art boards which she handed to Leslie while she freed a chair before the desk. Leslie was reminded of a trip to the principal. Mrs Small glanced at the mock-ups on Leslie's lap. When the door to the inner office had closed behind her secretary, she began in a clipped and measured voice.

'Why did you do it?' she asked. Leslie placed the mock-ups on the floor. 'Excuse me?' he said.

'Why did you scribble on my gravestone?' Leslie was too stunned to speak. The dog in Mrs Small's lap suddenly sat bolt upright and barked piercingly three times. Its tail wagged. The outer door opened. A draft cooled the back of Leslie's neck.

'What is it?' snapped Mrs Small. Leslie turned. Duane Clooney was standing filling the doorway. He was wearing a green mack, the sleeves of which did not reach halfway down his forearms. His fingers were stained bright pink with the abrasive compound he had been using on the blades of the mowers. His thin black hair hung in wet streaks across his broad flat forehead. His narrow eyes blinked out the rain.

'Use the washroom,' he said. His thick tongue did all it could to make the simple statement incomprehensible. Mrs Small seemed about to remonstrate, but change her mind. She frowned, nodded. Dripping wet, Duane entered the alcove where Leslie had hung his coat. A door was heard to slide open and shut.

Mrs Small's voice lowered a notch.

'If you are not the culprit then who are you covering up for, Mr Neil?'

The interruption had given Leslie time to collect his wits. 'I have no idea what you're talking about,' he said with as much conviction as he could muster.

Mrs Small stroked her dog. 'Charlie Metford saw you at the cemetery the night of the imposture,' she said. 'Please don't waste my time with silly denials. I can make things very uncomfortable for you, Mr Neil.'

'Is that a threat?' said Leslie.

'A threat?' said Mrs Small. 'I am the one being threatened.' Her dog jumped to the floor. 'That nasty bit of graffiti might have given a weaker woman of my age a heart attack.'

'Why did you ask me here?' asked Leslie.

'You don't really care about my feelings, do you?' said Mrs Small.

'I had nothing to do with the imposture, as you call it,' said Leslie. 'I'm sorry but that's all I have to say.'

'No it isn't,' said Mrs Small. 'Because I don't like the way that shocking bit of vandalism is being used by your paper as an excuse to forward the message of these VOICE people.'

'I'm not the editor,' said Leslie.

'No,' said Mrs Small. 'Cy Chaplin is the editor. I am acquainted with Cy Chaplin's political leanings and as long as the VOICE people are under suspicion he'll let them have a field day in his paper.'

Leslie shrugged. 'I don't see what Mr Chaplin's politics have to do with me,' he said.

'Simply that you are responsible for suggesting VOICE was behind the crime in the first place,' said Mrs Small.

'You suspected as much yourself,' said Leslie.

'But I didn't rush off and print it in the newspaper!' said Mrs Small. 'What's more, I believe you engineered the whole thing so that the *Times* could launch this smear campaign.' Behind the framed photographs and trophies and bound books a toilet flushed. A tap was turned on. Leslie imagined pink compound swirling down the sink.

'What do you want?' said Leslie.

Mrs Small leaned across her desk. 'I have a lot of friends in this town, Mr Neil. Commercial allies, let's call them. I also know the kind of budget on which the *Times* operates. *That*, I will discuss later with Mr Chaplin. As for you, I've been asking around town about Leslie Neil. Some people consider you a strange bird. A man at thirty-eight who still lives with his mother? A man who spends most of his spare time in the graveyard?'

'It's public property,' said Leslie.

'Not after hours,' said Mrs Small. 'Mr Spigott could get into considerable trouble with the Parks Board for knowingly complying with such a breach of regulations. For that matter, there are those who wonder about you and Mr Spigott.'

'We're friends,' said Leslie. 'We play cards.'

'Let's say I'm concerned about irregularities on civic property,' said Mrs Small, coolly. 'Obviously more concerned than you are.'

Leslie was speechless.

'Don't gape at me,' said Mrs Small. 'All I'm saying is that you know something which, for your own perverse reasons, you're not telling. I am not about to sit quietly while my husband's good name is impugned. Do you understand?'

A sliding door opened and shut. Mrs Small used this as a cue to get to her feet. Duane entered the room from the alcove.

'Thank you,' he said. Mrs Small shifted her attention to the intruder.

'Whatever your custom was while your mother was manager, I will expect you to use the facilities in the kitchen like the rest of the help from now on,' she said. With that she left, shutting the door behind her. Her purple companion whined at the door. Duane crossed the room and opened the door to the inner office enough for the dog to follow. He looked back at the muddy footprints on the pile carpet. He smiled at Leslie. Leslie breathed a long sigh of relief. Duane frowned.

'Why do you go there?' he asked. His speech was much improved, but Leslie looked blankly at him.

'The graveyard,' said Duane. 'I was listening. Somebody there?'

'Oh,' said Leslie. 'Lots of people. Some of the best folks in town.'

Duane nodded, but looked vague.

'You know Tressourville Centennial Park?' asked Leslie. Duane nodded. 'Well,' said Leslie, 'it's not really a park at all, is it? It's more like a bomb crater. There's this cinder-block legion hall and a baseball diamond and a french-fry truck that must have lost its wheels when the bomb dropped. The grass is all worn away like the knees of your jeans and trees we kids planted centennial year are all dead. Nobody wants to admit it, so they leave them there.'

Duane looked wistful. He wandered over to the window. He gazed out past the shed to the verdure of the golf course. The rain had almost stopped and the mist hung like finely-strung hammocks between the oaks and maples and tall pines guarding the fairways. A yellow flag stood limply in a hole but brightly, as if it were holding a morsel of the sun.

'I got no time for a place like that,' said Duane.

'Precisely,' said Leslie. 'You've got Rivercrest and I've got Paradise Gardens.' Now Duane seemed to understand. 'The cemetery was the last sensible decision the town council made,' said Leslie. 'That was eighty years ago. There were still rich people dying here in those days. They had to have some place to put them. Most of the rich have gone now and they've left Paradise behind for us. Suits me just fine.'

Duane nodded thoughtfully. Then suddenly he shook his head. 'The rich don't die,' he said. 'They just come out here and play golf.' Then his mouth slowly opened into a fist-sized grin and a belly laugh squeezed its way past his thick tongue and out into the office. It shook the glass in the windows. It shook Leslie a bit too.

The imposture was sanded and polished away but the protest it seemed to represent became a hot item in Tressourville. Increasingly the heat focused on the tiny offices of the Tressourville *Times* above Drews Bakery on Gladys Street. True to her word, Mrs Small commenced her campaign against the newspaper. Metford's Meats, Renata's Hair Salon, Holiday Travel, the A-Z Garden Centre and Doucette's IGA all decided, for the time being at least, that they needed the patronage of Small and her crowd more than they needed weekly ads in the *Times*. The rumour mills, never at rest in Tressourville, found new momentum in the turbulence. But apart from the odd queer look, Leslie did not believe Mrs Small had started her retaliatory campaign against himself. Not yet.

It was with this on his mind that Leslie Neil leaned against the plum tree in his mother's garden while Dorothy, in wellingtons and gardening gloves, attended to the tomato plants.

'What do they call people like Duane nowadays?' she asked, draping a fruit-heavy branch over a mesh support. 'People used to call men like Duane Clooney simple.'

'Simple will do,' muttered Leslie, though he wasn't sure it was entirely true.

'She wasn't from around here,' said Dorothy, straightening to get a crick out of her back. 'She was from down Merrickville way.'

Dorothy picked up an old jam can full of warm salty water. With her free hand she sorted through a ravaged section of tomato foliage.

'What'll you do when I'm gone?' she asked, without looking up.

Leslie thought a moment. 'Probably move to Vegas,' he said. 'Gamble away your savings and die of cirrhosis of the liver in some seedy dive on the outskirts of nowhere. However, I will have made previous arrangements to have my body transported to Paradise Gardens.'

Dorothy grunted approval. Her mind was elsewhere. Leslie's thoughts had drifted also. 'Merrickville?'

'That's what Hilda Sperling tells me,' said Dorothy. Suddenly her gloved hand darted into green and came out with a four-inch caterpillar between her fingers. 'Fern moved away just like that one day,' she said, examining the corpulent body wriggling helplessly in her grip. 'It was after the war. Everyone figured she'd met some soldier with an interesting tale to tell. Two years later she showed up in Tressourville with young Duane. She started working at the golf course soon after it opened. Worked her way up. Poor Duane,' she said. Then she dropped the squirming caterpillar in the jam can. It screamed. Leslie's gaze followed the caterpillar into the can. The water turned green. He saw it dimly floating to the bottom.

The next day was spent thinking up novel ways to fill the gaping holes in the newspaper where ads had once flourished. Photographs of bygone days and crossword puzzles would only go so far.

It was late afternoon before Leslie was able to get away. He drove straight out to Merrickville. He had already phoned Hilda Sperling, the librarian there. They had tea with an ancient soul called Mrs Hamilton and talked for some time about bygone days. Then the librarian locked Leslie up in the tiny library so he wouldn't be disturbed while she went for her supper. It was dark before Leslie let himself out. He drove straight out to Rivercrest Country Club. The lights were on in the club house lounge but he parked around back near the office and the work shed. The lights went out as he arrived. Linda was just locking up.

'He's out somewhere on the links,' she said, in answer to his inquiry. 'It's the only time he can turn on the sprinklers.'

Leslie watched Linda's car navigate the driveway to the River Road. He watched her tail-lights vanish beyond the woods of the conservation area. He walked out past the shed. He could see a row of lights bobbing low to the ground on a distant fairway. Worm pickers. He could not see the headlights of Duane's truck in any direction. He tried the door on the workshed. It was unlocked. Pulling the door to behind him, he found a light switch on the wall. A bare lightbulb lit up the workbench and little else. Directly under the lightbulb a space had been cleared of sawdust and grime, and there he found a pile of papers: government forms having to do with Fern Clooney's death; government forms having to do with the welfare of a simpleton. Leafing gingerly through the forms, Leslie found a picture of Fern as a young woman, country-fresh, slim-shouldered, deep-breasted. The kind of woman a man might make a fool of himself over. Leslie found Duane's birth certificate. Duane was his age. He did some math in his head. Distantly he heard the hum of music from the clubhouse, the occasional laughter of members on the patio. A pleasant sound. He ventured deeper into the workshed, sliding past the triangular framework of the gang-mowers. The air was pungent with oil and wood rot. In an open tool box at the back of the shed Leslie found a chisel with a damaged point and the finest trace of chocolate-coloured dust. Suddenly there was a noise behind him. Leslie spun around in time to see the doors click shut behind the massive frame of Duane Clooney. Leslie's gaze shifted to the large wood and iron contraption in Duane's hands.

'I been digging holes,' said Duane impassively. He held up the T-shaped tool as though he were an acolyte in a church parade. 'See them teeth?' he said. And Leslie immediately saw the teeth at the base of the instrument. Duane brought the point of the holedigger down on the earth floor between his feet. With a series of quick semi-circular twists the stainless steel shaft dug its way ten inches into the ground. With a heave, Duane pulled the shaft back out. 'This plug,' he said. 'I put it in the old hole. Now the golfers got somewhere else to shoot at. Simple.' Then he started down the workbench towards Leslie, who stood frozen in his tracks. Duane had to carry the holedigger high as he passed by the gang-mowers. As he passed under the single lightbulb, the cruciform shadow lunged towards Leslie and he backed away from it until his back came up against a large, unmoving steel drum.

'She was a teacher,' blurted Leslie with what voice he could muster. 'She was teaching in Merrickville in '46,' he continued, although Duane didn't seem to hear a word he was saying. 'Small was the inspector for the schools. He quit the following year, the year your mom left Merrickville. He's your father, isn't he?' Duane stopped six feet from Leslie. Duane turned away. He hung the holedigger on a cradle against the wall. He returned his attention to the trespasser in the shadows. He squinted. He saw the chisel in Leslie's hand.

'I ain't been taking so good care of things lately,' he said. Leslie slowly approached him. He handed him the chisel. Duane rubbed the tip with his calloused thumb. From his pocket, Leslie took a cap and, reaching up, he placed it on Duane's head. It was as far as he had reached to take it down from the low branches of the alder tree. Some Prince Charming, he thought. Some Cinderella.

'Small was okay about stuff,' said Duane. 'Gave us this place. Jobs. Mom was too proud to ask for more.' Duane took off the cap and combed his hair with his fingers, before replacing the cap snugly. 'I was at my mother's funeral,' he said, and now emotion impaired his speech. 'I seen the stone Small had. I see where it said Mrs Small was right there beside him.'

'And it made you mad,' Leslie volunteered. Duane's brow creased in a deep furrow. 'So you made a statement,' Leslie continued. 'You made a personal protest.'

'Something like that,' said Duane.

'Are you still mad?' asked Leslie. Duane looked around. The familiarity of the shed made him reflective.

'I don't think so,' he said. 'Except when Mrs Small finds out, then I'll get canned.'

Leslie was caught off guard.

'She doesn't know about Fern, about you?'

'No one knows,' said Duane, looking up. 'Except you and me.'

Leslie's mind was racing ahead. 'She's not going to can you, Duane,' he said. 'Leave it to me.' Duane ventured a hopeful glance.

'Just leave it to me,' said Leslie.

So Leslie told Mrs Small who he was covering up for, although he had had no idea when she first accused him. Only an inkling that what he had witnessed was more than it appeared to be. The news might have given a weaker woman her age a heart attack. Mrs Small was not weak. The hardest thing for her to swallow was Leslie's promise that he would remain silent about the other 'Mrs Small'. He didn't want anything from her except to call off her hounds. They established an uneasy truce. There was just enough time the next day before the *Times* went to press to pull her letter to the editor. She volunteered to make a few phone calls which helped to refill most of the advertising slots lost in the past few days of feuding. Mrs Small told her friends that she had over-reacted. That was all. She was rich and old. Nobody questioned her change of heart. In a gesture of mollification, Cy Chaplin offered to print a photo of her gravestone refurbished to its pristine state. But Mrs Small decided she had seen enough of her grave in the news.

Fletcher Spigott waited on tenterhooks but the week passed without reprimand from the parks authority. Duane Clooney's position at Rivercrest was tacitly assured (providing he did not use the washroom facilities in the manager's office), and so, although everything was not the same, everything returned to something like what it had been before.

So it was that on a Saturday night, not long after the dust had settled, the Tressourville Loonies took on the Merrickville Mavericks at Centennial Park. It was a golden evening for baseball. Leslie wasn't there. He had found another loose spoke in the fence at Paradise and was lying on his favourite spot, presently untenanted, just off Heavenly Way and in back of Golden Trumpet Path, when the first pitch was thrown. He lay for a while drinking in the view of the willows by the marsh and the swallows dipping low over Milkweed Creek before his eyes closed under the hum of gathering nightfall. He opened his eyes with a start to find Duane Clooney standing at his feet. He was wearing his cap. He was carrying a huge handful of cornflowers.

'I figured I might find you here,' he said. 'I wanted to thank you for what you done.' With the sun at his back, Duane was featureless. A shadow.

'That's okay,' said Leslie. Feeling a little vulnerable, he raised himself on his elbows.

'Nice view,' said Duane, looking down towards the marsh.

'That's why I picked this plot,' said Leslie. The sun's last rays were licking the creek, and every gravestone before them was like a minor eclipse. 'I want to enjoy it while I can,' said Leslie.

'Practising,' said Duane, thoughtfully.

Leslie sat up with a start. 'Precisely,' he said.

'You'll have the whole thing memorized by the time you go,' said Duane, encouraged by Leslie's response.

'Yes,' said Leslie. He'd never dared tell anyone of his plan.

'I got a place out at the course,' said Duane. 'A little rise, between these oaks all scarred up with gall. There's a deep bunker down to the right and there's a great view of the eighteenth hole. When my time comes I'll just disappear,' he said. 'Don't ask me how, but that's where I'll be.'

There was a silence between the two men. Then Duane said, 'I won't disturb you no more. I just come to put some flowers on mother's grave.'

'Ah,' said Leslie. 'I noticed she was in the new section off Angel's Walk.'

'Right,' said Duane. Unexpectedly, he winked. 'Well,' he said, 'I 'magine I'll see you around.'

'Right,' said Leslie. 'That'd be fine.' He watched Duane walk off. He lay down again on his back. The wink had disturbed him. He rolled over on his stomach and, edging up the rise, he watched Duane depart—not towards Angel's Walk but down Heavenly Way, down to Tranquillity Square. He watched Duane lay the cornflowers on Mrs Small's grave. Leslie rolled onto his back again, his heart pumping crazily. His skin was cold with sweat. Past the thumping of his pulse he heard a roar arise from the distant crowd in Centennial Park. The Loonies had scored again.

ELISABETH BOWERS · b. 1949 AND A.J. BELL

The Singles' Bar Rapist

Moira toyed with the plastic stick in her California cooler, gently stirring the ice-cubes, watching them bob and bump against the sides of the glass. Usually she just ordered a pint of draft, but today she'd felt like treating herself to something different. It was Friday—another week over with—and it had become her habit on Fridays after work to stop at Trilby's neighbourhood pub for a drink before going home on the bus. That way she missed the rush-hour crush, and put off her inevitable Friday-night-at-home-by-myself-again depression.

She'd discovered Trilby's six months ago, soon after she started working at Jamieson, Cheung & Pitch. Although she didn't usually go to pubs by herself, she felt comfortable here. The staff were friendly, and most of the customers were regulars, people who worked in the nearby businesses. She drank alone, sitting at her favourite table by the window, from where she could watch both the fashions passing on the sidewalk and the scene at the bar. But usually, at some point, someone would come over and strike up a conversation, buy her another drink, maybe ask her out to supper. She rarely accepted these offers, had learned, by now, that most of the men who hustled at Trilby's wanted a one-night-stand—but occasionally she met someone who seemed more promising and usually, of course, he turned out to be married. Nevertheless, it was better than sitting at home, watching television.

She'd been married herself once, straight out of high school. After the divorce, she'd concentrated on her career, taking courses at night, working her way up from being a receptionist to a legal secretary. Now she was twenty-eight—she had the job she wanted, and she was more than ready for another serious relationship. She was even debating putting an ad in the personals: 'Attractive, independent, fun-loving lady, looking for . . .' What? Whatever it was, she didn't seem to be able to find it.

It was six o'clock; Trilby's was filling up fast. People at the bar were standing three deep, crowded around those seated on the bar-stools.

Barry, who worked as a teller at the credit union, greeted her as he went to join a table of his co-workers; Duane, a salesman from one of the car lots, breezed in the swinging doors and swaggered up to the bar. Moira was careful not to catch his eye. Every woman at Trilby's knew Duane; he wasn't bad-looking, but he was a persistent hustler—a bit of a jerk, really—he had a young wife and three small children at home. At a table near the bar, the woman who worked behind the counter at the deli was holding hands with a man who had fat red cheeks and horn-rimmed glasses. Moira thought he looked a bit goofy. But they seem to like each other, she observed with a shrug.

Her glass was nearly empty; it was half past six. Rush hour would be over. She thought of the wait at the bus-stop, the long ride home, her empty apartment, the dirty dishes in the sink. She could go to the laundromat tonight, and get that job over with. Now there's something to look forward to, she thought, sarcastically.

She upended her glass to catch the last few trickles, placed it on the table—and found a man standing beside her, gazing down at her and smiling. He was tall, very handsome—and somehow, familiar.

'I know this sounds like a line,' he said, 'but don't I know you from somewhere?'

She stared up at him, mesmerized by his startlingly good looks. 'Yeah, I think . . . Ann Erskine.' Her voice was suddenly breathless. 'You're Ann's husband.' She knew his first name too—had taken many messages from him—but didn't want to admit that she remembered him so well. The miracle was that he had recognized her.

'That's right.' He sat down in the chair across from her and placed his glass on her table. She dropped her eyes, felt her whole body growing warm. He could have been a movie star: tall, tanned, athletic-looking; he had a square chin, bright blue eyes, a set of beautiful white teeth, and long dimples in his cheeks. She remembered the nudging and whispering that used to go on among the secretaries the few times he'd come into Seldridge's to pick up Ann.

'But your memory's better than mine,' he said. 'Help me out. Where do I know you from?'

'You don't know me,' she answered, bashfully. 'But I used to work at Seldridge's, with Ann. Well not with her, exactly—I was one of the receptionists—and I used to see you when you came to pick her up from work.'

'Oh yeah—now I remember. I guess the only time I ever talked with you was on the phone.' He raised an eyebrow, inquiringly. When she nodded he continued, 'But I've got a good memory for faces—especially pretty ones. What are you drinking?' He glanced at her glass. 'Why don't I buy you another?'

'Well, I—um—sure, I guess.' She pushed a strand of hair behind her ear, then dropped her hands in her lap, remembering to hide her fingernails, which were bitten to the quick. Were he and Ann still married?

He caught the waitress's eye; Moira ordered another cooler. 'Gerry,' he said, when the waitress had gone, and proffered his hand across the table. So Moira had no choice but to wipe her palm on her skirt and lay her hand in his. He gave it a friendly squeeze. She told him her name, withdrew her hand and curled her fingertips into her palms.

'So you don't work at Seldridge's any more?'

'No. Does Ann?'

He shook his head. 'We've got a little boy now—Tim. She's at home looking after him.'

So. They were still married.

'We're a one-income family now. Bucking the trend. It's tough.' He shook his head, ruefully, but his eyes continued to smile into hers.

'How old is Tim?'

'He's two. The terrorist age.'

Moira started to giggle, nervously, managed to subdue it into a smile. 'Is Ann planning to go back to work?' She felt like a fraud, talking about Ann in this way. She hadn't really known her, had only admired her from a distance. Ann had been one of the accountants at Seldridge's; she was beautiful, sophisticated, elegant, quiet; in Moira's eyes, the epitome of a lady.

The smile had left Gerry's eyes. 'I don't know. I don't know what she wants to do. She wants me to make more money, I think.' He gave a disparaging grimace.

'She likes being at home?'

He shrugged.

Oh, Moira thought, another marriage on the rocks. It seemed to her that everyone who was married wanted to be single, and vice versa. It was depressing, really. Ann and Gerry Erskine had looked like the perfect couple, but apparently they weren't doing any better than anyone else.

Her drink arrived. Gerry paid for it, and Moira watched the waitress, who was harassed and busy, thaw under his smile and linger a little longer at their table than was necessary. When she left, Gerry's eyes followed her legs, and Moira, in order to reclaim his attention asked, 'What do you do?'

His eyes came back to her, and his gaze was like a drug, transfixing her, making her thoughts slow and swirl to a stop. 'I go wind-surfing, scuba-diving, sailing—'

'For money, I mean.'

'Ah!' He sat back. 'See? You women are all the same.'

She started to protest, but he interrupted her: 'Actually, that is what I do. I work for a sports equipment outfit and we run courses in all sort of things. I'm one of the instructors.'

That explains the body, she thought—and the tan. 'Sounds like fun.'

'Well—I'd rather do it than teach it. But I meet a lot of nice people and the scenery is great. But like I say, it doesn't pay too well and that's a bit of a problem these days.'

He went on talking to her for almost an hour. He told her about his work, described some of the dangerous and exciting experiences he'd had. He was a real outdoors man, he'd done everything: whitewater rafting, hang-gliding, parachute-jumping, helicopter-skiing. . . . Listening, she felt transported into a world of wind and water, sun and adventure. Maybe she should try something like that—learn to ski, or sail. Of course it would be pretty expensive.

At seven-thirty he glanced at his watch and said he'd better be pushing off, that Ann and Tim would soon be home. 'And I'd better get there before they do,' he threatened, mockingly, 'or I'll be in trouble.' He stood up, pushed in his chair, then stood, gazing down at her, his eyes suddenly serious. 'She looks good from a distance, doesn't she?' he asked.

Moira pretended not to understand. 'Who?'

'Ann. I bet all you girls in the front office at Seldridge's used to admire her, eh?'

'Yes,' said Moira, slightly embarrassed. 'At least, I did.'

'I did too.' He was silent for a moment. 'But let me tell you something.' He leaned towards her, resting a hand on the table, his eyes only six inches above her face. 'Close up—you look a hell of a lot better.' He reached out a palm, ran it gently, swiftly down her cheek. 'It's been fun talking to you, kid. See you around.'

Then he was gone.

All the way home on the bus Moira's cheek burned where he'd touched it. She stared out the bus window at the passing storefronts, reviewing every minute of their conversation, every look, every gesture. That lasted her through supper, through her bath, right up until bedtime. Then she dreamed she was skiing through gusts of white snow, floating into snow-drifts, the sky so blue that it made her eyes ache.

Throughout the weekend she alternated between moods of elation and despair. What was wrong with her anyway? Why couldn't she find someone she liked? Did she put men off? (Yet he'd stroked her cheek, he'd said he preferred her over Ann. . . .) She looked up his name in the telephone book, but it wasn't listed. Perhaps Erskine was Ann's maiden name—not his? She didn't even know where he worked. Forget it, she told herself. One: he's married; two: he was just bored and looking for someone to flirt with; three: he's out of your league. Meaning? 'Look, Moira,' she said, staring at the reflection of her face in the mirror, 'you're not a frog—and one little kiss isn't going to turn you into a princess. You don't even know how to swim—let alone surf. Stick to reality.'

On Monday, at work, they had a big case to prepare for, and Moira didn't get her morning coffee break until it was almost noon. On her way out of the office, she picked up the morning paper that one of the lawyers, Julia, always brought in with her and left on the table in the reception area. Moira scanned the headlines as she walked next door to the deli. There she bought her usual: a coffee and a lemon Danish, and sat down at one of the tables by the window to read the newspaper.

Before Moira came to work at Jamieson's, she rarely read the newspaper—but at Jamieson's, where she took her coffee breaks alone, she started reading it every day. She had discovered which columnists and cartoons she liked best, and followed all the juiciest stories: murders, kidnappings, aeroplane crashes, car bombs. What a world it was! Sometimes she thought that people should just wipe themselves off the planet and leave it to the birds and bees and dinosaurs again. It would sure solve a lot of problems.

So when she read that yet another young woman had been picked up at a singles' bar and subsequently raped, Moira was not surprised. Lately there had been several such rapes: men picking up women in bars, offering them a drive home, then raping them at knife-point and abandoning them in the bush. Two of the women had resisted and been stabbed—though the wounds weren't fatal. Moira knew better than to climb into a strange man's car—but she dutifully read the police warnings and resolved to be extra careful.

The next Friday evening, she was in Trilby's again—trying (and failing) not to keep her eyes glued to the doors as if she were expecting someone to join her. You never saw him here before, she kept saying to herself, so why do you expect to see him here again? Then Barry, from the credit union, sat down and talked to her for a while. They'd talked before—and Moira quite liked him, but he never asked her out so she figured that he was either happily married, or gay. Usually she would have been glad of his company, but today she kept worrying that she would miss seeing Gerry. Barry ordered a second beer for both of them, and then began telling her about his younger sister, who was dying of bone marrow cancer. His sister was only seventeen; the doctors had tried, and failed, to find a donor whose marrow would match hers. Listening, Moira forgot all about Gerry—right up until he materialized at her elbow, a beer glass in his hand.

'Moira,' he said, surprise and pleasure in his voice. He dropped a hand on her shoulder, glanced at Barry. 'Mind if I join you?'

Moira introduced the two men, but Barry got up and said he had to leave.

'Hope I didn't interrupt anything,' Gerry said, sliding into Barry's place. 'I didn't mean to turf him out.'

'No, I think . . .' Moira trailed off; her eyes followed Barry as he moved towards the door. 'He was—' She glanced at Gerry, who was smiling at her, and she couldn't finish her sentence. Gerry's gaze drove Barry's troubles right out of her head. He was here! Again!

'So you're a regular,' he commented.

She smiled and blushed a little; now he probably thought she hung out here every night. 'No—not really. I just come here on Fridays. . . .'

This time they talked for more than two hours, and by the end of it Moira had drunk considerably more alcohol than she was used to. Moira told Gerry a bit about herself, and Gerry talked a lot about his relationship with Ann. 'I feel like all she cares about is appearances— the house, the garden, the furniture, the cutlery. You'd think the whole world was watching us, the way she goes on. But God— we've only got one life—why waste it worrying about that stuff? Let's have fun, let's do the things we really enjoy. Who cares what the neighbours think?'

Moira could see his point. She'd admired Ann's perfection—but perfection had a price. Gerry said that Ann was always tidying and fussing and wouldn't let Tim or Gerry relax. He intimated that this was affecting their sex life as well; Moira guessed that Ann was probably too worried about staining the sheets to enjoy herself. It was too bad, really, because Ann was a nice person. She was reserved, but not stuck-up, and unlike many of the other management types at Seldridge's, she always understood that the secretaries had many claims on their attention and couldn't necessarily drop everything else the moment she needed them. Moira felt sorry that it wasn't working out.

Just before he left, Gerry suggested they go out for dinner some-time—maybe next week. Moira gave him her phone number, then wondered what Ann would think. Gerry had told her that he and Ann lived pretty independent lives. ('We don't like the same people—she has her friends, I have mine.') But on her way home, Moira couldn't help asking herself: How independent? Did they have independent sex lives too? And would she want to get involved with a man who was married to someone else—even if his wife knew what was going on? No, she answered, fiercely, her stomach knotting at the very thought. But she also knew that if she and Gerry were ever alone together, if he made any moves . . . she'd get sucked into his arms like a moth into the light.

The following Tuesday at coffee-break, Moira read a long article about the man the newspaper was now calling the Singles' Bar Rapist. Apparently the police had concluded that this recent series of rapes was in fact the work of one man, whose modus operandi was always exactly the same. He struck up a conversation with a woman at a bar, offered her a ride home, or sometimes just suggested they go for a drive. Then he took her to a park or a stretch of beach, proposed a little walk, and raped her at knife-point, inflicting superficial wounds if she resisted. A composite sketch accompanied the article. The rapist was described as being in his early thirties, about six-foot-one; he had an athletic build, a dark complexion, blue eyes, dark brown hair. All his victims agreed that he was 'very good-looking', and said that he'd complained at length about his wife. He drove a dark blue, newish car, which one victim said she thought was an Altura.

Moira frowned, studying the composite. I wouldn't know an Altura if I saw one, she thought. And as for complaining about his wife—that could be just about anyone.

On Wednesday evening, Gerry phoned. When Moira heard his voice, her heart ricocheted around her chest like a bird trapped inside a house. 'Oh hi,' she said in a high, nervous voice, sounding half her age. He suggested picking her up after work tomorrow, going to an Italian restaurant for supper. 'Sure, that'd be great,' she enthused, trying to get her voice back down to its usual register. Afterwards, when she hung up, she wondered what Ann was doing that night. Maybe she has a lover too, she thought—and then caught herself: 'too'? 'We're just friends,' she declared loudly, and went to survey the contents of her closet.

The dinner date was both exhilarating and exhausting. When Moira had talked to Gerry at Trilby's she'd always been securely wedged behind her table—but now she had to negotiate all kinds of situations: getting in and out of his car, going through doors, taking her coat off—and she felt as awkward as a thirteen-year-old. Once they were seated in the restaurant, she relaxed a bit, and they started off their meal with a bottle of white wine—which helped. Unfortunately she was too nervous to really eat anything, but after Gerry had finished his meal, they sat and talked for a long time, sipping wine and then coffee, looking out the window to where the lights of the North Shore glittered against the black mass of mountains.

But when he started complaining about Ann again, she became uncomfortable. She tried to get him to talk about something else. She wasn't sure why she didn't like it—although she never liked it, really, when men complained about their wives. It always made her think: if I were married to him, then he'd be complaining about me. But today, for some reason, she was reacting more than usual. She wanted him to be different? Yes, she didn't want him to sound like all those other discontented husbands. And he was different, really—but his marital problems were uppermost on his mind, and all topics seemed to lead, inevitably, back to them.

By the end of the evening, her elation had worn off, and the strain was getting to her. She had the beginnings of a headache, and she knew she'd be hung-over the next morning. As they walked down the street to where his car was parked, he placed an arm, casually, over her shoulder. She felt her stomach clench. When they reached the car, he dropped his arm, and while she waited for him to unlock the passenger door, her eyes fastened upon a chunk of chrome script that decorated the front fender. 'Altura,' it read. He opened the door; her eyes scanned the rest of the car which looked black under the fluorescent streetlights, but which she now remembered was dark blue.

'Here you go,' he said, waiting for her to get in.

She swallowed. 'What kind of car is this?' she asked, sliding past him into the seat.

'An Altura. '89,' he said, closing the door.

As he walked round the car to his side, she tried to staunch the panic that was welling up into her throat. There's more than one dark blue Altura in the world, she reminded herself, and besides—I know who he is—so he isn't going to rape me. Even so, she found herself staring at the glove compartment, wondering if it contained the knife.

Driving home they chatted, desultorily, both tired—and she kept casting him surreptitious glances, studying his profile. Yes, he even fit the description: about six foot one, tall, dark, good-looking . . . She shook her head. No. But when they arrived at her apartment building, she still hadn't got over her scare and opened the passenger door as soon as he parked. 'Thanks a lot,' she called gaily. 'I really enjoyed that. I really did—thanks a million.' And again, like a thirteen-year-old, she bolted out of the car and fled up the concrete steps, almost tripping over the top one in her ungainly haste to lock herself into the security of her apartment.

Inside, she kicked off her shoes and collapsed on the sofa. Of course it's not him, she scolded herself. What must he have thought of her, running away like that? Overwhelmed with embarrassment, she covered her face with her hands. 'You idiot!' she cried, contemptuously. 'Don't you know that whenever the cops put out a description like that, they get hundreds of calls? Everybody wants to tell them that they know a guy who drives a dark blue Altura and complains about his wife. What's wrong with you anyway? He's the most charming, handsome, wonderful man you've ever met and you just treated him like a leper.'

The next day was Friday but he didn't show up at Trilby's, although she waited there until half past eight. Nor did he phone the following week. Just as well, she kept saying to herself, what you don't need is a married man. But she was definitely depressed; her life stretched before her, empty and flat, a vista of endless drudgery.

The following weekend, fortunately, brought a diversion. Her best friend, Chris, was driving down from Penticton to spend the weekend with her. Moira and Chris had gone to high school together, had counselled each other through their first boyfriends, subsequent marriages and divorces—and now Chris was on her second marriage. That Friday, therefore, Moira didn't go to Trilby's. She bought groceries and went home, cooked some supper in case Chris arrived hungry.

A little after eight, Chris pulled up in front of Moira's apartment building and they stayed up talking until two in the morning. On Saturday they went for a walk in Stanley Park, drove downtown, and spent the rest of the afternoon in Vancouver's biggest, newest, downtown shopping mall. They ate fish and chips at a restaurant on Denman Street, then went to an early movie. Afterwards, Chris suggested they visit one of their old haunts, a club called 'The Hot Spot'.

'I haven't been there in years,' Moira objected, 'and it's changed hands several times. It even has a new name. Who knows what kind of crowd they get?'

'If it's awful, we'll leave,' Chris said, cheerfully. 'Come on, I'm feeling nostalgic.'

The club was now called 'Lucky in Love'. The music was loud, but not deafening, and the crowd seemed to consist of people much like themselves: young working people between twenty and thirty-five. It seemed that this club, like Trilby's, had a regular clientele: groups stood in conversational clusters around the dance floor and people circulated freely among the tables.

After standing near the bar for a while, Moira and Chris got a table to themselves—and ordered Singapore Slings, for old times' sake. 'Who was that guy you went out with, the one who kept polishing his shoes all the time?' 'And remember that double date, where they decided to take us to a porno movie in Blaine and we escaped home on the bus?' But by the time they were on their second drink, the conversation grew more serious: Chris wanted to have a baby, but her husband, Mike, kept saying he wasn't ready yet; and Moira confessed that she didn't know why, but she couldn't seem to meet anybody she really liked. 'I guess I'm too idealistic,' she said. 'I want someone who's perfect.'

It wasn't until their third drink that Moira finally told Chris about Gerry—not about her paranoid attack when she'd suspected him of being the Singles' Bar Rapist (she wanted to forget about that)—but about her conflicting feelings concerning him. 'Already I'm head over heels—but at the same time, I don't want to get involved with a married man. And maybe he picked up on that—he hasn't phoned me since. So I should be glad, right?' Chris nodded, gravely, noticing that Moira looked close to tears. (She remembered that Moira cried easily when she was drunk.)

Chris got up and went to find the washroom. While she was gone, Moira watched the people at the bar and thought about Gerry. She knew that getting involved with Gerry would cause her nothing but heartbreak. Let's face it—it was causing her heartbreak already. Her eyes filled with tears; she stared unseeingly at the figures silhouetted against the brightly lit background—and she saw Gerry's profile moving, as if in a mist, past the laughing faces. She blinked, looked again—and yes—there he was! It looked like he'd just arrived—alone. He found a space at the bar, attracted the bartender's attention, and ordered a drink. What a coincidence! Her heart was fluttering; her palms were damp. But I'm with Chris tonight, she reminded herself, and it's our last evening together. I could go by and say hello, though.

Chris returned. 'I meant to tell you,' she said, 'remember Alison? From our softball team? She committed suicide last year. And she had two little kids. . . .' Finally, when they'd finished talking about Alison, Moira pointed Gerry out to Chris. 'See? At the end of the bar—in the grey sports jacket.'

Chris dug her glasses out of her purse and put them on to get a better look. 'Woo—' she commented, appreciatively. 'Who's the woman beside him? His wife?'

'What woman?' Moira glanced back at the bar. Gerry was talking to the woman seated on the bar-stool next to him. She was very sexy-looking; she wore a slinky black dress and she had teased, silver-streaked hair. 'No, that's not his wife. And he didn't come in with her.'

'I notice there's a lot of that going on in this place,' Chris commented, looking around.

'A lot of what?' Moira was still watching Gerry, whose dark head was almost touching the silvery one beside him. He must know her, she thought.

'You know—pick-ups. People cruising—girls as well as guys.'

'Oh yeah?' Moira glanced at her, then her gaze slid back to the couple at the bar.

Chris watched her, speculatively. 'Let's go, Moira,' she said. 'I have got to get an early start tomorrow.'

Moira gave her a panic-stricken glance. 'Sure,' she said, managing to sound nonchalant, but eyes slewed immediately back to Gerry.

'I'll just say hello on my way out.'

Chris swivelled, looked at the couple at the bar again. 'Too late,' she said, 'they're leaving.'

She was right. The woman with the silvery hair was standing up; Gerry had placed a hand on her shoulder, was guiding her through the crowd towards the far exit. Moira's gaze followed them all the way to the door and remained stuck there long after they'd disappeared through it.

Chris touched her hand. 'Time to go.'

Moira's eyes slowly focused upon Chris. Her face looked crumpled. 'Well!' she said, standing up suddenly and reaching for her jacket. 'I'm sure glad I'm not his wife.' But her bottom lip wobbled.

'Now you've got the right attitude,' Chris said, encouragingly, but she watched her friend with concern. Moira had always had a weakness for jerks, and it seemed to Chris that she'd just fallen for another one.

On Monday morning, Moira sat in the deli, staring at the screaming newspaper headline: 'Singles' Bar Rapist Strikes Again!' Her Danish lay untouched on the plate beside her, she'd read the article three times. No, she kept thinking—No! This doesn't happen! She tried to take a sip of coffee, but the rim of the cup clattered against her teeth, and she put it back down, her eyes compulsively returning to the fine print. 'Last Saturday night, the man police are now calling the Singles' Bar Rapist picked up another young woman, this time from the club called "Lucky in Love". According to his victim, he struck up a conversation with her at the bar, then suggested they move on to somewhere a little quieter, where they'd be able to talk. They left the club at around 11:30. He drove her to Ferguson Point in Stanley Park where he forced her down a path to an isolated stretch of beach. . . .'

Eleven-thirty! Even the time was right. She'd noticed a clock in a jeweller's window when she and Chris were walking back to the car. 'The victim, whose name has not been released, described her assailant as tall, tanned, and extremely good-looking, a description that matches that given by the other women who have been assaulted by this man. He was wearing a grey sports jacket and drove a newish, dark blue car. . . .' Moira closed her eyes. O.K., she thought—now talk me out of this one. It's the same club, the same time; he was wearing a grey sports jacket, he drives a dark blue car . . .

'Are you all right?'

She opened her eyes with a start and found the deli woman, the one whom she'd seen in Trilby's, peering at her anxiously.

'You're very pale. Are you feeling O.K.?'

'No,' Moira breathed. 'I mean, yes, I—' Her eyes skittered sideways to the article in the newspaper, then returned to the small brown eyes peering earnestly in her face. 'I mean, no.' She stood up. 'I'm sorry.' She indicated the lemon Danish. 'I don't think I can eat this.'

'I'll save it for you, shall I?' the deli woman offered. 'I'll stick it in a bag and you can take it home with you.' Before Moira could object, she'd whisked the plate from the table, went back behind the counter, and slipped the Danish into a small paper bag. 'Here you go,' she said, returning from behind the counter, proffering the bag. 'Looks like you'd better go home to bed.'

Moira took the bag. 'Yes. Thanks.' She turned towards the door.

'Don't forget your newspaper.' The woman retrieved the newspaper from the table, folded it, and handed it to her.

Moira thanked her again, went out the door. She stood on the sidewalk, staring at the traffic, clutching the bag and the newspaper, not knowing what to do next. Should she go to the police? But what if she was wrong? (What if she was right? What if she had to testify against him?) I'll go home and try to think, she resolved, in a panic. But she'd have to tell them at work first. She turned and stumbled up the sidewalk to the office.

The reception area was empty, but she could hear voices in Julia's office. She walked down the hall and stopped in the open doorway. Julia was sitting at her desk, Dave standing over her; together they were examining a document that had arrived in the mail that morning. They both looked up.

'Moira?' Julia got up from her chair, came towards her. 'What's the matter?'

Moira had intended, simply, to say that she felt unwell, but she found herself holding out the newspaper, as if by way of explanation. 'I have to go home,' she pleaded, her voice quavering.

'Of course. Do you feel sick?' Julia took the newspaper and glanced down at it, puzzled. As Moira watched, her eyes fell upon the headline. She looked at Moira inquiringly.

'I know him!' Moira blurted, her eyes flooding with tears. 'I even went out with him.'

'Who?' Julia stared at her.

'Him!' Moira sobbed, and pointed to the word 'Rapist'.

Footsteps passed in the corridor outside, a siren wailed over the steady clamour of downtown traffic. The police officer, sitting across from them, took out a handkerchief and blew his nose. Again Moira studied each face in the row of photographs that was spread out on the desk in front of her. Her eyes lifted to the detective's face. 'He's not here,' she said.

'No?' The detective put his handkerchief back in his pocket; his face was impassive. 'You don't recognize any of them?'

Moira shook her head, watching him doubtfully.

'So where does that leave us?' Julia asked.

The detective collected up the photographs one by one. Finally he sat back, tamping the photographs into a neat stack with his fingers, as if getting ready to deal out a new hand of cards. 'Nowhere,' he said. 'We arrested the man this morning.'

Moira stared at him, uncomprehendingly; Julia leaned forward. 'The rapist? You've got him?'

'Yes. But I was hoping you'd provide some—ahem—corroborative detail.'

'Is it—?' But Moira gagged on Gerry's name.

'Is it him?' Julia sounded exasperated. 'The guy she knows?'

The detective's eyes lowered to the photographs in his hand; he began shuffling through them, one by one. 'Apparently not,' he finally answered, and showed them the photograph that he'd moved to the top of the pile. 'This is the man we've arrested. And he's already been identified by two of his victims.'

Moira stared blankly at the photograph. He looked nothing like Gerry. He was dark—sure—and good-looking, she supposed, but . . . He's not a patch on Gerry, she thought, loyally.

'If you had seen this guy leaving the club on Saturday night,' the detective explained, 'we might have used you as a witness. But as it is. . . .'

Julia stood up, impatient to be gone. Moira glanced up at her. 'So you don't have to turn in your friend, after all,' Julia said to her, smiling, reassuringly.

Moira managed to return her smile, then remembering that Julia was due in court that afternoon and was in a hurry to get back to the office, she too stood up.

'Thank you for coming down with me,' Moira said, as they walked across the parking lot to Julia's car.

'Well, I couldn't leave you to face the detectives alone. Now—shall I give you a lift home? Or would you rather go back to work?' Julia asked her, sardonically.

Moira thought of her empty apartment, of the thoughts that were waiting to attack her there. 'Actually—I'd rather go back to work,' she confessed, as Julia slid into the driver's seat beside her.

'Good,' said Julia, 'then my brief will get typed.' She turned the key in the ignition.

On Thursday evening, he phoned again.

'I was wondering if I could lure you away from Trilby's tomorrow and convince you to take in a movie instead.'

'Oh,' said Moira. 'Oh, well I—actually, I'm doing something else this Friday.'

'All right. What about Saturday then?'

Again her heart was beating against her ribs like a bird thrashing itself against a window, and the phone receiver was slippery in her hand. 'Ah—you see—I'm seeing someone else now. And it—I don't think—it wouldn't work out.'

'Oh.' There was a silence. 'Well then.' Another silence. 'Guess I'll—ah—be seeing you around then, eh?'

'Yeah. Sure,' she breathed.

She hung up. She walked to the couch, sat down on the edge of it; she was shaking from head to foot, her limbs rattling like branches in the wind. It wasn't him, she reminded herself. You were wrong—the police said so.

But she couldn't help feeling that she'd had a very narrow escape.

PETER ROBINSON · b. 1950

Fan Mail

The letter arrived one sunny Thursday morning in August, along with a Visa bill and a royalty statement. Dennis Quilley carried the mail out to the deck of his Beaches home, stopping by the kitchen on the way to pour himself a gin and tonic. He had already been writing for three hours straight, and he felt he deserved a drink.

First he looked at the amount of the royalty cheque, then he put aside the Visa bill and picked up the letter carefully, as if he were a forensic expert investigating it for prints. Postmarked Toronto, and dated four days earlier, it was addressed in a small, precise hand and looked as if it had been written with a fine-nibbed calligraphic pen. But the postal code was different; that had been hurriedly scrawled in with a ball-point. Whoever it was, Quilley thought, had probably got his name from the telephone directory and had then looked up the code in the post office just before mailing.

Pleased with his deductions, Quilley opened the letter. Written in the same neat and mannered hand as the address, it said:

Dear Mr Quilley,

Please forgive me for writing to you at home like this. I know you must be very busy, and it is inexcusable of me to intrude on your valuable time. Believe me, I would not do so if I could think of any other way.

I have been a great fan of your work for many years now. As a collector of mysteries, too, I also have first editions of all your books. From what I have read, I know you are a clever man, and, I hope, just the man to help me with my problem.

For the past twenty years, my wife has been making my life a misery. I put up with her for the sake of the children, but now they have all gone to live their own lives. I have asked her for a divorce, but she just laughed in my face. I have decided, finally, that the only way out is to kill her, and that is why I am seeking your advice.

You may think this is insane of me, especially saying it in a letter, but it is just a measure of my desperation. I would quite understand it if you went straight to the police, and I am sure they would find me and punish me. Believe me, I've thought about it. Even that would be preferable to the misery I must suffer day after day.

If you can find it in your heart to help a devoted fan in his hour of need, please meet me on the roof lounge of the Park Plaza Hotel on Wednesday, August 19 at two p.m. I have taken the afternoon off work and will wait longer if for any reason you are delayed. Don't worry, I will recognize you easily from your photo on the dust-jackets of your books.

Yours, in hope,
A Fan.

The letter slipped from Quilley's hand. He couldn't believe what he'd just read. He was a mystery writer—he specialized in devising ingenious murders—but for someone to assume that he did the same in real life was absurd. Could it be a practical joke?

He picked up the letter and read through it again. The man's whining tone and clichéd style seemed sincere enough, and the more Quilley thought about it, the more certain he became that none of his friends was sick enough to play such a joke.

Assuming that it was real then, what should he do? His impulse was to crumple up the letter and throw it away. But should he go to the police? No. That would be a waste of time. The real police were a terribly dull and literal-minded lot. They would probably think he was seeking publicity.

He found that he had screwed up the sheet of paper in his fist, and he was just about to toss it aside when he changed his mind. Wasn't there another option? Go. Go and meet the man. Find out more about him. Find out if he was genuine. Surely there would be no obligation in that? All he had to do was turn up at the Park Plaza at the appointed time and see what happened.

Quilley's life was fine—no troublesome woman to torment him, plenty of money (mostly from American sales), a beautiful lakeside cottage near Huntsville, a modicum of fame, the esteem of his peers—but it had been rather boring of late. Here was an opportunity for adventure of a kind. Besides, he might get a story idea out of the meeting. Why not go and see?

He finished his drink and smoothed the letter on his knee. He had to smile at that last bit. No doubt the man would recognize him from his book-jacket photo, but it was an old one and had been retouched in the first place. His cheeks had filled out a bit since then, and his thinning hair had acquired a sprinkling of grey. Still, he thought, he was a handsome man for fifty: handsome, clever, and successful.

Smiling, he picked up both letter and envelope and went back to the kitchen in search of matches. There must be no evidence.

Over the next few days, Quilley hardly gave a thought to the mysterious letter. As usual in summer, he divided his time between writing in Toronto, where he found the city worked as a stimulus, and weekends at the cottage. There, he walked in the woods, chatted to locals in the lodge, swam in the clear lake, and idled around getting a tan. Evenings, he would open a bottle of chardonnay, reread P.G. Wodehouse, and listen to Bach. It was an ideal life: quiet, solitary, independent.

When Wednesday came, though, he drove downtown, parked in the multi-storey garage at Cumberland and Avenue Road, then walked to the Park Plaza. It was another hot day. The tourists were out in force across Bloor Street by the Royal Ontario Museum, many of them Americans from Buffalo, Rochester, or Detroit: the men in loud checked shirts photographing everything in sight, their wives in tight shorts looking tired and thirsty.

Quilley took the elevator up to the nineteenth floor and wandered through the bar, an olde-worlde place with deep armchairs and framed reproductions of old Colonial scenes on the walls. It was busier than usual, and even though the windows were open, the smoke bothered him. He walked out onto the roof lounge and scanned the faces. Within moments he had noticed someone looking his way. The man paused for just a split second, perhaps to translate the dust-jacket photo into reality, then beckoned Quilley over with raised eyebrows and a twitch of the head.

The man rose to shake hands, then sat down again, glancing around to make sure nobody had paid the two of them undue attention. He was short and thin, with sandy hair and a pale grey complexion, as if he had just come out of hospital. He wore wire-rimmed glasses and had a habit of rolling his tongue around in his mouth when he wasn't talking.

'First of all, Mr Quilley,' the man said, raising his glass, 'may I say how honoured I am to meet you.' He spoke with a pronounced English accent.

Quilley inclined his head. 'I'm flattered, Mr . . . er . . . ?'

'Peplow, Frank Peplow.'

'Yes . . . Mr Peplow. But I must admit I'm puzzled by your letter.'

A waiter in a burgundy jacket came over to take Quilley's order. He asked for an Amstel.

Peplow paused until the waiter was out of earshot. 'Puzzled?'

'What I mean is,' Quilley went on, struggling for the right words, 'whether you were serious or not, whether you really do want to —'

Peplow leaned forward. Behind the lenses, his pale blue eyes looked sane enough. 'I assure you, Mr Quilley, that I was, that I am entirely serious. That woman is ruining my life and I can't allow it to go on any longer.'

Speaking about her brought little spots of red to his cheeks. Quilley held his hand up. 'All right, I believe you. I suppose you realize I should have gone to the police?'

'But you didn't.'

'I could have. They might be here, watching us.'

Peplow shook his head. 'Mr Quilley, if you won't help, I'd even welcome prison. Don't think I haven't realized that I might get caught, that no murder is perfect. All I want is a chance. It's worth the risk.'

The waiter returned with Quilley's drink, and they both sat in silence until he had gone. Quilley was intrigued by this drab man sitting opposite him, a man who obviously didn't even have the imagination to dream up his own murder plot. 'What do you want from me?' he asked.

'I have no right to ask anything of you, I understand that,' Peplow said. 'I have absolutely nothing to offer in return. I'm not rich. I have no savings. I suppose all I want really is advice, encouragement.'

'If I were to help,' Quilley said. '*If* I were to help, then I'd do nothing more than offer advice. Is that clear?'

Peplow nodded. 'Does that mean you will?'

'If I can.'

And so Dennis Quilley found himself helping to plot the murder of a woman he'd never met with a man he didn't even particularly like. Later, when he analysed his reasons for playing along, he realized that that was exactly what he had been doing—playing. It had been a game, a cerebral puzzle, just like thinking up a plot for a book, and he never, at first, gave a thought to real murder, real blood, real death.

Peplow took a handkerchief from his top pocket and wiped the thin film of sweat from his brow. 'You don't know how happy this makes me, Mr Quilley. At last, I have a chance. My life hasn't amounted to much, and I don't suppose it ever will. But at least I might find some peace and quiet in my final years. I'm not a well man.' He placed one hand solemnly over his chest. 'Ticker. Not fair, is it? I've never smoked, I hardly drink, and I'm only fifty-three. But the doctor has promised me a few years yet if I live right. All I want is to be left alone with my books and my garden.'

'Tell me about your wife,' Quilley prompted.

Peplow's expression darkened. 'She's a cruel and selfish woman,' he said. 'And she's messy, she never does anything around the place. Too busy watching those damn soap-operas on television day and night. She cares about nothing but her own comfort, and she never overlooks an opportunity to nag me or taunt me. If I try to escape to my collection, she mocks me and calls me dull and boring. I'm not even safe from her in my garden. I realize I have no imagination, Mr Quilley, and perhaps even less courage, but even a man like me deserves some peace in his life, don't you think?'

Quilley had to admit that the woman really did sound awful—worse than any he had known, and he had met some shrews in his time. He had never had much use for women, except for occasional sex in his younger days. Even that had become sordid, and now he stayed away from them as much as possible. He found, as he listened, that he could summon up remarkable sympathy for Peplow's position.

'What do you have in mind?' he asked.

'I don't really know. That's why I wrote to you. I was hoping you might be able to help with some ideas. Your books . . . you seem to know so much.'

'In my books,' Quilley said, 'the murderer always gets caught.'

'Well, yes,' said Peplow, 'of course. But that's because the genre demands it, isn't it? I mean, your Inspector Baldry is much smarter than any real policeman. I'm sure if you'd made him a criminal, he would always get away.'

There was no arguing with that, Quilley thought. 'How do you want to do it?' he asked. 'A domestic accident? Electric shock, say? Gadget in the bathtub? She must have a hair curler or a dryer?'

Peplow shook his head, eyes tightly closed. 'Oh no,' he whispered, 'I couldn't. I couldn't do anything like that. No more than I could bear the sight of her blood.'

'How's her health?'

'Unfortunately,' said Peplow, 'she seems obscenely robust.'

'How old is she?'

'Forty-nine.'

'Any bad habits?'

'Mr Quilley, my wife has nothing *but* bad habits. The only thing she won't tolerate is drink, for some reason, and I don't think she has other men—though that's probably because nobody will have her.'

'Does she smoke?'

'Like a chimney.'

Quilley shuddered. 'How long?'

'Ever since she was a teenager, I think. Before I met her.'

'Does she exercise?'

'Never.'

'What about her weight, her diet?'

'Well, you might call her fat, but you'd be generous in saying she was full-figured. She eats too much junk food. I've always said that. And eggs. She loves bacon and eggs for breakfast. And she's always stuffing herself with cream-cakes and tarts.'

'Hmmm,' said Quilley, taking a sip of Amstel. 'She sounds like a prime candidate for a heart attack.'

'But it's me who —' Peplow stopped as comprehension dawned. 'I see. Yes, I see. You mean one could be *induced*?'

'Quite. Do you think you could manage that?'

'Well, I could if I didn't have to be there to watch. But I don't know how.'

'Poison.'

'I don't know anything about poison.'

'Never mind. Give me a few days to look into it. I'll give you advice, remember, but that's as far as it goes.'

'Understood.'

Quilley smiled. 'Good. Another beer?'

'No, I'd better not. She'll be able to smell this on my breath and I'll be in for it already. I'd better go.'

Quilley looked at his watch. Two-thirty. He could have done with another Amstel, but he didn't want to stay there by himself. Besides, at half past three it would be time to meet his agent at the Windsor Arms, and there he would have the opportunity to drink as much as he wanted. To pass the time, he could browse through the magazines and imported newspapers in the Reader's Den. 'Fine,' he said, 'I'll go down with you.'

Outside on the hot, busy street, they shook hands and agreed to meet in a week's time on the back patio of the Madison Avenue Pub. It wouldn't do to be seen together twice in the same place.

Quilley stood on the corner of Bloor and Avenue Road among the camera-clicking tourists and watched Peplow walk off towards the St George subway station. Now that their meeting was over and the spell was broken, he wondered again what the hell he was doing helping this pathetic little man. It certainly wasn't altruism. Perhaps the challenge appealed to him; after all, people climb mountains just because they're there.

And then there was Peplow's mystery collection. There was just a chance that it might contain an item of great interest to Quilley, and that Peplow might be grateful enough to part with it.

Wondering how to approach the subject at their next meeting, Quilley wiped the sweat from his brow with the back of his hand and walked towards the bookshop.

Atropine, hyoscyamine, belladonna. . . . Quilley flipped through Dreisbach's *Handbook of Poisoning* one evening at the cottage. Poison seemed to have gone out of fashion these days, and he had only used it in one of his novels, about six years ago. That had been the old stand-by, cyanide, with its familiar smell of bitter almonds that he had so often read about but never experienced. The small black handbook had sat on his shelf gathering dust ever since.

Writing a book, of course, one could generally skip over the problems of acquiring the stuff—give the killer a job as a pharmacist or in a hospital dispensary, for example. In real life, getting one's hands on poison might prove more difficult.

So far, he had read through the sections on agricultural poisons, household hazards, and medicinal poisons. The problem was that whatever Peplow used had to be easily available. Prescription drugs were out. Even if Peplow could persuade a doctor to give him barbiturates, for example, the prescription would be on record and any death in the household would be regarded as suspicious. Bar-biturates wouldn't do, anyway, and nor would such common products as paint thinner, insecticides, and weed killers—they didn't reproduce the symptoms of a heart attack.

Near the back of the book was a list of poisonous plants that shocked Quilley by its sheer length. He hadn't known just how much deadliness there was lurking in fields, gardens, and woods. Rhubarb leaves contained oxalic acid, for example, and caused nausea, vomiting, and diarrhea. The bark, wood, leaves, or seeds of the yew had a similar effect. Boxwood leaves and twigs caused convulsions; celandine could bring about a coma; hydrangeas contained cyanide; and laburnums brought on irregular pulse, delirium, twitching, and unconsciousness. And so the list went on—lupins, mistletoe, sweet peas, rhododendron—a poisoner's delight. Even the beautiful poinsettia, which brightened up so many Toronto homes each Christmas, could cause gastroenteritis. Most of these plants were easy to get hold of, and in many cases the active ingredients could be extracted simply by soaking or boiling in water.

It wasn't long before Quilley found what he was looking for. Beside 'Oleander' the note read, 'See *digitalis*, 374'. And there it was, set out in detail. Digitalis occurred in all parts of the common foxglove, which grew on waste ground and woodland slopes, and flowered from June to September. Acute poisoning would bring about death from ventricular fibrillation. No doctor would consider an autopsy if Peplow's wife appeared to die of a heart attack, given her habits, especially if Peplow fed her a few smaller doses first to establish the symptoms.

Quilley set aside the book. It was already dark outside, and the downpour that the humid, cloudy day had been promising had just begun. Rain slapped against the asphalt roof-tiles, gurgled down the drainpipe, and pattered on the leaves of the overhanging trees. In the background, it hissed as it fell on the lake. Distant flashes of lightning and deep rumblings of thunder warned of the coming storm.

Happy with his solitude and his cleverness, Quilley linked his hands behind his head and leaned back in the chair. Out back, he heard the rustling of a small animal making its way through the undergrowth—a racoon, perhaps, or even a skunk. When he closed his eyes, he pictured all the trees, shrubs, and wild flowers around the cottage and marvelled at what deadly potential so many of them contained.

The sun blazed down on the back patio of the Madison, a small garden protected from the wind by high fences. Quilley wore his sunglasses and nursed a pint of Conners Ale. The place was packed. Skilled and pretty waitresses came and went, trays laden with baskets of chicken wings and golden pints.

The two of them sat out of the way at a white table in a corner by the metal fire escape. A striped parasol offered some protection, but the sun was still too hot and bright. Peplow's wife must have given him hell about drinking the last time, because today he had ordered only a Coke.

'It was easy,' Quilley said. 'You could have done it yourself. The only setback was that foxgloves don't grow wild here like they do in England. But you're a gardener; you grow them.'

Peplow shook his head and smiled. 'It's the gift of clever people like yourself to make difficult things seem easy. I'm not particularly resourceful, Mr Quilley. Believe me, I wouldn't have known where to start. I had no idea that such a book existed, but you did, because of your art. Even if I had known, I'd hardly have dared buy it or take it out of the library for fear that someone would remember. But you've had your copy for years. A simple tool of the trade. No, Mr Quilley, please don't underestimate your contribution. I was a desperate man. Now you've given me a chance at freedom. If there's anything at all I can do for you, please don't hesitate to say. I'd consider it an honour.'

'This collection of yours,' Quilley said. 'What does it consist of?'

'British and Canadian crime fiction, mostly. I don't like to boast, but it's a very good collection. Try me. Go on, just mention a name.'

'E.C.R. Lorac.'

'About twenty of the Inspector MacDonalds. First editions, mint condition.'

'Anne Hocking?'

'Everything but *Night's Candles.*'

'Trotton?'

Peplow raised his eyebrows. 'Good Lord, that's an obscure one. Do you know, you're the first person I've come across who's ever mentioned that.'

'Do you have it?'

'Oh, yes.' Peplow smiled smugly. 'X.J. Trotton, *Summer's Lease,* published 1942. It turned up in a pile of junk I bought at an auction some years ago. It's rare, but not very valuable. Came out in Britain during the war and probably died an immediate death. It was his only book, as far as I can make out, and there is no biographical information. Perhaps it was a pseudonym for someone famous?'

Quilley shook his head. 'I'm afraid I don't know. Have you read it?'

'Good Lord, no! I don't read them. It could damage the spines. Many of them are fragile. Anything I want to read—like your books—I buy in paperback.'

'Mr Peplow,' Quilley said slowly, 'you asked if there was anything you could do for me. As a matter of fact, there is something you can give me for my services.'

'Yes?'

'The Trotton.'

Peplow frowned and pursed his thin lips. 'Why on earth. . . ?'

'For my own collection, of course. I'm especially interested in the war period.'

Peplow smiled. 'Ah! So that's how you know so much about them? I'd no idea you were a collector, too.'

Quilley shrugged modestly. He could see Peplow struggling, visualizing the gap in his collection. But finally the poor man decided that the murder of his wife was more important to him than an obscure mystery novel. 'Very well,' he said gravely. 'I'll mail it to you.'

'How can I be sure. . . ?'

Peplow looked offended. 'I'm a man of my word, Mr Quilley. A bargain is a bargain.' He held out his hand. 'Gentleman's agreement.'

'All right.' Quilley believed him. 'You'll be in touch, when it's done?'

'Yes. Perhaps a brief note in with the Trotton, if you can wait that long. Say two or three weeks?'

'Fine. I'm in no hurry.'

Quilley hadn't examined his motives since the first meeting, but he had realized, as he passed on the information and instructions, that it was the challenge he had responded to more than anything else. For years he had been writing crime novels, and in providing Peplow with the means to kill his slatternly, overbearing wife, Quilley had derived some vicarious pleasure from the knowledge that he—Inspector Baldry's creator—could bring off in real life what he had always been praised for doing in fiction.

Quilley also knew that there were no real detectives who possessed Baldry's curious mixture of intellect and instinct. Most of them were thick plodders, and they would never realize that dull Mr Peplow had murdered his wife with a bunch of foxgloves, of all things. Nor would they ever know that the brains behind the whole affair had been none other than his, Dennis Quilley's.

The two men drained their glasses and left together. The corner of Bloor and Spadina was busy with tourists and students lining up for charcoal-grilled hot-dogs from the street-vendor. Peplow turned towards the subway and Quilley wandered among the artsy crowd and sidewalk cyclists on Bloor Street West for a while, then he settled at an open-air café over a daiquiri and a slice of kiwi-fruit cheesecake to read the *Globe and Mail.*

Now, he thought as he sipped his drink and turned to the arts section, all he had to do was wait. One day soon, a small package would arrive for him. Peplow would be free of his wife, and Quilley would be the proud owner of one of the few remaining copies of X.J. Trotton's one and only mystery novel, *Summer's Lease.*

Three weeks passed, and no package arrived. Occasionally, Quilley thought of Mr Peplow and wondered what had become of him. Perhaps he had lost his nerve after all. That wouldn't be surprising. Quilley knew that he would have no way of finding out what had happened if Peplow chose not to contact him again. He didn't know where the man lived or where he worked. He didn't even know if Peplow was his real name. Still, he thought, it was best that way. No contact. Even the Trotton wasn't worth being involved in a botched murder for.

Then, at ten o'clock one warm Tuesday morning in September, the doorbell chimed. Quilley looked at his watch and frowned. Too early for the postman. Sighing, he pressed the SAVE command on his PC and walked down to answer the door. A stranger stood there, an overweight woman in a yellow polka-dot dress with short sleeves and a low neck. She had piggy eyes set in a round face, and dyed red hair that looked limp and lifeless after a cheap perm. She carried an imitation crocodile-skin handbag.

Quilley must have stood there looking puzzled for too long. The woman's eyes narrowed . . . and her rosebud mouth tightened so much that white furrows radiated from the red circle of her lips.

'May I come in?' she asked.

Stunned, Quilley stood back and let her enter. She walked straight over to a wicker armchair and sat down. The basket-work creaked under her. From there, she surveyed the room, with its waxed parquet floor, stone fireplace, and antique Ontario furniture. 'Nice,' she said, clutching her purse on her lap. Quilley sat down opposite her. Her dress was a size too small and the material strained over her red fleshy upper arms and pinkish bosom. The hem rode up as she crossed her legs, exposing a wedge of fat, mottled thigh. Primly, she pulled it down again over her dimpled knees.

'I'm sorry to appear rude,' said Quilley, regaining his composure, 'but who the hell are you?'

'My name is Peplow,' the woman said. 'Mrs Gloria Peplow. I'm a widow.'

Quilley felt a tingling sensation along his spine, like he always did when fear began to take hold of him.

He frowned and said, 'I'm afraid I don't know you, do I?'

'We've never met,' the woman replied, 'but I think you knew my husband.'

'I don't recall any Peplow. Perhaps you're mistaken?'

Gloria Peplow shook her head and fixed him with her piggy eyes. He noticed they were black, or as near as. 'I'm not mistaken, Mr Quilley. You didn't only know my husband, you also plotted with him to murder me.'

Quilley flushed and jumped to his feet. 'That's absurd! Look, if you've come here to make insane accusations like that, you'd better go.' He stood like an ancient statue, one hand pointing dramatically towards the door.

Mrs Peplow smirked. 'Oh, sit down. You look very foolish standing there like that.'

Quilley continued to stand. 'This is my home, Mrs Peplow, and I insist that you leave. Now!'

Mrs Peplow sighed and opened the gilded plastic clasp on her purse. She took out a Shoppers Drug Mart envelope, picked out two colour photographs, and dropped them next to the Wedgwood dish on the antique wine table by her chair. Leaning forward, Quilley could see clearly what they were: one showed him standing with Peplow outside the Park Plaza, and the other caught the two of them talking outside the Scotiabank at Bloor and Spadina. Mrs Peplow flipped the photos over, and Quilley saw that they had been date-stamped by the processors.

'You met with my husband at least twice to help him plan my death.'

'That's ridiculous. I do remember him, now I've seen the picture. I just couldn't recollect his name. He was a fan. We talked about mystery novels. I'm very sorry to hear that he's passed away.'

'He had a heart attack, Mr Quilley, and now I'm all alone in the world.'

'I'm very sorry, but I don't see . . .'

Mrs Peplow waved his protests aside. Quilley noticed the dark sweat stain on the tight material around her armpit. She fumbled with the catch on her purse again and brought out a pack of Export Lights and a book of matches.

'I don't allow smoking in my house,' Quilley said. 'It doesn't agree with me.'

'Pity,' she said, lighting the cigarette and dropping the spent match in the Wedgwood bowl. She blew a stream of smoke directly at Quilley, who coughed and fanned it away.

'Listen to me, Mr Quilley,' she said, 'and listen good. My husband might have been stupid, but I'm not. He was not only a pathetic and boring little man, he was also an open book. Don't ask me why I married him. He wasn't even much of a man, if you know what I mean. Do you think I haven't known for some time that he was thinking of ways to get rid of me? I wouldn't give him a divorce because the one thing he did—the only thing he did—was provide for me, and he didn't even do that very well. I'd have got half if we divorced, but half of what he earned isn't enough to keep a bag-lady. I'd have had to go to work, and I don't like that idea. So I watched him. He got more and more desperate, more and more secretive. When he started looking smug, I knew he was up to something.'

'Mrs Peplow,' Quilley interrupted, 'this is all very well, but I don't see what it has to do with me. You come in here and pollute my home with smoke, then you start telling me some fairy tale about your husband, a man I met casually once or twice. I'm busy, Mrs Peplow, and quite frankly I'd rather you left and let me get back to work.'

'I'm sure you would.' She flicked a column of ash into the Wedgwood bowl. 'As I was saying, I knew he was up to something, so I started following him. I thought he might have another woman, unlikely as it seemed, so I took my camera along. I wasn't really surprised when he headed for the Park Plaza instead of going back to the office after lunch one day. I watched the elevator go up to the nineteenth floor, the bar, so I waited across the street in the crowd for him to come out again. As you know, I didn't have to wait very long. He came out with you. And it was just as easy the next time.'

'I've already told you, Mrs Peplow, he was a mystery buff, a fellow collector, that's all—'

'Yes, yes, I know he was. Him and his stupid catalogues and

collection. Still,' she mused, 'it had its uses. That's how I found out who you were. I'd seen your picture on the book covers, of course. If I may say so, it does you more than justice.' She looked him up and down as if he were a side of beef hanging in a butcher's window. He cringed. 'As I was saying, my husband was obvious. I knew he must be chasing you for advice. He spends so much time escaping to his garden or his little world of books that it was perfectly natural he would go to a mystery novelist for advice rather than to a real criminal. I imagine you were a bit more accessible, too. A little flattery, and you were hooked. Just another puzzle for you to work on.'

'Look, Mrs Peplow—'

'Let me finish.' She ground out her cigarette butt in the bowl. 'Foxgloves, indeed! Do you think he could manage to brew up a dose of digitalis without leaving traces all over the place? Do you know what he did the first time? He put just enough in my Big Mac to make me a bit nauseous and make my pulse race, but he left the leaves and stems in the dustbin! Can you believe that? Oh, I became very careful in my eating habits after that, Mr Quilley. Anyway, your little plan didn't work. I'm here and he's dead.'

Quilley paled. 'My God, you killed him, didn't you?'

'He was the one with the bad heart, not me.' She lit another cigarette.

'You can hardly blackmail me for plotting with your husband to kill you when *he's* the one who's dead,' said Quilley. 'And as for evidence, there's nothing. No, Mrs Peplow, I think you'd better go, and think yourself lucky I don't call the police.'

Mrs Peplow looked surprised. 'What are you talking about? I have no intention of blackmailing you for plotting to kill me.'

'Then what . . . ?'

'Mr Quilley, my husband was blackmailing you. That's why you killed *him*.'

Quilley slumped back in his chair. 'I what?'

She took a sheet of paper from her purse and passed it over to him. On it were just two words: 'Trotton—Quilley'. He recognized the neat handwriting. 'That's a photocopy,' Mrs Peplow went on. 'The original's where I found it, slipped between the pages of a book called *Summer's Lease* by X.J. Trotton. Do you know that book, Mr Quilley?'

'Vaguely. I've heard of it.'

'Oh, have you? It might also interest you to know that along with that book and the slip of paper, locked away in my husband's files, is a copy of your own first novel. I put it there.'

Quilley felt the room spinning around him. 'I . . . I . . .' Peplow had given him the impression that Gloria was stupid, but that was turning out to be far from the truth.

'My husband's only been dead for two days. If the doctors look, they'll *know* that he's been poisoned. For a start, they'll find high levels of potassium, and then they'll discover eosinophilia. Do you know what they are, Mr Quilley? I looked them up. They're a kind of white blood cell, and you find lots of them around if there's been any allergic reaction or inflammation. If I was to go to the police and say I'd been suspicious about my husband's behaviour over the past few weeks, that I had followed him and photographed him with you, and if they were to find the two books and the slip of paper in his files. . . . Well, I think you know what they'd make of it, don't you? Especially if I told them he came home feeling ill after a lunch with you.'

'It's not fair,' Quilley said, banging his fist on the chair arm. 'It's just not bloody fair.'

'Life rarely is. But the police aren't to know how stupid and unimaginative my husband was. They'll just look at the note, read the books, and assume he was blackmailing you.' She laughed. 'Even if Frank had read the Trotton book, I'm sure he'd have only noticed an "influence", at the most. But you and I know what really went on, don't we? It happens more often than people think. Only recently I was reading in the newspaper about similarities between a book by Colleen McCullough and *The Blue Castle* by Lucy Maud Montgomery. I'd say that was a bit obvious, wouldn't you? It was much easier in your case, much less dangerous. You were very clever, Mr Quilley. You found an obscure novel, and you didn't only adapt the plot for your own first book, you even stole the character of your series detective. There was some risk involved, certainly, but not much. Your book is better, without a doubt. You have some writing talent, which X.J. Trotton completely lacked. But he did have the germ of an original idea, and it wasn't lost on you, was it?'

Quilley groaned. Thirteen solid police procedurals, twelve of them all his own work, but the first, yes, a deliberate adaptation of a piece of ephemeral trash. He had seen what Trotton could have done and had done it himself. Serendipity, or so it had seemed when he found the dusty volume in a second-hand bookshop in Victoria years ago. All he had had to do was change the setting from London to Toronto, alter the names, and set about improving upon the original. And now . . . ? The hell of it was that he would have been perfectly safe without the damn book. He had simply given in to the urge to get his hands on Peplow's copy and destroy it. It wouldn't have mattered, really. *Summer's Lease* would have remained unread on Peplow's shelf. If only the bloody fool hadn't written the note. . . .

'Even if the police can't make a murder charge stick,' Mrs Peplow went on, 'I think your reputation would suffer if this got out. Oh, the great reading public might not care. Perhaps a trial would even increase your sales—you know how ghoulish people are—but the plagiarism would at the very least lose you the respect of your peers. I don't think your agent and publisher would be very happy, either. Am I making myself clear?'

Pale and sweating, Quilley nodded. 'How much?' he whispered.

'Pardon?'

'I said how much. How much do you want to keep quiet?'

'Oh, it's not your money I'm after, Mr Quilley, or may I call you Dennis? Well, not *only* money, anyway. I'm a widow now. I'm all alone in the world.'

She looked around the room, her piggy eyes glittering, then gave Quilley one of the most disgusting looks he'd ever had in his life.

'I've always fancied living near the lake,' she said, reaching for another cigarette. 'Live here alone, do you?'

CHRYSTINE BROUILLET · b. 1958

First Love

When Sister Jeanne reviewed her geography notes that Sunday, she never suspected she wouldn't have to give any classes.

When Sister Jeanne welcomed the upper school boarders that year, she never suspected that among those forty-four teenagers there was one particularly passionate girl.

She never suspected a thing.

The term had begun in the same tiresome disorder as every other year.

September . . . Dear God, how good it would have been to enjoy it! To take advantage of the last real rays of sun, the golden light on the fields, the still-sweet scents of summer's end. Dear God, yes! Sister Jeanne would sigh, murmuring frequent 'Dear God's: it was both a conscious prayer and a habit. That morning of September 6, 197–, kneeling in front of the altar in the aisle of the chapel, she explained to her Creator that she gladly accepted her mission as supervisor, was even anxious to know 'her' boarders, but (she was sure He would understand) she would have liked to walk in the garden again just praying, without having to imagine forty-four problems. Sister Jeanne worshipped nature as the most perfect expression of the power and goodness of God.

She left the chapel a little before seven o'clock and went down to join her companions in the refectory. She was the youngest nun, only thirty-three. Her companions were as tense as she was. The convent itself was tense. In less than five hours the walls would ring with laughter and tears, cries, whispers, last goodbyes, final instructions. The seniors, separated for the summer, met again with unremitting exclamations of joy. The girls would rather think of the pleasure of seeing their friends than their sadness and resentment at leaving their families. They knew they were entitled to use the elevator, this first day back, because of their bags. The next day they'd be forbidden to use it again until the end of the school year.

The seniors who remembered their past apprehensions made

friends with the new girls, trying to reassure them, telling all the good tricks they'd pulled, mimicking the supervisors and department heads, laughing at any excuse. But laughing—it was important that their laughter be convincing.

Tonight only, Sister Jeanne had declared, bedtime would be at nine. There would be a little welcoming party, to get to know everyone, in room 142 at eight o'clock; the girls would put on their pajamas and dressing gowns before going down. It went off fairly well, all things considered: two students hadn't wanted to leave their rooms, sobbing their hearts out and clinging to stuffed bears and dolls. It was a senior, Louise Brisson, who succeeded in persuading them to come down and join the group. Three other seniors had kept to themselves during the party despite the exhortations of Sister Jeanne, who recognized them for rebels. However, this first evening could be considered a success, since the boarders had proved to be fairly docile when it came time to go to bed. Of course half the group were no sooner in bed than they got up to go to the bathroom. But all that was very normal. They would all fall asleep after giving one last thought to their parents.

All, except Edwidge. She wasn't thinking of her parents especially. She was thinking about her future. She wondered if she would know happiness, if she would make friends, if she would like her teachers. That evening she'd made an inordinate effort to take part, to blend in with the group. She'd never really had friends—at least, human friends. Her parents had chosen boarding school for her because they found their daughter strange; she talked to herself, she played by herself, and she read far too much. They hoped that some lively contact would bring her out of her dreamy torpor.

Did Edwidge dream too much? And was it wrong to dream of Prince Charming?

Edwidge wanted so badly to love.

She discovered friendship before love. Louise Brisson had the room next door. The very next day, she was knocking firmly at Edwidge's door and inviting her to breakfast. Edwidge accepted. Louise waited nearly fifteen minutes: the whole time Edwidge was brushing her teeth. Louise thought that was a little odd.

Breakfast was the best meal of the day; it's pretty hard to spoil toast, or not to manage to warm up rolls. There was cereal, too, and eggs. Coffee, tea, juice. They were entitled to one glass of milk per meal. After a week, all the boarders knew who drank milk and who didn't.

So the milk intended for those who abstained would be set aside in exchange for a better place in the line along the refectory walls.

Louise advised Edwidge to take a hot roll instead of toast. 'Sometimes it doesn't have enough butter on it. Take some cheese, it's good. At least it was, last year! We'll get the table by the window. Always try to sit near the window. There are plants—they're no use at breakfast, but when we have meatloaf for dinner you'll be glad to stuff it into the flowerpot.' Louise was laughing as she said all this. She laughed often. She had a face made for laughter: moon-shaped, with round cheeks, light blue eyes, and straight blond hair. To her despair. In fact, the reason she had made friends with Edwidge was because she was so impressed by her astonishing head of hair. Edwidge was dark, and her hair flowed over her shoulders in heavy, unmanageable coils. She had grey eyes. Slate grey. Rain grey. Grey as the sky before a storm. Storms were tirelessly brewing in her. But Edwidge didn't know it. She knew she wasn't the same as other girls her age; or rather she felt it, for she couldn't have said how she was different. Of course there was that special relationship with objects. . . Louise suspected none of this, but still found her strange. Strange, her way of answering too slowly, as if she never understood the question. Strange, that lost look. Strange, how impervious she was to rules: Edwidge seemed to accept all the many prohibitions, seemed happy to be a boarder. Now that was truly surprising and mysterious. Really!

At first Louise had thought that Edwidge's attitude would change after a few weeks in boarding, that she would criticize the authorities too. But no. She seemed to like it better every day. All the boarders had noticed this failing. Several had given her the cold shoulder, thinking they were dealing with some revolting little goody-goody, but they had reconsidered their position: Edwidge didn't respect the rules any more than they did. Only, when she was punished (deprived of television) she didn't react. As if it was all exactly the same to her.

Edwidge liked boarding school.

Sister Jeanne too had noted this peculiarity. And it worried her somewhat. There's nothing worse than still waters.

Edwidge's classmates tried to imagine her life: if she liked the convent so much, her parents must be monsters. Her father was a doctor—a butcher, obviously. Her mother must be a tart who didn't love her daughter. Who rejected her. These wild imaginings were never denied or accepted; Edwidge never knew about them. She never talked about her family, or about her past. She listened. And it was for this reason alone she had friends. If you were a little scared of her, on the other hand you could be sure to find an attentive ear in room 97. Edwidge could listen thirty-two times over to Lise or Hélène tell how a cousin or neighbour was dying for love of her.

Edwidge loved love stories. Even if they were a little simple.

In October she realized she was in love. And it was complicated. Desperate. Well, almost. Unlike her friends, she couldn't confide in anyone. She mustn't confide. She didn't want to. That would have sullied her love, even destroyed it. Her love was pure, and she would protect it in the face of all opposition. She had absolutely no intention of living out her love the way her friends did theirs. Stories of kissing and groping disgusted her. Edwidge didn't judge her friends—if they liked to have pimply adolescents hold their hands, that was their business. But for her—never!

She was distressed that she had the best marks in mathematics. She couldn't impress her teacher by doing better. What would she do to attract his attention? Edwidge thought about it for all one night; now that it was clear she loved Monsieur Levallois, she had to captivate him. He had to love her. They would love one another till the end of time. She was prepared to live this love in secret, of course. He would go on teaching math at the convent and she would continue her studies. They would meet in the garden, or in the field beside the nuns' property. He would marry her when she finished school.

After considering various strategies, Edwidge decided on the simplest one: she would sabotage her marks. She was first in the class: she would be last! He would worry and ask her questions, and she would confess her love. Her Love.

Those were the days when young girls idolized Cat Stevens. The first time Edwidge heard 'Sad Lisa,' 'Wild World,' 'Father and Son,' she realized that she would love those songs when she was much older, in five or six years, for they would remind her of the times when she was thinking of Monsieur Levallois. She'd tell him. She'd tell him everything. Everything. She hoped he would understand the strange, inexplicable things that sometimes happened to her. She'd have to tell him that objects liked her. She knew they had feelings for her. Of course, she was fond of them too; she always took care to put her clothes away properly, so they wouldn't be stiff in the morning; she closed her drawers tight so they wouldn't be in a draft; she never left an object by itself, lest it get bored. The objects repaid these attentions.

And then there were those strange signs on the walls of her room. Signs you couldn't see in daylight. That only she could see. She'd certainly have liked to know the meaning of the daggers enclosed by roses that she noticed from time to time in her room. There were also cats lying on their backs. Yet Edwidge knew very well that cats rarely lie on their backs. Sometimes she told herself it was her imagination that produced these images. A repeating imagination: she always saw the same signs. Every time she went back to her room at night she was aware of their presence.

For Edwidge went out at night. She left her room to walk where He had walked. She kissed the walls He had passed by. She stopped where He had stopped. By the principal's office, by that staircase, by her classroom—Edwidge was sure he'd deliberately stopped by her classroom that day. He wanted to see her. He didn't know it yet, but already He loved her. You can't escape your destiny. There was a reason she had come to study at this convent: it was where she would experience love. It was all very simple.

She had to fail three exams before Monsieur Levallois realized that this promising student, who intrigued him as she did all his colleagues, had a problem. He had put her failures down to the fact that she was extremely emotional. They discussed her case at a teachers' meeting; Edwidge did so well in every subject, but she was so withdrawn. Sister Jeanne, who was both her geography teacher and her supervisor, was completely frustrated. Even if it wasn't the sort of thing you talked about at meetings, she couldn't help mentioning what she had noticed: that Edwidge was obsessed with cleanliness: she washed her face six times a day, brushed her teeth eight times, and as for the times she washed her hands—incalculable . . .

'Maybe it's ridiculous of me to bring up all these details that don't really have anything to do with school, but I think this girl has problems. She never talks about herself. And if there's one thing everyone does at that age, it's talk about themselves. You'd almost think she wasn't conscious of her own existence! She's always got her head in the clouds.'

'But how do you explain her brilliant marks?'

M. Levallois sighed: 'You mean in the past. . . . But she still studies?'

'Yes . . . ' There was some hesitation in Sister Jeanne's voice. 'She studies. At least I suppose she does. In study period she always has a book open in front of her, but I don't think she's looking at it. It could be upside down and she wouldn't even notice!'

'Is that the reason she's been failing math?' asked M. Levallois. 'Until recently she was one of my most outstanding students. And God knows in fourteen years as a teacher, I've seen plenty. . . . What happened?'

Sister Jeanne turned to M. Levallois. 'I don't want to hurt you, but for a while now, the rare time they talk about teachers, or rather the rare time I'm there to hear, it's seemed that Edwidge has some very negative feelings towards you. She never says anything the rest of the time, but she joins in with the others when it comes to complaining about you. Have you said or done anything to shock her?'

'I've thought about that, but I really can't see what I might have done to disturb her to the point of failing her exams. You know it's hard to shock students with the square of the hypotenuse. And I've never really spoken to Edwidge—I've never had anything to find fault with. But as things stand, I'll have to do something . . . ' Monsieur Levallois pulled at his moustache. A big moustache. Brown with a few traces of white. Monsieur Levallois was very proud of it. Indeed, it was his one vanity. He knew he wasn't handsome. He had short legs, a red nose (though he didn't drink—it wasn't fair), and was losing his hair. And his illusions. At one time in his life he had imagined that maturity would give him a certain presence, if not good looks. Not even that. And now his best student detested him for no reason! What was wrong with her?

'Sister Jeanne, you seem to get along well with your boarders, do you think you could speak to Edwidge? I'd be glad to, but you know at that age it's rather complicated, as a man, to talk with young girls. If I keep her after class, at least fifty students will say I have a crush on Edwidge. I don't think that would help matters. If I have to, I'll speak to her, but first . . . '

'I can try, but I'm sceptical. She's very silent, very withdrawn. It's as if she's tormented by some terrible secret. I sound as if I'm romanticizing her case,' sighed the nun, 'but Edwidge really is . . . different.'

Edwidge herself felt strange. No—a stranger. A stranger to everything around her. Her friends, her courses, the nuns, the timetables, the rules, the activities. All that life was so unimportant. Now that she was really alive, Edwidge wondered how she'd survived without love. Without this Love. Monsieur Levallois, Georges, was so seductive, so handsome, so intelligent. Tall and strong, a face with character! And the expression in his eyes . . . how passionate, burning, sincere. Edwidge was totally, madly in love with Georges Levallois.

Had he known, he would have been astounded.

Sister Jeanne tried every excuse to talk to Edwidge and failed miserably. Edwidge was polite and pleasant, but would not on any account talk about herself. Neither her parents nor her friends, her desires nor her dislikes. Yet Sister Jeanne was convinced that Edwidge loved and hated intensely. Why did she hide it? What was she hiding? She had a desperate look, as if she was locked in some unbreakable silence. The good sister would gladly have helped her. As for talking about Monsieur Levallois, that needed more thought. And she would think about it again; certainly it was not the answer to try to talk about it with this bizarre girl.

Edwidge's friends had noticed that Sister Jeanne was taking an interest in her. There were two possible reasons for this sudden interest: either Sister Jeanne was on Edwidge's back because of her poor marks, or else she had a crush on her pupil, who was very naive. Lise, Hélène, and Louise had told her to be on her guard. Besides, Sister Jeanne's nocturnal visits to Sister Nicole were a classic joke. There was no proof, but . . . Edwidge had responded negatively to these revelations: all that had nothing to do with her, she wasn't interested, and what was wrong with it, anyway?

Lise, Hélène, and Louise were amazed by the vehemence of Edwidge's reaction; did she understand that they were talking about lesbianism? Did she approve of that horror, or was she so innocent she believed that those late-night visits were normal? Deep down, what did Edwidge think?

They didn't know, any more than Sister Jeanne did.

Edwidge decided to consign her amorous feelings to paper. When she confessed her love to Georges, she would give him the diary in which all her thoughts, all her transports, were inscribed. She was determined that he not think this love trivial; this was not a matter of girlish swooning, but of passion. Edwidge knew her love was not ordinary; it was no passing infatuation, no adolescent flirtation: she loved like a woman. For all her fourteen years, she had become a woman as soon as she loved. She had to make Georges understand that the great difference in age could not stand in the way of their love.

On November 26, 197–, at the school bookstore, Edwidge picked out a notebook with a cover as red as love. She had to wait until night, until the dormitory had fallen silent, to turn on her flashlight and, crouching in the wardrobe, write the first pages of her love diary.

November 26

My love

It's now more than 63 days that I've loved you. It seems to me as if this happiness, new as it is, has existed since the dawn of time . . . I feel as if we have always known, always loved one another. I was destined for you as you were destined for me.

Isn't it wonderful that after all this time that has gone by in silence, in fear that someone would discover my feelings, after all those days when I've had to speak badly of you so that no one would suspect, after all those days of failing math, at last the moment has come to reveal myself, to open my heart to you? I know I'll be able to speak to you soon. Didn't you write on my last paper: 'If you need help, don't hesitate to ask me—we can talk it over'? What beautiful words! What joy to read and reread those simple, transparent words. I know you have felt what is happening between us. Our love. This love is constantly renewed, an eternal rebirth! Sometimes I feel this love rising inside me like the springtime sap in young trees, and it's so strong, so intense, I think I'll die. . . . Sometimes love wraps itself gently around me and rocks me in a magic euphoria.

If only you knew how I hate the other girls who are rude to you and disrupt your classes! They have no right to act that way. I'd like to punish them: how can you be so patient with them? It's true that you have a noble heart. . . . But they bother me. And anyone who tries to interfere with this love I feel for you is as good as dead. I would kill for you.

I love you and will tell you how I love you every day of my life.

Edwidge's passion for Monsieur Levallois was so strong that she decided she had to have some object belonging to him. She wanted something he'd touched, held in his hands. She set her heart on a notebook he often had with him in class. It seemed to her that she'd feel a little like the notebook, feel herself touched, held, by Georges, if she possessed this relic. Besides, the notebook smiled appealingly at her.

Obviously the operation to borrow the notebook couldn't take place in daylight. Anyway, Edwidge was used to midnight outings! She knew it was a risk, especially since she'd found out that the nuns visited each other at night. She hoped she wouldn't meet Sister Jeanne or Sister Nicole, but if it happened, she'd pretend to be sleepwalking. They were entitled to have friends just the same as the students. If the latter had the opportunity, surely they'd go and chat with their friends late at night in their rooms, and not see anything wrong with it. Why was it wrong for the nuns? It didn't make sense.

Still, she'd be doubly careful when she went to get the precious object.

After two weeks of observation, she had learned that Monsieur Levallois kept the notebook in his box in the staff room. A room fortunately far from the dormitory. No one would be able to hear her break in. The only obstacle lay in the fact that the room in question was locked every night when the last teacher left the convent, and wasn't opened until seven o'clock the next morning. It was Sister Solange who had the keys. Two weeks had been enough for Louise to observe that the nun never forgot to lock the room; Edwidge couldn't count on her making a mistake if she was to get her hands on the coveted notebook. There was only one solution: to spirit away the keys from Sister Solange's room. The gods were with Edwidge: Sister Solange regularly left her door open; she wanted the boarders to feel welcome, that she was always ready to listen. She didn't teach but was more or less a nurse, and she knew that for many ills there is only one remedy: a listening ear combined with aspirin. Sister Solange had an industrial-sized bottle of aspirin, for it was the remedy she always administered, whether the problem was migraine, upset stomach, a sprain, sunburn, or a scrape.

On December 17 Edwidge suffered a violent headache. Sister Solange was hardly surprised: it was the day before the start of exams, and many students saw aspirin as a tranquillizer for their anxiety. She listened earnestly to Edwidge, gave her the famous aspirin, and advised her to go to bed early. It was fairly late anyway, almost eight o'clock. Edwidge thanked her politely. Sister Solange had the impression she'd helped Edwidge, for the latter left her room with a smile she wasn't wearing when she came in.

Edwidge did indeed have a little smile on her face—and the keys. It had been child's play: they were lying on the bed, and all Edwidge had to do was flop down as if in exhaustion. The keys had slid towards her, come closer still, and Edwidge had grabbed them. She wasn't so foolish as to keep them on her; there was no telling when Sister Solange would notice their disappearance. Edwidge only hoped she hadn't got the wrong set. There were two. But why would the keys betray her? She hid them in the linen cupboard, knowing that no one would go there at that hour. She went to bed as Sister Solange had recommended. And didn't fall asleep. She found the wait very long. When she got up, around two in the morning, everything was quiet. A boarder on her way to the bathroom almost saw her, but Edwidge slipped adroitly behind a half-open door. She walked down the great winding staircase that led to the classrooms. Dirty staircase! It was wooden and very old, with steps that could have won a creaking contest. She'd been careful to put on gloves; the wool would muffle the clinking of metal and ensure that she didn't leave any prints. After trying five keys, she was delighted to see the sixth run blithely into the lock. Edwidge entered the room and waited a few moments, long enough to get used to the dark. She quickly found Monsieur Levallois's notebook and took it. She slipped it inside her dressing-gown, went back up to the dorm, carried the notebook into her room, hid it at the back of the wardrobe, and went out again, to the bathroom. She flushed the toilet three times in a row, hoping to attract some mild attention. Immediately she left the bathroom and the dorm and headed for Sister Solange's room. She was hot and cold, she felt worse than before; she'd had nightmares and she felt sick.

'But why didn't you go to Sister Jeanne? She's the one in charge.'

'Yes, I know, but Sister Jeanne would have come to get you anyway, so there was no point in bothering her. I'm already embarrassed enough to have woken you up,' Edwidge explained, looking at Sister Solange with eyes that were truly tearful.

'Poor Edwidge, I think you're too nervous about your exams starting. Go back to bed, and I'll bring you some medicine that will help you sleep. You do look pale.'

She waited until the next night to look at Monsieur Levallois's notebook. How well he wrote! The way he formed his figures, the notes written in delicate red pencil in the margins. There were even some little drawings. At the end of the notebook she discovered a poem. He was a poet! She wasn't surprised: you can teach mathematics and still have the soul of an artist.

My child, my sister,
Think how sweet it would be
To go there and live together
To love at our ease
To love and to die
In the country that resembles you.*

What talent! Edwidge was convinced he'd written the poem for her, dreaming of her. Later she would tell him the joy she had felt when reading these lines.

Monsieur Levallois's notebook was red, like Edwidge's diary: these are signs that cannot be mistaken. They were made for each other. And this notebook was so nice, so truly refined, just like its master.

She didn't think it would do any good to fail her exams. It would even be useful to get the highest marks; he'd surely be surprised at such a reversal. Besides, Christmas was coming, and it would be a present for him.

But how sad to think she'd be separated from him for two weeks. Never had holidays caused anyone such pain. It was with a heavy heart that she left the convent to celebrate Christmas with her family.

She wrote every day of her grief, her sorrow at being far from him. She filled entire pages with her secrets—pathetic, dramatic, tragic.

On January 7 she was probably the only boarder who was delighted to return to the convent. Sister Jeanne, who noticed this delight, concluded that Edwidge had had a good holiday with her parents. 'That's better,' she thought. 'That girl had me worried. She's so wild, so complex, however docile she seems. Let's hope these high spirits last!'

The high spirits lasted. They even grew into exaltation. Edwidge couldn't sit still. She was feverish, excited, as if in the grip of some violent emotion. She had dark circles around her eyes and washed more frequently than ever.

She had decided to wash more to refine her skin. She wanted to be glorious the day she confessed her love to Georges.

Georges—who wondered where he could have mislaid his notebook. It wasn't the importance he attached to this object, but the mysterious aspect of its disappearance that troubled him. He was also thinking about Edwidge. A total mystery. He felt slightly uneasy in the presence of this student. She'd asked to change her seat, claiming

*Charles Baudelaire, '*L'Invitation au voyage*'.

she couldn't see the board properly from the back of the class, but Monsieur Levallois knew she sat at the back in all her other classes, and it didn't seem to bother her a bit. So she had moved to the front desk, directly facing the teacher's. She never took her eyes off Monsieur Levallois. And that made him uncomfortable. She never focused on him, but he could feel her gaze constantly hovering. Did she hate him? Even if Edwidge's marks really were better, Monsieur Levallois believed the problem continued. In fact, he was convinced the student detested him. It bothered him because he didn't know why. A natural antipathy, perhaps. It was aggravating. If it went on, he'd end up dreading group C because of the tension Edwidge created.

Three weeks after returning to the convent, Georges Levallois decided to have a talk with Edwidge; it was time to clear up this awkward situation. Awkward for both of them: he was well aware that the girl was ill at ease in his presence. Everything would be explained and things would return to normal. So he wrote on the corrected paper he was giving back to her that morning: 'Edwidge, can you come to my office at 4:00 this afternoon?' He thought she shivered when she read this message on her paper, but she made no sign of acknowledgement. Of course, she was embarrassed in front of the other students.

Edwidge flew that day. She was completely incapable of eating lunch, and obviously she didn't go for the four o'clock snack. She ran to get her diary and see the man of her life.

She was trembling when she entered Monsieur Levallois's office. He smiled kindly.

'Sit down, Edwidge. I suppose you're wondering why I asked you to come to my office.' His tone was truly friendly. Truly affable.

'Maybe.' And she said this in a passionate tone—to the extent that one can say 'maybe' in such a tone.

Behind his desk, Monsieur Levallois was wringing his hands. 'I think there is some kind of conflict between us. I may be mistaken. I hope so. But your attitude really is different from what it was in September. I'd like to know what's wrong. Have I done something you don't like? It's better to talk frankly, don't you think?' He went on wringing his hands. He was to wring them still more!

Stricken, Edwidge cried out. 'You thought I was angry? Me, my God! Me? Angry with you?'

'That's not it?'

'But I love you! I love you with all the strength of my being! For months I've thought only of you!'

'Me?'

'You!'

Monsieur Levallois had no idea what to say. It was the first time in his teaching career that anything like this had happened to him. It was also the first time in his life that such a thing had happened. He was utterly incredulous.

'Take this. Read any page of this diary, I've written for you every day.' Her nerves had given way to a fierce determination; was this man so humble that he didn't understand how someone could love him? She was going to make him believe it!

January 13

My love,

I'm pining for you. I'm dying, so far from you. What idiot invented vacations? I'm unhappy here without you. I need to see you every day, hear you, feel you near me. And you, do you remember me? Do you know how much I love you? For I love you more all the time . . .

M. Levallois saw that January 4, 5, 6, and 7 were similar in both form and content. The 8th, 9th, 10th, and following talked about the joy of meeting again. Edwidge was very serious. In short, she seriously imagined she loved him. Old, fat, ugly Georges Levallois. He was touched, moved, of course. And he didn't want in any way to hurt this young girl. But what could he say to her? . . . There was a long silence in which Edwidge's eyes devoured the marvellous man.

At last he said: 'I believe you love me sincerely. You know, though, that the situation is complicated—the great difference in age, the fact that I'm a teacher and you're a student, these are obstacles. You'll tell me that doesn't matter to you. I understand, but we live in a society; I know you're intelligent and will agree with me. I'm flattered and moved by your special attentions for me, and if there is any answer, it's that time takes care of things . . . '

Edwidge didn't reply to that.

Then they talked about trivial things so that they could part without embarrassment, to make it clear to one another that they could still talk.

When Edwidge left Monsieur Levallois she was soaring. He loved her, it was obvious! All he'd said was that they'd have to wait. Wait until they could love one another in the eyes of society. She would wait as long as necessary, for she would love him all her life.

In the face of all opposition.

Edwidge was always the last boarder to leave the convent on Fridays. The boarders went home every week. On Fridays before leaving they cleared their rooms, and the nun responsible for each level went to check whether each had done a meticulous cleaning. That is, to look under the beds to see if they'd quickly swept the dust under them, and to open the wardrobes to see what all was crammed in there. Sometimes the girls got carried away: in their joy at leaving the convent, they had a tendency to tidy up very quickly, throwing everything into the wardrobe.

Edwidge generally avoided these mistakes; she put everything away very neatly. Not out of concern for the rules, but out of affection for the things.

But that Friday she forgot—how could she forget?—to hide her diary in the third sheet on the second shelf from the top. She'd almost fallen asleep while writing the day before, in her wardrobe. In the morning, before going to class, she'd been careless when hiding her notebook and flashlight.

Around a quarter to four she went up to her room to find Sister Jeanne there on her tour of inspection. She always finished with Edwidge, knowing she was in no hurry to leave. Sister Jeanne was holding Edwidge's diary, and it was open in the middle. She'd read half of it.

Edwidge turned pale but didn't say a word.

Sister Jeanne didn't know what to say. So she told Edwidge she had found this notebook in her wardrobe, in a particular jumble, and that she had also found a flashlight. And that it was positively forbidden to read or write at night with the help of a flashlight. She would see what she'd decide; perhaps she'd speak with the principal. . . . She would make her decision on Monday. In any case, Sister Angèle, the principal, was away for the weekend; they would see on her return. She added that she hoped her room would be tidier in the future. She left Edwidge her notebook without a word about it.

But Edwidge knew that Sister Jeanne had read it.

It was a catastrophe: her love held up to ridicule, in the open! Georges's career ruined by an indiscretion! Their future destroyed!

Their happiness trampled underfoot!

Never! Never!

Edwidge had always thought she would protect her love. Only one solution was possible. Sister Jeanne must die.

Obviously, it had to look like an accident.

There must be no witnesses. And the accident had to be fatal. A fall down the stairs was thus out of the question, far too risky.

Edwidge considered it for much of the weekend and came up with the perfect crime. All she needed was a roll of masking tape and a pair of surgical gloves. They were easy to find, since her father's office was in the house. And in any case, she had an accomplice.

Edwidge had nothing personal against Sister Jeanne, she even liked her, but in the circumstances she had no choice. She preferred Georges.

She returned to the convent at the same time as every Sunday, spoke and acted as usual. She said hello to Sister Jeanne but didn't mention what had happened that disastrous Friday; she pretended she'd forgotten, in the hope that the sister had too.

Fortunately, Sister Jeanne was visiting Sister Nicole one floor below.

Edwidge waited until all the boarders were in bed. She got up at a quarter to eleven—the time when Sister Jeanne usually met Sister Nicole. Edwidge expected she wouldn't depart from her custom.

Edwidge slipped on her fine plastic gloves, put her roll of masking tape in her pocket, and walked one floor upstairs. She explained to the elevator what she expected of it. Heavy and slow as it was, the elevator was a metallic object, and Edwidge had always got along particularly well with them. It agreed to help her. She stuck the aforementioned roll in the lock of the elevator, against the latch. It was an old elevator, really likeable, with grills and a door that jammed or stayed open if the latches didn't fit tightly together. The tape would keep the elevator cage on this floor.

Sister Jeanne pushed the button and waited for the elevator. It didn't come. She got impatient, pushed on the grill, and looked down the elevator shaft. Edwidge pushed her. Sister Jeanne tumbled over the edge with a loud cry.

Edwidge rushed to the bathroom, threw her gloves in the toilet and flushed it. At the far end of the convent a door opened, a student had heard the cry; the other supervisor also came out of her room. They went by the bathroom door without stopping, running towards the cry. Edwidge returned to her room and slipped between the sheets.

She heard several doors open, then footsteps. She too went out to ask what was going on. Nobody knew very much. A cry had been heard, but no one knew where it came from.

The supervisor tried to calm the boarders, ordered them back to bed, and told them it would be looked into in the morning.

They found Sister Jeanne's body.

There was an investigation, because the likelihood of accidental death in an elevator is infinitesimal. The investigators found the little roll of masking tape.

It certainly wasn't an easy task to search for a murderer among two hundred and fifty-three boarders and eighty-seven nuns. Not only because of the number of interrogations, but also because the working conditions were particularly difficult: the sisters were so afraid of scandal that the investigators had to do their work virtually in the dark; they felt as if they were dealing in counter-espionage. Always speaking in veiled terms, almost in code; not telling names, so as not to disturb the students; avoiding too many meetings with the latter, who were so impressionable; trying to sort out this episode as quickly as possible, on account of the students' parents, who did not like this situation at all. Getting blamed by their superiors, who had no idea of the problems this investigation posed.

After a week of questions with and without answers, the investigators had succeeded in narrowing their field of action. Passive action—all they could do was listen. This had led them to the following conclusion: it was a student who had committed the crime, the nuns suspected of the murder being out of the question: they had faith, an ardent Christian faith that ruled out any possibility of a criminal act contrary to God's law, even if as individuals they experienced feelings of jealousy, joy, or desire. Ultimately, they dealt very well with these passionate feelings: they felt intensely alive, they committed mental sins. But never would it have occurred to any of them to kill. For, faith apart, there was the scandal; the nuns therefore were as anxious as the investigators for the affair of the elevator to be closed.

The elevator was equally anxious. It was being examined a lot these days, and it had led such a quiet life until now.

Edwidge was impatient for the results of the investigation. She'd never have thought it would be so long and complicated. But she didn't regret a thing. She wasn't really worried, just a little nervous. She knew her dear elevator would never betray her.

Yet she had good reason to worry: the investigators (there were two) were beginning to take an interest in her. Several people, students and nuns, had let slip some odd details concerning Edwidge. In fact, the investigators believed they were dealing with a schizophrenic. This student was definitely special. She could well have killed. Anyway, she was their only suspect, and somebody had to be guilty. They questioned the girl again, but she answered in monosyllables; she looked them straight in the eye, fearlessly, as if she had some secret power capable of obliterating them. It was ridiculous, but the kid sent chills down your spine. Still, they had to have proof that it was she who assassinated Sister Jeanne, and Edwidge wasn't giving them a single clue; she didn't talk, always repeated the same answers to the same questions. The investigators had permission to search her room when she was in class, but they found nothing strange or mysterious, apart from the fact that it was so perfectly tidy. Edwidge, obviously, hadn't kept either her notebook or Georges's in her room.

One of the investigators had the idea of bringing in a dog, a bloodhound. Of course the dog wouldn't smell anything now, but he might shake Edwidge up. Maybe she'd crack? The investigators felt very uneasy, hounding a little girl, but what if she was dangerous? If she struck again? For no reason? For they could see no motive that could have driven Edwidge to commit this crime. She killed simply because she was mad.

King nosed enthusiastically around everywhere. So many new smells, and all for him! The investigators made him sniff a sweater and some gloves of Edwidge's several times. Of course he understood what he had to look for. They took him to the elevator; he smelled the metal. Growled when they set it going. He absolutely would not go inside the cage. The investigators tried their best to flatter him, stroke him, encourage him, but they had to drag him into the elevator. King howled all the way down and all the way back up. It was only a few floors, but to him it seemed an eternity. What idiots these investigators were! If they wouldn't listen when he warned them of danger, why had they called on him? Men were strange. Like this machine . . . As soon as the elevator stopped, King leapt out the door. But the investigators didn't have time: the doors closed, and the elevator cage crashed to the ground. They should have trusted King.

He wasn't named that for nothing! He'd been one of the experimental dogs in a study of the ability certain animals have to discern strange phenomena. Of course he detected, sensed, earthquakes well before the humans and their complicated equipment, the seismographs; but if the experts had thought to push their tests further into the unknown, the inexplicable, they would have learned that certain animals, even certain humans, communicate with objects. It's very rare, for these animals, people, and objects don't often have the chance to meet. To love one another. It's not a question of dominance, like bending spoons or moving furniture—not at all. The human, or animal, and the object love and want to please one another. King howled because he knew the elevator was suffering, that it could no longer bear the presence of the inspectors. And that it wanted to protect Edwidge. If he, King, had succeeded in preventing the men from getting into the elevator, there wouldn't have been any trouble. But humans are stubborn and like to show they're the masters. It really was a pity.

The elevator was found to be outdated and dangerous. By this simple fact it was condemned.

So the boarders had to use the stairs every day of the year, even with all their trunks, suitcases, and bags.

Translated by Sally Livingston

NOTES ON AUTHORS

ALLEN, GRANT (1848-1899). Born in Kingston, Ont., at the age of thirteen he moved to Connecticut and a year later to England, where he spent the rest of his life. He wrote on scientific subjects such as psychology and Darwinism, but he was better suited for the writing of fiction. His novels include *The Scallywag* (1893), *The Woman Who Did* (1895), *A Splendid Sin* (1896), and *An African Millionaire* (1897). Allen's unfinished mystery novel *Hilda Wake* was completed after his death by his friend Sir Arthur Conan Doyle.

ARCHAMBAULT, GILLES (b. 1933). Humorist, broadcaster, jazz scholar, and novelist, Archambault is also the author of more than a dozen books. Among them are the novels *Une suprème discrétion* (1963), *La Vie à trois* (1965), *La Fleur aux dents* (1971), *La Fuite immobile* (1974), and *Le Voyageur distrait* (1981). He has published one collection of short stories, *Enfances lointaines* (1972).

BARR, ROBERT (1850-1912). Born in Scotland, he was taken by his family to Canada in 1854 and settled in Windsor, Ont. After working as a reporter for the *Detroit Free Press* he moved to England where, in 1892, he founded *The Idler*. His collections of short stories include *Strange Happenings* (1883) and *The Triumphs of Eugène Valmont* (1906). Among his novels are *In the Midst of Alarms* (1894), *The Victors* (1901), and *The Measure of the Rule* (1907).

BOWERS, ELISABETH (b. 1949). Born and raised in Vancouver, British Columbia, she won widespread praise for her first novel, *Ladies' Night* (1988).

BROUILLET, CHRYSTINE (b. 1958). Brouillet's third novel, *Le poisson dans l'eau* (1987), was the first Quebec title to be included in the prestigious French mystery series *Sueurs froides*. Her other novels include *Coups de foudre* (1984), *Chère voisine* (1986), and *Préférez-vous les icebergs?* (1988).

ENGEL, HOWARD (b. 1931). He is the Toronto-born creator of Benny Cooperman, who appears in *The Suicide Murders* (1980), *The Ransom Game* (1981), *Murder on Location* (1982), *Murder Sees the Light* (1984), *A City Called July* (1986), and *A Victim Must Be Found* (1988).

FINDLEY, TIMOTHY (b. 1930). He began his career as an actor, and published his first novel *The Last of the Crazy People* (1967) at the age of 37. This was followed by *The Butterfly Plague* (1969), *The Wars* (1977), *Famous Last Words* (1981), *Not Wanted on the Voyage* (1984), and the detective novel *The Telling of Lies*. A collection of essays, *Inside Memory*, appeared in 1990.

GODFREY, ELLEN (b. 1924). She is the author of two mysteries featuring a seventy-year-old anthropologist turned sleuth, Rebecca Rosenthal: *The Case of the Cold Murderer* (1976) and *Murder Among the Well-To-Do* (1977). She also published *By Reason of Doubt* (1981), a study of the Belshaw case, and *Murder Behind Locked Doors* (1988).

GOUGH, LAURENCE (b. 1944). A freelance writer living in Vancouver, Gough is the author of three mystery novels—*The Goldfish Bowl* (1987), *Death on a No. 8 Hook* (1988), and *Hot Shots* (1989)—and one spy thriller, *Sandstorm* (1990).

LEACOCK, STEPHEN (1869-1924). Born in England, he settled with his family in Ontario in 1876. His first collection of humorous pieces, *Literary Lapses* (1910), was followed by more than thirty volumes including *Nonsense Novels* (1911), *Sunshine Sketches of a Little Town* (1912), *Arcadian Adventures of the Idle Rich* (1914), and *Frenzied Fiction* (1918). An excellent selection of Leacock's work was edited by Robertson Davies under the title *The Feast of Stephen* (1974).

MAJOR, ANDRÉ (b. 1942). Poet, fiction writer, and playwright, Major was born in Montreal. Among his poetry collections are *Le Froid se meurt* (1961), *Holocauste à 1 voix* (1962), and *Poèmes pour durer* (1969). His novels include *Le Cabochon* (1964), *Le Vent du diable* (1968) and the trilogy *Histoires des déserteurs* (1974-76). He has published several collections of short stories.

McCORMACK, ERIC (b. 1938). Born in Scotland, he immigrated to Canada in 1966. He has published one collection of short stories, *Inspecting the Vaults* (1987) and one novel, *The Paradise Motel* (1989). He teaches English at the University of Waterloo, Ont.

MILLAR, MARGARET (b. 1915). Born in Kitchener, Ont., she has set several of her superb psychological thrillers in Canada. Most, however, take place in the United States, particularly in California, where she has lived most of her life with her husband, crime writer Ross Macdonald. Some of her best novels are *Wall of Eyes* (1943), *Fire Will Freeze* (1944), *Beast in View* (1955), *The Soft Talkers* (1957), and *How Like an Angel* (1962).

MUNRO, ALICE (b. 1931). Born Alice Laidlaw in Wingham, Ont., Munro published her first collection of short stories, *Dance of the Happy Shades*, in 1968. This was followed by several other collections: *Lives of Girls and Women* (1971), *Something I've Been Meaning to Tell You* (1974), *Who Do You Think You Are?* (1978), *The Moons of Jupiter* (1982), *The Progress of Love* (1986), and *Friend of My Youth* (1990).

PHILLIPS, EDWARD O. (b. 1931). Born in Montreal, he received a law degree and two master's degrees: one in teaching and one in English literature. He is the author of four novels: *Sunday's Child* (1981), *Where There's A Will* (1984), *Buried on Sunday* (1986), and *Hope Springs Eternal* (1988).

ROBINSON, PETER (b. 1950). Born in England, he immigrated to Canada at the age of 24 and attended university in Windsor and Toronto (York). He has published five mysteries, the first four featuring Chief Inspector Banks: *Gallows View* (1987), *A Dedicated Man* (1988), *A Necessary End* (1988), *The Hanging Valley* (1989), and *Caedmon's Song* (1990).

SKVORECKY, JOSEF (b. 1924). A native of Czechoslovakia, Skvorecky immigrated to Canada in 1968, after the Soviet invasion of his native country. Many of his stories and novels have been translated into English, among them two collections of detective stories: *The Mournful Demeanor of Lieutenant Boruvka* (1974) and *Sins for Father Knox* (1989). His novels include *The Cowards* (1970), *The Bass Saxophone* (1977), *The Engineer of Human Souls* (1983), *Dvorak in Love* (1986), and *The Miracle Game* (1990).

WOODS, SARA (1922-1985). Born Sara Bowen-Judd, in England, she was the author of numerous novels, including *Bloody Instructions* (1962), *Enter Certain Murderers* (1966), *Exit a Murderer* (1978), *Weep For Her* (1980), *Call Back Yesterday* (1983), and *Put Out The Light* (1985).

WRIGHT, ERIC (b. 1929). Born in England, Wright settled in Canada in 1951. His celebrated detective, Inspector Charlie Salter, first appeared in 1983, in *The Night the Gods Smiled*. His other novels include *Smoke Detector* (1984), *Death in the Old Country* (1985), *A Single Death* (1986), *A Body Surrounded by Water* (1987), and *A Question of Murder* (1988).

WYNNE-JONES, TIM (b. 1948). Born in England, he immigrated to Canada in 1952. His novel *Odd's End* won the Seal First Novel Award in 1980. He has since published two more novels, *The Knot* (1982) and *Fastyngange* (1988). He is also the author of several children's books.

ACKNOWLEDGEMENTS

GILLES ARCHAMBAULT. 'Mother Love'. English translation © 1991 Sally Livingston. Originally published in French as 'Amour maternel' in *Fuites et Poursuites*, Les Quinze, Éditeur (1985). Used by permission of Sogides Ltée.

ELISABETH BOWERS and A.J. BELL. 'The Singles' Bar Rapist', © Elisabeth Bowers and A.J. Bell. Reprinted by permission of the author and Georges Borchardt, Inc.

CHRYSTINE BROUILLET. 'First Love'. English translation © 1991 Sally Livingston. Originally published in French as 'Premier Amour' in *Fuites et Poursuites*, Les Quinze, Éditeur (1985). Used by permission of Sogides Ltée.

HOWARD ENGEL. 'The Three Wise Guys' © Howard Engel. Used by permission of the author.

TIMOTHY FINDLEY. 'Memorial Day' by Timothy Findley. Copyright © 1991 by Pebble Productions Inc.

ELLEN GODFREY. 'Common or Garden Murder' © Elllen Godfrey. Used by permission of the author.

LAURENCE GOUGH. 'Big Time' copyright © 1991 Laurence Gough. Used by permission of the author.

ERIC McCORMACK. 'Eckhardt at the Window'. Copyright © Eric McCormack, 1987. Reprinted by permission of Penguin Books Canada Limited.

ANDRÉ MAJOR. 'A Questionable Cast'. English translation © 1991 Sally Livingston. Originally published in French as 'Sueurs' in *Fuites et Poursuites*, Les Quinze, Éditeur (1985). Used by permission of Sogides Ltée.

MARGARET MILLAR. 'McGowney's Miracle' © 1954 by the Hearst Corporation. Copyright renewed 1982 by the Margaret Millar Survivors Trust u/a 4/12/82. Reprinted by permission of Harold Ober Associates.

ALICE MUNRO. 'Fits' from *The Progress of Love*. Copyright © 1985, 1986 Alice Munro. Originally published in *Grand Street*. In Canada, *The Progress of Love* is published by Douglas Gibson Books, an imprint of McClelland and Stewart Ltd. Reprinted by arrangement with Virginia Barber Literary Agency Inc. All rights reserved.

EDWARD O. PHILLIPS. 'Solstice' © Edward O. Phillips. Reprinted by permission of the author.

PETER ROBINSON. 'Fan Mail' © Peter Robinson. Used by permission of the author.

JOSEF SKVORECKY. 'An Intimate Business' from *Sins for Father Knox* by Josef Skvorecky, © 1973. English translation copyright © 1988 by Kaca Polackova Henley. Reprinted by permission of Lester & Orpen Dennys Publishers Ltd., Canada.

SARA WOODS. 'Every Tale Condemns Me' from *Winter's Crimes 17*. Used by permission of Macmillan, London and Basingstoke.

ERIC WRIGHT. 'Twins' from *Suit of Diamonds*. Used by permission of Harper Collins Publishers UK Ltd.

TIM WYNNE-JONES. 'The Imposture' originally published in The University of Waterloo *Courier*, September 1986. Used by permission of the author and Lucinda Vardey Agency.